P9-CMS-713

ROMANTIC TIMES RAVES FOR CAREER ACHIEVEMENT AWARD WINNER SANDRA HILL!

MY FAIR VIKING
"*My Fair Viking* is another entertaining story in Ms. Hill's Viking series . . . a great read."

THE BLUE VIKING
"Trademark Sandra Hill, *The Blue Viking* is filled with lots of humor, some of it laugh-out-loud fun."

TRULY, MADLY VIKING
"Once again the ingenious Ms. Hill brings a megadose of humor to her captivating and fun-filled time travels. Another winner!"

THE LOVE POTION
"The very talented Sandra Hill adds to her already impressive list of reading gems with this delightfully funny and sexy tale."

THE BEWITCHED VIKING
"A humorous, adventurous, sensual tale!"

THE LAST VIKING
"A fun, fast-paced page turner. The reader feels Sandra Hill's real joy in creating her story and the wordplay between the characters enhances the story."

THE OUTLAW VIKING
"Sandra Hill has written an entertaining battle-of-the-sexes romance that will keep readers laughing to the very end."

MORE *ROMANTIC TIMES* PRAISE FOR SANDRA HILL!

LOVE ME TENDER
"Leave it to Sandra Hill to take this fractured modern fairy tale and make it a wildly sexy and hilarious romp. Her fans will be delighted."

SWEETER SAVAGE LOVE
"A fast-paced, sensual yet tongue-in-cheek story peppered with plenty of dynamite dumb-men jokes and riddles. This funny and uplifting read will brighten any day!"

DESPERADO
"Humorous repartee and a high degree of sensuality mix well in Hill's tale of a wisecracking poor boy and the aristocratic woman he loves."

THE TARNISHED LADY
"Sandra Hill has written a sensual, vibrant, fast-paced tale of two proud lovers, their entertaining battle of wills and the steamy passion that overcomes them."

A T U R N I N G P O I N T

"Good Lord!" the woman murmured.

Did she think he was a lord? Well, he would correct that notion later. And good? He would hardly describe himself in that way, though he was not bad, either.

Even as he puffed out his chest at her blatant inspection of his body, every fine hair on Magnus's body stood at attention. Just looking at this woman made his bones turn to pudding and his fingers itch to reach out and touch her . . . to see if she was really . . . well, real. In all his thirty and seven years, he had never been affected by a female in such a way . . . and definitely not on a first meeting.

Is it a spell?

Is it a conjuring by the white-haired woman with the prayer beads?

Is it a joke by that jester god, Loki?

Does it matter?

She was staring at him as if equally poleaxed by the intense emotions swirling between them. Everyone around them probably noticed, but he did not care. Something important was happening . . . what, he could not say for a certainty . . . he just knew his life was a about to take a major turn.

Other books by Sandra Hill:
MY FAIR VIKING
THE BLUE VIKING
TRULY, MADLY VIKING
THE LOVE POTION
THE LAST VIKING
FRANKLY, MY DEAR . . .
THE TARNISHED LADY
THE BEWITCHED VIKING
THE RELUCTANT VIKING
LOVE ME TENDER
THE OUTLAW VIKING
SWEETER SAVAGE LOVE
DESPERADO

SANDRA HILL

The Very Virile Viking

LEISURE BOOKS NEW YORK CITY

A LEISURE BOOK®

March 2003

Published by

Dorchester Publishing Co., Inc.
276 Fifth Avenue
New York, NY 10001

If you purchased this book without a cover you should be aware
that this book is stolen property. It was reported as "unsold and
destroyed" to the publisher and neither the author nor the
publisher has received any payment for this "stripped book."

Copyright © 2003 by Sandra Hill

All rights reserved. No part of this book may be reproduced or
transmitted in any form or by any electronic or mechanical means,
including photocopying, recording or by any information storage
and retrieval system, without the written permission of the
publisher, except where permitted by law.

The name "Leisure Books" and the stylized "L" with design are
trademarks of Dorchester Publishing Co., Inc.

Printed in the United States of America.

Visit us on the web at www.dorchesterpub.com.

This book is dedicated to my mother, Veronica Cluston, who died just as I was finishing it. She was my greatest fan. I know she would have loved the idea of an overburdened Viking man with eleven children. Hopefully, she is cheering me on up in heaven. I will love you forever, Mom.

And to my paternal grandfather, who was named . . . guess what? Yep, Magnus. He came to the United States from Canada, but his family originated from the Orkney Islands, which were certainly Viking havens at one time. Like my Viking Magnus, my grandfather was an earthy adventurer. I could tell you stories.

My wish have I won: welcome be thou,
with kiss I clasp thee now.
The loved one's sight is sweet to her
who has lived in longing for him.

. . . Now has happened what I hoped for long,
that, hero, art come to my hall.

Heartsick was I; to have thee I yearned,
whilst thou did long for my love.
Of a truth I know: we two shall live
our life and lot together.

—*"Svipdagsmál,"* from *The Poetic Edda*

Chapter One

Autumn, the Norselands, A.D. 999

In days of old when men were . . . whatever . . .

Magnus Ericsson was a simple man.

He loved the smell of fresh-turned dirt after spring-time plowing. He loved the feel of a soft woman under him in the bed furs . . . when engaged in another type of plowing. He loved the heft of a good sword in his fighting arm. He loved the low ride of a laden longship after a-viking in far distant lands. He loved the change of seasons on his well-ordered farmstead.

What he did not relish was the large number of whining, loud, bothersome, needful children who called him *"Faðir."* "Father, this . . . Father, that . . ." they blathered night and day, always wanting something from him. Ten in all! That was the size of his brood, despite the loss of a son and a daughter to normal childhood ills and mishaps. Holy Thor! The large

1

number was embarrassing, not to mention unmanage-
able. He could not go to the garderobe without stepping on one or the other of them. Like rats, they were,
or fleas.

And, of a certainty, he was not pleased with their
mothers. Over the years there had been four wives, six
concubines, numerous passing fancies, and at least
one barley-faced maid. That latter could only be at-
tributed to a fit of mead-head madness on his part, he
was quick to tell any who dared ask. Not all of them
had shared his bed furs at the same time, praise be to
Odin, though some lackwits claimed it to be so, just
because he'd practiced the *more danico* during some
halfbrained periods of his life. He'd learned by now
that one woman at a time was more than enough for
any man to manage. All of his women, one by one,
had had the temerity to die on him, desert him, or,
ignominiously, divorce him, as his most recent wife,
Inga, had done last summer at the Althing. Claimed
she was tired of playing slave to all his babes, she did.
Norsemen from here to Birka were still laughing about
that happenstance.

He suspected as well that they were taking wagers
on how many more whelps would land on the doorstep of his longhouse by year's end.

None, if he had his way.

It had not been so bad when his father, Jarl Eric
Tryggvason, and his mother, Lady Asgar, had still been
alive and living on the adjoining royal estate. Or when
his brothers had been nearby. His mother had seemed
to have better luck in arranging help for him. But his
mother and father had both died this year, within
months of each other. The healers said it was due to

lung sickness brought on by an especially fierce winter, but he believed that it was heartsickness over his missing brothers, Geirolf and Jorund, whose ships had presumably sunk in distant waters beyond Iceland. He and his sister, Katla, were the only family left, and Katla, happily married to a Norse princeling these many years, lived in far-off Norsemandy, which some called Normandy.

There was much pressure on him to take over his father's jarldom, especially from his uncle, the high king of the Norselands, Olaf Tryggvason. But that would mean giving up his own lands and the farming he cherished. Further, he would knowingly be immersing himself in the political pressures that faced all the minor kingdoms in the Norselands as they squabbled for power. He was a farmer, at heart, not a man ambitious for power.

Besides, did he not have enough pressures within his own family?

That is a pointless question.

Where would his children fit into such a scenario?

Wherever they could squeeze in.

Would he have to take another wife?

For a certainty.

Did he want another wife?

Bloody hell, no!

But how long had it been since he'd lain with a woman?

Far too long! I am afraid to look at a woman these days, for fear my seed will fly into her womb.

Would the marriage bonds be worth the bother of another squawking woman following him about like a shadow? Or producing even more babies?

3

Bonds . . . that is an accurate description.

And would a woman of his choosing be willing to take on all his offspring?

Probably not. Nay, I should not wed again.

But the sex . . .

Aaarrgh!

The problem, as far as he could tell, always came back to the children and the burden of his virility. If he were free, he could make decisions based on his own wants, or needs, or the good of the people of Vestfold. But he had ten other individuals to consider.

Magnus had seen seven and thirty winters. Sometimes, when he was in a daze from too much youthling noise, or when he was suffering from the ale ache, he wondered how he had begotten so many children. But, of course, he knew how.

Magnus Ericsson was a lustsome man.

And therein lay the Viking's problem.

Winter, the Norselands, A.D. 999

Trouble comes in small packages. . . .

"You have another child," Magnus's eldest son, Ragnor, said with disgust, trying to hand a girl barely out of swaddling clothes into his arms.

Magnus promptly folded his arms over his chest in refusal.

"Her name is Lida," Ragnor persisted, and tried once again to hand over the child, who couldn't be more than a year old.

Magnus took one step backward and shook his head vehemently.

"Goo!" Lida said, favoring him with a gummy grin.

She shook her little head from side to side as well, no doubt thinking he was playing a game with her.

He was not moved. Nor was he in the mood for games. "Take her away." He stepped to the side and used a poker to stir the yule log in the center hearth of his great hall; the burning of the log was a Christian tradition his family had always followed. Though he was Norse by birth, he also practiced the Christian faith of his mother. God bless her soul. He hoped she was at rest with the saints she'd revered. Just as he hoped his father was revelling in Valhalla. Sometimes he wondered if heaven and Valhalla might be the same place, but it was a far-fetched opinion he kept to himself. Regardless, 'twas best to appease all the gods. Unfortunately he seemed to be personally blessed—or was it plagued?—by Freyja, the goddess of fertility.

Meanwhile, the Viking comrades who sat about his great hall drinking ale and playing the board game *hnefatafl* snickered amongst themselves while they viewed his son trying to hand him another babe. Once again he and his potency would be the subject of jests. Well, he would not stand for it this time.

"There is no proof," he contended. "She is not mine."

"I beg to differ. She looks just like you."

"Goo!" Lida repeated. Blond spikes of hair stood up in disarray about her tiny head. Freckles speckled her rosy cheeks. She smelled like a privy.

"Sarcasm ill suits you, boy," Magnus snapped. His son knew full well that his father was considered an attractive man. Magnus prided himself on a well-honed body and his inherited good looks. Aside from his big ears, which he covered vainly with long hair, he was nigh perfect. Many a maid had told him so. And this whelp was anything but attractive or perfect. But then he noticed something. *Oh, for the love of Frey! Are those excessively big ears on the mite?*

Ragnor snickered, noticing the direction of his father's stare.

"You are not so big at sixteen years that I cannot put you over my knee," Magnus declared, sinking down to a bench. Of course, his sitting down gave three-year-old Kolbein the excuse to climb up onto his lap. Kolbein should be acting the little man at his age, like five-year-old Hamr did. Begged him constantly for his very own bow and arrows, the bothersome boy did. "You'll shoot your eye out," was Magnus's response. Kolbein, on the other hand, had always been a needsome child, having lost his mother at birth. Even six-year-old Jogeir with his club foot asked for no special indulgence. Some said Magnus should have exposed Jogeir to the elements in the frozen north when he was born, as some Vikings fathers were wont to do. Life in the Norselands was harsh for whole persons. Those weak or handicapped from birth would face nigh insurmountable obstacles to survival. But he had not been able to do it, and Jogeir worked hard each day to prove he had made the right decision. *Poor boy!*

"Ha!" Ragnor said, jarring him back to the present. Apparently Ragnor was still reacting to his father's comment about being able to spank him. Ragnor's one word said it all, though, for Ragnor might not yet have reached his father's massive height, but he was fast approaching it. And both of them had muscles aplenty.

"I could hold Ragnor down for you whilst you give

him a well-deserved whomping." It was his other sixteen-year-old son, Torolf, speaking now. Torolf loved to tease his older brother more than anything, though Ragnor was older by only one sennight. They were born to different mothers in different lands within days of each other. Magnus must have been particularly lustful that week nine months beforehand, but, in truth, he could barely recall the details of the women or the couplings. All he knew was that Ragnor had the black hair and pale blue eyes of his Frankish mother, while Torolf favored Magnus's first wife, Sigrun, with pale blond hair and honey-colored eyes. That was when Magnus's troubles had first begun. Sigrun had threatened to cut off his man part when she heard about Ragnor's birth. Two years later she was gone— ran off with an Irish priest, she did—leaving Torolf behind. It had been the beginning of a trend in Magnus's life.

"I would like to see you try," Ragnor told Torolf with his usual arrogance. He gave Torolf a punch in the shoulder with his free hand. Meanwhile a giggling Lida dangled from the crook of his other arm.

"Anytime, brother. Anytime." Torolf punched his brother back and grinned, just to annoy him. The two were like overgrown puppies. Soon they would be down in the rushes wrestling each other.

"Goo," Lida contributed.

Magnus had a sudden inspiration. "I cannot take the child. She needs a wet nurse, and as you know, we cannot even keep maids here at the farmstead to care for the older children, let alone a wet nurse."

"Lida is weaned, smart little one that she is." Ragnor fairly smirked at him.

7

"Take her back whence she came," Magnus demanded.

"I cannot," Ragnor said. "She came on that trading *knorr* from Hedeby. Sent by a craftswoman there by the name of Gyda the Goldsmith. She claims her daughter, Helga, gave birth to Lida a year ago. Helga died recently of the brothel disease."

Helga? Unfortunately that name sounded familiar to Magnus. He seemed to recall a comely maid in a red gunna serving mead in a Hedeby alehouse. Her face had been sprinkled with freckles.

"The captain of the *knorr* says the fjords are already freezing over. And besides, he is not taking a smelly-arsed, squalling babe back with him. Those were his exact words." Ragnor smirked again.

With a sigh of resignation, Magnus opened his arms and welcomed the newest addition to his family. He could not swear that Lida was his. But that could be said of half his brood.

"Goo," Lida cooed, tugging at the war braids on either side of his face.

"Goo to you, too, little one," Magnus replied.

Still wintertime, the Norselands, A.D. 1000

"It is disgraceful, *Faðir*. Really, it is. All these children, and no one to care for them. Tsk-tsk! Mayhap you could hire another nursemaid or two. Or better yet, a whip master for the older ones."

It was Magnus's eldest child, seventeen-year-old Madrene, who had started berating him from the moment he entered his keep. He was frozen to the bone after making his way, along with a half dozen workers, through chest-high snow from the stables. He had spent the past eight hours delivering one foal, two calves, and a litter of piglets. He and his helpers had pulled in enough feed to get the animals through tonight's upcoming blizzard; then they'd mucked out the stalls . . . who knew when they'd be able to do it again! And who knew horses and cows could produce so much smelly waste! Ah, well, 'twas part of a farmer's life and he did not mind all that much. Industrious little six-year-old Jogeir had come along with them. Even dragging his lame foot along, he was able to accomplish as much as many a laggard man he'd met in his time. Finally they'd made the trek home on the slippery ice path, carrying baskets of hen and duck eggs for Gunnhora, his head cook, who was preparing for Madrene's wedding feast next week. It was ridiculous, really, having a wedding feast in the middle of winter, but once Madrene got an idea in her head, she was like a dog with a bone; she would not give it up for anything.

"And furthermore . . ."

Bloody hell! His daughter was still wagging her tongue. What he did not need was more complaints, especially from one of his own children.

He decided to ignore Madrene, who was too full of herself by half now that she was to become a wife. Instead he walked up to one of the three blazing hearths in his hall and proceeded to remove his ice-crusted furs and undercloak. Madrene followed him, the pestsome wench. 'Twas a wonder she did not start on him about the puddle he was making in the rushes. He shook his body like a shaggy dog, creating a shower of droplets, just to annoy her more, but all she

9

did was make more of those clucking noises women fancied so much.

Blah, blah, blah! Does her tongue ever get tired? "What is the problem now?" he asked, knowing full well she would not leave till she'd spouted everything on her mind.

"Lida has soiled another nappy, and Kirsten and Dagny refuse to change her again." Kirsten and Dagny were his fourteen- and twelve-year-old daughters, and, to tell the truth, he did not blame them at all. The girls did more than their fair share of household chores, especially since another nursemaid had quit on him last sennight, claiming to be overburdened by his wild and numerous progeny. And Lida did seem to have bowels that worked all too well. "Ask one of the kitchen thralls to help," he advised. "Or how about the new chambermaid? What is her name? Arnora . . . that is it . . . Arnora. Came to us on that last trading ship, searching for work."

Actually he knew her name precisely. The voluptuous young woman had been swishing her hips afore him in invitation every time she passed by. And he was tempted—sorely tempted, considering how long it had been since he'd last lain between a woman's thighs. Six months! Ever since Inga had divorced him. It was not yet spring, but his sap was running high. So far he had resisted temptation, but he was not sure how much longer he could remain chaste. If nothing else, he was going to be drooling sap before long.

Weren't there any attractive women beyond child-bearing age? Mayhap he should look for one next time he went to Birka. He would have to mention it to Toki the Trader, who was wintering here in Vestfold till the fjords thawed. Toki knew everyone in the market towns.

"Arnora! Hmpfh! That is another thing," Madrene said, frowning with consternation.

Gods! The girl is still chattering away, even when I am not listening.

"Ragnor and Torolf were seen entering her sleeping chamber this morn, and they have not come out since."

Any temptation he had felt for the maid flew up to the rafters. His rising sap lowered like a lake before an unplugged dam. "Together?"

She nodded.

Magnus's eyes widened at that news. And his first thought was, *Double the chance of impregnating the lass.* That was all he needed. More babes being bred in his family. From sixteen-year-old boys, yet! He had known they were no longer untried youthlings. In truth, they tried too hard. But this was a situation he would have to stop. Two to one? What could they be thinking? Well, actually, what they were doing did not involve thinking at all.

Just then he noticed yet another son, Storvald, sitting by the hearth, whittling away at one of his fine woodcarvings—a rendition of a longship in intricate detail. He squinted in the firelight to make up for his poor vision. It was not a real handicap for the boy; he had trouble seeing only tiny details close up. But now Storvald, at thirteen years, was listening with great interest to their conversation. No doubt he thought it would be great fun to join Arnora in the bed furs, too . . . even at his young age—*especially* at his young age.

"Do you want me to go get them?" Storvald asked, blinking his eyes with exaggerated innocence.

11

"Nay, I do not want you to go get them," Magnus said. "I will handle it myself." *And I am looking forward to it about as much as if I were about to pull the hairs out of my nose.*

And off he stormed, even as Madrene continued to call out her list of grievances. "And Kolbein ate three bowls of custard that Cook had put aside in the scullery, and now he is suffering belly cramps. Dagny got her first monthly flux and will not stop weeping. Kolbein saw the bloody rag and thinks she is dying. Hamr broke Asa's broom, pretending it was a sword."

"Is that all?"

"Nay, that is not all. Do you want to know what Njal and his friends are doing?"

Nay. "Do I have a choice?" Njal was his nine-year-old son. A more mischievous boy had never been born.

"Njal and his friends are breaking wind, deliberately, every time they pass the weaving room, and the girls there say they will not work in such a stinksome place."

Magnus sighed loudly and put a palm to his aching forehead. At least his groin was no longer aching.

He could not wait till the wedding feast, when Madrene's besotted young jarl would take her away from all this misery. At least then he would have one less child to worry over. At least then he would be a little less miserable himself.

Wouldn't he?

Still wintertime (would it ever end?), the Norselands, A.D. 1000.

"We think we have the answer to your problem, Magnus."

Resting his bleary head on the trestle table, Magnus was sitting on the dais above the central hearth when he heard someone addressing him from below. He'd had only one horn of ale to drink this eve, but he was overtired from a day of shoveling snow to make paths to the various outbuildings of his vast farmstead. Already the snow was eaves-high and still falling. And ice had to be knocked off the roofs lest the thatch come crashing down under the heavy weight. The skies were black day and night, except for about an hour each day, which was the pattern in the Norse-lands. Everyone was tense from the confinement, especially his energetic children. *Will winter ever be over?*

He raised his head reluctantly to see his best friend and chieftain of his *hird* of fighting men, Harek the Huge, waiting expectantly for his answer. Harek—who was . . . well, huge—stood in the aisle that separated the dais from the open-sided hearth, taking up most of the space. Crowded on either side of Harek were Atli One-Ear, Kugge the Archer, and Sidroc of the Forked Beard. They were all grinning up at him.

Uh-oh! "You say you have an answer to my problem, Harek. Which problem would that be? It cannot be Madrene. She is two weeks wed and gone with her bridegroom to her new home. Ragnor? Torolf? Kirsten? Storvald? Dagny? Njal? Jogeir? Hamr? Kolbein? Lida? Which one has caused the *problem* this time?"

"Freyja's tits! How do you remember them all?" Kugge wanted to know. Kugge was an expert marksman, but he was thickheaded as a woolly sheep.

"How can I forget them?" *They will not let me forget.*

13

Magnus arched an eyebrow at Kugge and took a sip of stale ale.

"They—your children—are not the problem we refer to," Harek said.

Magnus noticed then that dozens of men about his hall were watching them expectantly . . . with much amusement. Norsemen ever did enjoy a good jest. But what—or who—was the subject of this particular jest? He came suddenly alert.

"You have been very peevish of late," Atli remarked, pulling at his disfigured ear, as if the lobe had not been lost to a Saxon sword.

"Peevish?"

"Yea, you nigh bite the head off of anyone and everyone for the least little reason," Sidroc added, jutting out his forked beard, daring him to disagree. "And we know the reason."

"You do?"

"Frustration," Harek explained. "Your male humors must needs escape on occasion, or you will explode. Happened to Halfdan the Hermit, it did. He went barmy in the end for lack of a good swiving. Yea, you have been too long without a tupping."

All the men nodded their agreement.

"You men push the bounds of friendship. My body humors are naught of your business." *Can anything in the world be more embarrassing than this? Methinks I should go live in a cave. But nay, I cannot do that. My children would follow me, and they would freeze in a cave. Aaarrgh!*

"But here is the best part . . ." said Ottar the Oarsman, a new entry to the company.

"We heard you were looking for a more . . . uh . . . mature woman. One who could give you pleasure in the bed furs without popping out a babe every nine months," Harek explained.

"A mature woman who is still attractive," Atli quickly added.

"Well, reasonably attractive," Kugge further added.

"Leastways, not repulsive," Sidroc further added.

Oh . . . my . . . gods! Magnus glanced to the left . . . then glanced again. He could scarce believe the scene unfolding before him. A line of women—a dozen in all—were being led from a far corridor, all ages and sizes and types of attire. One thing they had in common, though: only one of them appeared to be under the age of forty.

"Where . . . why . . . what . . ." he sputtered out. "I mean, oh, bloody damn hell! Tell me, Harek, where have all these women come from—in this weather—and why?"

"They come from your father's estate and other neighboring jarldoms—come to be your bedmate, they have. Well, candidates for your bedmate. You get to pick," Harek explained pridefully, as if he had done Magnus a great favor. "Some of them have been here for several sennights, in secret. The more recent additions came aboard sleds."

Magnus's jaw dropped with incredulity at the bizarre "candidates" who stood before him.

"This is Bertha." Harek drew the first woman forth. "She has had five children, but she is past the breeding age now."

"I would think so," Magnus commented as Bertha smiled up at him. She was toothless and her face re-

15

sembled a dried apple. "You cannot be serious," he told Harek.

Harek shrugged, as if it were of no matter. After all, he had eleven more "candidates" to offer. "How about this one? Leila comes from the Eastlands."

"East of where?" Magnus scoffed. The woman—probably a dockside harlot—a Norse dock, that is—had attempted to slant her eyes with kohl, but mostly she just looked like a sad raccoon.

"Well, surely you will like Eadgifu then. Comes from London, she does," Atli offered, shoving a woman midway down the line to the forefront. "She is the youngest of this lot, but she is barren due to a childhood illness."

Eadgifu also weighed about as much as a warhorse, and that was no exaggeration. He misdoubted a man could even find her woman's portal in all that flab. And if she flipped him over, he would be crushed in the coupling.

Magnus just scowled as one by one his comrades paraded their candidates before him.

Hervor used a cane because her one leg was swollen with some malady.

"Is she crippled?" he asked in an indignant whisper to Harek.

"Nay. 'Tis just the gout. Comes and goes," Harek replied, waving a hand dismissively.

"Her ankle is the size of a ham."

"Do you not think you are being a bit picky?"

Magnus frowned his disapproval, but Harek just ignored him and motioned for more candidates. There was Olga, whose eyes were crossed. And Sybil, who stuttered so badly that spittle ran down her quivering chin.

"Blanca has a special talent she employs with her tongue," Atli told him with a wink and a chuckle.

"That would be fine if one could overlook her mustache."

He thought he heard several of the men mutter, "Picky, picky" under their breath.

Next was Gunnhilde, who looked more like a man than a woman, and not just because of her height; there was a bulge in front of her gown at an inappropriate spot.

Valda was a comely lass, but clearly pregnant, though 'twas true she would not be growing *his* seed, leastways not for the next few months.

Thea's raven-black hair was so thin her white scalp showed through.

"Do my eyes play me false, or is that woman nigh bald?" Magnus's eyes bulged with incredulity.

Kugge, who had led that woman forward, made a *tsk*ing sound at his words. "Thea merely has some head sores which caused her hair to fall out. It will soon come back," he said. After a moment, he added, "I think."

The last straw, so to speak, was Dagmar, a dairymaid from the Danish lands. Even as she stood before him, she could not stop scratching herself—her head, her underarms, even her groin. The woman was clearly infested with lice.

"Enough!" Magnus roared, rising to his full height and pointing a forefinger at Harek with the silent message that he should remove the candidates from his presence at once.

"We were just trying to please you," Harek said defensively. But Magnus saw the grin twitching his lips. In fact, looking about his hall, he saw that some of his men were laughing so hard they were bent over at the waist. He wouldn't be surprised if a few of them wet their *braies*, so overcome with mirth were they.

Magnus could not be angry at his friends . . . leastways, not for long. They were only teasing. The fact that it was a sore and serious subject for him was beside the point. Magnus and his misdeeds would no doubt be the subject of a skaldic saga at the next Althing. It would be titled something ridiculous, like "Magnus the Virile and His Wild Seed."

Magnus could not go on this way much longer.

Something would have to be done.

At last . . . springtime, the Norselands, A.D. 1000

Magnus had made a decision, and it was a momentous one.

"Hear me, one and all," he shouted out to those in attendance at the springtime feast taking place outdoors on his farmstead, where large trestle tables had been set up and canvas tents erected. The fields had been plowed and planted. All the chores left over from winter were completed. Fallen timbers were cleared from streams. New baby animals were being born. It was a time of celebration after weeks of grueling hard work. Many of his men would go off a-viking now, or lend their sword arms to King Olaf in his never ending battles to hold the all-kingship of the Norselands. They would return at harvesttime, though.

But not Magnus.

It was a season of new beginnings for the farm.

It would be a season of new beginnings for Magnus, too.

"I, Magnus Ericsson, have decided to take a vow of celibacy," he announced over the din of celebration.

Slowly silence fell over the crowd, and he could hear murmurs as his words were repeated from group to group. Once his meaning sank in, laughter began to burst forth in waves. They thought he was jesting.

He held up a hand for quiet. In his other hand he raised high his drinking horn. "Wish me well, my friends, for I am serious. And that is not all."

"Now, now, Magnus, are you still chafing under our little joke last winter?" Harek had come up to stand beside him.

He shook his head and smiled at his good friend.

"And that is not all," he repeated. "I will be leaving the Norselands for a good long time. I am off to that new land beyond Iceland which was discovered a dozen or so years ago by my father's cousin, Erik the Red. 'Tis Greenland I refer to, of course. Or mayhap I will venture even farther to that place which his son Leif is exploring. Vinland is supposed to be warmer, if naught else."

The laughter of the crowd had become shocked silence.

"But why?" Harek was gazing at him with a frown of puzzlement on his forehead.

Magnus wished he could explain the missive he'd received a sennight before. It had arrived on a trading ship that had come in contact with some sailors from that new land of Leif's. In a linen-wrapped parcel was his brother Jorund's sword. Tied to the sword were two small portraits—one of Jorund with some strange woman and two twin girls, and the other of Jorund and Geirolf with arms looped over each other's shoulders, standing before a huge archway sign that read, *Rosestead.*

The portraits, if they could be called that, were done on peculiar parchment paper unlike any he had ever seen before. And the attire worn by all of them was strange. But most important, Jorund and Geirolf looked happy. After much pondering, Magnus had decided that it was a message from the gods . . . or from his brothers.

Geirolf's dragonship had been lost in the oceans beyond Iceland almost three years past; he was presumed to have drowned in a shipwreck. Then Jorund's dragonship had done the same two years ago when he'd gone to search for Geirolf.

But were they really dead? Or were they alive in some new land? Magnus had to find out for himself. It was a mystery he must at least investigate.

"It is something I must do," was the only explanation he could give Harek. He put on a mirthful face then and added, "Besides, there is not enough good land in Norway for all my children. Ha, ha, ha!"

People nodded and laughed, tentatively, at his half jest, half truth. Arable land had always been scarce in the Norselands. Thousands of Vikings were settling in other countries for that very reason.

"Who will rule here . . . in your absence?" Atli called out to him.

"Madrene and her husband, Karl, will rule in my place here at the farmstead. Ragnor will represent me at my father's estate. The rest of my children—all nine of them—will come with me." *May the gods help me,* he added to himself.

He could see the disappointment in Jogeir's face. The boy was a farmer at heart, like him, and he loved this land. But there would be new farms for Jogeir, of that he was convinced, or he would not go. Besides, they would come back someday.

As his people began to assimilate his news and accept it—all Vikings loved a good adventure—Magnus sat down with a sigh and took a long draft from his horn of ale. He felt good about his decision. If nothing else, it was a time for new beginnings.

Besides, it would be a lot easier to honor his vow of celibacy in the new land, where there were surely not very many women. And those who were there must be dog-ugly—Why else would they settle in the back of beyond?—though the one in Jorund's portrait had been more than passable.

For the first time in a year or more, Magnus was excited, and it had naught to do with the throb betwixt his legs.

As sure as dragon piss, it was a good sign.

Chapter Two

Sonoma Valley, June 2003

Whining in Wine Country . . .

The sign read, *Blue Dragon Vineyard*.

Angela Abruzzi made a smooth slide of her hand on the leather steering wheel of her BMW, turning it up the drive to the rambling Victorian house she had once called home. With a deep sigh, she slowed the Beamer to a crawl and tried to enjoy the familiar scenery, despite the knot in her stomach, which had been tightening since she'd left her apartment in L.A. this morning. The tension was not due to trepidation at coming home; that was always a joy. It was due to the formidable task she had to accomplish today.

The stately, unique species of oak trees that lined the drive always brought a smile to her face. The trees, with their rare speckled bark, had been a whim of the original builder a hundred years ago . . . and too expensive and showy not to be kept up by all the owners since then. The low stone walls on either side of the road were dotted every ten feet or so with enormous, dragon-design terra-cotta planters spilling over with lush red geraniums that were painstakingly cared for by her seventy-five-year-old grandmother. Wildflowers in a myriad of pastel colors dotted the lawns leading up to the house and beyond, on either side of the stream that fed into a large pond. The pond acted as a reservoir for the much-needed irrigation system. Ancient willow trees surrounded the pond like Southern belles with wide lacy crinolines; they'd been her make-believe playhouses as a child. Behind the house as far as the eye could see, for two hundred acres or more, were row upon row of grapevines, bright green now in the June sun but soon to be filled with clusters of purple globes—the lifeblood of Blue Dragon. A large vegetable garden was also located in the back—far too big for the single inhabitant of the house.

As she pulled up to the wide circle in front of the house with its wraparound porch, her grandmother, Rose Abruzzi, was already coming down the steps to greet her, a welcoming smile on her face. In many ways they resembled each other, especially the thick masses of curly hair spilling down over their shoulders, although Angela's was coal black and Grandma's was now pure white. And they both had coal-black eyes and a tiny black mole just above the upper lip on the right, something Grandma preferred to call a beauty mark.

People were always surprised when they met her grandmother for the first time. To say she was not the usual senior citizen would be a vast understatement. Today she wore a white tank top and denim coveralls over her still-trim figure. A Virginia Slims cigarette dangled from the fingertips of her right hand. Grandma had been a chain smoker for more than fifty years and was not about to stop now, despite all the health warnings. Her feet, still a petite size six that she prided herself on, were covered with muddy, formerly white sneakers.

"Angela, darling," her grandmother crooned, opening her arms wide for a one-armed embrace, meanwhile holding her cigarette expertly in the air to avoid catching her granddaughter's hair on fire. Even as she hugged, she shook off the long ash. Before she'd discovered Virginia Slims, Grandma had used a cigarette holder, and what a pretentious sight that had been! Dungarees and an eighteen-karat-gold Tiffany cigarette holder! Her grandfather had matched her conspicuous consumption with Cuban cigars. But those had been the days of prosperity . . . before the year of the drought, before the year they'd had the fire in the warehouse just after harvest, before the year they'd had so many strange machinery breakdowns, before the year they'd lost their prize vintner to a French winery, before the year they'd been hit with phylloxera. Now they just eked by, growing grapes for other wine makers, hoping for a miracle that would allow them to bottle wine again.

Thank God for her job in the city, which allowed her to make huge commissions selling Beverly Hills homes to the rich and famous. Without her annual input of $100,000 to $200,000 into Blue Dragon, they would be looking at one dead mythical serpent . . . so to speak.

"Grandma!" she squealed affectionately, and hugged back, giving an extra squeeze. It had been only a month since she'd visited last, but she missed the old lady and was desperately worried about her and the vineyards these days . . . with good reason. "How have you been? Is Miguel taking his heart pills? Did you fix the aerator? Where's Jow?" Miguel was the foreman, just as old as Grandma and still working as hard as ever, despite his doctor's precautions. And Jow was "Just One Week," the German shepherd she'd bought for her grandmother and grandfather so they wouldn't be lonely eight years ago after she married the man they had all come to refer to as the Creep. They'd vowed to keep the dog for "just one week" because having a rambunctious animal amidst delicate grapevines could be a problem. Besides, even as a puppy, they'd been able to tell by his huge pointy ears and enormous feet that he was going to grow into the horse of a dog he was now. Well, they'd kept Jow, her marriage had ended after only one year (too bad she hadn't made the one-week vow about the Creep), and grandpa had died three years ago of a sudden and massive stroke, brought on in part by the series of unexplained mishaps in his precious vineyard.

Grandma shrugged and began to lead her up the front steps. "Everything's fine. Jow is out with Miguel inspecting the new roots in the west field. You know, that damn dog has the greatest nose for aphids. And he saved a dozen of the rootstock last week by scarfing up slugs. Eats like a horse, and not just slugs. He ruined three of my prize rosebushes this spring because he insists on peeing there, close to the house. But at least the damn dog is of some use." She sniffed with disdain as she spoke, as if to hide the fact that she adored "the damned dog." She took a long drag on her cigarette, blew out the smoke in a circular cloud, then ground out the stub in a special sand-filled tub near the front door, placed there especially for that purpose by a disapproving Juanita, the Mexican housekeeper who had been a fixture at Blue Dragon forever. She was Miguel's wife.

"When are you going to quit smoking, Grandma?"

"When are you going to find yourself a good man and come back home to Blue Dragon?"

Never, apparently. "I heard you have a buyer interested in Blue Dragon. Gunther again?"

"As always," her grandmother said in a voice of pure disgust. If it wouldn't have been unladylike, she probably would have spit, too.

Gunther Morgan was a neighboring vintner who had been wanting to buy the Blue Dragon for years, since even before her grandfather had died. They suspected, but had never been able to prove, that he was responsible for some shady tactics to coerce them and other property owners in the region to sell. A more despicable fellow was not to be found in all of the Sonoma Valley.

"At least he's upped his offer this time," Angela remarked.

"Who told you that?"

"Carmen."

"Pfff! My great niece has a big mouth. She ought to use it to mind her own business. In fact, she ought to use it to find herself a husband and a father for that girl of hers."

"Grandma!"

"Well, it's true. If Carmen would spend more time teaching her daughter some traditional values, instead of preaching all that man-hating nonsense to college girls, she'd be a lot better off."

The best Angela could come up with was, "Tsk-tsk-tsk!" Then, "That statement is outrageous, even for you, Grandma. You know very well that Carmen is a respected professor of women's studies at Merryvale College. True, she goes off the deep end with some of her feminist philosophies, but she is by no means a man-hater."

"Ha! I heard her on the college radio station one day. She said any woman who lusted after George Clooney was a brainless twit."

Angela frowned in confusion. "Why would Carmen be discussing a movie star on a public radio station? She's not usually into entertainment issues."

"She was talking about how young girls are given the wrong standards in picking a man. Seems she's writing a new book, *Men to Avoid in the New Millennium.* She said women would be better off using logical standards to pick a mate, like a Bill Gates–type fellow, rather than lusting after a hunk of the month, like George Clooney."

Hunk of the month? I wonder if that's Carmen's phrase, or Grandma's? "That doesn't mean she's a man-hater."

Grandma was already lighting up another Virginia Slims. She inhaled deeply before replying in a puff of smoke: "Honey, any woman who fails to lust after George Clooney has to be a man-hater."

Angela had to laugh at that. "Even you, Grandma?"

"Especially me."

"I suspect that Carmen's point was, in this postfeminist era, women should have learned at least one thing: Looks aren't everything."

Grandma waggled her eyebrows at her. "They don't hurt."

"Furthermore, Grandma—"

"Uh-oh! I know I'm in trouble when you start a sentence with 'furthermore.' "

"Furthermore, Grandma," she continued, shooting her grandmother an exaggerated scowl for interrupting her, "I know better than anyone that all the man-pleasing acts in the world by a loving wife aren't going to keep a bound-to-stray, overly attractive husband at home."

Grandma nodded gravely. "Perfect example: the Creep."

"Precisely."

"Ay-yi-yi!" a feminine voice shrieked. "Is that a cigarette I smell in my nice clean house?" Juanita came barreling down the hallway that led from the kitchen to the front anteroom, all five-foot-nothing of her. But then she noticed Angela, and a smile spread across her face. "Angela, I didn't know you were here already. I made your favorites for lunch . . . chicken frijoles and 'spicy-dicey ricey.' " That latter was the name a much younger Angela had given to Juanita's special jalapeño-pepper-and-wild-rice dish.

"Oh, Juanita, I've missed you—and your cooking—so much." Angela, at five-foot-seven, had to bend over to hug the tiny housekeeper, who had been a second mother to her since she was a toddler. That was when her mother and father had died in a car accident, and Grandma and Grandpa had stepped in as her parents.

"How about *my* cooking?" Grandma asked, clearly miffed. "I thought my penne pasta with pesto marinara was your favorite."

Grandma and Juanita had been fighting a gentle battle for years in the kitchen over whether the Italian dishes of her homeland were better than the Spanish dishes that Juanita preferred. It had not been unusual to have lasagna and tacos on the dinner table at one time.

"Now, now, I love both of your cooking," Angela said.

"Hmpfh! Well, come then, Angelina. I've set the table out on the side porch. Hope that damn dog doesn't get a whiff of my frijoles, or he'll be galloping down from the hills faster'n a cat with a hot tail. Ate a whole ham I baked last week before I could catch him."

Grandma made sure she got the last word in, though. "We're going to eat *in bianca* for dinner tonight. All white. Chicken in garlic sauce, angel hair pasta with shrimp, cauliflower fresh from the garden, even white fudge mousse." Grandma took one last drag on her cigarette then.

That caught Juanita's attention, if Rose's insistence on an Italian menu had not. "Put out that stinkin' cigarette."

Sometimes it was hard to tell who was mistress of Blue Dragon.

Sometimes it just did not matter.

Sometimes it was so good to be home.

Pride goeth before . . .

Rose lit a cigarette and leaned back in her wicker chair.

She and Angela were sitting in the shade of the side porch, replete from Juanita's wonderful lunch. Rose squabbled constantly with Juanita, as two old women were wont to do, but she knew that Juanita was a good cook and a priceless friend. She also knew that Rose returned her affection in equal measure . . . aside from the smoking.

She and Angela were sipping from stemmed Lalique crystal wine goblets glistening with a splendid 1997 dry chardonnay, the last year they'd made their own wine at the Blue Dragon. The lunch and the visit with her beloved granddaughter both contributed to making it a perfect day in the house and on the land she loved dearly.

The only thing missing was the sound of children. It had always been a shortcoming, in Rose's opinion, but in fifty years here at the Blue Dragon all they'd had was Angela, and Angels's father, Marcus, before her. Oh, it hadn't been her fault that she'd given birth to only one child; she would have had a dozen kids, if she could have, but a hysterectomy had been necessary when she was only twenty-five. And her son, Marcus, had had only the one child, Angela, before his untimely death. And, God knew, she couldn't blame Angela for failing to have children with the Creep. Still, this was a huge house made for loud, energetic children.

Inhaling sweet smoke from her cigarette deep into her lungs, she exhaled slowly and studied her granddaughter. Such a good girl she was . . . though hardly a girl anymore at thirty-two. And she worked so hard. They rarely talked about it, but Rose knew how much money Angela plowed back into the Blue Dragon to keep it going. Rose never protested, though it rankled her pride mightily. In effect the Blue Dragon belonged to Angela . . . or it would as soon as she passed on. Before then, she hoped for a miracle; she was saying a novena every night for just that purpose. There had to be a way for Angela to be able to return to Sonoma and run the vineyards and reopen the winery.

"Why are you looking so wistful, Grandma?"

Rose laughed. "I was thinking about miracles . . . and great-grandchildren."

Angela laughed right back at her. "From me? It would take a miracle, and more, since there are no likely fathers on the horizon for me."

"You could do that artificial-insemination thing, couldn't you?"

"Grandma! You don't really mean that."

She shrugged. "I guess not, but I thought maybe I could shock you into action."

"We have more important things to discuss today, Grandma."

By the serious expression on her face, Rose knew she wasn't going to escape this time. "What is it now? Bounced check? Increased taxes? That sleazeball Gunther?"

"No, it's more than that. We need a big influx of money into this estate, Grandma. Bigger than I can provide from my job."

She exhaled a nicotine cloud. "How much?"

"Five hundred thousand would be nice. Two hundred thousand would pay off our bills and enable us to make some much-needed improvements. The other three are a cushion we've got to have. We can't go on month to month anymore."

31

Rose nodded. She understood the pressure all these money woes put on Angela. But five hundred thousand! Where would they ever get that kind of money? It was impossible. That must be what Angela was trying to tell her. "I am not going to sell the Blue Dragon, if that's what you have in mind . . . and certainly not to Gunther. I'd rather sell my jewelry, the antiques, everything in this house first." Actually, she'd already sold some of her most valuable possessions and replaced them with reproductions.

Angela reached across the table and patted her hand. "I know that, Grandma. I have an idea that might work, though."

Rose narrowed her eyes at Angela with suspicion. There was a shifty cast in her granddaughter's pretty black eyes . . . the kind that meant she was going to try to talk her into something she would not like. "What idea?"

"I sold a Bel Air mansion recently to a Hollywood producer. He's about to make a film—a romantic saga—about an old California family after World War Two. And here's the best part. . . ."

Rose waited. That crafty cast was still in Angela's eyes.

"It takes place in a vineyard."

"So?"

"I think I could talk him into filming the movie here."

"For five hundred thousand dollars? Is he nuts?"

"No. He offered two hundred thousand—tentatively—conditional upon a personal tour and approval by his film crew. But I think I can negotiate him upward once he sees the place."

"When would this be? And for how long?"

"August . . . possibly into September."

"Angela! That's prime growing season . . . maybe even harvesttime. We can't have strangers stomping around here then."

"Maybe I could negotiate a time deadline, and put a limit on the number of people. It's the only way, Grandma."

"Oh, Angela," she sighed. "I can't believe we are reduced to this."

"It's not such an awful thing. Really. Lots of vineyards rent themselves out to movie studios . . . even to cooking shows on TV. In fact, we might be able to get you a bit part in the movie."

She pretended to brighten up. "Like Sophia Loren."

"Yeah. An older version of Sophia Loren."

"Ha! Sophia Loren is no young chick."

"I forgot."

"Any chance you could negotiate George Clooney into this movie? That would be the clincher for me."

Angela smiled warmly at her. She knew she had won. They were going to have a film crew here at the Blue Dragon.

"Just one thing, Angela."

"Anything."

Ha! Smart women know never to say that. "If I'm willing to give in on this point, I want you to agree to something."

"Anything."

Yep. Very unsmart of you, sweetie. "I want you to try to look a little harder for a man. You need someone to love, who will love you in return."

"And give you great-grandchildren?"

At least Angela wasn't offended. "An added bonus," she conceded.

"Okay, I'll look harder. I promise. It will be at the top of my list." She pretended to be writing herself a note on the palm of her hand. "One . . . good . . . man."

"Oh, I don't know about good. Virile would be better."

Angela had just begun to take a last sip of wine from her goblet and she started to choke. When she was able to talk, she asked with an arched eyebrow, "Virile?"

"Very virile."

Vinland, a month later . . .

Drowning in children . . .

Magnus and his nine children had been at sea for two sennights. Furthermore, he had not lain with a woman for eleven months. He wasn't sure which of those facts was driving him the barmiest.

"Are they all asleep?" he asked Torolf.

"Yea. Finally," his son answered, clearly disgusted. The younger children—all eight of them—were strung out between them on bed furs spread on the ship's cold planking. Most important, a long rope tied one ankle of each to that of the next, with Magnus and Torolf on either end. He would take no chance that one of them might sleepwalk over the side into the frigid water. Then there was Jogeir, who had developed a passion for fishing over the side of the boat and was becoming quite successful in his efforts. His lameness mattered not when casting a net or pulling in a heavy cod. Jogeir might decide to go night fishing and fall overboard. Or, in Hamr's case, he might just get it into his reckless head to go whale hunting . . . in the dark . . . with a stick.

It was the strangest thing . . . a lack-witted female killer whale had been shadowing his longship for days now, as if she were a long-lost friend. *Click, click. Squeal, squeal. Chirp, chirp,* the whale went on endlessly, which was enough to give a grown Viking an ache in the head. The whale seemed to be communicating with them in whale language, which Magnus of course did not understand, despite being fluent in the language of five countries, including Saxon English, which was very close to Old Norse. Perhaps the whale's vision was bad, and she thought his longship was a male whale.

Torolf saw the direction of his stare and said, "I am never going to have children. They are far too bothersome."

"Going to be celibate, are you, son?" he asked with a laugh.

He could barely see Torolf's face in the moonlight, but he suspected that it had turned green at the prospect. Celibacy at sixteen years of age must sound horrific. But then, celibacy at his age was not so pleasant, either.

"Nay, I am not as lack-witted as you to take such a vow."

The boy is far too impertinent by half.

"I will find a way to get the pleasure without the pain, so to speak."

Ha, ha, ha! Immature braggart! And I am going to find a beautiful young woman who loves to tup and cannot bear children. Well, actually, I am not. Now that

35

I have taken my celibacy vow, I could not tup her, even if she dropped down in front of me . . . which will probably happen now, some twisted joke of that jester god, Loki. Mayhap then my vow would be invalid . . . because of the interference of a god. Aaarrgh! My brain is splintering apart here, and all from lack of a good tupping . . . or from too many children. Or whale talk.

"I have heard that the Saracens have invented a method to prevent conception."

Is the pup still on the selfsame subject? "That must be why there are so many children running about the desert harems I have seen in my travels," he replied with dry humor. Young men always thought they knew more than their elders . . . not that he considered himself an elder at seven and thirty. He was in his prime. Too prime, if truth be known. "Besides, I cannot see a true man donning a sheep's intestine . . . even to prevent the flowering of his seed in yet another woman's womb."

Torolf grimaced. "Is that what they do?"

But Magnus had more important things on his mind. "Do you think we should turn our ships back to Greenland on the morrow?"

"Would Erik the Red allow us back in his settlement?"

Torolf had a good point there. "Probably not." For some reason, Magnus and his children had not endeared themselves to Erik whilst visiting at his not-so-great hall, *Brattalid*. After Njal had wrestled with a baby polar bear, causing the enraged mother and father to run into the settlement and stomp on Erik's precious oat field and vegetable garden, the Viking chieftain had not been in a very good mood. That mood had grown stormier when he'd accused Torolf of flirting with his wife, Thjodhild. As if Torolf would flirt with a fifty-year-old woman! Lida had pulled off her nappy and pissed in the great-hall rushes, right in front of one and all, which made it appear as if *he* had no manners. Then Storvald had sculpted a figure of Erik's eldest daughter, which showed her to have an unflattering set of oversize buttocks . . . which she did. Dagny and Kirsten wouldn't stop weeping with homesickness. The coal that had caused the pot to boil over, though, was Magnus's innocent remark that Erik had put on a little bit of extra weight about his middle. Some Vikings were so vain!

They'd chosen the wisest course the next day—which was a sennight ago—and decided to visit the new settlement in Vinland recently discovered by Erik's son, Leif. And that was a whole other saga . . . how Leif was luring Norsemen to his new land under the pretext that it was some kind of paradise, when in fact it was not. Oh, 'twas true there were grapevines here and there, and much greenery, and there did appear to be more arable farmland than there had been in Iceland or the Norselands, and the climate was a bit warmer.

But there were also wild native people of red-hued skin, who ran about almost totally naked, wielding sharp axes and emitting strange war cries. He did not understand the guttural tongue they spoke, but it would be his guess that they did not want to share their grapes. That supposition was confirmed when one of Leif's Irish slaves confided to him that these native inhabitants liked to take the scalps of white men. He and Leif had gotten into a fist-throwing exercise starting when he'd merely commented that Leif might be called Leif the Lucky, not because he'd saved some men in a shipwreck one time, but because he still had a scalp. The man had no sense of humor.

All the men, and a few female maidservants from this longship, *Fierce Dragon,* as well as his other two longships, *Fierce Wind* and *Fierce Hammer*, were sleeping on land tonight in Leif's crude settlement. Leif had told him that he and his brood were not welcome until Magnus said he was sorry. *Ha!* It would be a hot day in Niflheim when he apologized to the likes of that ill-bred Norseman.

"Perhaps we should go home," Torolf suggested.

"Nay!" Magnus said without hesitation. They had come too far, and they had not given any of these new lands a chance yet. But then he wondered if he was being selfish. "Do you want to go home?"

"It is not that, Father. It is just that . . . well, Erik and Leif are strong-willed men, as you are. I wonder if there is room in Greenland or Vinland for two strong-willed leaders. I cannot see you taking orders from those two."

Hmmm. Torolf had a good thinking head on him. He made good points. "What would you think of our traveling a bit farther south? Would it not be a noble enterprise for us to discover our own new land?"

Torolf's voice was bright with enthusiasm when he answered. "Yea, I like that idea. And who is to say there are not many other lands beyond Vinland? No doubt there are dozens."

"We will have to put it to a vote in the morning when the men return to the ships. It is not a decision to be made on their behalf. We will give them a choice."

Even in the dim light he could see Torolf nodding. And he could see how excited Torolf was at the prospect of such an adventure. "Even if some of the men decide to stay behind with Leif, or return to Iceland, we can offer them one of the longships," Torolf pondered aloud. "Two will be enough for our purposes. Bloody hell, even one would suffice."

"Let us pray to both the Norse gods, and the Christian One-God that they bless our journey," Magnus concluded in the end.

"Let us also pray for new worlds to conquer and brave exploits to give fodder to the skalds for their sagas," his son added.

So it was that he and Torolf fell asleep finally, dreaming of brave new worlds. It was a strange slumber, though, because the skies went pitch black and a thick fog covered the horizon as far as the eye could see. In the stillness of the night, the only sounds were the lapping of the waves and the shrill squeaking of the killer whale. The giant mammal seemed to be trying to give them a message. How strange!

And, strangest of all, during the night, the anchor slipped from its mooring, and *Fierce Dragon* drifted off on its own mystically directed quest. Of course, Magnus was unaware of this event till morning. But he did hear the whale make a sound that he would swear was laughter.

And as he slept soundly that night, he kept dreaming of an old, white-haired woman who was fondling prayer beads as she chanted, "Holy Mother, I offer this novena that you may grant my petition. Please send a man. . . ." The words of the supplication always drifted off, but Magnus had a fearsome suspicion.

He was the man the old woman was calling for.

Lost in a fog (more than usual) . . .

When Magnus awakened the next morning, he knew immediately that something was wrong. He just felt it in his aching bones like the premonition of danger most Vikings sensed afore battle.

But he was not about to be attacked.

Was he?

He stood abruptly and drew his sword. His movement jarred Lida, whose ankle was still tied to his. She began to whimper. He made a shushing sound. She gooed at him, then fell back asleep. Only then did he gaze about, unable to see much of anything in the thick fog. He did notice that his longship was moving, and that should not be the case if it was firmly anchored.

"What is it, Father?" Torolf asked in a hushed whisper. He was standing, too, with drawn sword.

"I do not know. Dost think we have been overtaken by some sea monsters? Perchance the whale? The old legends speak of such fanciful things. The air does reek of some mystery."

Torolf made a scoffing sound of disbelief. "The old myths speak of a veil dividing this world from the underworld, but then they also speak of two-headed dragons and fire-breathing sea monsters. I have ne'er believed those stories of magic and mayhem."

"Me either," Magnus said.

But he and Torolf were clearly having second thoughts. Wasn't a fog somewhat like a veil?

Just then the sun shone through the fog, and in the parting mists he saw the most unbelievable thing. There was a mountain, and on its side was a huge sign that read, *Hollywood*.

"Holy Thor!" Torolf exclaimed. "We have entered the world of Holly and Wood. Dost think it is heaven or hell? Or somewhere in between?"

"I am hoping for in between," Magnus said. "That would mean we are still alive. Besides, a land plentiful in greenery and wood must be a prosperous. A land of opportunity, I am thinking."

They were unable to speak any more because the fog pressed down on them, causing an unnatural drowsiness to overcome them. He and Torolf dropped to their knees, then spread themselves flat on the bed furs, succumbing to the mystical haze that appeared to be entering their bodies.

Just before the vapors overpowered him totally, a question occurred to Magnus . . . one that disturbed him mightily.

Where will we be when we awaken?

Chapter Three

Hollywood, land of dreams . . .

"You've got to be dreaming!"

Angela wasn't surprised by Darrell Nolan's reaction to her counteroffer of five hundred thousand dollars to use the Blue Dragon as a setting for his new movie, *Grapes of Sin.* In fact, she'd known beforehand that she was going to have to engage in some of the high-powered persuasive techniques she'd perfected these past years as a successful real estate agent. "No, I'm not dreaming. You have to see my grandmother's vineyard to appreciate how perfect it would be as a backdrop for this movie. It's worth every cent."

"Oh, I would definitely require a firsthand inspection if I am going to pay out *two* hundred thou."

"*Five* hundred thousand," she repeated.

"Honey, I could get the Taj Mahal for a half mil."

She shrugged and tried to appear unconcerned and

not desperate, as she really was. At the same time, she gritted her teeth over the producer's use of the word *honey*. The aging Lothario with the thick, wavy white hair and George Hamilton tan was living in another era. He didn't understand how offensive the endearment was in today's work environment. Next he would be pinching her behind. Putting her irritation aside, she said, "My price is firm."

"So is your butt," he said, waggling his eyebrows suggestively as he walked around his desk, and, yep, pinched her behind. He didn't even check to see what her reaction was. Instead, he strolled toward the set of windows that covered two walls of his posh office in the Universe Studios building. The man was a sexual-harassment suit waiting to happen . . . even here in Hollywood, casting couch of the theatrical world. On the other hand, he was a genius of a producer, highly regarded for his movie credits across the world.

"Look, Angie . . ." he began.

Angela hated that nickname—with a passion. If she didn't watch herself, she was going to grind her teeth down to the gums.

". . . I already have money problems casting this production."

Angela had heard rumors that Angelina Jolie and Benjamin Bratt were to play the leads. So, yeah, big bucks were probably involved. Her five hundred thousand would be a pittance.

"I've got to cut costs somewhere."

That hangdog expression isn't winning me over, buster. "But time is money, Darrell. I have a ready-made movie set for you . . . a spectacular working

43

vineyard. Every week you spend searching for a cheaper site is going to cost you."

"You have a point there."

"Why don't we schedule a day when you can come to visit? Don't dig in your heels on the price till you've seen the place." Angela was confident that once he got a look at the Blue Dragon, money would be a moot point.

He conceded and told her that he and a crew would be there a week from Thursday. "Actually, I have bigger problems than the location for my next film. I've got to finish my current project, a remake of that old Kirk Douglas classic, *The Vikings,* and Dirk Johansson has walked off the set . . . again. God, what a prick he is! First he didn't like his costar. . . ."

Angela frowned. "I thought I heard that Pamela Templeton was starring in this movie."

"She is . . . she is," Darrell said, nodding. "And, hot damn, what red-blooded male wouldn't want that blond goddess as a costar? Only the world's biggest egotist, that's who."

Angela had to smile. She'd read enough *Variety* magazine articles to know that Johansson was renowned for his high opinion of himself. Supposedly there were so many mirrors in his Beverly Hills mansion that it resembled a brothel. Pamela Templeton was outrageously sexy and beautiful . . . the perfect match for a Norse warrior, you would think. But he must view her beauty as competition.

"If that wasn't bad enough," the producer was rambling on, "Dirk—*the dick!*—doesn't like the drab clothing that Vikings wear. Says he doesn't look good in brown. He does like the fur cloak, though. You should see the outfit he wants to wear. Pfff! Better suited to a gay pimp than a Viking hunk."

Angela wanted to tell Darrell that none of this was her concern . . . that all she cared about was getting some cash for her grandmother to continue operating Blue Dragon . . . but, of course, she didn't. Some of her most important house sales were made by employing a little diplomacy.

"The latest foolishness on Dirk's part is that he gets seasick . . . on a fake longship, for chrissake! On an artificial ocean. He made us turn off the wave-making machine. What does he think . . . that longships sailed in calm seas. That Norsemen *rowed* halfway across the freakin' world?"

"I saw the longship as I drove up, sitting in that fake lake. It was beautiful . . . a wonderful reproduction. I understand how frustrating it must be for you," she commented, just to make conversation. Now that Darrell had agreed to visit the Blue Dragon, she just wanted to escape. She stood and gathered her briefcase and purse, easing her way toward the door. "Well, I've got to be going."

"Oh . . . my . . . God!" Darrell exclaimed.

Now what? Angela turned slowly to see the producer staring out the window, slack-jawed with disbelief.

"Who is that guy, and what the hell does he think he's doing on my ship? Where's security? And who the hell turned that wave machine back on?"

This was the perfect opportunity for Angela to escape, but she couldn't help herself. Curiosity compelled her to turn around and walk over to the window.

"What?" she asked, standing next to Darrell.

"Look . . . look . . ." he sputtered, pointing down two stories to the lot that she had passed earlier . . . the one with the longship floating on a man-made lake.

Now it was her turn to exclaim, "Oh . . . my . . . God!"

Standing with legs widespread on the prow of the longship was a man who could only be described as . . . well . . . a Viking. He was six-foot-five, at least, with long, light brown hair streaked with blond highlights—probably from riding a surfboard and not because he'd been riding the ocean waves on some ancient dragonship. He was over thirty years old, but, hey, there were lots of overage surfers in California, living the perpetual quest for the perfect wave.

This Viking, who must be part of some publicity stunt, was wearing a thigh-length leather tunic over wide, muscled shoulders. The outfit was accented by a thick belt around a sinfully narrow waist. His sinewy legs were bare, except for cross-gartered boots. His arms, also roped with muscles, were bare, too, except for etched silver bracelets on his biceps. In one hand he held a huge sword. In the other arm he held a little blond-haired girl dressed in an old-fashioned pinafore-style gown. The most amazing thing of all was the group with this . . . this . . . Viking on a longship. Not just the toddler in his arm but a bunch of other kids as well. She quickly counted. Nine in all, each dressed in ancient attire that she surmised was the way the old Norse would have been garbed.

Her gaze went back to the man then, as if compelled to do so. He was staring about the set and acting profoundly baffled, but still protective of his family . . . if that was what the children were.

In a town that was loaded with gorgeous men, this man took the prize. His features were not perfect. In fact, when the wind blew intermittently, she noticed that he had rather large ears. Furthermore, he was too tall—and too bulked up—for her tastes. Despite all that, he was as handsome as a Viking god. Kevin Sorbo in his role as Hercules . . . but better.

For some strange reason, Angela's heart was racing. And she felt like laughing and crying at the same time. If she didn't know better, she would think this was love at first sight. But, of course, she knew better.

"Who is he?" she finally managed to ask.

"I have no idea," Darrell said, still gaping goggle-eyed out the window. "But I'm sure as hell gonna find out."

The tone in his voice made Angela instantly suspicious. "Why?"

"Why? I'll tell you why." He was chortling with glee. "Screw Dirk Johansson. Who needs him now?"

"Why?" she asked again.

"I've just found my perfect Viking."

Out of the fog, but someplace hot . . .

"By thunder! It's hotter than the fires of Muspell here." Magnus wiped sweat off his forehead with a forearm— the same arm that held his favorite sword, Head Lopper. In his other arm he held Lida, who was *gooing* at every bird or breeze that passed by. The wee one certainly had a pleasant disposition, but in this case her good mood was probably due to her nappy being filled with some stinksome substance.

"I have heard of such hot weather in the deserts of

the Eastlands," Torolf answered him. He also was perspiring profusely under the blistering sun, as evidenced by the beads of moisture on his forehead and upper lip and by the underarm stains on his leather tunic.

"How could we have gone from the cold of Vinland waters to this excessive warmth in such a short time? The fog was confusing, but I am fairly certain we did not travel eastward. Dost think we have entered the Land of the Dead?"

"That fiery first level of the Norse underworld, comparable to the Christian hell?" Torolf shook his head. "I hardly think my younger brothers and sisters have done anything wicked enough to merit such punishment. Bloody hell, I have not been so bad myself . . . except for that time when I put honey on the privy seat when I was a youthling . . . or when I seduced the smithy's daughter . . . or when I got *drukkin* on Frey Day and . . . Oh, never mind. Besides, those people over there look alive . . . and normal. Well, not normal, considering their clothing and hair. But not dead. 'Tis strange, this place, though." Obviously his rambling son was equally puzzled by the scene surrounding them.

They were still on his longship, and they were still at sea, if the waves lapping at the sides of *Fierce Dragon* were any indication, but the land that was visible a short distance away was anything but familiar. The irksome whale was gone, he noticed. *Thank the gods for small blessings.* In the distance he could see huge letters propped against the mountainside: H-O-L-L-Y-W-O-O-D . . . the same sign he had seen in his dreams. Or was it through the fog? Next he expected to see the white-haired lady with the prayer beads pop out of one of the puffy clouds. If that happened, he might just jump overboard and end it all.

The only thing certain in this uncertain happenstance was that they had entered the land of Holly and Wood. But where this strange new land was, he had no clue. There were enormous buildings unlike anything he'd ever seen before; the longhouses reached far up into the sky. And moving horseless vehicles fairly shot along the roads that crisscrossed all the land as far as his eyes could see. In addition, at the beginning of one of the roadways, much closer than the Hollywood sign, was another sign that said, *Universe Studios*. He tried to sound the words out, "You-knee-verse Stew-dios." It was all so confusing.

The most alarming thing to Magnus was the lack of farmland, or open spaces where cultivation of the land would be possible. What would he do in this new land if he could not farm?

The people who were gathering along the shore were strange, as well. The hair on most of the men was short, in the Frankish style. Some of the women had short hair, too, which made them look rather mannish. And the clothing! Not a man in sight wearing a belted tunic over *braies*. And the women! Some of them wore men's breeches, and some wore short *gunnas* that were so tight as to be a second skin, ending barely beneath their womanplace.

"For the love of Frigg!" Torolf exclaimed, as his eyes riveted on the same scandalous attire of the women. Soon an appreciative smile spread across his son's face. "Could this be a land of harlots?" He did not appear displeased at the prospect.

"I would like to be around when one of them bends over to churn some milk or feed the chickens," Magnus remarked, not often sharing such lascivious thoughts with his son, but too shocked to restrain himself.

"Nay, *Faðir*, did you misremember your vow? 'Tis best that you not view such sights and be tempted. I will look for both of us."

Magnus glowered at Torolf, but the cocky cub just laughed.

But women were not the only ones in the gathering crowd, and some of the men arriving looked angry, especially those with matching dark blue *sherts* and *braies* with shiny, star-shaped brooches on their chests. They carried objects in their hands that Magnus suspected were weapons, though they were not the spears or battle-axes with which he was familiar.

"I sure hope they are not as vicious as those natives in Vinland," Torolf commented, noticing the direction of his stare. He fingered his sword, Skin Slicer, as he spoke. "I have grown accustomed to a hairy scalp on my head." Torolf had a misplaced sense of humor betimes.

Just then Magnus's attention was drawn to a movement overhead. "Hamr, get away from there this instant. If you climb that mast pole one more time, I am going to chain you in some dungeon till you are at least"—he had to quickly do a mental count to remember the rascal's age—"six years old."

"Which dungeon, *Faðir*?" Hamr called out, an impudent grin on his face as he slid down the pole. "Do they have dungeons in this new land?"

"I have no idea," he said in a snarl. "If they do not, I

will build one . . . just for the likes of you."

"Goo!" Lida said with a wide toothless grin. Drool drizzled down to her chin. The brave imp, who was teething, almost never cried. *Thank the gods for another small blessing!*

Kirsten and Dagny were behind him, cowering in fright, and weeping as they had been doing ever since they'd left the Norselands. Storvald and Njal were wrestling on the ship's plank floor, trying to settle one insult or another that had been uttered just to start such a wrestling bout. Jogeir was making some observation about the ocean here not really being an ocean at all. Kolbein was clinging to Magnus's thigh like a barnacle. Every time Magnus tried to move, it felt as if he were dragging an anchor with him. And wasn't that another odd thing? Suddenly his longship, which had been drifting through a dark, eerie fog for a day and more, had discovered its anchor and stood firmly in place now, as it should have been back in the waters off Vinland.

"GET . . . OFF . . . THE . . . SHIP!"

Magnus jumped at the sound.

"GET . . . OFF . . . THE . . . SHIP!" was repeated once again, at an exceedingly loud pitch.

He looked left and right, trying to discover the source of the order that passed through the air like a roar from the heavens. Was it one of the gods calling for him? Finally he ascertained that the noise came from a large horn being held by a man on the shore. Over and over the order was repeated through the horn, as if he were deaf and could not hear properly, or as if he were a dunderhead. He would like to purchase one of those horns to take back with him when this adventure was over. It would be useful when laying siege to a Saxon castle, as King Olaf was ofttimes wont to do.

"COME . . . AND . . . GET . . . US," Magnus yelled back, as loudly as he could, which was nowhere near as loud as the man with the horn. All of his children could swim, except for Lida, of course. But he was not about to get them or himself wet needlessly. Nor did he want to risk their drowning. Many a skilled swimmer had sunk in strange waters with undertows and other unknown perils.

At first he did not think he was heard, or understood. But then the man with the horn muttered something like, "Arrogant bastard!" He had no time to be offended because a small boat with two oars was being launched to come for them. He still kept his sword drawn, though, as did Torolf. They were taking no chances.

No sooner did the two men in the boat climb up the rope ladder to his ship than the white-haired one of foppish appearance stepped forward, obviously the leader. He motioned to his companion, one of the men in all-blue attire with the shiny chest brooch, to put down his weapon, even though both of them were eyeing the swords he and Torolf still carried with some trepidation. "They're just props," the leader told his comrade.

Magnus glanced quickly at his broadsword, then Torolf's, and wondered what they might prop up with their swords . . . except for some enemy's gullet. Was that what he meant?

"I'm Darrell Nolan," the chieftain explained, "as if you didn't already know. Ha, ha, ha! Great publicity stunt, young man. Great publicity stunt! Ha, ha, ha! Although why you brought along all these children is beyond me. Well, whatever! An interesting touch, I suppose. Ha, ha, ha! I must admire your enterprise in avoiding the usual audition procedure. Great job! What is that putrid smell, by the way?"

Lida said, "Goo."

Dare-all turned slightly green with comprehension, but then he made a deliberate effort to smile widely at Magnus, exposing the whitest, most perfect teeth Magnus had even seen on a man his age. Not a bit of wear or staining. Most Viking teeth were worn down somewhat by the time they reached old age because of the bits of stone in their bread, which resulted from the stone-quern process of milling the flour.

The man was still smiling after a prolonged silence.

"I think he's waiting for a response from you," Torolf prodded in an undertone, out of the side of his mouth.

"Huh?" was Magnus's brilliant response. *Thor's toe-nails!* He understood much of what was spoken in five languages, and he was fluent in three of them, including the Saxon English. But this English that Dare-All No-Land spoke was different. Surprisingly, Magnus could understand most of it, except for some words, such as pub-less-city and odd-itch-on. Even his children seemed to understand what was being said. How odd! But then, how odd was it to be overcome by a weird fog and end up in a new world?

"Is this hell?" he asked of a sudden, deciding to ignore the smile on the man's face—a smile that implied that Magnus was a tasty morsel he'd just been handed. That made Magnus mighty distrustful.

"I beg your pardon?" Dare-All said.

"Why?"

"Why what?"

"Why are you begging my pardon? Did you do something that needs pardoning?" Yea, he'd been right to be wary of this ingratiating miscreant. Was he a sodomite? Nay, he did not think that was it. Perchance a pirate out to rob him of his longship and treasures? Yea, that was more likely. Best to be on guard. He gave Torolf a quick eye signal to indicate that he remain on guard, as well. "Be prepared," he whispered.

"I need a sword," Hamr said.

Magnus swatted him on the head. "Not now, half-ling."

"Let's go get *Faðir's* spare sword, Heart Piercer," Njal offered. He was too far away for Magnus to swat.

"I have a big piece of wood I was going to start carving. We could use that for a club." It was Storvald speaking now as he squinted at the two visitors on the longship.

Magnus groaned. *Does life get any better—or worse—than this?*

"Good idea, Stor." Hamr patted his older brother on the back. "And I warrant there are bows and arrows somewhere on this ship. Someone keeps hiding them from me."

Guess who? "I have a better idea," Magnus said. "How about I drop three bothersome boys overboard for a good dunking?"

Dare-All shook his head as if to clear it. "Let's start over," he suggested, and extended his right hand toward him.

Magnus took one step backward. What now? Did Dare-All want him to hand Lida over to him? That hardly seemed likely after his grimace at her odor. *Ha!* It must be his sword. "I am not handing over Head Lopper. So just forget about that."

"Head . . . Head Lopper?" Dare-All stammered.

"My sword."

Dare-All turned rather green again, but then he regained his composure with a nervous laugh. "You seem almost like a real Viking. I swear, if this is acting, you've got a job. What's your name, by the way? Are you union?"

"My name is Magnus . . . Magnus Ericsson," he revealed, but said no more. 'Twas best not to give the enemy—or potential enemy—too much information.

"Are you from L.A.?"

"Ell-aye?" Magnus shook his head slowly. "Nay, I am from the southwestern coast of Norway. Vestfold, to be precise."

"Norway?" Dare-All exclaimed. "My God, you are too good to be true. A pure-blooded Viking, to the bone. Hey, those are some armrings you're wearing, buddy. Look like solid silver, but of course they must be fake. Right? They sure look authentic. Holy shit! And I love those tunics you and your 'sons' are wearing. Couldn't get Dirk Johansson to wear anything resembling what you've got on. Too plain."

Plain? There is naught plain about me. "Dirk?" His head was starting to hurt from all the questions bumping about inside his brain. That and the sun. "Dirk is a new name, even for a Viking, and we have some of the oddest in the world. Halfdan of the Wide Embrace. Ragnor Hairy-Breeks. Ivan the Ignorant. But ne'er have I heard of a man named for a knife. Dirk. Hmmm. I like it." Now, why he had decided to home in on the peculiar name, rather than all the other things this strange man had said, was a wonder to Magnus. Probably because his brain was being baked in this hot sun.

"Yeah. Dirk the Jerk. Dirk the Dick. You get it? Ivan the Ignorant. Dirk the Dick. Ha, ha, ha!"

This fellow was acting a bit demented. Magnus wasn't sure he wanted to be associated with him. Narrowing his eyes suspiciously, he asked, "What country is this?"

"Are you for real? This is carrying the stunt a bit far, don'tcha think? Oh, well, I'll play along. It's America. Ha, ha, ha!"

"Ah-mare-ee-ca," he sounded out. "Is that anywhere near Vinland?"

"Vinland? Where the hell is Vinland? Oh, you mean that place where the Vikings were supposed to have discovered America about a thousand years ago."

A thousand years ago? Yea, this man is barmy as a bat. "Look, Dare-All, my family and I have been aboard this longship for days. May we board your small boat to go ashore and get our land feet, and perchance refresh ourselves afore departing for other shores? A small repast would be much appreciated, as well. In all truth, I am sick of *gammelost* and moldy manchet bread."

At first Dare-All appeared confused, but then he brightened. "Sure. Sure thing. Let's all go ashore and get a repast. Ha, ha, ha!"

Dare-All's incessant laughter was beginning to grate on Magnus's nerves. Besides that, he suspected that if he looked up, he would see a five-year-old, soon-to-be-arse-paddled young boy at the top of the mast pole . . . swinging his father's second-best sword.

In less than an hour they were all ashore, though not without much grumbling and consternation—the latter on his part. Dare-All had balked at the idea of his taking four heavy wooden chests into the small boat. "Why the hell do you need those chests? And how did they get on my longship anyhow?"

"*Your* longship?" Magnus had asked in an icy voice. "I beg to differ. This is my longship, *Fierce Dragon*. It was built by my brother Geirolf five years past, and a better ship has never sailed the seas." He deliberately failed to inform the man that the chests contained much treasure, which he intended to use in whatever new land he settled . . . obviously not this one, which was already settled.

Dare-All had said, "Whatever!" Then he'd quickly added, "But, please, put those freakin' swords away. There are laws against carrying weapons in public places, you know?"

He and Torolf had sheathed their swords, though they had not understood half of what Dare-All had said. What was a free-can sword? And what weapon laws?

"Let's go up to my office," Dare-All suggested.

Magnus wasn't so sure he wanted to visit any of this man's orifices, but perhaps he'd misunderstood. Meanwhile, dozens of people were milling about, gaping as if he and his children were freaks of nature, when in fact the onlookers were the odd ones.

Just then he noticed Hamr trying to climb atop one of the horseless vehicles standing at rest by the roadside. He grabbed the child by the scruff of the neck and shook him. "Behave yourself, boy. Do I have to tie you to my other leg, like Kolbein here?"

Hamr looked horrified.

One lady, apparently aghast at his treatment of his son, chastised him. "Is it necessary to be so violent with that child? He's only a little boy."

Hamr cast her a sweet smile.

"Perhaps you need some anger management classes."

"Perhaps you need to mind your own business, you old biddy."

"What is that putrid smell?" she said, then looked at Lida. "When was the last time you changed her Pampers?"

"When did I last pamper her? *Blód hel*, I pamper her way too much, if truth be told."

"I think she's referring to her diapers," Dare-All explained, still smiling.

"And what, pray tell, is a die-purr?"

"The cloth you put on the baby's ass to catch the piss and shit," Dare-All practically shouted, finally becoming exasperated with him.

"Well, why did you not say nappy to begin with?" he told the woman, who was slack-jawed with amazement. "I used the last one yesterday."

The woman gasped some more. "Oh . . . oh . . . oh! Is that boy limping? Did you hit him . . . or kick him . . . or something?"

Magnus glanced at Jogeir, who was blushing profusely at being singled out in such a way because of a handicap he chose to ignore. If this woman were a man, Magnus would call him out for such an insult. He would never kick a child. Never.

"Someone ought to call Child Protective Services."

Really, he had had enough for one day . . . in fact, for one year . . . and what he did not need was a meddling crone telling him what to do. On the other hand. . . . hmmm . . . "Are you interested in employment, my good woman?"

"Em . . . em . . . employment?" she sputtered out. "As what?"

"A nurse maid for my nine children, that's what."

"*Nine?* I'll have you know, I'm a noted chef in one of the city's most exclusive restaurants. I'm just touring the studio."

Magnus hadn't a clue what she'd just said.

"I think a chef is a kind of cook . . . for royalty and such," Kirsten explained to him. His daughter fancied that she was an authority on the lifestyles of the royal families of not just Norway, but England and Frankland, as well. Probably hoped to wed some prince, or at least a lower level atheling.

"Well, I would not mind a nurse maid who could cook a fair meal, too," Magnus told the woman.

"You have some nerve," the woman said, and stormed away. That was what women did whenever they knew they had lost an argument with a far more intelligent man. He had made her a perfectly reasonable offer, after all.

"Step away, everyone. Go back to work," Dare-All ordered, and surprisingly people began to obey him. He must be a chieftain here, after all, though Magnus could hardly credit that possibility. The man had no muscles to speak of. But then, Magnus knew of one Danish jarl, Sven Spear Thrower, who was short and stout, which he made up for by being mean as a snake.

As the crowd parted, Magnus got his biggest surprise of the day. It was a woman. But not just any woman.

"Good Lord!" the woman murmured.

Did she think he was a lord? Well, he would correct that notion later. And good? He would hardly describe himself in that way, though he was not bad, either.

Even as he puffed out his chest at her blatant inspection of his body, every fine hair on Magnus's body stood at attention. Just looking at this woman made his bones turn to pudding and his fingers itch to reach out and touch her to see if she was really . . . well, real. In all his thirty and seven years, he had never been affected by a female in such a way . . . and definitely not on a first meeting.

Is it a spell?

Is it a conjuring by the white-haired woman with the prayer beads?

Is it a joke by that jester god, Loki?

Does it matter?

She was staring at him as if equally poleaxed by the intense emotions swirling between them. Everyone around them probably noticed, but he did not care. Something important was happening . . . what, he could not say for a certainty. He just knew his life was about to talk a major turn.

This woman was no longer young. She was at least thirty years old. But comely. Nay, more than comely. Beautiful. Masses of curly black hair surrounded a heart-shaped face. Her parted red lips were full and sensuous and immensely kiss-some. To the right of her mouth was a small black mole, which, rather than being repulsive, was sinfully tempting. Oh, the things that could be done to that very spot by the tongue of a man with expertise in the love arts . . . which he had in excess. Thick black lashes shadowed eyes of so dark a brown they appeared black.

She wore a two-piece garment of white silk, which left the creamy skin of her neck and part of her chest bare, where a small gold cross on a thin chain rested tantalizingly. She was tall for a woman, but curvy. The hem of her garment ended just above her knees. Her long legs were covered with transparent silk hose, and on her feet were black leather shoes with thin, high heels. If his hands were not occupied with the babe, he would be unable to restrain himself from touching that long, long stretch of winsome leg. Not just touching, either. Licking would be good, too.

His heart began to race madly against his chest walls as he gazed upon her. He could scarcely breathe. If he did not see her chest heaving with the effort to pant for air, he would have thought her a goddess, or one of the Valkyries, not a living, breathing woman.

"Faaa-ther!" Torolf groaned. "Do not appear too anxious. Your tongue is practically hanging out."

He cast a quick glower at his son, whom he was beginning to think he should have left behind with Ragnor. Almost immediately he returned his attention to the woman. He was not going to let her out of his sight. Still, without looking at him directly, Magnus remarked to Torolf, "I have not yet seen the day when I will take advice from a pup such as you. I have bred thirteen children, for the love of Odin! Do you not think I have learned a thing or two?"

"Oh, God! I can see it all now. More children."

"There will be no more children," he declared. *I hope.* "Shut your teeth now. I need to concentrate."

Torolf muttered some rude opinion about where his concentration was lodged.

"You know, Torolf, you could learn something from your elders. My mother, Lady Asgar—your grandmother—was always of a whimsical bent. She believed that for every man there was one special woman. A soul mate."

"*Faðir*, you just met the woman."

"It matters not. Mother always told me and your two uncles that we would recognize that person when she came. I suppose she told your Aunt Katla the same thing, in reverse, but I was never around for that discussion."

Torolf grunted his opinion.

" 'Women may come and go in your lives, my sons, but there will be only one who will touch your heart to the quick, and change your world so that it will be forever empty without her.' That is what my mother always said."

Torolf grunted again.

"Geirolf and Jorund and I scoffed with disbelief behind Mother's back, but now I know she was right. This is my woman . . . my destiny."

"Destiny has boiled your brain," Torolf grumbled.

"I think what Father said is beautiful," Kirsten stated.

Dagny sighed deeply in agreement.

Hamr and Njal snorted.

Jogeir looked unimpressed.

Storvald was eyeing a nearby piece of what appeared to be fake driftwood, uncaring one way or another.

Kolbein clung tighter, probably fearful that Magnus was going to toss him aside in favor of some lady love.

Lida *goo*ed.

Magnus did not care what any of them thought. The only thing that mattered in this moment was how *she* felt.

Even so, how would she fit in with his vow of celibacy?

And did she like children . . . like eleven of them? Well, nine only, if you counted those with him. Nine was not such a dreadful number. Was it?

What if she was already wed? Mayhap even to Dare-All the Laugher? Nay, he could not countenance even the remote possibility. It was such a mismatch.

Was it really possible that he had had to go through four wives, six concubines, and numerous passing fancies before finding "the one" for him?

Did she feel their instant connection, too?

Would she be willing to live on a farm . . . assuming there were farms somewhere in this crowded land?

Better yet, would she return with him to the Norselands, if that was what he was called to do?

In essence, what did fate have in store for him now?

Chapter Four

The man was a tree . . .

Angela tried to calm her erratic breathing . . . such an odd reaction to a man who should be unattractive to her. It must be the heat, worry over her deal with Darrell Nolan, and this bizarre scenario taking place on one of his sets. It was not that she was attracted to this man. Definitely not.

Such a blatant display of pushiness—bypassing the usual audition route to garner attention for himself. How arrogant! How egotistical! How like an actor!

He reminded her of her ex-husband. The Creep had always liked to be the center of attention, demanding a better table when they ate out, insisting on Rodeo Drive labels for his "Hollywood" wardrobe. Being naturally reticent, Angela cringed even now in memory.

This man was tall . . . at least six-foot-five. She was not short, being five-foot-seven, but standing before him was like standing before a tree. Even his arms and legs, which were exposed by the belted leather tunic he wore, resembled tree limbs. And he was a big man in bulk, too—probably two hundred and fifty pounds—with lean muscles everywhere.

Angela had never been a fan of muscle men . . . as evidenced by the fact that she'd donated the Creep's Nautilus equipment to Goodwill the moment he moved out. The act had been symbolic of her disdain for the Creep's obsession with physical fitness.

Back to the man before her. His light brown hair had sun-bleached streaks and thin, intricate braids hanging on either side of his face, which were intertwined with amber beads. Thick golden lashes framed whiskey-colored eyes. He wore ornately etched, wide silver bracelets on his upper arms. A gold brooch of writhing dragons was attached to a short shoulder mantle. *God spare me from a man with a passion for jewelry. The only thing missing is the Las Vegas–style gold chains. Oops! There is a chain there . . . one holding a gold pendant. Jeesh!*

And he carried a sword, for heaven's sake. How juvenile! Or rather, how like a man with his macho toys! The Creep had insisted on a loaded revolver in their bedside nightstand . . . even though they lived on the fourteenth floor of a high-security apartment building.

Worst of all was the numbers of children surrounding him, ranging from age sixteen or so to a toddler of little more than a year. And one of the little boys appeared to be lame. If all of them were his children, as he had proclaimed in his strange accent, then shame on him. Angela was not a rabid feminist, like her cousin Carmen, but some people just overpopulated the planet like rabbits, uncaring of the children's welfare or that of the environment. A man who felt the need to reproduce himself nine times over was a pig, pure and simple, in her opinion.

"Uh-oh, Father," the teenage boy said with a hoot of laughter. "Methinks your destiny is frowning at you. Not a good sign. Best you pull out some of that far-famed expertise."

"Leave off, son," the big man replied in a deep, deep voice. The whole time he continued to stare at her in the most disarming manner. It was rude, actually.

Noticing the direction of the Viking's gaze, Darrell motioned her forward. Reluctantly she stepped up to the tree. That was the only way she could describe how he looked and felt next to her.

"Angela, I'd like to introduce you to Magnus Ericsson."

"Angel? You are an angel?" The tree asked with a mixture of horror and glee.

"No, I'm not an angel. And don't you dare call me that. 'Angel baby' won't work either. Believe me, 'angel' as a pickup line is not cool."

"Huh?" the tree said.

"The name is Angela."

"Oh."

Oh, God! Dumb as a . . . a . . . tree.

"Magnus is going to be the new star of *The Vikings.* I hope," Darrell interjected.

"She is an angel who does not want to be called an angel, and you want me to be a star. Are you sure I am not dead?"

Really, this language-miscommunication game of his was getting tired already.

"And Magnus, this is Angela Abruzzi, a Hollywood realtor and possible business partner of mine."

Angela liked that last part, and she extended her hand toward the tree. No need to be impolite. "How do you do?"

At first he just stared at her hand. Then, seeming to come to some sudden comprehension, he took her hand in his huge one and squeezed tightly as if he would not ever let her go.

"How do you do?" she repeated.

"I do fine," he answered in his gruff, accented voice. Then he smiled at her . . . a slow, purely male smile that was so sexy she felt her knees begin to buckle. Luckily he was still holding her hand, or she might have fallen. *It must be hormones,* she thought. How else to explain her lust-laden reaction to a man she didn't even like? *Maybe I'm turning into a bimbo . . . a desperate single woman dying for the first man I meet.* "I do not suppose that you live on a farm, do you?"

A farm? Where did that come from? "No, I live in a condo in Century City. Do you live on a farm?"

He nodded. "Dost bother you?"

"Dost . . . does what bother me?"

"That I am a farmer. Well, betimes I am a warrior, too, but mostly I am a simple farmer." The brute was still holding on to her hand.

I am beginning to think there is nothing simple about you, Mr. Tree. She was still fluttering inside at his mere touch. *Bimbo, bimbo, bimbo. Next I'll be humming the theme song of* "Sex and the City." *Is there a theme song? Aaarrgh!* She cocked her head in confusion. "Why should your being a farmer bother me?" She tugged on her hand, but he wouldn't release it.

The little girl in his other arm reached out a hand to her, too, imitating her father's action, and said cheerily, "Goo." The tree finally released Angela's hand.

Angela felt a peculiar distress at that loss of contact, but then she smiled at the sweet thing and shook her tiny hand. "How do you do, munchkin? Aren't you the prettiest thing?"

"Goo!" the toddler said, flashing her a drooly grin.

"Her name is Lida," Magnus pointed out. "Not Munch-Kin."

Angela looked at the big man to see if he thought she had seriously believed the baby's name was Munchkin. He had. Holy moley, he *was* a good actor.

"And these are my other children," the tree said. Starting with the oldest, he pointed and called out their names: "Torolf, Kirsten, Dagny, Storvald, Njal, Jogeir, Hamr, and Kolbein." The last one, about three years old, was holding on to the man's thigh as if he would never let go.

"You have nine children?" she asked with amazement.

"Actually I have eleven living children. Two of them stayed behind in the Norselands. And two of them passed on at a young age . . . Ivan drowned and Ilsa died soon after birth."

"Thirteen children!" She had to force her slack jaw shut. *Is he for real? No, of course not. He is an actor. This is all a script to him . . . make-believe.*

"I do not think she is impressed," the teenage boy said to his father. "Mayhap you should tell her of your *expertise*."

She had no idea what response the tree gave, because Darrell called her aside, telling the big guy that they would be right back and not to move.

"Angela, I need your help with *The Viking*," Darrell said right off.

"Me?" she squeaked out.

He nodded quickly. "He's perfect for the part, but I can't let the press get a whiff of him till my lawyers release me from the contract with Dirk."

And, in Angela's opinion, to make sure that Magnus didn't know how desperate Darrell was and demand more money for the part the tree so clearly wanted. "So? What has this to do with me?"

"Take him and his brood home with you," he said bluntly.

At first she was shocked that he would suggest such a thing. Shock soon turned to indignation. "No! Absolutely not!"

"It would only be for a day or two. A week at the most."

"Are you crazy? I live in a two-bedroom high-rise. That guy's head would touch the ceiling in my place, and with eleven people we would be stepping on each other. No way!"

"How about the vineyard up in Sonoma? The Blue Dragon? You know, the one you think is worth five hundred thou for a one-week movie shoot?" He said the last in a subtly threatening tone.

"Are you suggesting that unless I help you out with this, the deal is off?" She had to fist her hands tightly to keep from socking the jerk a good one.

"No, what I'm suggesting is that, if you do this, I will be much more likely to agree to your terms."

She folded her arms over her chest and tapped one

high-heeled shoe with indignation. *The nerve of the louse!*

"Come on, Angela. You said your grandmother has a big old house at the Blue Dragon. Surely it's big enough for all these kids. And it would only be for a few days."

Her shoulders slumped in surrender. Really, she had no choice. Darrell might not know it, but the Blue Dragon was in dire straits, money-wise. Without his cash, there might not be a vineyard much longer.

She looked at Darrell; then she looked at the Viking, who still stared at her with an intensity bordering on hunger—Criminey, she couldn't remember any man ever looking at her with hunger—then she looked back at Darrell again.

"My price just went up. Seven hundred thousand."

"Agreed."

His quick response made her think she should have asked for more. "My grandmother is going to kill me," she said.

When they walked back to the group and informed Magnus of their decision, he just nodded, as if his going with her had been a given all along.

Soon after, they all moved toward a studio van that Angela was going to have to use. Her BMW would never hold the bunch of them, and Magnus claimed not to be able to drive a car.

"You remind me of someone," he said.

"Oh, great! The oldest line in the book! Let's get one thing straight from the get-go: no hanky-panky."

"Hank-what?"

"Never mind."

"Do you happen to know an old lady with white hair

and prayer beads? And what is a no-veen-ah anyway?" the tree asked her all of a sudden.

Angela's heart skipped a beat and she stumbled. When she righted herself, with his hand under her elbow, she examined him in a new light.

Something strange was going on here.

No place like home (wherever that is . . .)

They were all crammed into a very large horseless cart, known as a van, and were speeding down a free-road . . . or, rather, a free-way. Magnus assumed that was a thoroughfare with no toll. But he did not want to ask. His stomach was too queasy from the harrowing experience of traveling faster than a speeding arrow. Other horseless vehicles were driving by them at even more excessive speeds. Angela claimed to be going only forty miles per hour, as if he would be comforted by that fact.

As things turned out, they were not going to be able to go to the Blue Dragon place right away. That didn't bother Magnus all that much. He wasn't sure he liked the idea of taking his children to a dragon's lair anyhow . . . though Hamr had practically wept with disappointment. It was his lifelong wish, or so he had proclaimed loudly, to kill a dragon.

Storvald and Njal were sitting with their filthy hands folded in their laps, at his orders. The pair had crawled under the van while it was still standing still, looking for a hidden horse, before he'd been able to pull them out of harm's way. They now resembled ragpicker's children, not the sons of a Norse noble.

Angela had just stared with bewilderment at the lot

of them. He was confused himself. How could he blame her?

When Angela had spoken to her work master a short time ago on a little black box called a tell-of-own, Master Blackman had reminded her that a big buyer coming in from some other country required her personal attention. This buyer, known as a custom-her, represented very large amounts of payment to her employer, who had to be out of town himself on a vay-kay-shun, which meant a time to have fun. How odd that people here had to schedule a special time just for having fun!

In any case, Angela continued to be distraught at the news that she could not take them away from the city immediately, but he assured her he could handle the close accommodations of her home. After all, he'd been living on a longship with all of his children, and more people besides, for weeks now. Surely it would be no tighter than that. "Besides, I need more time to hone my sword if I am going to have to kill a blue dragon," he told her.

"Have you killed any dragons before, Rambo?" she'd asked him with one arched eyebrow.

"Nay, but how much harder can it be than killing a wild boar, or an angry polar bear? Some of the black bears in the Rus lands are as big as dragons, I warrant."

She gave him another of her disbelieving looks, which he was becoming accustomed to.

"I am loath to remind you . . . my name is Magnus, not Ram-bow." The wench might be a bit half-witted, he feared, to have such a poor memory for important matters . . . like the name of her destiny.

"Whatever."

That was a favored word in this country, he noticed. People used it whenever they had lost an argument. It was a handy word he would have to recall when he got home to the Norselands. He knew just how the word would come in handy.

Like when one of his comrades taunted him, "That is the seventh game of *hnefatafl* you have lost, Magnus."

"Whatever."

Or a woman chided him: "Go clean out the midden, Magnus."

"Whatever."

Or numerous people commented, "Thirteen children, Magnus!"

"Whatever."

At the time of this mental conversation with himself, he'd had to smile at his own wit, which had caused Angela to look askance at him.

Whatever.

So now they were all strapped into the van, with Lida fast asleep in her very own seat, despite the din created by eight of his other children talking at once inside a confined room the size of a privy . . . which was not such a far-fetched comparison, considering the stench from Lida's still-unchanged nappy. Despite the size of this horseless cart, he and Torolf had to sit with their heads touching the roof and their knees practically touching their chins. Mayhap they did not have such tall men in this country, but then Norsemen were known for their great height . . . and good looks. He was hoping the latter would weigh in his favor with his newfound destiny.

"Will your husband not object to your bringing us

back to his keep?" he asked, wanting to make sure she was an unmarried lady.

Despite her continuing scowl, his hopes were fulfilled when she answered. "I have no husband, and the *keep* is mine, thank you very much."

Well, that is a relief. Her bad disposition he could handle. A husband would have been much more difficult.

"Stop smiling," she ordered.

He winked at her.

"And no winks, either. Look, I don't mean to be . . . well, mean, but get this through your head: I . . . am . . . not . . . interested."

"In what?"

"You. Jeesh!"

"I like the way your face gets all flushed when you are excited."

"Not excited. Angry."

"I like the way the sun brings out the silver highlights in your beautiful silken black hair."

"Silver highlights!" she exclaimed. "Oh, my God! I must be getting some gray hairs."

He laughed. "I like your sense of humor."

"Give it up, Magnus."

"Is there naught you like about me?"

"Pathetic! Our *faðir* is pathetic," he heard Torolf mutter behind him.

Angela thought for a while . . . too long a while, actually. Then she answered, "I like your big ears."

Yes, he liked the woman's sense of humor. Magnus leaned back in his seat as best he could, well satisfied with his progress thus far. His life was definitely taking a turn for the better.

74

His previously chattering children went suddenly silent as they gazed out the windows at the passing marvels of this new land. Not only were there horseless vehicles racing across the ground, but there were vehicles speeding through the skies, as well. Magnus still wasn't sure if they had landed in the otherworld or just some new land. For his children's sake, he was trying to maintain a facade of calm, but inside he was roiling with anxiety.

"I guess we'd better stop at the Super Wal-Mart and get some diapers for the baby," Angela said to him.

"By Thor, woman, you are a wonder. You can drive a horseless vehicle and talk at the same time." 'Twas best to compliment women on occasion to smooth their ruffled feathers. That was his philosophy, leastways.

"Yeah, yeah," she said. "Save your Viking act for Darrell. I told you . . . I'm not interested."

"Why are you so angry with me?"

"Damn, I have no time for this crap. I need to stay on good terms with Darrell because . . . well, just because. And you showing up like that put me in an untenable situation. Where do you live anyway? Can't I just drop you off there?"

"I already told you—or rather Dare-All—I live in the Norselands. And by the by, coarse words ill suit you, m'lady."

"What coarse words?"

"Damn and crap."

"Give me a break."

"Huh?"

She flung a hand out in disgust.

There was a clicking noise under the wheel she was

steering, and they began to veer to the right into a very large open area containing many, many other horseless vehicles of all shapes and colors. "Where are we?"

"Super Wal-Mart."

He rolled the words around in his head and asked, "Mart . . . is that like a market?"

"Sort of," she said with a shrug as she pulled her vehicle between two white lines.

Finally, something he could understand. He had gone to markets in many a trading town. "Is this where we will buy cloth for Lida's nappies?"

"We can buy disposable diapers here."

"What does disposable mean?"

"It means throwaway."

He gasped. "You cannot mean that you throw the dirty linens in the midden after every use? Surely you do not practice such waste in this country."

"I have a suggestion, Magnus. Let's not talk."

The new World's Greatest Marvel: Wall-Market . . .

A short time later they were in the market building, a structure so large that hundreds of people were able to bustle about its numerous aisles.

Angela had tried to talk him into staying inside the van and waiting for her, but he had refused adamantly. There was no way he was letting her out of his sight, especially in light of her rampant hostility. She did not recognize yet that she was his destiny. He needed more time to convince her.

Angela was steering a metal cart with Lida strapped into a special baby seat. He was steering a second cart with Hamr sitting in the body of the cart, his arms wrapped around his bent knees, scowling fiercely at him. Torolf had an equally scowling Njal in his cart. Kirsten pushed Kolbein and Jogeir. Storvald and Dagny were permitted to walk on their own, with strict orders to stay next to the carts.

"First things first," Angela said once they had all passed the wall-market greeter, who shook each and every one of their hands—something Magnus now recognized as a gesture of greeting in this country. "We've got to change this baby before they have to fumigate the store."

As she led their entourage of carts skillfully through the aisles—a difficult job when his children kept *ooh*ing and *aah*ing over every blessed thing they saw.

"Have you had much experience with babies?" he inquired casually. "Do you have any of your own?"

She laughed and grabbed a box off one of the shelves. It was a toddler-size box of Pampers. Apparently Lida was a toddler. "No, I've never had a child of my own, but one of my officemates brings her little girl into the office sometimes. Believe me, changing a diaper requires no particular talent." Next she put a package of wet cloths in the cart, along with a sweetly scented powder made especially for babies. Kirsten and Dagny were equally fascinated by the adjoining shelves, where products were sold that specifically handled the problem of what to do about a female's monthly flux . . . as if a rag would not suffice. Kolbein was exclaiming over something called "soap on a rope."

Then Angela steered them all toward a "ladies room," where females went to relieve themselves. Like a privy it was, but indoors. More like a garderobe, he supposed. There was a "men's room," too. Amazing, really, that people had to have such facilities even when they were marketing.

"Stay right there," Angela ordered, pointing a finger first at him, then at each of his children in turn. "Anyone moves and I'm out of here. You're on your own."

M'lady, if you knew what it does to me when you talk fiercely like that, you would be shocked. Bloody hell, it shocks me. "Whatever you say, sweetling," he agreed, trying to be pleasant in the face of her . . . unpleasantness.

All he got for his pleasantness was a scowl.

"You really need to work on your expertise, Father," Torolf said.

"I want one of those mirrors we passed, Father. And a comb," Kirsten said. "No one told me my hair was such a tangle."

"That is all you need, daughter, more boosts to your vanity."

"I want a bottle of bubbles for my bath, Father. 'Lavender Garden,' " Dagny said.

"You will attract every bee in sight."

"I want some new carving knives, Father," Storvald said.

"Better that you get your first sword and start practicing to be a warrior."

"I want a bye-sigh-call," Jogeir said. "Then I will be able to move as fast as the other children."

"You move fast enough, boy."

"I want some boxing gloves, Father," Njal said.

"I would like to box something on you, boy. Like your ears."

"I want a bow and arrows, Father," Hamr said.

"You will shoot your eye out."

"I want a wagon, Father. A red one," Kolbein said.

"If it will stop you from clutching my leg all the time, the answer is yes, yes, yes."

"I want a pair of den-ham *braies*, Father," Torolf said. "All the men wear them in this country, and see how fine their arses look."

"Your arse looks fine enough, thank you very much."

How his children had managed to see so many things in the short time they'd been in the mart was beyond him.

It seemed like an hour but was only minutes later that Angela returned with a fresh-smelling, *gooing* Lida. If he was not already half in love with this woman, he would be now. Her gentle treatment of his daughter touched him deeply.

"Dare I hope that one of those chests you insisted on bringing with you in the van contains a change of clothing for this baby?" she asked.

"Nay," he answered. He might consider her his destiny, but he did not trust her enough yet to let her know he had left a fortune back in her locked vehicle.

"By the way, what in God's name is this?" She tossed a soft cloth belt at him that was exceedingly heavy. It had been wrapped around Lida's middle, and Angela must have discovered it when she'd changed her nappy.

"It is a coin belt," he said, raising his chin defiantly at her glance of condemnation. "All my children wear them, as I do. What if we had been shipwrecked? We would need some means to survive once we were rescued, wouldn't we?"

"I guess so." She was shaking her head at him, though.

On the way back from the baby department, where she picked out several outfits for Lida called "onesies" and "sleepers," a "sippy" cup, and a "teething ring," which the baby instantly began to slobber over, Angela led them to the toil-a-trees section for some hair moose she wanted to buy herself. That was something he really wanted to see . . . till he discovered it was just a container of some foamy substance and not a large, hairy animal. Was it moose drool she intended to put on her silky hair? He shuddered with revulsion at the thought. While there, he noticed a long aisle of shelves filled with nothing but different types of dee-odor-ants. When he asked Angela what they were, she said, "They prevent excess sweating and foul body odors." She looked pointedly at him when she said the latter.

"Do I smell?" he asked, fully expecting her to say no.

"To high heaven."

The woman just said I stink. No one has ever dared insult me so. Shall I lop off her head? Mayhap later. She had already turned away from him and was heading toward the food department. He lifted one arm and sniffed himself. Yea, she was right. He was a mite odorsome. He noticed that Torolf was doing the same. Their gazes connected of a sudden and they both shrugged sheepishly. Neither of them had ever had a female tell them that they stank "to high heaven." Probably because the women they'd known were also a bit fragrant. He grabbed a half dozen of the products marked "Old Spice," and put them in Torolf's cart.

"What in the name of Thor is that?" Torolf was pointing to a headless, armless figure of a man wearing a tight-fitting garment around his arse and man parts.

Angela's face turned pink with embarrassment before she murmured, "Jockey shorts."

"Jaw-key shorts?" Torolf repeated. "What purpose does such attire fulfill?"

"It's male underpants. Some men—and boys—wear those, and others wear the looser boxer shorts." She pointed to another headless, armless figure as an example. "Surely they have the same kinds of things in your country."

"Nay, they do not," he and Torolf said at the same time.

"Loincloths suffice for most men, or small clothes made of linen for those of a more refined nature, or nothing at all," Magnus explained.

They bought jaw-key shorts for him and his sons in six different sizes. Hamr grumbled that he would rather go bare-arsed and buy a bow and arrows. That purchase prompted Kirsten and Dagny to demand lace-trimmed undergarments of their own, including special dual-cupped pieces of cloth to support their tiny, almost nonexistent breasts.

He wondered idly if Angela's breasts were being "supported" by such an outrageous garment. That was a sight he would love to see. With luck, it was a sight he would see . . . someday.

Nay, nay, nay! I cannot see that . . . not if I keep my vow of chastity.

Well, I could look, couldn't I? And not touch?

Ha!

Finally they ended up in the food department, but

not before Angela complained, "The whole lot of you are giving me a huge headache."

"I know a surefire method for getting rid of a megrim," he told her.

"Get a life," she responded. There was a frown on her face as she spoke, so he assumed that expression was a negative directive and not a sincere offer of goodwill.

"That is precisely what I am trying to do," he murmured under his breath.

Torolf just laughed, way too amused at his father's lack of success with the wench.

Of all the things that had amazed him thus far in this amazing land, one of the most amazing was the vast array of foods that were displayed in this market. With little care for price—and surely they were priceless—Angela tossed rare oranges and succulent grapes into her cart, along with cakes, already sliced bread, and milk. There was not one, but eight different kinds of crisp apples, both green and red. There were also wild greens, onions, turnips, beets, cabbages, parsley, horseradish, mushrooms, carrots, and many other vegetables he had never heard of.

His frugal nature was disgusted by the excess of this land, and the waste that must surely ensue each day with the products that were not sold. But as a farmer, he had to appreciate the vast array of produce. And he speculated that perchance farming would be a lucrative occupation in this land of luxury.

Almost immediately Angela had had to caution his children to take only one of the samples being offered by ladies standing before several small tables in the food department. Kolbein particularly liked the "shrimp grasshoppers," though Magnus could not bring himself to try the delicacy himself. All of them liked the little cups of cherry Kool-Aid, an overly sweet beverage. And he was partial to the hot-dog roll-ups, even if the meat came from a pet animal. Some people objected to horse meat as well, but when people lived in the frigid north, betimes it was necessary to eat what was available . . . not that he had ever eaten dog before. Another lady gave them samples of a cold delicacy known as ice cream. It was strawberry flavored and sinfully delicious. Even Lida got a taste, and she nigh purred with delight. Angela put three kinds in her cart.

Something about this whole scenario was perplexing to Magnus. "All these people in this mart . . . are they all royalty, or of the landed class of upper wealth?"

"No, actually, Wal-Mart prides itself on catering to the middle classes. Working people," Angela said.

"How can that be?" he remarked, gazing about him at all the wonders of the world gathered in one place. "All this richness, and it is available to *everyone?* Surely this passes the bounds of logic."

Angela stopped pushing her cart and turned to stare at him directly. For the first time her expression was soft as she looked at him. "You're serious, aren't you?"

He nodded.

"You must have come from some really isolated area to be so shocked by what you've seen thus far. It's nothing, believe me. Nothing."

They had finally reached the head of a long line where they were expected to pay for their purchases before leaving the mart. "Do you have money to pay?" Angela asked him.

"Of course," he answered. What did she think? That he was a pauper? He opened the pouch attached to his belt and handed a gold coin to the store person, who wore a white brooch that read, *Kimmie*.

Kimmie stared at the coin, then at him. "This is what you intend to pay with? Oh, man, it's almost time for my break, and I gotta get a loony-bird."

"What is it?" Angela asked, peering around his body. She was always muttering something about him being big as a tree. Well, of course he was. He was a Viking, wasn't he? What did she expect? A dwarf? "Some antique coin?"

"Now what? My coin is not good here?" Magnus confronted Kimmie. "Gold is gold, m'lady. Do not try to tell me different."

Kimmie spoke into a black square attached to her "station" by a black coiled cord. Her voice echoed throughout the store, just like the horn back at the longship site. "Manager to register three. Manager to register three."

"Shhhh," Angela intervened. "I'll pay and you can reimburse me later." She pulled out some parchment pieces from a black leather pouch that hung over her shoulder.

"Parchment!" he scoffed. "They will not accept my gold, but they will accept your parchment?"

"Shhhh," she cautioned once again. "Let me pay so we can get out of this store without causing an even bigger scene than we already have."

He looked around and saw that she was right. People were staring at them with great interest. Was it their unique attire, or the fact that he had so many children, or the sight of his gold coin?

"Listen, Magnus, I saw a small coin shop in the strip mall outside, next to Wal-Mart. Why don't you go there and see what they'll give you for your coin while I take care of things here? I'll meet you at the van."

He agreed, reluctantly, and stomped off with Njal and Hamr trailing behind him. No way was he letting those two out of his sight in this land of myriad mischief opportunities.

When they were all strapped into their respective seats in the van a half hour later and all their packages were stowed in the back with his chests, Angela asked him, "Well, how did you do? Did they buy your coin?" There was a smirk on her face which led Magnus to believe that she had no confidence in his ability to make such a transaction.

Wench, did no one ever tell you that 'tis unwise to push a Viking too far? You will learn that there is payment to be exacted for every insult you toss a Norseman's way. "Yea, I sold my coin," he said, but he injected a miserable tone into his voice. "I suspect I was cheated. The coin merchant was too happy over our transaction. In truth, he begged me to come back with any other coins I have."

"How much?" she demanded to know.

He shrugged. "The worst part is that it's all in parchment."

"Parchment?" she inquired.

"Yea, just like yours."

She frowned. "You mean paper money. Come on, Magnus. Spill the beans. How much did the man give you?"

It was with much hesitation and even more feigned embarrassment that he pulled a pile of parchment from his belt pouch. The pile was so high he had barely been able to stuff it all into his pouch.

"Magnus!" she exclaimed. "Those are hundred dollar bills. Let me see."

She took the pile into her lap and began to count. It took her a long time to finish. When she did, she gazed at him with amazement. "There's ten thousand dollars here and a check for forty thousand more."

"Is that a great amount?"

"It is a very great amount. Do you have any more of those coins?"

Chestfuls. "A few," he lied. "How much do I owe you?"

She took one of the parchment sheets from him.

"Only one?" His eyes grew wide as he comprehended just how valuable the coin must have been.

"It must have been an antique coin."

"Antique! 'Tis no more antique than I am."

"Well, don't sell any more till I put you in touch with some reputable dealer."

"Why did you send me to this man if he was not reputable?"

"How was I supposed to know you had some authentic antique coin?"

"I am telling you, that coin was not antique. Here, look at this coin. It is just like the one I sold." He took another coin out of his pouch and showed it to her.

"*Eoforwic?* Where is that?" she asked, turning the coin over, examining both sides carefully.

"That is the Saxon name for Jorvik . . . or York. Jorvik is the Viking capital of Britain. And as far as I know, those coins were minted last year. Does it not have an imprint on it of Aethelred the Unready, the British all-king?"

She stared at him for a long time before asking in a suffocated whisper, "Who . . . are . . . you?"

Chapter Five

No rest for the weary, or confused . . .

It was almost midnight, and Angela sat exhausted at her kitchen table, reading over the day's mail as she sipped from a stemmed crystal glass filled with a fine 1997 Blue Dragon zinfandel.

Her "guests" were asleep in their assigned beds or pull-out sofas. Magnus and Torolf were in her king-size bed, with Lida between them. Njal, Jogeir, and Hamr were wrapped in comforters on the floor. In her second bedroom, in twin beds, slept Kirsten and Dagny, who'd gotten teary-eyed when she'd first shown them the soft pastel sheets and flowered wallpaper. Even clothes hangers and closets had made the girls almost swoon. Storvald and Kolbein were on the sleep sofa in her den, while the living room sofa was all hers. She'd already taken all the necessary clothes out of her bedroom so she could leave for work by seven the next morning without awakening anyone in her room.

What a day she had had! What a night she had had!

She had thought she'd seen everything at the Wal-Mart, but it had gotten worse. First she'd had to get the motley crew from the van in her condo parking lot up to her fourteenth-floor apartment. Her doorman took one look at the lot of them and almost swallowed his false teeth. Magnus had balked at getting into the elevator, but not his kids. They had been game for anything, especially those rascals Njal and Hamr. Finally, after a hair-raising, white-fisted climb upward amidst much squealing and laughter and requests that they do it again, they had reached her apartment, all of them carrying bags from Wal-Mart along with Magnus's numerous wooden chests.

While her "guests" had walked about touching everything, asking question after question, she had called Domino's and ordered pizzas and soda for their supper. The television in the den had, of course, been the biggest attraction. To say the children had been stunned was a vast understatement. While most of them sat watching cartoon after cartoon, alternated with MTV videos, Angela herded them one at a time into the shower, which was another fascination to them . . . that and the toilet, which they kept flushing and flushing. The girls she had put into old flannel nightshirts of hers and the boys into loose jogging pants or nylon jogging shorts. Meanwhile she had dumped their clothes into the washer and dryer—two loads thus far. She had no idea how the leather tunics would come out, but she was giving it her best shot.

Lida, the little darling, had been toddling about the apartment in nothing but a diaper, falling, then picking herself up over and over, till Magnus had caught up with her and tickled her and rolled with her on the carpet. The scene—all of it—overwhelmed Angela's well-ordered mind, not to mention her previously tidy apartment. And the way he interacted with his children—whether it was tenderness with Lida, or gruffness with the needy Kolbein, or sternness with the rascals Hamr and Njal—something deep inside her melted, then grew. She could not give it a name. In fact, she was afraid to examine the new emotion too closely.

The pizza was something else again. She'd been in the bathroom, trying to explain to the girls that the shampoo was a concentrate and they needed to use only a dab of it, not half a bottle, when the delivery guy knocked on the door. Magnus, who answered, apparently almost frightened the young man to death with his massive size. Then he forgot his earlier experience at Wal-Mart and tried to pay for the food with a gold coin. In the end he had paid for the six large pizzas and three six-packs of Coke with a hundred-dollar bill. She assumed the stunned delivery guy had just kept the change as a tip. All she knew was that he was gone by the time she came out. Magnus and his children had devoured the pizzas in a short period of time, declaring it food of the gods. Even Lida had gummed a crust happily, though Angela had given her some canned vegetable soup just before that. Afterward they'd had ice cream for dessert—three half gallons of it, strawberry, butter pecan, and chocolate.

These people had taken over her life.

"I am sorry," she heard a gruff male voice say behind her. She jumped with surprise and almost spilled her wine. She'd thought everyone was asleep by now.

"Sorry for what?" she asked over her shoulder.

Magnus walked around the table, into her line of vision, then sat down in a chair across from her.

"You're naked!" she accused him. "Go cover yourself."

"I am not naked," he said. "I have wrapped one of your towels around me, and I am wearing a pair of those jaw-key shorts under that. Wouldst like to see?" He stood and was about to remove the towel.

"No!" she shouted. *Holy moley!* Could her heart really stand such an intimate view of six-feet, five inches of drop-dead-gorgeous bare skin and muscle? Angela had never been wowed by good-looking male hunks. They were a dime a dozen in Hollywood. But this man . . . well, all she could say was, *Holy moley!*

"No?" he repeated, and sat back down.

"Why are you sorry?" she managed to get out, trying to look everywhere but at his bare chest, which was— *okay, let's admit it*—pretty near spectacular.

"For putting you to this inconvenience. Oh, do not mistake me; I believe this is where I am supposed to be. My destiny. I but regret making you unhappy."

She accepted his apology with a nod, then homed in on one word: "Destiny? What could you possibly mean? By the way, would you like a glass of wine?"

"I prefer mead or ale, but thank you, yea, I would."

She rose and poured wine into another glass for him. When he took a sip and smiled his appreciation, she told him, "It's from my family's vineyard."

"Really?" He was clearly surprised. "Why would you live here in this crowded city when you could live on your family lands, which are presumably not so crowded?"

"My salary here helps to keep the vineyard going." Now, why had she revealed that to him?

"The vineyard is not self-sufficient?"

"It used to be, but we ran into some problems a few years back, especially after my grandfather died. We stopped making wine, but we still grow the grapes in hopes that we can start up again someday. My grandmother is the only one left there, but it is her fervent desire that the Blue Dragon wines will be made once again." She shrugged to indicate the matter was out of her hands.

"I know a little about growing grapes," he offered, twirling his wine about in his glass before sipping it speculatively.

"You do?" Angela's heart skipped a beat at his words, and she had no idea why.

"I am a farmer. There are many similarities betwixt farmers and grape growers. Both depend on earth, sun, rain, love of the land . . . luck." He shrugged. "It is what I do."

"You're not an actor?"

"What is an act-whore?"

"Please don't play these games with me."

He gazed at her with absolute sincerity.

"If you aren't an actor, what were you doing on a movie set? Why are you here, then?"

"You . . . I think." He took one of her hands in his. The sharp contrast between his huge hand and her much smaller one was startling. She should have been repelled, but instead she felt a strange thrill at the difference. "You are the reason I am here in this country."

"I beg your pardon," she squeaked out. Despite all logic and all her best instincts . . . despite everything she knew about good-looking men and their lines . . . despite all that, her heart began to beat madly.

"Wait here. I want to show you something." He got up and walked out of the kitchen and into the living room. She was too upset by the idea of his not being an actor even to notice his state of undress. When he came back, he was carrying a small framed photograph that had been sitting on her mantel. "Who is this person?"

She cocked her head to the side. There was an ominous buzzing in her head, and it wasn't due to the wine, either. Something important was about to happen . . . she just knew it.

"It's my grandmother, Rose. Why do you ask?"

"By your leave, m'lady, she is the one who called me here."

A glass of wine later . . .

Angela waited till Magnus had gone off to bed again and, bolstered by another glass of wine, she dialed the cordless phone that sat on the table before her.

"Grandma? Sorry to call you so late. Were you asleep?"

"No, honey. The older I get, the more trouble I have sleeping soundly at night."

Angela knew the insomnia was mostly due to her grandmother missing her grandfather, who had been gone these past five years.

"Actually, I was reading in bed. The latest Maeve Binchy." Grandma seemed to catch herself then. With

93

concern in her voice, she asked, "Is something wrong?"

"No, I just wanted to tell you that the movie people will be there next Thursday."

"Ah, that's good. Did Mr. Nolan meet your price?"

"He might go up to seven hundred thousand."

She could hear her grandmother's gasp over the phone line. "You are a wonder woman, Angela. How is that possible?"

"It's complicated. We can discuss the details when I see you in person."

"You're coming with the film people?"

"I'll be there, all right. Actually, that's the real reason I called . . . and the reason Darrell Nolan is being so accommodating. He wants a favor . . . from you."

"Uh-oh. I can hear the nervousness in your voice."

"Can I come out to the Blue Dragon tomorrow and stay for a few days—" she started to say, all in a rush.

"Angela! Of course you can come, anytime. Why would you even ask?"

"I wasn't finished."

"Oops, sorry."

"Can I bring some guests with me?"

"Of course. How many, dear?"

"Ten."

There was a telling silence. Then Angela heard the strike of a lighter and the deep inhale of her grandmother's breath before she continued: "How many men? Women? Couples? I'll need to know so I can make sleeping arrangements."

"One man. Nine children."

Grandma started to laugh.

"What's so funny?"

94

"You. I'm trying to picture you with all those children. Where are they now?"

What would you say if I told you there was a six-foot-five-inch hunk in my bed this very moment . . . actually, two hunks? Angela really, really hated to admit the predicament she was in. With a groan, she confessed: "Here. In my condo."

"Angela! You truly amaze me. How long have they been there?"

"One day." *So far.*

"Amazing," her grandmother murmured. "What are the ages of the children?"

"The six boys are three to sixteen. And the three girls are fourteen months to fourteen years."

"A baby! Fourteen months is practically a baby. My goodness, dear, you have a baby with you? Oh, this is going to be such fun!"

Yeah, great fun!

"How long do you think they'll stay?"

"I was hoping for a day or two, but the way things have been going, I suspect it will be till next week, when the film crew arrives for the property inspection."

"And the man, Angela . . . what about him?"

Angela's grandmother was too perceptive, by far—even over the telephone. "His name is Magnus . . . Magnus Ericsson. Darrell wants to put him in one of his movies, but he has to keep him under wraps for a bit. He doesn't want the press to get a whiff of him yet. Does that name ring a bell? Magnus Ericsson?"

"For heaven's sake, no. Should it?"

Whew! "Well, he claims you are the reason he is here. He says he saw you in a dream or a fog or some

95

such thing, and you were conjuring him here with some prayer beads."

"Conjuring? Now, that's a strange way of saying it."

"Saying what? *Do* you have an explanation for this?"

"I do, Angela. At least, I think I do."

"Come on, Grandma. No secrets here. I can hear the self-satisfaction in your voice. What's your explanation?"

"God works in mysterious ways."

Three days in the New World, and almost barmy . . .

"I think I am in love," Torolf said with a long sigh.

"Now where would you have had the opportunity to meet a wench—uh, lady—in this new world, confined in this prison con-dough as we all are?" Magnus was just entering the den, where he banged his head for about the hundredth time on the low archway. "Ouch!" he exclaimed, followed by a crude expletive.

This "new world," as Magnus had come to regard the country where they had landed, was full of marvels, but, truth to tell, he was all marveled out. Three days! And not a clue as to where exactly they were. Vikings were not meant to be indoors all the time. Soon his muscles would soften. His brain was surely already turned to gruel.

And there was another truth to tell: Magnus was randier than a bull, with all this time to sit around and ponder his favorite subject. He needed some good, hard exercise to expend his energy.

He had just put Lida down on the big bed for a nap. He guessed she was all tired out from watching Bert and Ernie on the tell-a-vision box, or waddling endlessly about the place like a duckling. They were all becoming more adept at this country's form of the English language, thanks to the tell-a-vision, but his children were also learning some foul words, which he'd had to halt a time or two already. A great number of them were gleaned from Hamr and Njal's latest hero, a rascally little fellow called Bart Simpson. Some of the words, like *free-can*, Magnus had decided couldn't be too bad. But he still misliked the word *suck* as an expletive. In fact, he wasn't sure what it meant when someone said, "That sucks!" So he'd told the children they could say "free-can" but not "That sucks!" Of course, the most perplexing one was "friggin'." Since Frigg was a goddess and the wife of Odin, he could not figure how "friggin' " became a bad word; so he'd decided to forbid that word, too, if for no other reason than to avoid offending the gods.

"Did you hear what I said, Father? I am in love."

At your age, young men are always in love . . . or lust. Same thing. "I heard you, Torolf. I heard you."

Torolf was lying on the low pallet, known as a sofa, arms crossed under his neck. He was watching some loud music event on the tell-a-vision box. Kirsten and Dagny were stretched out on the rug watching as well. The three of them seemed oblivious to the screeching that was taking place in the living chamber where Njal and Hamr were practicing something called kung fu, which they had learned on the tell-a-vision box from a person known as the Carrot-y Kid.

Only soft murmurs came from the kitchen, where Storvald was teaching Jogeir and Kolbein how to do a puzzle, which Angela had left for them. Nay, it wasn't the kitchen whence their murmurs emanated. It was the bathroom . . . again.

"If anyone flushes that toilet again," he shouted, "there is going to be a young Viking boy going down the hole with all that water."

Immediately he heard the bathroom door slam and murmurs traveling along the corridor and back to the kitchen. "No one ever lets us have any fun," Storvald grumbled.

"Let us make some mica-wave popcorn," Kolbein suggested to his brothers.

"Do not free-can burn it this time. The building master said we are in big trouble if we make the free-can smoking alarm go off again," Jogeir said.

"*That* is the object of my affection." Torolf, who somehow managed to ignore all the noise emanating from the other rooms, nodded his head toward the tell-a-vision screen, where a nubile young woman was gyrating and shaking her female parts as if she were having a fit . . . an erotic fit, he had to admit. " 'Tis Britney Spears."

"Britain Spear? Ha! That will be the day I allow my son to align himself with a Saxon wench. And a warlike wench she must be, too, if she carries a spear in her name."

"Daaa-aaad!" Kirsten groaned.

"*Dad?* What is this 'Dad' business?"

"*Dad* is what children in this land called their fathers."

"We are Vikings, no matter where we are. You, my Viking maid, will call me Father."

"Father, then," Kirsten conceded. "It's Britney . . . not Britain."

"Same thing," he said. "By thunder, is that young woman really wearing so little clothing?" The girl's skintight *braies* started below her hips and barely covered her nether cheeks. On top, only her breasts were covered . . . just barely.

"Yea, is it not great?" Torolf grinned up at him and winked mischievously.

"It is grate, all right. Grating on the nerves, if you ask me. Is there no soft music in this land? Why does it have to be so raucous all the time?"

"I love it," Dagny said. "Can I get my navel pierced, like Britney? Can I, can I?"

"Why would you want your navel pierced when no one is going to see it? Because I am telling you now, Dagny, afore you ask . . . you are not purchasing such nonattire."

Dagny gave him a look foreign to her usual biddable self. If he did not know it afore, he did now: this land was having a bad influence on his children.

"I am considering a tattoo," Torolf said. "Mayhap a dragon or a hawk. But I do not know whether to put it on my shoulder or my thigh."

"How about a jackass on your buttock?" Magnus suggested. And he was serious.

"Well, if I were going to be pierced, I would rather have a gold ring in my nose. Just a small one. On the left nostril. I saw a girl on *Sex and the City* with one, and it was so cooool. No one else at Uncle Olaf's court would have the same. What do you think of that, Da . . . Father? May I put a gold ring in my nose? May I?" Kirsten asked. And she was serious, too.

"Only if you intend to moo and give milk into a wood bucket twice a day," he told her. "And, by the by, I thought I told you girls not to watch that sinful program on the tell-a-vision."

"I saw the nose ring afore we turned it off," Kirsten said, but he could tell by the blush on her face that she was telling an untruth.

Magnus could hardly blame her. There were too many temptations in this New World. And the biggest, as far as he was concerned, was the black-haired witch who locked them in every day before she went out to work, promising, "Just one more day."

The tell-of-own rang suddenly, and he picked it up off the low table. He did not understand this device at all, but he had learned how to use it in the short time he had been here. How else would he have learned how to order endless pizzas for his family from Dome-nose? And for himself, too, he acknowledged. He had grown partial to the pepperoni-and-sausage thin-crust delicacy.

"Greetings!" he said into the palm-sized black device.

"Magnus?"

He smiled at Angela's voice. Even when she was chastising him for some misdeed, like coming out of the bathing room in naught but his jaw-keys, or eating all of the cold cream from the freezer, he loved the sound of her voice.

"Yea, 'tis me."

"I have good news," she said cheerily.

You are going to join me in the bed furs . . . rather, bedsheets?

Nay, that would not be good news. Because of my vow, I could do nothing.

But I would really like to do something.

Nay, I would not . . . because then, sure as sunshine, there would be another babe . . . or babes.

Oh, but what pleasure there would be in the making! I am pitiful. Really pitiful. The woman does not even like me.

But I could convince her to like me.

"Magnus, are you there? What is that loud noise I hear? Is it music?"

"Yea, I am here. And what you hear is Britain Spear."

"Huh?" she said. Then: "Never mind. What I wanted to tell you is that I'll be home soon. We settled the deal a few minutes ago. Guess where we're going this afternoon?"

To bed? Ha, ha, ha. Just jesting. "Vinland?" he offered hopefully.

"No, silly! We are going to—"

No one in the world had ever dared called him silly afore. So it took a stunned moment for Magnus to realize that Angela was still talking.

"—the beach. I'll stop for some swim suits on the way home."

"Wonderful," he said, but what he thought was that new word he had learned, *Whatever.* He could hardly credit her enthusiasm for going to a beach. He had a stone-stubbled beach bordering the fjord right in front of his farmstead in the Norselands, and people did not come to visit it. In truth, it was mainly used to beach longships.

"And the best news of all is that we're going to the Blue Dragon tomorrow after my closing."

"Hamr will be glad to hear that. Dragons, at last."

Closing? Her closing? He decided not to ask what part

of her body she was closing. He feared he would mislike the answer.

"What did you say?"

"Nothing."

"You don't sound very excited."

If you only knew! Excitement is my second name when I am around you. Magnus the Excited! That is what they should call me. Especially when I see those sheer hose hanging in the bathing chamber every time I go to piss. "Dearling, I am very excited, if it means we will finally be able to leave this confinement." *And I am very excited about some other things, too. Forbidden things. Think bulls, m'lady. Excited bulls.*

The minute he clicked off the tell-of-own with Angela, it rang again. It was Dare-All No-Land.

"Darrell Nolan here. Is that you, Magnus?"

"Yea, 'tis. Greetings."

"I have great news here, my boy."

More grating news. I can hardly contain myself.

"I've just about tied things up with that dick, Dirk."

He has tied the man up? Now, this is interesting.

"Give me a few more days and we should be able to arrange your audition."

"What precisely is an odd-itch-on?"

"Ha, ha, ha! You are such a kidder, Magnus. Really, you are going to be perfect for this role. I just know it. You won't even need a dialect teacher."

"Let me make one thing clear, Dare-All. You are not tying *me* up."

"What?" Dare-All squawked. "Oh, you and your language act! I keep forgetting. Well, anyhow, don't do anything I wouldn't. Ha, ha, ha! Bye-bye!"

Magnus frowned at the tell-of-own for a long moment before clicking it off. He really did not like Dare-All, nor did he trust him.

"What was that all about?" Torolf asked, jarring him back to the present. "Was it Angela?"

He nodded. "It appears we are going to the beach."

"Why?" Torolf wanted to know.

Magnus shrugged. "To look at the ocean, I suppose."

"This is a strange land," Torolf commented.

Magnus agreed.

Good vibrations (not!) . . .

Angela was totally confused by this strange group who had entered her life . . . taken it over, really. And they *were* strange, no doubt about that.

For example, why were they so surprised by people lying about a sandy beach, getting a suntan, or swimming in the surf, just for the fun of it? Why had the older ones never heard of surfboarding? Or volleyball? And why were they so shocked by the scanty attire females wore when swimming?

She and Magnus were lying on a blanket on the beach in Santa Monica . . . he on one side in his new boxer-style bathing trunks, and she on the other side in her most conservative one-piece bathing suit, a flame-red maillot cut high on the hip. Actually it was her only bathing suit . . . one she'd bought for her honeymoon with the Creep aeons ago. In between them was Lida, fast asleep on her tummy, with her adorable diaper-clad rump up in the air. Lida had been like an Energizer bunny, running along the edge of the water and squealing with delight every time a wave came in and wet her toes. Angela was surprised at the time and care Magnus took with the toddler, sitting in the sand to teach her how to dig and make sand castles, after Angela had first shown him how.

"Father," Torolf said, running up to their blanket, sand and water droplets showering them. He dropped his rented surfboard to the ground near their feet. "This is Crystal. We are going up on the boardwalk to buy a Coke. Can I have some paper . . . uh, money?"

Crystal smiled at all of them. "Afterward, we're going jogging. It's, like, so cool to jog on the beach here. And the waves are awesome. And Tor is so buff. He's gonna give us some pointers."

"Well, *Tor,* just do not get too *buff,*" Magnus drawled.

Torolf shot him a look that pretty well translated to, "Faaaa-ther!"

Torolf was a good-looking young man, who closely resembled his father, except that his hair, which was tied back now with a leather lace, was true blond, whereas Magnus's was light brown with hints of blond. Torolf was almost the same massive height as his father, too. And they both had wide-shouldered, narrow-waisted, cover-model bodies. You could see why Torolf was having no trouble drawing young women to him here at the beach. Even more women ogled Magnus when he passed by.

Magnus took one startled look at the teenage girl with Torolf—a typical blond California girl wearing a thong bikini. Magnus's gaze went wide at her outfit, and Angela just knew he would be rolling his eyes if the girl were not watching. Reaching into his leather pouch, which lay beside the still sleeping baby, he was about to hand Torolf a hundred-dollar bill. Angela halted him with a hand over his and took out a ten-dollar bill instead. Magnus nodded his thanks to her. He still hadn't mastered the currency values.

Once they were gone, Magnus asked, "Do you ever wear one of those thongs?"

Not where anyone can view my backside. "Not on the beach."

"Other places?"

Hardly ever . . . unless it's in a dark room, and my backside is hidden. "Sure," she said. "There is thong underwear, too, you know."

"Is it not uncomfortable?"

"No. In fact, a good pair, properly fitted, can be more comfortable than traditional underwear." *Angela, you are such a fraud. Victoria's Secret material you are not, and never will be.*

"I can hardly fathom that."

She smiled. "Would you like me to buy you a male thong?"

He looked horrified at the suggestion. "Absolutely not."

She couldn't see him in such attire, either. He was male enough without such a blatantly teasing garment. It would appear obscene on him.

"I would like to see you in yours, though. I would *really* like that." She could tell by the smoldering glint in his eyes that he meant his words. But that was a road she did not want to travel with this man . . . especially this man who claimed she was his destiny, of all things. Best to change the subject. "Where is the mother of all these kids?"

"There is no *one* mother. There have been four wives, six concubines, numerous passing fancies, and at least one barley-faced maid, which I can only attribute to a fit of mead-head madness on my part. All of my women, one by one, have had the temerity to die on me, desert me, or, to my shame, divorce me, as my most recent wife, Inga, did publicly at an Althing. Claimed she was tired of playing slave to all my babes, she did. Norsemen from here to Birka are still laughing about that happenstance."

She could tell this long spiel of Magnus's was a pat answer he gave to a question he'd no doubt been asked many times.

"You're embarrassed," she teased.

He shrugged. "I do not have much woman luck . . . leastways in keeping women. Attracting them and pleasing them has never been a problem, though."

Not much trouble pleasing women, huh? Now that posed some interesting questions that she was not going to ask.

Apparently disapproval was evident in her expression, because he asked, "You disapprove of my children?"

"Just the number of them."

"I take good care of all my children. They want for nothing," he informed her defensively.

"How about a mother? Children need a mother."

"There is that lack, but I try to make up for it." Whatever anger he had felt at her condemnation quickly melted as he admitted, "It *is* an excessive number of children. I cannot help that my seed is so virile, but—"

Oh, my God! Did he really say that?

"—that is why I took my vow of celibacy. There will be no more babes born of my loins, if I can help it."

Oh, my God! Did he really say that? "You . . . you are celibate?" she finally sputtered out.

"I am trying."

My mind is boggling here. A man this hot, and he's celibate. Well, at least he's not gay. "All those sizzling looks you keep giving me, and you are celibate?" Those words were blurted out before she had a chance to curb her tongue.

"I said that I took a vow, m'lady. I did not say that my man part fell off." He gave her a haughty stare, then turned the tables on her. "How about you? Why is there no husband?"

"There was, but we got divorced seven years ago."

"Did you divorce him?" He was probably envisioning his own ignominious public divorce.

She nodded. "The Creep was cheating on me . . . a lot. Couldn't keep his pants on for the life of him."

"The *creep?*"

"Creep, jerk, whatever word you want to use to describe a most detestable fellow."

"Aaah," he said. "We call such a man a *nithing* in my country. A man of no honor."

"Sounds good to me."

"I mislike divorce very much, but I must admit to being pleased that you are unencumbered. It makes things so much easier for us."

"Us? *Us?*" Angela was spared an explanation of that outrageous statement by the shrill blast of the lifeguard's whistle. Before she could locate the source of the problem, Magnus was already on his feet and running toward the water. He dove under a large wave, then began swimming steadily after he emerged on the other side. Two lifeguards with yellow bullet-shaped buoys slung over their shoulders were following in his wake. In the distance—the far distance—she could see Hamr and Njal, sitting big as you please on their boogie boards. They didn't appear to be in distress, but there were rules on this beach that limited how far out swimmers could go. The boys had exceeded that distance, by a lot.

Soon they all returned safe and sound to shore, where the two lifeguards were now talking and gesticulating wildly to Magnus and his sons. Magnus was nodding his agreement with whatever they were saying, while Hamr and Njal hung their heads. Torolf and the rest of the children walked up to join the group. Angela stayed on the blanket with Lida.

Finally Magnus returned to the blanket, towing Hamr and Njal behind him. "Sit," he ordered, "and do not move."

She saw equal parts anger and concern on his handsome face. It must be hard being a parent, she thought, balancing discipline with love.

He turned to her then and said, "I think we have had enough beach playing for one day. Shall we go back to your keep?"

She nodded.

"Mayhap we could stop at that Scotsman's place on the way . . . to break our fast."

"Scotsman's?"

"McDonald's. I saw a picture of his food on the tell-a-vision. Methinks we could all do with a few Big Macs and Frankish fries."

"I found a piece of driftwood. Can I bring it back with me to carve?" Storvald was holding a hunk of wood the size of a small telephone pole.

"If Stor is bringing wood, then I'm bringing my

crabs," Jogeir said. He was holding a plastic bucket loaded with sand crabs.

"I want some dome-nose," Kolbein said softly.

"Njal pissed in the ocean," Dagny informed everyone, as if anyone needed to know that.

"I saw your teeny, tiny tits when a wave pulled your bathing suit down. So, hah!" Njal countered, sticking out his tongue for good measure.

"Njal, you are still in trouble, you know. I would not push too far," Magnus told his son.

"Kirsten has a suitor. He kept splashing her, and she kept giggling. Just like this. Tee, hee, hee, hee. His name is George, and, whooee, does he have pimples!" Hamr piped up.

Kirsten smacked her brother on the shoulder and started to sob with embarrassment.

Truly, the little imp had a death wish, if his father's growl was any indication.

All his brothers and Dagny glared at Hamr, and the rascal asked with exaggerated innocence, "What? What did I do? I was only telling the truth."

"Hamr," was all his father said, but it was in a level, angry tone.

Just then Lida woke up. Rolling over to her back, she sat up agilely, wiped her eyes with her two tiny fists, smiled toothlessly at them all, and said, "Goo!"

As far as Angela was concerned, that about said it all.

Chapter Six

On the road again . . .

They had been driving in the van for about five hours, with two stops along the way to eat and use the resting rooms, before Angela finally turned the van at the sign, *Blue Dragon*. They were in the Sonoma valley—wine country, Angela had explained to him a while back.

For the first four hours of their journey, Magnus had thought he was going to lose his mind . . . or his temper.

"*Faðir*, are we there yet?"

"*Faðir*, I have to stop and make water."

"*Faðir*, I am hot."

"*Faðir*, I am cold."

"*Faðir*, are we there yet?"

"*Faðir*, Dagny won't stop looking at me."

"*Faðir*, what smells?"

"*Faðir*, are we there yet?"

On and on and on his children had persisted . . . question after question . . . complaint after complaint . . . even when Angela had turned some music on the raid-he-oh by the Blessed Mother—or was it the Madonna? He could understand their restlessness, because it *was* stifling inside the confines of the van.

But now, fortunately, the children were either napping or engaged in a contest he had thought up for them . . . a special prize to the child whose tongue could touch his or her chin. In the blissful quiet, he was able to enjoy the view unfolding at this moment before him. In truth, nothing—not even his loud, demanding children—would have been able to penetrate the strange ripple of recognition he felt on entering the lands of Angela's family. For a certainty, he had never been here before, and yet he felt as if he were coming home.

He opened the windows of the van and breathed deeply. "Aaah!" he said with a long sigh.

She turned to give him a quick glance, then immediately focused her attention back on the road. *She likes me. She likes to look at me, but she does not want to show her attraction*, he thought with his usual immodesty. *Or could she be repelled by me, and I am misreading the signs?* Magnus misliked his lack of confidence. What was a Viking without his swagger?

Tall oak trees, unlike any he'd ever seen before, were spaced evenly on either side of the long roadway leading to her family keep. At regular intervals along a low stone wall, huge pottery bowls spilled over with bright red flowers. Everywhere there was the scent of fields and tilled earth that he recognized so well. He inhaled deeply and exhaled with a sigh of pleasure.

111

There was also the scent of the woman next to him. The perfume she sprayed lightly on herself each morn was appealing, but just as appealing was her own woman musk. Magnus had a nose for these things when it came to the fairer sex, and it wasn't because he had a big nose. His nose was just fine, or so he had been told. 'Twas his love of the female sex that gave him this talent. And 'twas his love of the female sex that had given him thirteen children, he reminded himself ruefully.

Angela gave him a curious sideways glance as she steered the van through the picturesque corridor. "What are you doing?"

"Breathing," he answered. "I think it is the first time I have really breathed since I entered this land of yours. Do you not love the smell?"

"What smell? Fresh air?"

"Earth. The wonderful, pungent smell of earth and trees and growing things. That is what I have missed since entering this new land."

"You like to smell ... dirt?" Instead of acting surprised, she almost seemed frightened.

He nodded. "Is that so odd?"

"Actually, no. My grandfather used to say the same thing. He even tasted dirt sometimes to see if it was missing some nutrient." She paused before adding, "I got a sort of eerie feeling, hearing someone repeat his words."

"He must have been a wise man, your grandsire."

Tears sprang immediately to her eyes. "He was. Oh, not so much in book learning, but in simple truths. I swear, Gramps had a hokey proverb for everything. We teased him by calling him the Italian redneck philosopher."

"I wish I could have met him."

She pondered what he'd said, then changed the subject. "I didn't realize that you were so unhappy back in L.A."

"Not unhappy, precisely. I do not understand half of the marvels of Ah-mare-ee-ca. There is so much more wealth than in the Norselands, so many more efficient ways of doing things, so much entertainment for your vast amount of free time. And yet I have been dissatisfied here. Until now I did not realize why. There are just too many people crowded into too small a space, too much ease and excess, too many complications that add nothing to the betterment of everyday living."

"But those are the things that make life better. High-rise buildings. Televisions. Cell phones. Cars."

He shook his head adamantly. "All a man really needs is home and hearth . . . and occasionally a bout of a-viking when adventure calls, or fighting when warrior skills are required by one's king." *And lovemaking . . . good lovemaking . . . often . . . preferably twice a day. Aaarrgh! There I go again. My brain in the bed furs.* "I am a farmer at heart, and the land is what I have missed most."

She laughed. "I'll tell you one thing, Magnus: if this is all an act . . . you are bound to get an Oscar someday."

"I would not mind a car, though I do not know what an oss-car is, but you could not pay me to live in one of those high-rise keeps. Pretty prisons, they are, if you ask me."

113

"You are really a strange person," Angela said with a laugh.

Strange, eh? Well, leastways she did not say I was a repulsive person. Or a slimy toad, as Inga once called me. Yea, I was correct. She likes me. "Good strange or bad strange?"

"I'm still trying to figure that out."

Or mayhap not. He looked at her and could tell she had answered honestly. Good enough . . . for now, he thought.

The children were chattering away, having given up on the tongue game. They too were excited about finally reaching the end of their journey.

"Look over there," Dagny shrieked. "It is a pond. And those trees . . . their leaves look like green hair. Dost think fairies live there?"

"Or trolls," Njal offered, making a scary face at his sister.

"Those are weeping willow trees," Angela told them. "I loved those trees when I was a child. I have so many memories of playing games under their wispy branches. Personally, I think they resemble fine ladies with flowing dresses, especially when there's a breeze." Angela's face turned pink then, as if she were embarrassed at revealing so much about herself.

"Weeping willow? What a pretty name for a tree! We do not give trees such fanciful names in our country," Dagny said dolefully. "We just call them oak, pine, or elm."

"Are there fish in that pond?" Jogeir wanted to know.

"Yes. I think so," Angela answered, to Jogeir's delight.

"There is a swing hanging from one of the trees,"

Kolbein pointed out. "Are there children living here?"

"No," Angela said. "It was my swing when I was a little girl."

"It must be a really old swing then," Kolbein blurted out, then turned red-faced when everyone laughed at his blunder.

"Not *that* old, young man," Angela remarked when she was able to stop laughing.

"I have never seen so many wildflowers together, and so many colors. It is beautiful." Kirsten's nose was pressed to the window on her side.

"Where are all the free-can dragons? That's what I want to know?" It was Hamr speaking. *Who else!*

"They are off stoking up the fire in their bellies so they can flame little boylings like you," Magnus said.

Angela made a *tsk*ing sound. "Do you think it's wise to scare children like that?"

"Are you scared, Hamr?" he asked.

"Bloody hell, nay! But I will tell you what is scary: sending a wee boyling off to fight dragons without a bow and arrow."

Magnus exchanged a quick smile with Angela, who must be starting to understand his son's persistence about owning a weapon.

In the far distance Magnus could see row after row of grapevines, many, many hectares of land . . . all filled with growing things. And, if his eyes did not play him false, there was a large vegetable garden closer to the house. He couldn't wait to explore everything.

He turned slightly in his seat and his eyes connected with Jogeir's. He saw the same appreciation of the land reflected there. *My little farmer boy.* They both smiled.

But first there was the Blue Dragon keep and its mistress, Grandmother Rose, to be met. He glanced at each of his children in turn, cautioning them to be on their best behavior. After all, this might very well be the goddess who had called them here.

The van came to a stop. He took Lida out of her car seat and stepped out onto the cleared area in front of a large wooden house of a most unusual design. It had covered verandas all around and highly carved eaves and rails. His blood began to race, and there was a peculiar buzzing in his ears as he observed his surroundings.

Of a sudden he noticed the very lady from his dream fog—an older replica of Angela with white hair. But this goddess was wearing full-length, shoulder-to-ankle den-ham *braies*, and she had a smoking stick dangling from the fingertips of one hand, which she immediately dropped to the ground and stomped on with one white cloth-shod foot. Then she held both arms out wide, not for her granddaughter, Angela, but for Lida, crooning, "Oh, you adorable baby, you. Come to Grandma Rose."

And Lida, to everyone's surprise, did just that, with a wide, smiling, "Goo!"

Grandmother Rose took Magnus's measure then, head to toe, with a pause at his armrings and Viking attire. Then she nodded to her granddaughter. "You're right. He's like a tree."

Magnus arched an eyebrow in question at Angela and mouthed, *A tree?*

Angela shrugged at him with a winsome blush on her face.

His other eight children began to pile out of the van,

and Grandmother Rose's eyes grew wider and wider at the sight of each of them.

"For the love of a troll!" Kirsten exclaimed. "They have a horse which they keep indoors."

Everyone turned to see the large animal loping down the wooden steps in front of the keep. It must have emerged from inside the building.

"Kirsten, you are such a lackwit," Njal declared with a superior sniff. "That is a dog, not a horse."

It was indeed a dog—the size of a small horse—and it was licking the face of each of the children, wagging its tail in a friendly fashion.

"It's Jow," Angela told them, laughing as the giant dog licked her in welcome, too.

"Jowl. 'Tis an odd name for a pet," Magnus said.

"Not Jowl, Jow. It stands for Just One Week. That's how long he was supposed to stay."

That made as much sense as anything else that had happened to him in this land . . . which was not much.

Angela smiled at him as she spoke.

He hated when she smiled at him like that. It made his stomach knot and his lungs go breathless.

Between the dog licking, which gave him certain carnal ideas, and her winsome smiles, he was going to be in a sorry state before the afternoon was over.

Finally, as the barking and giggles and squeals died down a bit, and Angela stopped smiling at him, the grandmother shook her head as if to clear it of the amazing scene unfolding around her. Then she returned her attention to him. Stretching out an arm, she shook his hand firmly, "Hello, there, young fellow. Welcome to the Blue Dragon. I'm Rose Abruzzi. You can call me Grandma Rose."

He nodded and said, "I am Magnus Ericsson. And these are my children." He pointed to each of them in turn. "Lida, Kolbein, Hamr, Jogeir, Njal, Dagny, Storvald, Kirsten, and Torolf."

She laughed merrily as she nodded one by one at his children, concluding with a loud kiss on Lida's cheek. Then she turned back to him and said, "It's about time you got here, boy."

Looking for trouble . . .

It was dark when Angela emerged onto the back veranda of the house, searching for Magnus.

Torolf, Kirsten, and Dagny were in the library watching an action-adventure film on TV, with a worn-out Jow laid out at their feet, on his belly with his legs widespread like a rug. The other boys were in an upstairs den playing a computer game. Grandma was upstairs, too, putting Lida down for the night.

Juanita was cleaning up in the kitchen after their sumptuous supper feast—chili-lime quesadillas, nachos and guacamole, blackened chicken, a family version of Spanish rice, better known as "spicy-dicey ricey," a nickname that delighted Magnus's children, shrimp chimichangas, taco salad, and cinnamon-topped Mexican fried ice cream for dessert. No one complained about how spicy the food was. It was a good thing Juanita and her grandmother had prepared such a large quantity because the children and Magnus seemed to have insatiable appetites. Heck, she did, too. There was a special dry red wine served to the adults and frosty tumblers of lemonade for the children.

Both Juanita and her grandmother had done nothing but smile and fuss over the children since they'd arrived. They were delighted when every bit of food disappeared from the table. They didn't even frown at the noise the children made. Truly this house was made for children, as her grandmother had always said.

"Miguel, have you seen Magnus?" she asked now as the manager approached the house. He'd eaten with them earlier, then had gone out to make his nightly inspection of the vines, taking Magnus with him.

Miguel walked wearily up the steps to the porch, nodding the whole time. "He's still over near the west vineyard. Who is this man, *chiquita?* He is amazing."

"Magnus is an actor—I think—although he claims to be a farmer."

"The man knows a lot about the land—not grapes, of course, but he has a great curiosity about them. So many questions. The right questions. How long is the growing season? The hazards of growing grapes? How dependent are we on climate? How profitable are grapes, compared to oats or vegetables?"

"You're impressed," Angela commented in a surprised tone. It took a lot to impress Miguel, who could see through phonys in an instant.

"Yes, I am. You did good, little one."

"Oh, no! You misunderstood, Miguel. There is nothing between us. He's just a visitor here. He'll be gone in a few days . . . a week at most."

Miguel looked skeptical. "He says you are his destiny."

Angela's heart swelled with some strange emotion,

despite herself. "You must have misunderstood," she said weakly.

Miguel still looked unconvinced. Then he shrugged as if it were no concern of his. "In any case, your visitor has asked me to teach him everything about grape growing. Starting tomorrow he will be my assistant." Noting the distress on her face, he added, "Just while he is visiting here, of course. And he will work for no pay. Where else can we get a no-salary worker? Ha, ha, ha!"

Miguel went into the house then, leaving her behind on the porch, poleaxed by the Viking—*again*, even when he wasn't present. But then she heard Miguel talking to his wife through the open window.

"The Norseman looks like a tree, Juanita. He picked up the back of a tractor all by himself when I wanted to check the oil pan. Can you imagine the Italian-Viking children he and Angela would make together?"

Juanita giggled, then cautioned, "Shhhh! The worst thing you can do is tell that stubborn-headed Angela that you like her young man."

He's not my young man, Angela wanted to shout. *And he's not my destiny, either.*

With that thought in mind, Angela went stomping off in search of her . . . destiny.

Here comes trouble . . .

"Magnus, we have to talk."

Magnus had just turned off the lever of the hollow metal rod that came up out of the ground spurting water. He'd washed his hands and splashed water on his face. Now he wet-combed his hair behind his ears with his fingers as he watched Angela approach. *Uh-oh!* he thought. *When a woman tells a man she wants to talk, it usually means she has a long list of grievances to lay on him. And she's stomping. Yea, stomping and a desire to talk are sure signs of a riled-up woman.*

"Shall we sit down . . . to talk?" he inquired, pointing to a nearby bench. "I can tell I am in trouble."

She frowned in confusion, even as she sat down. "Why do you think you're in trouble?"

"The stormy expression on your face. Either I have done something wrong, or my children are the culprits. Either way I am bracing myself for a lengthy tirade." He sat down beside her and was immediately assailed by her woman scent, a combination of some light floral perfume and her own female essence. Magnus loved women . . . and he loved each and every individual scent they carried. That alone had probably contributed to his downfall.

"No one is in trouble . . . exactly," she started to say, then practically jumped off the bench when he slid his arm along the back and took a strand of her raven-black hair in his fingertips. He rubbed the silky filaments sensuously. "I mean, what I'm trying to say is . . . uh . . . hmmm . . . uh . . . you've been saying and doing some things I object to, but, uh, once I set the record straight, I'm sure there will be no more, uh, trouble." She groaned softly at the end of her sputtered explanation, which was no explanation at all. She almost leaned into his palm, which was caressing her hair, then pulled back sharply, as if correcting her baser instincts.

Like a skittish mare, she was. Mayhap even a mare in heat, he thought. *Skittish mare?* He was too earthy

121

by far . . . or so he had been told by more than one
female, usually when they were about to spread their
thighs for him. His crudeness came from being a
farmer, he supposed. But if there were two things he
knew well and good in this world, it was women and
farm animals. This woman was fighting his appeal,
crude or not.

"Don't you look at me like that. Don't you dare," she
said, and shuffled her rear end a bit to remove herself
from his touch. Her hair slipped from his fingertips as
she'd intended, and she raised her chin in challenge.

Never challenge a Viking, my dear. Never. He immediately shuffled his own rear end, closing the distance between them. This time he slid his hand under
the long skein of her hair and cupped her nape, drawing her closer. "How am I looking at you, dearling?"

"Like a horny toad about to hop my bones."

*Inga called me a slimy toad. Now Angela calls me a
horny toad. Next time I see a mirror I must check myself
for warts. And what does she mean about hopping
bones? Oh. She must mean I want to lay my body on
hers and have* . . . For a moment—only a moment—
he was shocked by her blunt words. He supposed
women could be earthy, too, but he was not sure he
liked it. After a brief two seconds of pondering, he
decided he did . . . in moderation. With that in mind,
he chuckled and pulled her resisting body even closer.
"I am not all that *horny* . . . yet. I merely want to thank
you for bringing me to your home . . . to the Blue
Dragon. It is truly a paradise."

"Do you think so?" she asked, clearly pleased at his
appreciation of her beloved homestead.

He decided to take advantage of her momentary

lapse in guardedness and took her by the waist, lifting her onto his lap. Angela's head came only to his shoulder. He wanted—nay, needed—to have her body parts better aligned with his.

After a surprised squeal of dismay at his quick maneuver, she squirmed and shoved and tried to escape his embrace. "What do you think you're doing?"

Oh, lady, you do not really want to know. "Thanking you. I told you that I wanted to thank you for bringing me here, and that is what I am doing."

She stopped wriggling for a second and stared at him with wide-eyed question. "This . . . *this* is your way of thanking me?"

It is a beginning. "Nay, this is," he said, and lowered his mouth to hers, softly at first, gentle and persuasive. "A thank-you kiss."

Her lips were full and slightly parted with surprise. The two of them fit together perfectly, like dovetailed pieces of wood that his brother Geirolf used in crafting his ships. Like two pieces of a cracked pottery jug, whole again. Like the age-old mold created by the gods, joining man to woman.

The air was charged, as if with sparks during a summer lightning storm. Something momentous was happening—or about to happen—and he was joyous to be part of it.

At first Angela resisted, but he held her tightly by the nape and waist. He sensed the moment of her surrender when her entire body seemed to soften and lean into his. He did not need her moan into his open mouth to know that she wanted him . . . perchance as much as he wanted her. Nay, his want was greater. Nothing could surpass its intensity.

He brushed his lips back and forth across hers, shaping her. Against the dewy wetness he whispered, "Thank you."

To his immense satisfaction, she reciprocated by tracing the tip of her tongue along the outline of his mouth and whispered back, ever so softly, "You're welcome."

Well, he was a Viking, and he was virile. Hell, he was a man. He needed no more invitation than that. He plundered her mouth with his hot tongue, thrusting in and out, imitating the sex act itself. Instead of foiling his efforts, she opened her mouth wider for him and put her arms around his shoulders. The whole time, she was brushing her cloth-covered breasts to and fro over his tunic-covered chest. They did not need to be bare-skinned. So heightened was their arousal that even fabric could not lessen the delicious sensations.

"Too fast," he said on a groan.

"Too slow," she said on a groan.

Everything was happening too fast, no matter what she said. Furthermore, in the back of his mind was a nagging reminder of something important that he could not for the life of him recall now. Besides, with her words of encouragement, he did not even want to think of anything that might put a damper on these spreading fires.

He lifted her by the hips so that her legs in their denham *braies* straddled his thighs, her knees on the bench. Then he adjusted her so that her buttocks rested on his thighs and her woman cleft rode the hard ridge of his manhood.

In the light of the full moon, he saw her eyes go huge with wonder. And her lips parted and stayed open on a long sigh, which then evolved into soft panting breaths.

His hands moved upward from her waist, over her tea-*shert,* along her rib cage. His hands remained at her sides, but, with just his thumbs, he skimmed the sides of her breasts.

She arched her back so that her head was thrown back and her breasts thrust forward. "More," she demanded huskily.

More? Any more of this love play and I will come in my breeches like an untried youthling. "More what?" he choked out, as if he did not know . . . as if he wanted to torture himself.

"Touch me, Magnus. Touch . . . me," she said, and further arched her chest at him. The action caused her crotch to move against him, and Magnus saw stars before his open eyes. By all the gods and goddesses, was he *that* randy, or was it this woman who brought such an instant reaction from him? He was usually able to pace himself better than this.

But she had asked, and he was willing . . . more than willing.

He molded her breasts in his hands then, taking all of each in his big palms . . . pushing up, rubbing in a circular fashion, then lifting them again so that his thumbs could strum the pebbled nipples into hard peaks . . . then harder still and longer.

"Ride me," he encouraged.

And she did.

Magnus had not expected her to comply so readily. Therefore he was unprepared for the immediate assault on his senses. *Holy Thor, forget about senses!* Every male part of his body came to immediate attention, and that included his thick male brain, not to mention his thick male . . . nether part.

Magnus had not tupped a girl fully clothed since he was a boy, and, oh, the sheer joy of it was beyond description.

While she undulated her hips against him, he slid his hands under her *shert* and shoved her lacy undergarment aside. Taking her nipples between his thumbs and forefingers, he tweaked and strummed; he pinched and soothed. She was nigh wailing her pleasure as her woman's cleft slid back and forth along the ridge of his erection.

Gasping for air, he directed her, "Harder. Ride me harder, sweet angel. Bring me to heaven."

He knew Angela did not like to be called *angel*. The word had slipped out. And luckily she did not seem to mind at this moment, for she began to pound against him now, belly against belly.

"It's been too long for me. A year. I'm so embarrassed," she confessed.

"You are embarrassed! Ha! It has been nearly a year for me, as well. And I am a man," he confided.

"That is such a sexist thing to say."

"I am a sexy man," he replied, assuming *sexist* meant the same as *sexy*.

She tried to laugh but it came out as a gurgle. Then she was unable even to gurgle. "Oh, oh, oh, oh . . ." she moaned as her peak came.

He let out a roar of triumph at his own climax. Holding both her buttocks in his hands, he pressed her hard against him and let his man part jerk against her woman place . . . once, twice, numerous times . . . till he was depleted.

126

Her head was resting in the crook of his neck. His hands were wrapped about her waist, softly caressing her back. They were both panting to regain their breath.

"You certainly know how to say thank-you," she finally said with a soft laugh.

"Wait till you see how I say, 'Thank you *very much*,' " he answered, also with a soft laugh.

She pulled her head back to look at him. "I came here to talk with you."

"I like the way you talk."

"That's not what I meant," she said, and swatted his shoulder playfully. "Magnus, you have to stop telling people that I'm your destiny."

"Why?"

"Why? Because I'm not your destiny."

He was nibbling at her neck now, and she squirmed on his lap, which caused a part of his body that had gone dormant to come to life again. Really, this was beyond belief. He was *not* going to come in his *braies* twice. He was not, not, not. With determination bred of some iron will he had not known he possessed, Magnus lifted the squirming wench off his lap and set her next to him on the bench.

Only then did he consider her words. Not his destiny? *Ha!* "What do you call my being called halfway 'round the world to your country, if not destiny? What do you call my seeing your grandmother in my dreams, if not destiny? What do you call the breathlessness I experience whene'er I see you, if not destiny? What do you call the unplanned happenstance that just occurred betwixt us, if not destiny?"

"You get breathless whenever you see me?" she

127

asked, homing in on what was surely the most irrelevant part of all he had said.

Women ever do want to know that they can weaken a man. She must see my breathlessness as a weakness. "Why does that surprise you?"

"Because I get a teeny, tiny bit breathless myself," she admitted.

On the other hand . . . Thank you, God! Magnus could not see in the dim light, but he was betting her face was flushed at the admission. "A teeny, tiny bit, eh?" he teased. "Sounds like destiny to me."

"Whether you get breathless or I get breathless is beside the point," she said huffily. Then she seemed to think of something else. "What about your celibacy vow?"

Oh, so that is what my conscience was trying to call to mind when my sap was rising. The damned vow. Nay, the necessary vow. I cannot have any more children . . . not even with this comely lady. "I forgot, but not to worry. This kind of lovemaking does not count."

"Oh, really?" She twisted sideways on the bench so she was facing him. "There are rules for celibacy vows, are there?"

He knew she was teasing him, but he was a Viking, and Vikings took their vows seriously. "No rules. Just common sense."

"I mean, a man could still be called celibate if there is no completion . . . that is, if there is no satisfaction. . . ." *Any more satisfaction and my eyes will be permanently crossed.* He stopped himself and exhaled with frustration at his difficulty explaining himself. "Oh, hell, what I mean to say is that the vow is still intact if there is no insertion of a male part into a female part. What we did is called a dry tup in my country, and, for a certainty, it does not count."

He would have been patting himself on the back with congratulations at his final response if she were not laughing so hard.

When her laughter died down and she wiped tears of mirth from her eyes, she informed him, "I do not blame you for what happened here tonight, Magnus, but it cannot happen again."

"Definitely not," he agreed.

They stood then and began to walk back toward the house.

And both of them thought, *Ha!*

When all else fails, pray. . . .

Rose Abruzzi stood at her bedroom window, staring out at the vineyards she loved so well.

In one hand was the rosary she used for her nightly novena. In the other hand was a cigarette—the first Rose had had since the children had arrived early this afternoon. She was going to try not to smoke in front of them.

For the past fifteen minutes or so, she had been unabashedly watching her granddaughter and the handsome Norseman. Tears misted her eyes. She remembered too well how first love felt . . . though it had been fifty years and more for her. And it *was* first love for Angela—Rose was convinced of that, despite her granddaughter's failed marriage.

Already her brain was rushing forward, making plans. A wedding at the Blue Dragon . . . wouldn't that be a wondrous event? And more children . . . even with all the Viking already had. Baptisms, birthday parties, family holidays. Most of all, dare she hope that someday the winery would reopen and flourish? But first there would have to be a wedding. That was the first step . . . well, no, love was the first step, but she could already see that the two of them were starting along that road, even if they did not know it yet.

Rose watched the couple a little bit longer and saw how he kept reaching for her hand, and she kept swatting him away. He was laughing at something she said. She was raising her chin haughtily. Not exactly lover-like.

Rose decided then and there that she'd better say two rosaries tonight.

Chapter Seven

The roar of silence . . .

Angela overslept the next morning.

When she finally awakened at nine A.M., two hours past her usual rising, she realized that what had penetrated her deep sleep was the silence. No automobile traffic outside her apartment building. No musical wakeup from her bedside radio alarm. No children shrieking and squabbling.

Just birdsong outside her windows.

And a herd of mice running back and forth along the corridor outside her bedroom, then up and down the stairs . . . over and over . . . back and forth . . . up and down . . . usually accompanied by a "shhh" from one or another of them. The mice were, of course, the children—at least four of them, would be her guess. They must be running about on tiptoe, trying their best not to awaken her, no doubt at her grandmother's and

131

Juanita's orders. Instead their very silence had penetrated her sleep, along with the incessant tiptoeing, which probably meant they were up to some mischief.

Angela stretched and yawned openmouthed at the satisfaction she'd gained from her long, deep sleep—something she rarely indulged in. Only then, midyawn and midstretch, did she remember another satisfaction that had come her way recently.

Magnus, she thought, and groaned with dismay as images flashed before her eyes of the kiss he had used to thank her, for God only knew what. The kiss was not just a kiss. No, it was much more than that. And she, who was usually so careful, had participated fully.

She disliked men like Magnus. He was totally irresponsible to have brought thirteen children into the world. Forget about celibacy vows; he should have had a vasectomy ten children ago.

And this continual acting gig of his! Really, enough was enough! She had heard way too many " 'tis"es and " 'twas"es and mispronunciations of common words.

And those swords of his and Torolf's that were parked in the Weller pottery umbrella stand in the front hall! *Do I need a daily reminder of the violence that is a part of society today? Did 9/11 teach me anything?*

Despite all that, she had let him kiss her. Worse, she had kissed him back.

What could I have been thinking?

I wasn't thinking. That's the problem.

Maybe it's a good thing to toss logic to the wind sometimes. To listen to my heart, instead of my brain.

Maybe I'm engaged in a little morning-after rationalization.

I don't even know the man.

I knew the Creep for two years before we got married; so that shoots that argument full of holes.

Why am I arguing with myself?

Angela ran her hands over the front of her cotton sleep shirt and stopped at her breasts. They felt full and achy, and the nipples were still tender from Magnus's fondling. Oh, the things he had done! Whether he was a farmer or a Viking or a movie actor, one thing was certain: the man was a supreme lover. He knew *things* about pleasing a woman. If he could bring her such pleasure fully clothed, imagine what he might do if they really made love.

Moving her hands lower, she put a palm over her lower belly, where an unfulfilled emptiness existed that hadn't been there twenty-four hours ago. Last night was not nearly enough, she realized.

So much for good intentions. So much for her and Magnus agreeing that there could be no repeat of that kind of sex play between them. The bottom line was, she wanted him—more today than she had last night . . . and that had been a lot. How could she have been so blind to what was happening?

With crystal clarity, she admitted to herself, *I am attracted to a man who claims to be a Viking, and a farmer. And he has eleven children.*

Criminy! Could her life get any worse than this?

La vida loca, *for sure . . .*

The house was empty by the time Angela had showered and dressed in her usual Blue Dragon attire—

jeans, athletic shoes, and a T-shirt . . . a stretchy one that read, *Wine Away!*

She heard soft singing coming from the kitchen. It was Juanita, and she was singing, of all things, "La Vida Loca." So the house wasn't totally empty after all.

The Blue Dragon kitchen was huge, with commercial appliances and a ten-foot oak pedestal table in the center to accommodate all the entertaining that had been done here at one time.

She did a double take as she entered the kitchen. Juanita—the short, elderly, plump cook—was doing a cha-cha from the stove to the sink and back again, all the time singing that old Ricky Martin song.

Juanita's audience was a laughing Lida, who was perched happily in a wooden high chair, which Grandma must have brought down from the attic. The baby was keeping time with Juanita's singing and dancing by banging a spoon on the wooden tray, where a dish of mashed bananas sat, half-eaten. The other half was on Lida's drool-covered chin.

"Goo," Lida said, noticing her arrival.

"Good morning, sweetheart." She leaned down to kiss Lida on the top of her head. Angela went immediately to the coffeepot and poured herself a cup. "Good morning to you, too, Juanita."

"Good morning," Juanita answered cheerily, and stopped cha-chaing . . . for the moment, anyway. "I will make you a big breakfast . . . just like when you were a little girl. Ho-kay?"

"Not too big," she protested.

"Okey-dokey!"

Okey-dokey? Jeesh!

"A little breakfast then," Juanita said, and managed

to whip up within minutes a Spanish omelette with whole-wheat toast, home fries, fresh sliced tomatoes, and orange juice. Angela ate every bit of it.

In between bites, some of which managed to get in Lida's mouth, too, Angela asked, "Where is everyone?"

"Well, Magnus was up at four—"

"Four! Are you kidding me?" The men whom Angela knew—especially the Hollywood types—slept till noon and partied or business-schmoozed all night.

"I am not kidding. He was up at four and was out weeding and hoeing your grandma's vegetable garden when me and Miguel got up at five. Jow was there with him. That man sure does know a lot about growing things. Didn't know what a tomato was, which is strange. Or a potato. Everyone knows tomatoes and potatoes. But he knew to pull the suckers off some plants, leave them on others. Which plants need transplanting to get more sun or shade. Which plants got too much fertilizer. That kind of thing. Have some more coffee, honey."

Angela held out her cup to be replenished, which prompted Lida to hold up her sippy cup to be refilled, too.

"Where is he now?"

"Everyone had breakfast at seven—not a puny little breakfast like you had, but sausages and bacon and scrambled eggs and corned-beef hash and blueberry waffles. And sides of oatmeal and Frosted Flakes. Lordy, Lordy, I used three loaves of my homemade bread. Guess I'll have to bake another batch this afternoon—a double batch." Juanita beamed, obviously in cook heaven over all these appreciative mouths at her table. "Anyhow, after they all ate, the older boy, Torolf, and the boy with the limp, Jogeir, went with their father and Miguel to work in the fields. Been gone 'bout two hours now."

"And the rest of them?"

"The two girls and one of the boys went to the mall with your grandma—the boy who was squinting at the food on his plate last night. Grandma thinks he needs glasses. The boy didn't even know what glasses were. Can you imagine that? Magnus gave your grandma a pile of money and told her to buy clothing for him and all his kids. Betcha it was three thousand dollars. Jeans, T-shirts, sneakers . . . that kind of stuff. And deodorant. He sure does have a thing about deodorant. Your grandma measured everyone first . . . even traced their feet on pieces of paper. I'm surprised you didn't hear all the giggling down here."

Angela blinked with astonishment at the rambling Juanita.

Juanita took a deep breath, then continued: "The rest of the kids are over by the pond, fishin' and playin' on that ol' swing. Guess I'll hafta be makin' lunch soon."

Angela couldn't remember seeing Juanita this happy. All because extra work had landed in her lap, and children filled the house. She suspected her grandmother was feeling the same way.

The problem was that they might be getting too accustomed to all this company. She would have to remind them both that Magnus and his children were just visitors. They would be leaving soon.

She would have to remind herself of that fact, too.

Lida smiled up at her and said, "Goo."

It was probably baby talk for "Who are you kidding?"

Juanita was back to shimmying across the kitchen floor while singing "La Vida Loca."

The crazy life, Angela translated mentally. *For sure!*

The Farmer and the dell . . . uh, vineyard . . .

The sun was shining brightly overhead when Angela walked the half mile or so to the south fields, where she hoped to find her missing Viking. It was a pleasant stroll through aisle after aisle of "little men with outstretched arms." That was how she'd always viewed the vines when she was a little girl, and the image had stayed with her.

There were two hundred acres on the Blue Dragon's gently rolling hills—a modest size by most vintners' standards—and a dozen different grapes were planted. When they had been making their own wine, the grapes would have gone into highly prized blends of chardonnays, cabernet sauvignons, sauvignon blancs, pinot noirs, and zinfandels. Now they were sold to another vintner.

The south field was where they grew their sangiovese grapes, an Italian import that could trace its roots all the way back to the Etruscans. Her grandfather had loved this particular grape, though it did not produce their most popular wine. He probably had an affection for it because it originated in his homeland. Or maybe because this grape carried a "fingerprint," which usually meant a hint of cherry or cranberry flavor in its various blends.

"Hi, everyone," she called out when she saw Magnus, Miguel, and the two boys.

Torolf and Jogeir were on their knees in the next aisle, along with several of the dozen full-time workers from the Blue Dragon. They were cluster-thinning the grapes with small curved knives to prevent over-cropping. This process would hasten the ripening process and would also prevent a weakening of the vines.

Magnus had been listening intently to something Miguel was explaining to him. His knees were bent so he could be at the manager's level and look through the magnifying glass Miguel was holding up to one of the vines. They were probably searching for any sign of mold or pests. Inspection of the vines was a daily task in any good vineyard.

Magnus looked up at her greeting and straightened to his full, impressive, treelike height. Then he smiled.

And, oh, what a smile it was! There was welcome in it. There was pure male self-confidence. There was innate sensuality. And, more than anything, there was an awareness of the intimacy they had shared the night before. It was a bone-melting, sexy smile, and it was directed right at her.

What woman wouldn't be flattered by that?

He did the most outrageous thing then. He walked up, leaned down, and kissed her lightly on the lips before saying softly, "Good morning to you, m'lady slugabed."

He kissed me! As if he has every right in the world to do so! I'd better be careful or he'll charm the pants off me . . . so to speak. Oh, God! "Uh . . ." *Well, that was brilliant.*

Magnus smiled some more, as if he knew what she was thinking.

He couldn't possibly.

Could he?

Behind him, Miguel was chuckling. On all sides the vineyard workers were grinning. To the right, Torolf commented to Jogeir, loudly enough for them to overhear, "Whoo-whoo! I guess Father's getting his knack back."

"What knack?" she asked Magnus.

"I have no idea," Magnus said, and shot Torolf a glare.

Before she had a chance to pursue the subject, Miguel diverted her attention.

"Magnus is a great student, Angela. He asks so many questions. Soon he will know more about the vines than I do," Miguel informed her, laughing jovially.

Jow raised his lazy head from where he lay nearby, watching the boys work. He had just come back from the hard rigors of chasing the other children at play by the pond and attempting to catch a fish himself.

She walked the aisles with Miguel and Magnus then, inspecting the vines. There were neuron probes to measure the amount of moisture in the plants, but nothing could take the place of hands-on examination.

"The Norselands, where I live, are not good for grapes," Magnus said conversationally, as they walked. "It is too cold in the winter and the summer is too short. Still, I have wild grapes that I allow to grow in the fruit trees."

"There are still some small vineyards in France that do it that way . . . the ancient way," Miguel said.

"Miguel and I have been talking about all the similarities between grape growing and simple farming," Magnus informed her, even as he laced the fingers of her hand with his. She was too stunned by his audacity to pull away. Heck, who was she kidding? She didn't want to pull away. It felt so good.

"Yet each man brings his own expertise and ways of doing things to the land. And each man is different. You have so many horseless machines and other marvels to lessen your work"—Magnus waved a hand to indicate the tractors and aerators beside the fields—"but in the end, 'tis the hand of man that makes all the difference. Without his hands, the land yields nothing."

She glanced down at Magnus's hands, the one that was free, and the one still holding hers. They were big. And blunt. And callused. Short-nailed. Dirty today from hard work—honest dirt, her grandfather would have said.

She thought they were beautiful.

Magnus gazed off into the distance, as if caught in some old memory . . . probably of his own farmlands in Norway.

Miguel leaned up to her ear then and whispered, just as he had the night before, "You picked good this time, little girl."

She wanted to tell him once again that he was mistaken.

But she didn't.

The calm before the storm . . .

Magnus had never felt more at peace in his entire life.

And he had never felt more troubled.

140

He was sitting at one end of the big kitchen table, and Grandma Rose was at the other end. Juanita and her husband, Miguel, sat on long benches across from each other near Grandma Rose. Angela sat on his right. All his children were in between, except for Lida, who was in a high chair at the corner between him and Angela.

They had just finished a meal comprised of rigortone-he covered with a red sauce and big meatballs, which was delicious; a salad made up of greens covered with oil and vinegar, which was not so delicious (who ever heard of eating grass and weeds?); warm bread, fresh from the oven, covered with garlic and butter; and two double-layer chocolate cakes, which he and his children had devoured to the last crumb.

He leaned back in his chair with contentment, gazing about him. Everyone appeared to be talking at once, but not in an unpleasant way.

Storvald was ecstatic over the glass eye adornment that Grandma Rose had bought for him, after an examination by some eye healer at the mall—a large indoor marketplace. The object, which fit over the nose and looped behind the ears, was called eyeglasses, and Storvald pronounced them a miracle. He claimed not to care how he looked in them. His close-up vision was much improved, and that was all that mattered.

Grandma Rose had also bought Storvald some paints. So now he could put color on his wood sculptures, as well. Dagny had gotten a water paint set, and she was already showing some talent using it. Kirsten had purchased a palette of face paints, which did not sit well with Magnus, who had asserted, "I am not raising a harlot here." But then Angela had explained that they were just pale lip glosses suitable for a young girl. At least Kirsten had not come home with a tattoo or a body ring.

"Did you know that children in this country go to school from the time they are six years old—and earlier—till they are eighteen years old? Even girls," Kirsten pointed out.

"Never!" Magnus exclaimed with disbelief. "What is there to learn for"—he did a quick mental calculation—"twelve years?"

"Reading, writing, history, math, science . . . and much more," Angela told him, a puzzled frown on her face. "Surely there are similar education requirements in Norway. Aren't there?"

"There are not," he declared scoffingly. "Unlike some men, I have no objection to women learning . . . even learning to read and write, but . . ." Magnus could see that not just Angela, but Grandma Rose, Juanita, and Miguel were staring at him incredulously.

"We'd better hope Carmen doesn't bop in for a visit," Juanita said with a chuckle.

"She'd whack him over the head with her NOW manual," Grandma Rose said, also with a chuckle.

Magnus continued, despite their obvious scorn for his opinion on the subject. "What is there to learn from a teacher for all those years that cannot be learned from doing? Like managing a household or a farm. Fighting wars. Building ships. Forging weapons. Tell me, for it seems a mighty waste of time."

"You've got to be kidding!" Angela said at his side, even as she attempted to mop up the tide of red sauce that Lida kept slathering on her face, the high chair, the floor, and everywhere about. "Have you ever been to college?"

"I think not. Is it near the Rus lands? Or the Orphrey Islands? Methinks I heard of a place there by that name."

Once again, she exclaimed, "You've got to be kidding!"

Before he had a chance to react to Angela's comment, Torolf brought up an equally perplexing notion. "Do you know what I learned today, *Faðir*? In this vast country, they have only one all-king, which they call a press-a-dent. And, although there are many military troops—arm-he, knave-he, mare-eens—they all serve only one chieftain, Mist-her Bush."

"Is this true?" Magnus asked Angela.

She nodded, gazing upon him as if he'd grown two heads.

"And the laws here! Whoo-ee!" Torolf continued. "People cannot purchase an ale or wine till they are twenty-one years old, even though they may drive on the highways at sixteen and serve in the military at eighteen."

"Who told you such nonsense, Torolf?"

"Juan Franklin. One of the vineyard workers. He is a student at You-See-Ell-Aye." His son was sipping at his third glass of iced tea as he spoke, a delicious beverage served in this country with many of the meals.

"They can die for their chieftain, but they cannot have a cold mead at the end of the day? I cannot fathom such illogic."

He turned to Angela, who was still gazing at him as if he'd grown two heads . . . actually, three heads now.

"By the way, Juan invited me to a concert next week in Ell-Aye. Can I go?"

Magnus was tired of always having to ask what certain words meant. Njal, who sat next to Torolf, saved him from the embarrassment by piping in, "What is a concert, lamebrain?" Apparently *lamebrain* was a new word he had learned . . . probably from that Bart Simpson character.

"A performance put on by musicians, *half-wit*," Torolf answered, giving his brother a friendly jab in the shoulder. "In this case, No Doubt."

"No doubt what?" Magnus asked.

"No Doubt is the name of the musicians," Dagny explained.

"I saw them on Em-Tee-Vee."

"Are they the ones who sing 'Don't Speak'?" It was Kirsten speaking now.

His children were watching entirely too much tell-a-vision.

"Let me see if I understand you, Torolf. You want to go hear some musicians called No Doubt who want to preach you a song message of 'Don't Speak'?"

"Exactly!" Torolf beamed at him.

Magnus threw his hands up in surrender. "You people are demented."

Lida threw her hands in the air, imitating him, which prompted everyone to laugh.

Best he be careful what he did around the little imp.

"One other thing," Torolf said to him.

Uh-oh!

"I would like to purchase a Hog."

"A hog? A hog? I can hardly credit what I am hearing. Must be I have a buildup of wax in my ears. Are you not the same fellow who would have naught to do with the hogs back on our farmstead?"

"Oh, *Faðir*, not that kind of hog. The Hog I refer to is also called a moat-or-sigh-call. It is a horseless vehicle, like a car, except it has only two wheels, and it goes at excessive speeds."

"Nay."

"Nay?"

"You heard me, boy. 'Twas bad enough when you talked me into that Saracen stallion last year and broke your leg. I will not countenance your 'galloping' off on a moat-or-sigh-call."

"I never get what I want."

Magnus raised his eyebrows in a manner that indicated the subject was closed, and if it was not, Torolf was going to lose some of what he had already gained, like No Doubt.

"If Torolf gets a moat-or-sigh-call, I want Rollerblades," Njal injected.

"I would be content with a bye-sigh-call," Hamr said.

"Can I have a pony?" It was Dagny speaking now.

"See what you started, Torolf? No one is getting anything, and that is that."

All of the children glared at Torolf, except for Lida, who drooled red spittle down her chin.

Grandma Rose must have decided to change the subject, for she asked him, "How do you like the purchases I made today, Magnus?"

He smiled at the old lady, who had been so kind to him and his family since their arrival. "Wonderful. Did I give you enough money?"

"Oh, yes, although we may have to make another trip in a few days."

"Can I go? Can I go?" all his children chimed in.

"Goo? Goo?" a red-faced Lida asked, too. She had a marvelous new stroll-her device, which would make such a trip possible, not that the little one knew that. She would be just as happy riding his shoulders.

He and all of his children were now wearing den-ham *braies*, which he had to admit felt comfortable. On top, their attire varied from tea-*sherts* to tanking-tops to soft fabric *sherts* that tucked inside the *braies*. Lida's garment was also den-ham but it was something called a coverall. Around her neck was a cloth mantle called a bib, which caught all the baby's slop and drool.

The most amazing thing to him was the fastening devices they used in this land. Zip-hers, they were called. He did not think he would ever be able to explain their workings to his sewing women back in the Norselands. Buttons, on the other hand, were such a simple concept that he wondered why people had not thought of them earlier or why news of them had not spread from this country to his.

And that was the problem.

This land—Ah-mare-ee-ca—was more than strange to him. In the back of his mind an uneasiness kept niggling at him. Something was wrong, and he could not figure out what it was.

It was not apprehension at discovering a new, possibly dangerous land. Vikings, and adventurers from other countries, had been discovering new lands since the beginning of time, though he did not think they had discovered lands so fully populated. He was willing to accept that he had come across an already settled country that no one knew about. Somehow his longship had gone so far off course as to enter territory never seen before.

But all the marvels that this land held . . . they did not just boggle the mind—they were unbelievable. Impossible, really.

Magnus had never been a fanciful man. He'd always disdained the old Norse legends of enchanted isles beyond Greenland and the unknown places north of the Rus lands, but if this Ah-mare-ee-ca did not count as an enchanted isle, he did not know what would.

That was the problem he had to puzzle out.

Was this journey a dream? Or was it real?

Was it permanent? Or would they suddenly awaken back on his longship off the shore of Vinland?

Why had he been called here by the elderly woman?

What exactly was his destiny?

And where did Angela fit into this madness?

Chapter Eight

Still calm, but picking up steam . . .

Angela swung back and forth slowly on the old swing near the pond, watching her guests with newfound admiration and progressing alarm.

She admired Magnus for the way he cared for his children. While loudly protesting what a bother they all were, he calmly kept them in line and taught them good life lessons. Right now he was lying on his back in the newly mown grass near the pond with a bare-footed Lida waddling around him. Lida was picking wildflowers, which she kept carrying back to him one at a time. Each of them he praised as if they were precious objects and she were the most talented girl in the world.

Lida had learned a new trick—kissing. Every time someone said the word *kiss*, she would cheerily place a slobbery smack on lips or cheek or whatever skin surface she could reach. Right now Magnus was saying *kiss* every couple of moments, which would cause Lida to halt in her busy tracks, turn around, waddle back, give a smiling kiss, then continue on her merry way.

To give Magnus credit, he *was* a good father. She admired the work ethic of his children. Dagny was inside helping Juanita clean up the kitchen. Afterward the cook had promised to show the young girl how to make homemade pizzas . . . "better than Domino's."

Kirsten was with Grandma, pruning and spraying her prize collection of one hundred species of rosebushes. Grandma—*God bless her soul!*—had sneaked off to have a cigarette in the potting shed, but Kirsten had found her there and urged her to show her the roses. Grandma might kick the habit yet . . . and all because of these children.

Torolf was having great fun mowing the lawns with a tractor, under Juan's tutelage. The wildflowers that were permitted to grow in the grass got cut off in the process, which was a shame, but they would soon grow back.

Njal and Hamr had been given the ignominious task of picking up Jow's poop in the lawn with small trowels and buckets before Torolf's mowing. Jow had helped them, running to each of the piles and barking loudly. The two rascals had been given that job as punishment because Magnus had caught them smoking one of Grandma's cigarettes that afternoon.

Now, the poop patrol completed, the two boys—along with Storvald and Jogeir—were playing in the shallow pond, doing more splashing than swimming.

She eased off the swing and went over to stand

beside Magnus. His hands were crossed behind his neck. His feet were bare and planted firmly in the grass, his knees raised. He wore a plain black T-shirt and blue jeans. His hair, which appeared dark blond today in the sun, was held back off his face with a rubber band.

"Do you like what you see?" Magnus asked, turning his head on his hands to look at her.

Oh, yeah! "I was just checking out your new duds. You've adapted to our attire already. Are you sure you haven't worn jeans and T-shirts before?" She forced herself to look at his face, and not his tight jeans. All those muscles and bulges. *Jeesh!*

He arched his eyebrows at her, not fooled by her diversionary tactics. "Are you staring at my big ears?"

Nope. It's that other big part that draws my attention, honey. "No, I'm not staring at your ears. For heaven's sake, why would I?"

"They are my one shortcoming," he confessed dolefully.

He was actually serious. *The fool!*

"From the time I was a youthling, my brothers teased me about my big ears. Do you mind overmuch?"

"Actually, I think they're rather endearing."

"Endearing ears? I like that," he said, and winked at her.

Good Lord, is my heart really pumping so fast just because of a wink? Well, not any wink. I must remember how much I dislike this brute. I must, must, must.

"Why do you have your hand over your heart?" he inquired in a too-silky voice.

He knew. The brute knew what effect he had on her.

Then she recalled something else he'd said. "Your big ears are your *only* shortcoming? My, my! You can't say that you suffer a humility problem, can you?"

"Are you making jest of me, m'lady?" he asked, and, quick as a wink, he grabbed her ankle and pulled her down beside him, hard on her rump, then flat on her back.

"Good work, Father," Hamr yelled from the pond.

"Go dunk your head, Hamr," his father yelled back.

"Jogeir gave me a wedgie in the pond," Njal complained.

"What is a wedgie?" Magnus wanted to know.

"I did not," Jogeir said, and shoved Njal underwater, which caused Njal to pull him under, too. They both came up laughing.

Shaking her head at all the unfamiliar commotion, Angela raised herself on her elbows. Lida noticed her just then and rushed up like a tiny Energizer bunny, gurgling, "Goo, goo, goo," and handed her a bunch of dandelions mixed with pink daisies, all smushed together.

"Oh, Lida, how pretty!" she cooed. "Can I give you a thank-you kiss?"

The precious darling leaned her cheek forward for the thank-you kiss, a trick Magnus had been teaching her today—probably to remind Angela of his own thank-you kiss the night before.

She gave him a quick sideways glance. *Uh-oh!* She saw the gleam in his eyes, the way his gaze lingered on her lips, then made a slow perusal of her body down to her breasts, then back to her lips again. *Yep, he's remembering the same thing I am.*

No way was she waiting for him to bring it up. "Darrell called a bit ago. He wants to know if you've had a chance to read the script he express-mailed to you today."

He shook his head, and his face flushed with some embarrassment. "I do not understand why he wants me to read this script thing. In truth, I am not proficient in reading your version of the English language. I have no trouble with Saxon English, but Ah-mare-ee-can English is vastly different. Oh, I can pick up words here and there, but it would take me a week to read those parchment pages he sent. I have better things to do, like learn grape growing."

Darrell was not going to be pleased by this. Would he blame her? Would Magnus's reluctance jeopardize Darrell's deal with her? She'd better try to smooth this wrinkle out . . . and soon.

"I could teach you to read English . . . *our* version of English." Really, though, wasn't the written English in Britain the same as in the United States . . . or nearly the same?

"Maybe . . . if I have time," he conceded.

"You don't have to work with Miguel, you know."

"Yea, I do."

"Why?"

"Because, if for some reason I am unable to return to the Norselands, I must adapt to this country . . . learn new skills."

What does he mean, "unable to return"? I wish he would stop playing games with me. "You could be a farmer here, too," she said, more testily than she had planned.

"I could, but I am developing a taste for"—he gave her a hot look, which spoke volumes—"grapes."

"Don't you dare jiggle your eyebrows at me."

He jiggled his eyebrows at her some more, supposedly to appear lascivious, but actually charming her with his parody of himself.

Time to change the subject. "You mentioned your brothers teasing you ... tell me about your family back in Norway."

He rolled over on his side, his head propped on one hand. "I have no family back in Norway ... not to speak of anyway. Just my daughter Madrene, who is married, and running my farmstead. And my son Ragnor, who is sixteen and taking my place at my father's estate in Vestfold. My parents died a few years back. My sister, Katla, is long wed and lives in Norsemandy. My brothers, Geirolf and Jorund"—his voice cracked—"they are missing ... presumed dead."

"You were close to your brothers, weren't you?"

He nodded.

"What happened?"

"Geirolf went off on a quest ... an important errand ... for my father. He never returned. Then Jorund went off in search of Geirolf, and he never returned either."

She understood suddenly. "That's why you and your children made this trip ... you're looking for your brothers?"

"That is part of the reason," he admitted, "though my instincts tell me it is hopeless. They have gone to the other world—that is my conclusion." He made his face a blank, as if he did not want to discuss it any more. "I would rather talk about you ... rather, us," he said. "What are we going to do about us?"

"Us?" she replied, suddenly breathless. "There is no us, Magnus."

Sandra Hill

"Ah, yea, there is, sweetling." He put a fingertip to the mole beside her mouth and caressed it as if it were something special.

Who knew a mole could be an erotic spot?

Then he traced her lips with several fingers.

I already knew lips were erotic spots. How could I not know, after last night?

"I want you very much, Angela."

Oh, my! Oh, my, my, my! That was certainly up-front and blunt enough. If my heart beats any faster, I'm going to blow a vein. "And your vow?" she managed to get out in a surprisingly calm voice.

"The vow," he repeated with a long sigh. "I keep trying to forget it."

This guy is so smooth. I'd better watch myself . . . or him. "Would you break it . . . for no reason other than you want to?"

"I could not do that. I am honor-bound, but . . ." He stared at her for a long moment with a look of intense longing in his eyes, and said, "Meet me tonight . . . in the garden house." He motioned toward the gazebo on the far side of the pond with its open trelliswork and climbing roses. It had been her playhouse as a young girl with Barbie dolls and dreams. But she was no young girl now; the Barbies were long tucked away, and she had no dreams anymore.

Did she?

She was spared an answer because Jogeir screamed just then, *"Lida!"*

All eyes turned to the little girl, who was about to waddle right into the pond.

Magnus was up like a shot and running across the grass, with Angela right after him. The four boys in the water were rushing toward the bank, hoping to catch

154

Lida. Jow was barking up a storm. All to no avail. She went under.

Magnus was the first to grab hold of her and yank her out of the water. After she'd sputtered and spit out water and swiped at her eyes with both hands, one of which still held a clump of wildflowers, Lida's little chin began to quiver. There was such a sad expression on the child's face that everyone began calling out her name and saying soothing things to her. Jow was still barking wildly.

Lida looked from one to the other, her chin still quivering.

Everyone waited with bated breath for the sure-to-come howl.

But what Lida did was burst into a goofy smile and reach out her arms to the water.

Lida said, "Goo, goo, goo," as her father dunked her tush in and out of the water, and her brothers demanded more kisses.

Angela was about to walk out of the shallow water at the end of the pond, satisfied that another crisis had been averted, when Magnus put a hand on her arm. *Tonight,* he mouthed.

She didn't answer.

She couldn't.

The logical part of her brain said, *No way!*

The other side of her brain—the one with a mind of its own—said, *Hmmmm.*

Let's make a deal. . . .

Angela approached the gazebo later that night. There was no hesitation in her step or her mind. She had made her decision, and it had been a surprisingly easy one. Especially since she'd downed two quick glasses of pinot noir to bolster her nerve.

The question was, would Magnus agree to her "terms"?

She entered the shadowy confines of the large, octagonal gazebo, where light from the full moon was filtered through the lattice walls. There was enough light for her to see that Magnus was already there, and—*Oh, good heavens!*—he was barefooted and bare-chested, wearing only a pair of gray sweatpants, low on his hips. The only thing showing was the edge of the waistband on his low-riding jockey briefs. She was pretty sure his belly button was exposed, but didn't dare look too closely for fear she would appear to be ogling. Water from a recent shower still dampened his hair and beaded on his shoulders. In fact, she could smell the Irish Spring soap and Old Spice deodorant from here.

In other words, he posed an extremely potent temptation.

As if she weren't already tempted.

"You came," Magnus said.

Not yet, she thought with a silent giggle, but didn't have the boldness to voice such an earthy sentiment aloud. *Sex and the City* gal, she was not. Instead she nodded, taking only one step inside before stopping. He was in the center . . . several yards away.

Opening his arms, he started to approach her.

She put up a halting hand. "Wait!"

He stopped and tilted his head in question.

"I want to make sure we understand each other before we do . . . uh, anything. Let's talk first."

"Talk?" His voice sounded raspy with disbelief. You'd think she had suggested they walk on hot coals as foreplay.

"Is that not just like a woman? They must talk every blessed thing to death. You want to talk? Now? Before we do . . . *anything?*"

"That's right." She put her hands on her hips to show she meant business.

He put his hands on his hips to show he meant business, too.

"First off, why did you invite me here?"

He said something so crude and blunt that she should have been offended. Instead her stomach dropped like a lead weight and settled between her legs. A hot, pulsing lead weight.

"That is not precisely accurate," he immediately corrected himself, watching her warily as she walked a slow circle around him, beyond the stretch of his arms, examining his body from every angle.

Boy, oh, boy, does he have angles!

"I invited you here because I want—nay, I need—to hold you, and kiss you, and touch you."

Who turned up the temperature? Why is it suddenly so hot out here? "And that's all?" she squeaked out. At the moment she was scrutinizing his backside in the form-hugging sweatpants. And a very nice backside it was, too. But—*jeesh*—the man really was like a tree. So tall and muscled and, well, just darn big.

"There will be no consummation, if that is what you mean by 'all.' A dry tup is the best I can offer you," he replied.

Is a dry tup what I think it is? "Because of the vow?"

157

"The vow," he agreed. "I apologize for that, but I promise I will give you pleasure nonetheless."

Oh, baby, you'd better. "Like last night."

"Oh, nay, m'lady. Much more than that."

More? Oh, geez! Am I in over my head, or what? Angela was afraid she was going to lose her cool; in fact, she was already very hot. But she had to make herself clear to this oversexed Viking—or whatever he was—before they started . . . *anything*. "Don't apologize for not being able to have intercourse. Actually, that fits in better with my plans."

"Your plans?" he said in a suffocated whisper.

Angela did not have a lot of sexual experience, aside from the Creep. And she would never describe herself as a sensual woman. But, good grief, she felt like a goddess, knowing she could reduce this big man to a suffocated whisper. It was a heady, heady feeling.

"Let's sit down," she suggested, pointing to the round wicker table in the center of the gazebo with its high-backed rattan chairs on four sides.

"Why?" He seemed disappointed at the suggestion.

Slow down, Magnus. It's going to be a long night. I hope. "Why not?" She slid into one of the chairs and tightened the belt of her full-length Chinese silk robe.

"Why not? I will tell you why not. You mentioned 'plans,' and I assume you meant plans that involve something other than sitting at a table and blathering on and on till the cows come home. Are you teasing me? If so, my brother Geirolf had a name for such women. Or is it that this is the manner of seduction in your country? My brother Jorund has an even more colorful name for women like that." He plopped down heavily into the chair next to hers—not opposite her, as she had expected—and glowered at her.

"You . . . you . . . you . . ." she sputtered, even in the midst of admiring him. She had to admit he looked just as good leaning back in the thronelike chair as he had standing up. It was all that bare chest and oozing masculinity, she supposed. He'd thrown too many outrageous accusations her way for her to reply immediately. That, and the bare chest and oozing masculinity. "I am not a tease," she declared finally. "And I wouldn't know how to seduce a man if my life depended on it. Furthermore, I'd like to give both your brothers a piece of my mind."

He smiled, and she realized that he'd deliberately provoked a reaction from her.

"I'm not liking your brothers very much."

"They are much better-looking than I am. And more charming."

I doubt that. "Fishing for compliments, are you, Magnus?"

He shrugged; then, reaching out an arm, he touched a forefinger to the mole at the side of her mouth. "I love your beauty mark. I saw such on a desert houri one time, but hers was not real. Can I kiss it?"

Yes, yes, yes! "No, you can't kiss it. At least, not yet . . . not till I discuss my . . . uh, terms." His fingertips were stroking the line of her jaw now. To say she was disconcerted would be like saying George Clooney was okay-looking—which would be a vast understatement, in her grandmother's book—and, frankly, hers, too. She swatted his hand away and, still seated, moved her chair several feet to the left.

He grinned and slid his chair closer to hers, not about to allow that much space between them.

"Terms, eh? I like the sound of that," he said in a deep, husky voice that implied he had his own idea of *terms*. Under the table, he stretched his leg over toward her leg and caressed her calf with his bare toes.

She felt the zing all the way to her fingertips, the hardened nipples of her breasts, and all the erotic places in between. The man had to have the sexiest toes in the world. He would probably be great at toe sex, if there was such a thing. *Maybe I should ask . . . later. Yeah, right. Only if I've had a few more glasses of pinot noir.* "Behave yourself," she said. "I need to say what I have to say."

"Then can I misbehave?"

She had to laugh at the man's persistence. And he was adorable. He really was. "If we agree on terms, yes. In fact, I'm counting on it."

He raised his hands in surrender and leaned back in his chair, waiting for her to explain.

"I must admit to admiring a man who would take a vow such as you have," she started out, "and stick to it."

"You admire celibacy vows?" He asked the question as if she were demented.

"No, I admire your honor in taking a stand on something. Not that I understand what this particular stand is all about, but that's not important. What is important is that, much as you might like to do differently, you made a promise, and you will adhere to it."

"Why is that so surprising?"

"Most men I've known—except for my grandfather—would break a vow in an instant . . . if it became inconvenient."

"I am feeling very inconvenienced at the moment."

"But you won't break your vow, will you?"

He tapped his chin with a forefinger, as if actually considering the possibility, then shook his head.

"My ex-husband is the perfect example."

"The Creep?" he inquired.

She nodded. "He lied. He cheated. He made promises, which he broke over and over."

"Pfff! Your husband was a *nithing*. Put him out of your mind."

"I have, but I've learned a lesson from him . . . and other men I've known as well. A committed relationship isn't in the cards for me. Oh, don't go looking all sad on my behalf. Not everyone needs to be married and have a dozen kids."

"Was that an insult directed at me?"

"No. It was an assessment of my own life, and the future I want for myself."

He frowned. "What has this to do with us . . . and tonight?"

"I just wanted you to know that what you consider less than appealing—unconsummated sex—is rather appealing to me." She felt her face heat up and thanked God that Magnus could not see.

"You are blushing," he accused.

Darn right I am. Any normal woman would be. "How can you tell?"

"Your body speaks to me. The tilt of your head. The shrug of your shoulders."

Oooh, I like that.

He added, "Are you saying that you do not enjoy the sex act . . . the complete sex act?"

"No, no, no. I'm not making myself clear. Let's face it, Magnus, you are a very attractive man, and—"

161

Sandra Hill

"Even with my big ears?"

The man has an ear fixation. Well, most women have a rear fixation, so I guess that's okay. "Tsk, tsk, tsk!" she said at his interrupting her. "What I was saying is that I can't hide the fact that I'm attracted to you. And making love—*really* making love—would no doubt be spectacular . . . but there is also an appeal in just making out. It reminds me of high school days, kissing and petting for hours. In those days a guy did everything in his power to turn a girl on in order to convince her to go to bed with him. The whole exercise was about her . . . and her pleasure."

"I do not understand all your words, like 'making out' and 'petting,' but if you are implying that your pleasure would not be foremost in my mind, whether the sex was consummated or unconsummated, then you have never made love with a Viking. And you have certainly never made love with *me*, m'lady, for if you had, you would not be impugning my lovemaking skills."

Arousal rippled over Angela's skin like erotic fantasy fingertips. "That's all well and good, Magnus, but are you willing to accept that this is all there will ever be? You and I can use each other's bodies . . . for a while?"

"Are you *drukkin?*"

"Just a little tipsy," she admitted. "I drank two glasses of wine for fortification. Should I have brought some for you?"

"Ha! I need no fortification. I am already a bit . . . what did you call it? . . . tipsy. *Drukkin* on you, that is what I am."

What a nice thing to say! I wonder if it's just smooth talk, or if he really means it. I think he means it.

He put a hand to his forehead to ease the furrows. "Seems to me that this is the kind of proposition most often made by a man. It is women who want marriage and commitment and lifetime promises."

"Not this woman."

He gazed at her as if trying to figure her out. "Methinks this is all about lust. Methinks you are as randy as a mare afore being mounted by her stallion."

A full-body flush swept over her at his words. "There may be a little truth to that, but that's not all of it."

"Ha! And do not dare be embarrassed. I am in the same condition. You could say I am randy as a springtime bull whose blood has been heating all winter long. And believe you me, it has been a long winter for me."

How could she respond to such an earthy comparison . . . both on his part and her own? Magnus was different from any man she'd ever met, and that was a good thing.

"Well, what's your answer?" she prodded.

"You have discussed your terms. Now I will discuss mine. Do not look surprised, sweetling. Didst think I was so lustsome for you that my brain was too muddled to understand all the implications of what you offer? Well, actually, I am that lustsome, but that is neither here nor there."

Uh-oh! Have I backed myself into a trap here? "Get to the point, Magnus."

He grinned at her impatience. "I would love to engage in this half-lovemaking with you, and I will, but you must accept some things, as well."

"Like?" she asked suspiciously.

"Like you are my destiny." He put up a hand to stem

her protests. "I have no idea why I am here in this country, but an inner voice keeps telling me that it is you who drew me. At the same time, I have no idea how long I will be here . . . mayhap a day, mayhap forever. So commitments are not within my promising power, anyway. And lastly, this buzzing in my ears . . . this breathlessness I feel . . . this speeding of my heart every time you are near . . . well, I have ne'er felt it afore with any other woman. It has to mean something, does it not?"

Angela wanted to disagree, but she was experiencing many of the same symptoms. And all for a man who was presumably uneducated . . . who had eleven children, for God's sake . . . who carried a sword like some modern-day gladiator (except he was lots better-looking than Russell Crowe)! She had never felt this instant chemistry with any other man. What could it be but destiny?

"Is it settled then?" he asked.

She nodded.

He stood and kicked aside his chair and the one next to it. Then he slid the table over.

She stood and kicked her chair aside, too. There was empty space now between herself and the most handsome hunk she'd ever met in her life. And she was going to make love with him . . . sort of. She had to smile at the prospect.

He cocked his head to the side in question. But a grin of anticipation crept over his lips. Magnus was obviously waiting for her cue in this strange love game they were about to play.

"Oh, I forgot," Angela said suddenly. "There is one last term I forgot to mention."

Magnus put his face in his hands. "Spare me, Odin. The woman is going to talk some more."

"Now, now," she teased. "I just wanted to say that you can't touch me unless I ask. You have to let me be in control."

"Cannot touch you? Cannot touch you?" His voice was harsh with outrage. "I refuse your terms."

Don't be so hasty, Magnus. Wait for the other shoe to drop. "I will do all the touching."

"You? You will touch me?" She could see his glower change to a twitch of a smile as the implications of her words sank in. "Well, I might reconsider. . . ."

"It will be better than the best sex you've ever had." *I cannot believe I just said that. Where is all this nerve coming from? I must be operating on hormone overload here.*

"Hmmm."

"I will even . . ." She said something then that was so provocative, Magnus's eyes widened, and she wondered if she even knew how. *Yep, Hormones "R" Us.*

"Agreed," he said before she had a chance to reconsider. "Unless you change your mind, of course, about wanting my touch. I ever was persuasive in the bedsport." He waggled his eyebrows at her.

Angela did the most brazen thing then—so brazen she surprised even herself. She untied the cloth belt of her silk robe and stepped out of it. She was totally naked . . . except for tiny red lace bikini panties.

Magnus gasped. She was pretty sure he was as surprised as she was.

"M'lady, if you are not my destiny, then the gods are playing a cruel jest on me."

"Does that mean you like what you see?" It was difficult for Angela to bare herself so blatantly. Not that she was humble about her attributes. Good genes and regular exercise were responsible for the not-so-bad appearance she knew she presented.

"Are you trying to torture me, m'lady?" he choked out.

"What do you mean?"

"You are naked, in case you hadn't noticed." He wagged a forefinger at her in playful chastisement. "I thought we were only going to engage in a little love-play. Naked equals *big*, to my mind. Naked in no way, in no country, in no culture equals a *little* anything. Naked portends something much more serious than 'a little loveplay.' Methinks you are trying to seduce me into breaking my vow."

"Uh-uh! No way! That's not what I meant, and I'm not totally naked, by the way."

He gave her a look, head to toe, that said she was splitting hairs.

"I just want to fool around . . . naked. Perhaps we will torture each other a little bit." Her defensive explanation sounded weak, even to her ears.

"Whatever," Magnus said with a slow smile. It was becoming one of his favorite words, she'd noticed.

"Does that mean that you don't object?"

"Object? If I were any more willing, certain body parts of mine could start a bonfire." He gave her a rueful look, then added, "But if you are going to torture me, it is only fair that I do the same." With a slow smile he shimmied out of his sweatpants and underwear, both at the same time, and Angela was faced with an astounding fact. Magnus resembled a tree in height; she'd known that from the first. Now she knew that he had some very impressive branches . . . one in particular.

She must have gasped, as Magnus had, because he winked at her . . . just before he pulled the jockey shorts back up. She knew why, too, and it was not just to mirror her attire. *Dry tupping.* That required some item of clothing separating them, didn't it? And actually, he looked just as good in his revealing briefs.

Destiny was pretty appealing right now.

Chapter Nine

Even Vikings get lucky sometimes. . . .

Magnus could not believe his eyes.

The woman he had been waiting for all his life—
without knowing it, of course—was standing before
him practically naked. And she wanted him. *Him . . .*
the most lack-witted Viking in all the Norse world. He
had to be lack-witted to have wasted all these years
with so many other women. Why had he not gone
searching for her? Why had he bred babe after babe
in meaningless encounters when he could have
shared a love child with her?

Although she was not the most comely woman Magnus had ever coupled with, she was beautiful. Though
tall for a woman, she barely reached his shoulder. But
then he was exceptionally tall, even for a Viking. He
had been with some women who could have kissed
his navel, they were so short . . . not that there hadn't

been an appeal in that activity at the time. But he knew now he'd been a fool to waste his time so.

Angela's hair formed a cloud of black silk about her heart-shaped face. Her lips were painted crimson red . . . to match the enticing undergarment, he supposed. He could not wait to kiss it off—the lip color, that is.

Her body was rounded in all the right places. Narrow waist, wider hips. Long, shapely legs. And her breasts . . . ah, her breasts were high and full and rose-tipped.

He wished he had met her many years ago.

"Why?" she asked.

He hadn't realized that he'd spoken aloud.

"Because I would not have made so many mistakes in women. Because I would not have had so many children with other women. Because I would have been worthy of you then."

"And because you wouldn't have taken the vow?"

The woman is too perceptive, by far. "That, too," he admitted with a laugh, and opened his arms for her. She had said she wanted to do the touching, but they had to start somewhere. Much more dithering and he was going to do something really disgraceful . . . like beg. And he knew—not from personal experience— that the sight of a Viking on his knees was not a sight to be relished . . . unless, of course, the man in question was doing something interesting sexually. That latter he did know from personal experience. Slightly. Only slightly. *Holy Thor! Why am I feeling guilty over things I did years ago? It is as if even when I did not know her, I was betraying her.*

Angela took one look at his open arms, crossed her own arms over her breasts in delayed modesty, and strolled right by him. *The impudent wench!* But he got an opportunity to gaze at her saucy behind in the skimpy red undergarment, so he didn't mind her by-passing him too much. She pointed to a long, low piece of furniture made of white cane, which was referred to in this country as a "chaise," and ordered him, "Lie down."

Be still, my heart . . . and other body parts. If m'lady thinks I am going to balk at her erotic orders, she had best think again. I am game for anything she might toss my way. Well, almost anything, as long as it does not involve breaking my vow . . . or perversions. Actually, it depends on the perversion. "Do I have to?" he griped in his best youthling whine.

"You agreed to the terms, honey."

Honey? I like that as an endearment . . . almost as much as sweetling. Mayhap I will use that term myself on occasion. With Angela only, of course. Not with any other woman.

"Lie down," she repeated.

Let the chase begin, he thought as he immediately obeyed. "What now, sweetling?" He was on his back, arms folded under his neck, ankles crossed, staring up at her. Even in this dim light—even with his jaw-keys—he could see his man part standing up like a tent pole. He could also see Angela trying her best not to notice his . . . uh, tent pole, which was an impossibility. 'Twould be like ignoring an elephant in a brass tub. 'Twas one of the best things about Vikings, his brother Geirolf always said—their *tent poles.* His brother Jorund claimed it was the Viking ability to maintain erections for an impressive period of time. Usually his brothers had imbibed a huge amount of mead when expounding these wisdoms. Personally he agreed with both philosophies.

"Move over," she said.

He didn't have to be told twice. Now he was on the far side of the chaise, on his left side, facing Angela, who carefully folded herself down beside him, lying on her back, the whole time holding one forearm over her breasts. *What a talented lady!* What she didn't know was that he could see her endowments anyway. *What a talented man!*

"You can kiss me," she said, "but that is all. There is no harm in that."

Ha! I will show her just how much "harm" I can do with no touching at all. Magnus leaned over and placed his lips against hers, but in the process he made sure that his chest brushed against her breasts, just a slight whisper of a caress, but enough for her to gasp against his mouth. He smiled even as he moved his lips over hers, shaping and testing. This lady was sorely misguided if she thought she could beat him in the game of bedsport. There were some arenas where he was confident of his expertise. This was one of them.

"I want to make love to you so badly," he confessed.

"Don't," she said on a soft groan.

He raised his head. "What? Speaking is forbidden, as well as touching? You cannot keep changing the terms, Angela."

"No, speaking is not forbidden, you fool."

Ha! I will show her just how much of a fool I am. He kissed Angela then. And kissed her. And kissed her. Long, endless kisses that alternated between gentle and demanding, soft and hard, wet and . . . well, wet. Mostly openmouthed. And sinfully expressive of his sexual need . . . and hers, as well. Angela was giving as good as she was getting. Mayhap their kissing bout did not go on for hours and hours, as she had described "making out" as a young girl, but it seemed like hours to him. And she was certainly panting prettily. So was he . . . though probably not as prettily.

While he was complying with her no-touching order, she was following a different rule. Her hands caressed his shoulders, his back, his buttocks through the thin cloth of his jaw-keys, both sides of his face as if holding him in place for her fervent kisses. He found her touch to be exceedingly arousing, and he would have relished returning the favors, but he did not because of his promise. He was a man who kept his vows.

But who was to say what amounted to touching? He decided that touching meant hands. Therefore he could caress her in other ways . . . with his mouth, or teeth, or tongue. Even with his legs. Yea, that would be his interpretation.

"Why are you smiling?" she asked.

Like a wolf in the sheep pen, I am. All that is missing is my howl, and that might just come soon. "You make me happy," he replied, which was not really a lie. He began his own assault in earnest then. Moving slowly, so as to give her a chance to protest his interpretation of the rules, he kissed his way along her jaw, down to the pulse point in her neck—and thank the gods it was jumping nicely!—on downward toward her breasts, the points of which were pressed enticingly against his own skin.

He traced the contours of her lovely breasts, first one, then the other, with his tongue. He nudged her from side to side with his cheeks. There was no waiting for permission when he took one of the engorged nipples into his mouth—all the way—and began to suckle rhythmically with the tip hitting against the roof of his mouth.

She let loose a long, high-pitched moan, and at the same time she arched her back upward and put her hands against his nape, encouraging more. He played her breasts then, employing every trick and talent he had developed over the years; in truth, he invented some new ones with Angela, whose breasts were beyond beautiful, and so very responsive. Like the kisses, his mouth-fondling of her breasts seemed to go on for hours. He wasn't sure either of them could stand much more. Angela was keening softly and writhing from side to side. His blood was racing beneath his skin at breakneck speed, and the erection inside his jaw-keys was nigh to bursting.

Without thinking, he rolled himself atop Angela and parted her thighs with his own legs, thus placing his rampant desire against her rampant desire. Even then, he did not touch her. Instead, he braced his arms on either side of her head and began to move against her, simulating the sex act. He could not control the woofing sounds he made as he attempted to control his out-of-control arousal. He would have been embarrassed, but Angela was counterpointing his woofs with little noises of her own: "Oh, oh, oh, oh . . ."

They reached their peaks at the same time, his with a triumphant roar, hers with an elongated, "Oooooh!"

It was the best "dry tupping" he had ever had. In fact, it was almost as good as intercourse itself. Almost. He and Angela were well matched for sexplay. Of that there was no doubt.

Magnus started to say, "Thank you," for the gift of pleasure she had given him, but instead, out of nowhere, other words entered his head, and he said, "I love you."

Angela was just as surprised as he was.

Who knew a Viking could rock her world . . . ?

Angela was stunned.

The man—almost a perfect stranger—had just said that he loved her. Well, not a perfect stranger, after what they'd just done. She had to say she knew him intimately now . . . sort of.

And Magnus appeared just as stunned as she by his unexpected admission.

"Angela," he murmured.

She was about to tell him that he didn't have to ply her with smooth talk. She'd already made it clear from the beginning that theirs would be a no-commitment relationship. She had no chance to say anything, though, because Magnus had other ideas.

"It is my turn now, sweetling." He was leaning over her once again, and the expression on his face could only be described as determined.

"Your turn?" She almost swallowed her tongue.

He nodded. "The no-touching rule is over. Now we play the game my way." Before she could blink, or raise another question, or a protest, if she was so inclined, Magnus placed a big hand on her tummy, then slid his fingers under the waistband of her panties, skimming her pubic hair, and delving right into her cleft.

"Wet," he pronounced with great satisfaction, and smiled at her.

"Well, of course I'm wet. What did you expect?" Mortified, she tried to squirm away from his probing fingers, but he would not allow that. "Oh, no . . . Magnus! . . . really, I don't think—"

"Shhhh!" he whispered against her ear. "Let me."

And she did.

Angela had no idea she had the expertise, or the nerve, or the moves. She had somehow turned into a sex goddess. Within moments—way-too-short, embarrassing moments—she climaxed again.

He raised a brow in amusement when she tried once again to squirm away and avoid his scrutiny.

"What can I say? I must be a slut."

He laughed. "Nay, I just have talented fingers."

"No one can accuse you of humility," she said. "It's more likely that I'm just pathetic."

"Perchance we are both pathetic . . . in our need for each other."

"Whatever," she said.

Magnus threw back his head and laughed. What an odd reaction to such a simple word.

But then she had no more time to think about simple things . . . like words. Magnus was aroused again. She knew by the way his new erection pressed against her thigh. And he could tell that she knew, as evidenced by his soft chuckle as he rolled over on his back and adjusted her astride him. The change in position was a feat in itself, since the chaise longue was not all that wide.

He had a self-satisfied expression on his face, which she couldn't let stand . . . although she hated to move away from the delicious sensations created by her crotch resting against his crotch. Still . . .

She slid her bottom down his thigh, tugged on the waistband of his shorts, and let his penis spring forth. His very huge, very hard penis. Her eyes probably bulged with amazement before she took him in both hands and moved.

"Holy Thor!" he said through gritted teeth. Then, "Holy, holy, holy Thor!"

Before she could move the circle of her hands up and down the smooth column more than two times, Magnus swore again, shoved her hands aside, pulled up his pants, and jerked her up to straddle him again.

"Ride," he ordered.

And she knew just what he wanted. But, golly, she would have thought that she would be the one in control when she'd ordered him not to touch her. Somehow she had quickly lost control. And now, when she'd reversed roles and taken him in hand, she was the one out of control again.

"I want you to be wanton, Angela," he pleaded hoarsely as he put his hands on her hips and showed her the movements he liked. "No inhibitions. Lose control . . . for me."

Is the man a mind reader, too?

But Angela soon lost the thread of that thought as her control melted like butter under a hot knife, and that hot knife was stabbing at her most erotic places with a delicious rhythm. She imagined that her eyes were rolling in their sockets like a pinball machine. When they came this time, powerful shudders shook them both and she lay collapsed across him like a rag doll.

It was more than sex, more than a physical act. In a way she could not explain, she felt as if some electrical current had zigzagged back and forth between them, burning and bonding them. Aftershocks shook them both.

And they hadn't even had intercourse.

Amazing!

Finally she raised herself up on her arms and stared down at him. He was as solemn and incredulous as she was.

"What just happened here?" she asked.

He thought for a moment and then replied, "Destiny."

The morning after . . . sort of . . .

First thing the following morning, Angela was having second thoughts.

Who was that person who bared her body like a horny harlot?

What could I have been thinking?

When did I start engaging in stranger sex? Stranger in more ways than one . . .

Where can this relationship possibly go but nowhere?

Why has this one man become so important to me?

So what did Angela do about her misgivings?

She had almost-sex with Magnus midmorning against a tree in the empty west vineyard. She would never smell chardonnay grapes again without certain memories.

Then she repeated the almost-sex that afternoon on a picnic table in the orange grove.

That night, not to be outdone, she slipped into Magnus's third-floor shower with him—wearing panties, of course—after all the kids were asleep. Her knees could barely hold her upright by the time she crawled into her own bed.

She was going to lay down the law . . . tomorrow.

Tomorrow, tomorrow . . . tomorrow is another . . . yeah, right, Annie!

Magnus was having second thoughts. Not just about the constant loveplay of the last twenty-four hours. But about his own feelings.

He had told the witch that he loved her. *By thunder!* Magnus racked his brain and could not recall ever having told a woman *that* before. Had she put a spell on him?

As to all the "fooling around," as Angela called it, he had to ask himself certain questions.

Who is she?

What am I doing, tempting myself so dangerously?

When will this sexual yearning end?

Where will I be tomorrow, or next week, in this strange journey I am on?

Why can I not keep my hands off the woman?

Enough was enough! Well, not nearly enough . . . but enough lest he go insane from an overabundance of nonsex . . . which came close to nonsense, to his mind. Nonsex, Nonsense, same thing. So he was off to set some ground rules with Angela about this nonsense. No more "making it." Or was it "making out"? *Whatever!*

But he got waylaid in the kitchen, where Juanita—the goddess of cooking—was whipping up batter for blueberry waffles, his favorite morning feast in this land . . . next to scrambled eggs, Froot Loops, fried ham, strawberry jam, fresh orange juice, and toasted, butter-dripping muffins, that is. If he was not careful, he would soon lose his fine physique. And wouldn't that be an outrage—a fat Viking?

Until the meal was ready, he decided to crawl under the table and play hide-and-find with Lida. Hamr, Kolbein and Njal were under there with Magnus, pretending to be quacking ducks. It was amazing the way the reticent Kolbein had lost his shyness now that they were at the Blue Dragon. The boyling no longer felt the need to be attached to his father like a bothersome burr. Kirsten and Dagny were doing an outrageous Britain Spear–type dance around the kitchen to some raucous music on the raid-he-oh, trying further to distract Lida. Jow was barking wildly, making sure he was part of the activity. Torolf and Jogeir had aprons on and were helping Juanita serve up the food. Grandma Rose was no doubt off in the downstairs bathing room smoking one of her toe-back-hoe sticks in her usual surreptitious manner, as if she were fooling anyone.

That was when Angela walked into the room. Her eyes practically bugged out at the scene they all presented; then she burst out laughing. But he'd also seen the gleam in her eyes as she'd watched him playing with his children. Angela liked him. She really liked him.

Therefore, Magnus did as any thinking man would do. Or was that nonthinking man? *Whatever!* He took Angela's hand and discreetly led her off with him to the nearby pantry, where he locked the door behind them. Then, hoping they'd be momentarily forgotten in all the chatter and activity of a huge breakfast, he and Angela engaged in some more nonsex. And that was *before* he had eaten any blueberry waffles . . . which was saying a lot.

His resolution to end this nonsense was further thwarted that afternoon when Angela came out to the machine shed, where Miguel was teaching him how to check over the motor of a clanking tractor. She was wearing a white tanking-top over den-ham *braies* that were cut off practically at her woman parts, and skimpy leather sandals on her bare feet. He wasn't sure which made him randier, the nipples visible through her tanking-top or the pink toenails peeking out of the sandals. Not that it took much to make him randy these days. Randy could become his second name. Magnus the Randy. *Aaarrgh!* Naturally he and Angela ended up having more nonsex on the seat of the vibrating, still-running tractor when Miguel went off to buy a new car-burr-ate-whore.

That night, he was determined to end this nonsense before he did something really foolish, like break his vow. In fact, it would be more than foolish. It would be dishonorable. That, he would not—could not—do.

His downfall, this time, was a guard-her belt . . . the most scandalous, tempting garment ever invented by man . . . or woman. *Whooee!* The things a man could do to a woman in a black lace guard-her belt with sheer black hose and high-heeled shoes. By midnight, when Angela had left his third-floor bedchamber, the bed linens were in a shambles, his knees were scraped raw, his lips were swollen, his legs were shaky, his cock ached from lack of a female sheath, and his muscles were tense and trembly. In essence, he felt wonderful. No wonder he forgot what it was he had been going to tell Angela.

All shook up . . .

Magnus was shaken the next afternoon, upon returning from his vineyard work, to learn that Angela had gone back to the city where work presumably beckoned her.

Apparently Dare-all had called and canceled his visit for the next day, postponing it till the following Monday. That gave her some free time to go back to work in her office and earn more money, or so Grandma Rose explained. He could have given her any money she needed, he had started to say, but halted himself, knowing Angela was a prideful woman and probably wouldn't accept what she would consider charity from him. If their positions were reversed, he would feel the same way.

It was all for the best, he supposed. They needed some time apart . . . a resting period during which each could evaluate this irresistible force that drew them into a fiery sexual maelstrom every time they were within kissing distance of each other.

But then Miguel took him up to the old winery, which had been closed down the past few years. That was when Magnus's world came apart with a crash.

Miguel, with tears in his eyes, held up a bottle of wine from the last vintage, six years past, and pointed out the label to Magnus. It read, *Blue Dragon Vineyard, Sonoma, California, 1997.*

Magnus was thickheaded at times, 'twas true. So it took several moments for the fact to sink in that the

181

wine label read 1997—supposedly six years past—
which would mean that this was 2003. In other words,
if he was to believe what he was seeing, an entire mil-
lenium had passed since he'd left the Norselands.

"Miguel, what year is this?" he asked, just to make
sure.

"Two thousand and three," Miguel said, casting him
an odd, questioning look.

"Are . . . are you sure?"

Miguel nodded. "Magnus, are you all right?"

"Nay, I am not all right," he murmured as he stag-
gered out of the winery and off toward the house.

How was it possible? A thousand years! Impossible!
But so many perplexing things about this land began
to make sense to him now. Like the turning pages of
a book, he saw the modern inventions that he had
tried to explain away as just the innovations of a different land and culture, the peculiar manner of speaking English, the intuitive sense he had had all along
that there was some puzzle to be figured out. All these
things, and more, convinced him that the answers had
been there all along, and he had not recognized them.

But if he accepted that he was living a thousand
years in the future, then he would have to accept that
he and his children had traveled through time. Para-
doxical. Wasn't it?

Torolf caught up with him at the pond, where he
was sitting on the grass, staring off into space. Miguel
must have sent for Torolf, concerned about Magnus's
behavior over a mere wine bottle he had shown him.

"*Faðir?*" Torolf asked, sinking down to the ground
beside him and placing a hand on his back. "What is
it?"

Join the Historical Romance Book Club and GET 4 FREE* BOOKS NOW!

A $23.96 Value!

Yes! I want to subscribe to the Historical Romance Book Club.

Please send me my **4 FREE* BOOKS.** I have enclosed $2.00 for shipping/handling. Each month I'll receive the four newest Historical Romance selections to preview for 10 days. If I decide to keep them, I will pay the Special Members Only discounted price of just $4.24 each, a total of $16.96, plus $2.00 shipping/handling ($23.55 US in Canada). This is a **SAVINGS OF AT LEAST $5.00** off the bookstore price. There is no minimum number of books I must buy, and I may cancel the program at any time. In any case, the **4 FREE* BOOKS** are mine to keep.

*In Canada, add $5.00 shipping/handling per order for the first shipment. For all future shipments to Canada, the cost of membership is $23.55 US, which includes shipping and handling. (All payments must be made in US dollars.)

NAME: _____

ADDRESS: _____

CITY: _____ STATE: _____

COUNTRY: _____ ZIP: _____

TELEPHONE: _____

E-MAIL: _____

SIGNATURE: _____

If under 18, Parent or Guardian must sign. Terms, prices, and conditions subject to change. Subscription subject to acceptance. Dorchester Publishing reserves the right to reject any order or cancel any subscription.

The Best in Historical Romance!
Get Four Books Totally FREE*!

A
$23.96
Value!
FREE!

**PLEASE RUSH
MY FOUR FREE
BOOKS TO ME
RIGHT AWAY!**

Enclose this card with $2.00
in an envelope and send to:

Historical Romance Book Club
20 Academy Street
Norwalk, CT 06850-4032

"We are time travelers," Magnus informed him bluntly.

"What?" Torolf squawked at him.

Ha! He would have squawked at anyone who'd suggested such to him, too, if he wasn't seeing evidence of that fact all around him.

"I have just learned that this is the year two thousand and three. We must have traveled somehow into the future a century and more from our own time of one thousand."

"I cannot credit that notion," Torolf said, shaking his head from side to side. "Oh, I know that the old sagas speak of such, but I always thought they were mere folklore."

"Me, too," Magnus agreed. "Me, too."

"Why? Why would such a thing happen to us?"

Magnus shrugged. "Methinks it is our destiny. All along I assumed that Grandma Rose and her prayer beads cajoled the gods into bringing us to a strange country. Little did I know that her prayer beads could bring us across time."

"But what will we do now that we know?"

"We must bide our time and see what happens. What will be will be," Magnus said philosophically.

"Now that I think on it," Torolf mused, "something Juan told me about one of the greatest inventions of all time begins to make sense. Of course, I did not believe him at the time, but if we have indeed time traveled, mayhap it really is possible."

"What great invention?" Magnus asked with little interest. What did he care about another modern marvel when his world had been turned upside down?

"Birth control."

"Birthing control?" Magnus asked, his interest piqued in spite of himself.

Torolf nodded vigorously. "Not only do they have pills that women can take to prevent conception, but men can wear extremely thin sheaths over their man parts called cone-domes, or men can even have a cutting operation performed that prevents them from impregnating a woman. And none of these interfere with the man's or woman's pleasure."

Magnus literally gaped at his son. "Can this be true?"

"I see no reason why Juan would lie to me."

"As a jest?" Magnus suggested.

Torolf thought a moment, then shook his head. "Nay. At the time, Juan was telling me about his girlfriend, Anna. They are both call-ledge students with three more years to go till graduation. They practice this birth control so they will not have children afore they are able to marry."

The implications of all that Torolf had told him suddenly began to sink in. "She knew! She knew, and she did not tell me!" he exclaimed, standing suddenly in outrage.

"Who knew? And what?"

"Never mind!" he said. But what he thought was, *Someone is going to pay for this withholding of information. Someone is going to pay for torturing me needlessly. Someone is going to find out just what it means to be my destiny.*

Then he recalled his vow. Even if he had known about this modern birthing control, there was still his vow to be reckoned with.

"Where are you going?" Torolf called after him as he began to walk away, not toward the house, but in the direction of the road leading away from the house.

He turned around and informed his son, even as he was backing away, "I must needs find an expert on vows."

"With all due respect, Father, have you lost your senses?"

"Probably."

Chapter Ten

Give me a vowel . . . I mean vow . . .

Grandma Rose was sitting on the side porch off the kitchen peeling apples when he walked up the steps. Juanita was sitting across the table from her snapping string beans. The apples made his mouth water, because he knew they would probably go into a pie or some such sweet delicacy to end the dinner meal. The string beans on the other hand, he could do without. Although he was a farmer, and should appreciate fresh produce, he still contended that they served far too many vegetables in this land. Even worse were the greens that they put in salads; no matter how they tried to hide them under various sauces and dressings, they were still weeds.

Torolf scurried up the steps to stand beside him. His son was sticking to him like a thorn in a bear's behind, not to be helpful—oh, nay, not that—but to see what kind of mess his lack-witted father would end in next. Magnus couldn't wait to see himself. Still, he told Torolf, "Best you wipe that smirk from your face, son. I am still bigger than you are."

"Not by much," the impudent lad countered, and continued to smirk at him.

Magnus shook his head at Torolf's silliness and turned his attention to the ladies on the porch. "M'lady Rose, I come to you seeking advice."

"Yes?" she said, always eager to help.

"I must needs speak to a man about some vows," he started out, "and I was wondering if—"

"Vows!" Grandma Rose exclaimed, exchanging a quick glance of happiness with Juanita. They both beamed as if he'd offered them a plate of gold.

"Yea, vows. There is an important matter regarding vows that I must discuss with . . . well, the appropriate person."

"A priest?" Grandma Rose and Juanita suggested at the same time.

"A God man? Hmmm. That might work. Since vows are usually made in the name of the gods, or a specific god, like your Christian One-God, I assume that a representative of that god would be the man I need. Where might I find such a person?"

"There's one in the village. Father Sylvester at Saint Agnes Church."

"Ah, I recall passing it on our way here."

"Have you discussed this . . . uh, vow business . . . with Angela?" Grandma Rose inquired.

"Not yet, but you can be sure that I will."

Grandma Rose practically swooned at his words. She must need a toe-back-hoe stick, she was acting so strangely. "See, Juanita, I told you my novena would work."

"I did not tell you, Rose, but I have been saying novenas, too," Juanita admitted.

"Do you think it would be too soon to plan a ceremony for September, right after the harvest?" Grandma Rose was tapping a forefinger against her closed lips, as if deep in thought.

"That would be perfect, but all the planning! Ay-yi-yi!"

"Would that be enough time?" Grandma Rose asked him.

"Huh?" He had no idea what these two were talking about. All he was concerned about was his celibacy vow. But what he said was, "Sure." That was a shortened way that people in this country denoted, "For a certainty." He liked that word almost as much as *whatever!* He stood, not about to waste any more time prattling about unimportant matters when he had to see a priest about a vow—a vow that could affect the rest of his life. "Well, I am off to see the priest, then." He began to walk away. Grandma Rose and Juanita barely noticed, so busy were they with planning some ceremony . . . to celebrate the harvest, he presumed.

"That church is at least five miles away," Torolf reminded him. Apparently the thorn was still sticking to his backside.

"Go away."

"You are going to walk that far?"

"I am."

"Why?"

"If you were not such a half-brain, you would know. Because a priest is God's representative on earth. I need to speak with someone in authority about vows."

"And the breaking of them?" Torolf asked with a laugh.

"That, especially," Magnus conceded. "If I have traveled through time, hard as that is to believe, and endured all the rigors and hardships of such a mind-boggling journey with nine bothersome children, including one especially bothersome, insolent sixteen-year-old, I must deserve some compensation."

Torolf was still laughing as his father stomped off.

Goin' to the chapel . . . uh, rectory . . .

"Are you the God-man?"

The man sitting on a stone bench in the backyard of Saint Agnes's rectory reading a Bible practically jumped out of his monk garb at Magnus's simple question. "Ga . . . ga . . . ga . . ." he sputtered, looking up the long length of Magnus's frame to his impatient face. He did not appear frightened by his size, just stunned. "God man?" he finally got out.

"Yea, I am looking for the priest named Father Sylvester . . . the God-man."

"Oh. That would be me. Ha, ha, ha! What can I do for you, son?"

"I need advice on vows."

"Sit down, please. I'm getting a crick in my neck." The priest motioned for Magnus to sit on another stone bench facing him. "Now, tell me, what kind of vows do you have in mind? Baptismal vows? Wedding vows?"

"Holy Thor, nay! A celibacy vow."

"Aaahhh," the priest said. "You are considering taking religious orders and are not sure if you can handle the celibacy vows. Well, I can only tell you of my own experience and that of my fellow priests."

"Huh?"

"As a first step, I would suggest making an appointment with the bishop of our diocese. After an initial interview, he may or may not recommend a seminary for you. I personally like—"

"Halt, halt, halt, halt, halt!" Magnus held both palms out in front of him to stem the priest's words. "I am not interested in entering the priesthood. For the love of Frigg, I have bred thirteen children of my loins. 'Tis a little late to consider such a path in life."

"Thirteen children! Well, well, well! You certainly take the church's ban on birth control seriously, don't you?" The priest laughed jovially. *Bloody hell, even priests know about birth control. Am I the only person in the world who did not?* Then the priest added, with another laugh, "Thirteen children and you now want to take a celibacy vow? Isn't that like closing the barn door after the horse has fled?"

"Sarcasm ill suits your priestly role," Magnus snapped. "Let me explain myself better. I made a celibacy vow after having all these children because I did not want to have any more. At that time and place, 'twas a wise decision. I had no knowledge that there was any other method of birth control besides abstinence."

"Where have you been living, boy? Another century?"

"You could say that." Magnus explained further, though not bothering to tell of his time-travel theory.

190

He was having trouble believing it himself. What might a stranger think?

The priest nodded his understanding of the situation thus far. "Go on, my son."

"My question is, Can a vow be broken when the circumstances surrounding the vow have changed?"

"Surely you do not expect me, a priest, to say that it is proper to practice birth control. You know the Vatican's rule on that, don't you?"

Actually, Magnus did not, but that was neither here nor there. "I do not come to you soliciting your sanction of birthing control. I merely want to know how the gods—your God in particular—feel about vows. Are they ironclad?"

The priest pondered for several moments, then said, "I will tell you the same thing I tell my parishioners on many subjects: God can be stern, but more than anything, he is a loving father. He wants what is best for us. He wants us to be happy, within his rules. And if the best thing for us requires flexibility, bending the rules on occasion, I cannot believe that God would be offended. Mostly our actions should not hurt others. So, in my humble opinion, when you must question whether some decision is right or wrong, ask yourself if anyone will be hurt."

"In other words," Magnus interpreted, "this is a decision between me and God."

"Precisely."

Magnus stood up, feeling as if a huge weight had been lifted from his shoulders.

"One other thing, my son . . ."

"Yea."

"If my instincts are correct, and you are headed in

the direction I think you are, I would suggest your taking vows of a different sort."

"And those would be?" Magnus smiled broadly. He was in a cheery mood now that the priest had given him a dispensation of sorts from his vow.

"Wedding vows."

Magnus's smile disappeared.

Oh, Lord, spare me from the fury of a Norseman. . . .

It was nine o'clock on the second night since Angela had left the Blue Dragon. Only a day and a half, but she missed everyone miserably—not just her grandmother, as usual, but all nine of the "Viking" children, each in his or her own way, and most especially Magnus, the most endearing of all to her. The only way she'd been able to handle her loneliness was to bury herself in work. As a result, she'd just returned from the office with a briefcase loaded with "homework."

That was when she heard a loud banging on her door.

Looking through the peephole, she saw nothing but the chest of a very tall man. *Uh-oh!* She knew only one person who was that tall. *Magnus.*

How did he get here?

How did he manage to get past her doorman?

Had something happened back at the Blue Dragon . . . something so bad it required personal delivery of the news? *Oh, God! Oh, God! Please don't let it be Grandma . . . or one of the kids.*

Quickly she opened the door. It was open only a crack when Magnus shoved it wide. With barely a glance in her direction, he stormed past her and into the living room, leaving her to close the door. Was it ominous that he was back to wearing his Viking attire—wide-belted tunic and cross-gartered ankle boots? The only thing missing was his sword.

"Magnus! Is something wrong at the Blue Dragon? Is someone hurt?" Angela followed him into the living room, where he was pacing like a caged animal. He'd placed an old overnight bag of her grandfather's on the floor. He slammed the leather fanny pack that Grandma had bought him several days ago onto the coffee table. It looked as if he was planning an extended stay. "How did you get here?"

"I paid a friend of Juan's to drive me here. In his Jeep. My ears are still ringing from the heavy iron music on his raid-he-oh." He cast her such a look of hostility that she reeled. "Nothing is wrong at the Blue Dragon, and no one is hurt . . . except me."

"You? You're hurt? Have you been to a doctor?"

He waved away her concern. "Not that kind of hurt."

Reaching for his fanny pack, he unzipped it and asked her in a cool voice, "Have you ever heard of birthing control, Angela?" Before she had a chance to answer, he held up a very long strip of foil packets. Condoms. At least two dozen of them.

She tilted her head to the side in question. "Of course I've heard of birth control. Who hasn't?"

"I have not."

"Oh, come on, Magnus. Everybody over the age of puberty, and even those younger, have heard about birth control—pills, IUDs, injections, the works."

"I have not," he repeated. If looks could kill, the one directed at her then would have done just that.

"Magnus, I don't understand any of this. Why are

193

you so angry? Why are you pretending to be unaware of stuff that is common knowledge *everywhere* in the world?"

Instead of answering her question, he asked, "Do you take pills that prevent conception?"

She nodded. Even though she hadn't been sexually active for a long time, it was a habit she had never dropped.

He appeared to breathe a sigh of relief, despite his continuing fury. "I cannot believe that you have tortured me these past few days with all that half-sex nonsense when we could have had whole sex anytime."

"I thought you liked the way we fooled around," she said, more than a little bit hurt at his criticism. "You said you were satisfied with almost-sex."

"I lied. Or else I was muddle-brained with frustration." He arched an eyebrow at her sardonically. "I like half-sex. I *love* whole sex."

"But what difference does it make? You took a celibacy vow. That was why we couldn't have sex."

"Are you really that lack-witted, lady? I took the vow because I did not want to have more children."

"Why didn't you just practice birth control?"

"Aaarrgh!" he said, pulling at his own hair, which was tied back into a queue. "How could I practice what I did not know existed?"

"You're really confusing me, Magnus." *And, frankly, scaring me a bit, too.*

"Do men use these cone-domes"—he shook the foil strip in her face—"at the same time their women take birthing-control pills?"

"Not necessarily . . . usually only when they are with

194

new partners and they fear the transmission of some disease."

"I have no disease. I tell you that now . . . just in case you might be interested."

Angela was totally baffled. "Magnus, there have been so many things this past week that have surprised you and your children. Normal, everyday things. And now birth control, which has been around for a very long time all over the universe. How is it possible that you don't know all this stuff?"

"That I will explain to you later. It is an unbelievable story, one I just learned about yestermorn, but I have a more important task to take care of now." He undid his belt and sat down on the couch to remove his boots. Then he stood and drew his thigh-length tunic over his head. All that was left was his jockey shorts.

Be still, my heart. If Magnus decides not to take an acting job, he can always model underwear. He'd do Michael Jordan out of a job any day. "Wh-what important task?"

"Tupping." He was already moving toward her on the other side of the room, and there was a determined glint in his eyes.

Tupping. I know what that crude, archaic word means. I also know what its vulgar modern counterpart is. Should I be offended? Nah. Maybe later. "But what about your vow?"

For the first time since he'd arrived, Magnus smiled, but it was a feral smile, and she was the target. Without thinking, Angela backed up a bit.

"I got a dispensation . . . sort of."

"From whom?" she asked in a strangled whisper. Magnus had backed her up against the wall and was beginning to unbutton her blouse. The enticing fragrance of Old Spice deodorant enveloped her, along with Magnus's very own male scent.

"The God-man at Saint Agnes," he murmured against her ear, even as he pulled her blouse out of her skirt and off her shoulders, and tossed it aside.

"Father Sylvester?"

"The very one." How he got the words out, Angela had no idea because his eyes were riveted on her breasts, which were encased in a flesh-colored lace bra. As he removed the bra it was obvious he had nonpriestly ideas dancing in his head.

"And he told you that you don't have to obey your celibacy vow anymore?"

"Not precisely."

Magnus shimmied her skirt down her thighs, leaving her in nothing but her panty hose and black pumps. Then he flicked the nipples of both breasts with his thumbs, sort of as an afterthought.

Oh . . . oh . . . some afterthought! She tried to keep her eyes from rolling back in her head and asked in as calm a voice as she could, "What, precisely?"

Magnus straightened and looked down at her, a small smile of satisfaction on his face. "The priest said it was a decision that I had to make with God." He inserted the fingers of both hands in the waistband of his underwear and dropped them nimbly to the floor.

Oh, geez! Oh, boy! Wow!

Magnus was sporting nothing but his two silver armrings, as usual, and an erection that was anything but usual.

He grinned and did the same with her panty hose.

The look on his face as he gazed at her was the highest form of compliment.

"And what did you and God decide?"

"Of course, I did not talk to God," he chided her with a playful flick of his fingertips to her chin. "But I did hear a voice in my head . . . sort of."

She had to smile at that. "And did the voice say, 'Go for it'?"

"In so many words." He returned her smile. "Or mayhap it was wishful thinking on my part. Whatever."

She let her eyes roam downward again, unable to stop looking at the immense erection pressing against her belly.

Noticing the direction of her stare, he ducked his head sheepishly. "Do not expect such a spectacular show all the time, dearling. This one has been building for quite a while."

Oh, good heavens! Is he really calmly discussing the size of his penis with me? But while he is on the subject . . . "Listen, Magnus, I'm sorry to be a spoilsport here, but it's been a long time for me, and I don't think I can take all—"

Before the words were out of her mouth, Magnus had lifted her off the floor by the waist, parted her dangling legs with his own, and entered her wetness with a surprising surge. To the hilt. *I . . . do . . . not . . . believe . . . this.* Apparently she could hold his impressive length and width, after all. Angela felt incredibly full, almost to the point of pain, but her inner muscles shifted and soon accommodated his size.

Meanwhile, Magnus had his head thrown back, and veins were sticking out on his neck. His eyes were closed and his teeth bared and gritted. Down below, he was imbedded in her, but unmoving.

Angela felt like a rag doll, pinned to the wall, bare shoulders to bare buttocks—not by a stickpin, but a spear . . . a most erotic, welcome spear.

Magnus opened his glazed eyes finally and blinked at her. Then he did the most outrageous thing. He pulled out of her, sank to the floor, and put his face on his arms, which were folded over his bent knees. She'd landed on her feet, but continued to lean back against the wall.

Oh, my God! He's changed his mind. He doesn't want me after all. Is it my body? Now that he's really seen me naked, I'm probably not that desirable to him. "Magnus? What's wrong?" She barely got the words out, so empty and bereft and, yes, still very aroused did she feel.

Without looking up at her, he said, "I came here in anger. I just realized that I do not want to make love to you in anger. Not the first time. Not ever."

If I were a squealing kind of girl, I would be yelling "Yippee!" about now. Angela's heart lurched at his words. Trying for a lighter tone, she asked, "How long do you think this anger will last?"

He turned his face on his arms without raising his head. "Why?"

Dumb, dumb, dumb! Does he really need to ask that? "Because I'm feeling a bit lonely and vulnerable standing here like a naked vestal virgin."

"Naked vestal *virgin*, eh?" Magnus had raised his head and a small smile was twitching his beautiful lips. "Exactly what are you trying to say, wench?"

"I want you." *That was certainly blunt.*

"Well, why did you not say that afore?" He threw his

hands in the air with mock disgust. Then he stretched out one arm, gesturing for her to sit down on the carpet beside him. With an arm looped over her shoulder, he kissed the top of her head and said, "We make quite a pair, do we not?"

"Without a doubt. The vestal virgin and the virile Viking."

He laughed, but then he rose smoothly to his feet, leaned down just as smoothly and lifted her into his arms, and began to carry her toward the bedroom. Just before he laid her on the bed, he whispered against her ear, "I hope you slept well last night, sweetling, because there will be no slumber this night."

Angela thought that was the best offer she had had in a long, long time.

An-tic-i-pa-tion . . .

Magnus looked down at Angela, who lay naked on her bed, awaiting him, and knew he was blessed. If this was his destiny, he welcomed it.

"You are so beautiful," he said, and he meant it, too. Some men liked women with more flesh on their bones, but not him. Her body was perfect in terms of curves and slimness—not too skinny and not too fat. And he loved her round breasts with their rosy peaks, just the right size for his big hands. He also was partial to her indented navel . . . and her raven black woman curls . . . and the mole above her kiss-some red lips . . . and the arch of her foot . . . and her long, long legs. Plus, he liked the way she was not embarrassed by his perusal of her body.

"You are beautiful, too," Angela said.

Well, of course, I am. I am a Viking, am I not? He was about to remind her of his big ears, but stopped himself. It pleased him that his appearance pleased her, even if he lacked the proper humility.

What the future held for them, he had no idea. He still had the time-travel notion to deal with himself, and to discuss with Angela, especially concerning how long he would even be here in this time and this land. For now, all he could control was the present. And he was determined to make their coming together the best either of them had ever experienced. But how was he to do that when his need for her was so out of control?

If he were back home in Vestfold, he would probably take her to the sweathouse, or lay her down on his sensuously soft bed furs, or show her the famous Viking S-spot. That latter could be employed in any culture or time, but he would save that discovery for more advanced sexplay . . . mayhap later tonight. For now he went over to Angela's high chest to see how he might improvise. With a hoot of, "Oh, ho!" he pulled several silk scarves out of the drawers. Now, these had possibilities.

"Magnus?" she inquired tentatively, drawing his name out slowly.

"Shhh!" he said, and tied her wrists together with one scarf, securing them over her head to the spindle on her bed frame.

"Magnus?" she inquired, more shrilly this time. "Why are you doing this?"

"Because I want to?" he offered. It was as good an answer as any. *She probably thinks I am a pervert. Well, I could be, if that is what she wants. Ha, ha, ha! Bloody hell, my brain must be melting from the heat of my excitement if I am laughing at my own unspoken jests.* He ran the back of his hand over his mouth to make sure he wasn't smiling and inquired sweetly—or as sweetly as a six-foot-five-inch Viking with an erection the size of a battle lance could ask—"You are not frightened, are you?"

"No. Just confused. We could have had sex against the wall in the living room, but you stopped because you didn't want to take me in anger. Now you're tying me up, even though you must know I'm willing. Is this some kind of Viking rape-and-pillage fantasy?"

Fantasy? Did she say "fantasy"? Praise the gods! A woman who likes fantasy play. That was what he thought, but what he said was, "Huh?" He was a lackwit, after all. Then he blundered on: "Oh, why must everyone repeat that rumor about us Vikings? Rape and pillage, rape and pillage. 'Tis just the bad reputation jealous Saxon clerics choose to give us. All I have in mind is a little forceful seduction." *Glory be to the saints and goddesses! Where did I think up that one? Forceful seduction, indeed!*

"Well, tying someone up is a bit more than forceful seduction, don't you think?"

"Do you want me to untie you?" *Please, please, please say no.*

"Yes . . . no . . . I don't know. I just want you to be aware that you don't have to do this. After all, I am willing."

Talk, talk, talk. Why do women always feel the need to talk? "That is the problem."

"Pardon me. My being willing is a problem?"

Mayhap I should put one of these scarves over her

mouth as a gag. Nay, that would not be a good idea. Then I would be unable to kiss her, and I very much want to kiss her. "You are overeager . . . as am I," he said, pointing to his still-rampant erection. "I am determined to make our first coupling special . . . I want it to last a good long time . . . but if I allow you to touch me—and I know that you would if you were unrestrained—the bedsport would be over afore it began. That I cannot allow. I want you begging for completion before I ever enter your body. I want to touch every inch of you, most especially your secret places. I want you so out of control for me that I could do anything to you, and you would not protest." *Sometimes I am so good I surprise even myself.*

A flush covered Angela's face and swept downward. A full-body flush. He took that as a good sign. *Yea, smooth as cream on fresh-churned butter, that is how smooth my tongue is betimes.*

"Are you sure this isn't about revenge?" she asked in a raspy voice. "For my 'torturing' you this past week, as you put it?"

Revenge? Hmmm. She did put me through hell. She does deserve "punishment" for that. He thought a moment. "Perchance a little bit of it is for revenge . . . but mostly it is for my lady's pleasure." *Did I go too far that time? Too much sweetness can make a person gag.*

"Oh, boy!"

Apparently not. "I am no boy."

"Oh, man!"

"That is better. Now, should I tie your ankles to each of the posts at the bottom of the bed?" *By thunder, the erotic fantasies that conjures up. But if I am not careful, this cock of mine is going to get so big, just with antic-*

ipation, that it will explode afore the main event. "Nay, I do not think that will be necessary," he said with a coolness that he did not know he had in him. "Just one more scarf here." He folded the piece of fabric and tied it over her eyes.

"Oh, I don't know about this, Magnus. I want to see what you're doing."

Since I am not sure what I will be doing, perchance that is not a good idea. There is no battle plan here, dearling. Just me, acting on instinct, and my instincts in the love arts are mighty rusty. He laughed softly. "It will enhance your sense of touch."

"I think it is enhanced enough."

"Nay, not nearly enough." Magnus had never been much into sex games. Simple lovemaking was his style, and it had sufficed well over the years. But it was so very important that he please Angela. He would do anything, try anything to make their time together memorable . . . for as long as they might have. He hoped he wasn't trying too hard. "Now be still, dearling, and ponder over what I will do next. I will be back shortly."

"But . . . but . . ."

With that, Magnus left the bedchamber and headed for the bathing chamber, where he intended to take a cold shower—or spill his own seed . . . anything to slow down his arousal for this love game he had started. In the meantime it would be good for Angela to anticipate what would come next.

Not that he knew what that would be.

He hoped she didn't fall asleep waiting.

Chapter Eleven

Let the games begin. . . .

Angela was in the dark . . . in more ways than one.

Magnus had been gone for what seemed like a long time. She'd heard the shower running, but that had ended at least fifteen minutes ago . . . though it was hard to judge time with her eyes blindfolded.

He had been right about one thing, though: cutting off her vision had indeed heightened her other senses. She was more aware of her own body than if she'd been looking in a mirror or touching herself. *Where did that latter thought come from?* Fine hairs stood out all over her skin. Her nipples were turgid and upright; she knew that without seeing them, because they literally ached for touch—Magnus's touch . . . or his mouth. Hot liquid pooled between her legs at the image in her mind, and she squirmed restlessly on the bed.

"Magnus," she whispered, sensing his presence in the room. Yes, she could smell the pungent scent of Irish Spring soap. And she could swear she felt his body heat as he drew closer.

"Yea, sweetling, I am back. Did you miss me?"

Is that a trick question? She nodded.

"Speechless, are you? Now, that is a wonder."

"Are you mocking me?"

"Nay, just gazing at your body . . . and wondering where to begin. Do you have any preferences?"

Man, oh, man, is that a loaded question? "Come lie down beside me. I want to feel your body heat."

He did as she asked, placing himself on his side, up against her, very close. She imagined his head was propped on one hand. She could feel a hard part of him prodding her hip. "Are you cold?"

She laughed. "Are you kidding? I'm hot, hot, hot."

He laughed, too, a low, throaty chuckle. Then he placed one hand gently on the side of her neck and leaned down to kiss her.

She whimpered at that mere whisper of a caress, so needy was she already for his touch.

His lips moved over hers, persuading her to open for him. Then his tongue delved inside, exploring her moistness before stroking in and out with carnal hunger. The kiss went on forever, employing both hard and soft lips; tongue; and teeth, till Angela's whimper became a continuous vocal moan of arousal.

Only then did he move to new territory.

He stroked her shaven armpits and kissed her there . . . first one side, then the other. "I like the way women in your land are clean-shaven here, and on your legs. It makes you different from us men, as if

205

there are not enough differences." His lips tickled, and she shivered with pleasure. "And you smell good, too."

Thank goodness for Lady Speed Stick.

He touched the tips of her breasts with the tips of his fingers, and she arched upward at the sheer ecstasy. For a long time he fondled her breasts, teasing them to a throbbing ache, till finally she moaned, "Please."

"Please what, dearling?" he replied, his warm breath blowing on one distended nipple.

He knew what she wanted. He knew, but he was going to force her to say it.

Pride goeth before the fall. Wasn't that how that old saying went? Well, she was falling fast. "Please put your mouth on me."

"And?"

She moaned. "Suckle me."

That hard part of him jerked against her side, but then he put his mouth over her right nipple and began to suck. His mouth was so very hot and wet. The rhythmic action of his lips was so tantalizing that Angela did the unthinkable.

She climaxed.

She stiffened and tried to stop the small ripples that passed through her female parts, inside and out.

Magnus raised his head and seemed to understand what was going on, because he placed a palm over her pubic area.

Oh, Lord! How mortifying!

And then he gave similar attention to her other breast, which caused the ripples to continue, seemingly without end. She writhed from side to side, trying to remove his mouth from her breast, but he held fast, and pressed his palm harder against her mound.

When she was done, tears streamed down her face. "I am so embarrassed."

"Why?" Genuine surprise rang in his voice. "I love how responsive your body is. Do you not know how much pleasure I get from your pleasure?"

She felt him use the edge of a sheet to gently wipe away her tears. Then she lost her sense of where he was. *Oh, no! Oh, geez!* When had her legs gone widespread? Was Magnus really kneeling between them, as she suspected? And why was he so quiet?

"What are you doing?" There was a nervous gurgle to her voice.

"Just looking."

Oh, geez! Don't be looking. Not there. "Looking?" The gurgle was more pronounced. "At what?"

"You."

"There?"

"*There.*"

Is this not every woman's nightmare? All her private secrets exposed? Her most intimate parts examined . . . and possibly found wanting? "Well, don't," she said, and tried to push him away with her knees and feet. The unsuccessful maneuver left her knees bent and her legs even wider apart.

He just laughed. "Do not go shy on me now, sweetling. You are beautiful *there.*"

Oh, my goodness! "What are you doing now?"

"Still looking."

I am going to give him till the count of five, and then I am going to insist that he stop . . . looking. One, two . . . But then she felt his breath *there* and she lost her power of speech . . . or ability to count.

Magnus pressed one palm flat on her lower stomach and trailed the fingertips of the other hand over her pubic hair, barely touching, just a hint of a caress. He did it over and over till she wanted to scream out her yearning.

But then he moved to more interesting territory— the hot, slick channel between her legs. Suddenly she felt something inside her. So surprised was she that she yelped, "Magnus! Is that you . . . your penis?"

"Angela!" Magnus exclaimed indignantly. "You malign me greatly. 'Twas a mere finger." He withdrew it instantly.

In retrospect, she should have known the difference, but with her eyes blindfolded how was she to tell? She giggled at her mistake.

"You find humor in making mock of my manliness, do you, wench?" There was amusement in his voice now. "Ne'er have I had a woman compare my man part to a finger afore. The skalds would write a saga about this event, if they ever found out . . . which they will not. 'Magnus the Needle-Cock' or some such ignominious title, I would imagine."

"Really, Magnus, you make much ado about nothing."

"Ha! Do not ever tell a man the size of his man part is nothing."

Angela was about to tell Magnus that he had nothing to worry about in that department when he began to touch her most sensitive places with light strokes that bespoke an expertise she didn't want to think about. When the light strokes turned to thrumming vibrations against the heart of her, she felt a new climax coming, and she didn't want it to happen this way again.

"Enough, Magnus! Untie me. I do not want to come again without seeing you, or touching you."

"You are a demanding mistress," he said in a growl, but immediately followed her commands. *Thank God!*

She blinked her eyes several times to adjust to the light. Then she noticed how she lay spread-legged on the bed with Magnus kneeling between her thighs. The erection that stood out from the thatch of hair at his groin was thick and blue-veined and very, very impressive . . . a compliment to herself, she chose to believe.

Opening her arms, she leaned upward, "Come here, darling. Enough games! Let's make love."

"Whate'er you say, dearling." Magnus braced his elbows on either side of her head and gently settled his much heavier body over hers. Then, holding her eyes, with his fingertips bracketing her face, he began to enter her . . . inch by glorious inch by glorious inch . . . till she was full with him.

She whimpered softly, but not from pain. It was all the delicious sensation assailing her. Magnus spasmed slightly as her inner walls shifted around him. Her breasts ached with torturous ecstasy. Her heart thrummed madly.

"Come . . . *with me*," he encouraged.

As if she needed such encouragement!

At first he withdrew and entered her with long, slow strokes that were a delicious torment. Her body was tensing for some cataclysmic event, and she wanted more. "Harder! Quicker!" she finally pleaded. *I can't believe I actually said that aloud.* But her arousal was making her frantic, clouding her mind, loosing her tongue.

Instead he moved even slower. But he was panting as he did so, and Angela knew he was as turned on as she was. He was just able to control it better.

She pounded his chest with her fists when the stubborn man stopped altogether, fully imbedded, and watched the play of emotions on her face, especially when he deliberately shifted his hips from side to side, just once, and a miniorgasm caused her to convulse around him. "Oh, oh, oh . . ." she cried out.

Now he would surely start the real business. Now he would end this pleasure-pain that had her writhing from side to side, keening endlessly. Wouldn't he?

No.

Instead, in one fluid motion he sat up on his heels, bringing her with him so that she straddled his thighs. "Like this, Angela," he said huskily. He began to thrust his hips against hers and at the same time put his hands on her buttocks to show her the counterpoint rhythm he wanted her to follow.

Her orgasm came as she bucked against his belly, the pistonlike strokes of his penis inflaming her senses. But it was not enough. Even as she convulsed around him, he continued to pound her, and she wanted more. She threw her head back and strained against the terrible/wonderful tension that continued to ripple over her entire body. When he leaned his head down and took one breast into his mouth and bit gently on the nipple, she climaxed instantly . . . a hard, dramatic spasming that started in her woman folds and went out in seemingly endless waves to her belly and breasts and down her thighs.

When that died down, she realized that she was on her back once again. As she was inhaling and exhaling harshly to catch her breath, another realization came to her: they were not nearly finished, and Magnus— her magnificent Viking—still hard as a rock and positioned at the edge of her cleft, had not been satisfied . . . yet.

"Are you ready?" His brown eyes were glazed golden with passion. His lips were parted and panting. His nostrils were flared as he attempted to control his surely approaching climax.

Need you ask? "No, I'm not ready. I mean, yes, I'm ready, but don't you think we should wait—"

Whoosh! He was in her again, and this time he meant business. No playful jests. No games. No half-sex, or extended foreplay. This was the big time. She saw that in the serious expression on Magnus's face, and the purely masculine growl he emitted as he began to plunge into her hard and fast, the way she had wanted it all along.

In, out, in, out, in, out, inoutinoutinout, in, out, in, out, in, out, inoutinoutinout, IIIINNNNN,OOOUUTT!

"Oh . . . my . . . God!"

"Oh . . . holy . . . Thor!"

Angela screamed.

Magnus howled.

They came together in such a powerful climax that Angela's body shook and Magnus's hands trembled. In the aftershocks that swept over them both, as Magnus finally grew limp within her, he fell upon her heavily and rested his face in her neck, which was damp with perspiration, hers and his both.

They fell asleep then, or passed out from lack of blood to the brain. But before they did, Magnus put his lips against her ear and whispered, "I knew it would be like this, heartling."

Heartling? I like that. "Like what?" she asked, caressing his hair and shoulders.

"Destiny is sweet," was all he said.

She couldn't argue with that.

Man (even virile Vikings) cannot live on love alone. . . .

Magnus awakened a short time later, totally invigorated. There was naught like a good bout of swiving to replenish a man's juices.

He looked down at Angela, who was sleeping soundly beneath him. Poor lady! He had worn her out. He gave himself a mental pat on the back for his prowess, which apparently hadn't been diminished by a year of abstinence.

He was tired, too, but in a sated sort of way. Mostly he was hungry . . . famished, in fact. After all, he hadn't eaten since morn, when he'd consumed eight waffles, six sausage links, four scrambled eggs, and two slices of buttered toast.

Carefully he lifted himself off of Angela, gently kissed the mole above her lip, and eased his body off the bed. After visiting the bathing chamber, then pulling on a pair of jaw-keys, he made his way to the scullery. Opening the cold box, he leaned against the door and looked inside for a long time. *What I would not give for a horn of mead!* No such luck! He settled for half a carton of orange juice and drank it straight down in a series of long gulps. There was nothing else in the cold box that would satisfy his huge hunger . . . certainly not those thin slices of cheese in clear wrappers.

So he called the dome-nose on the tell-of-own to order two large sausage-and-pepperoni pizzas. While he waited for the delivery, he settled down at the table with a bowl of granola—which was the same as grain and nuts, but tasted like bark—with milk and five spoonfuls of sugar. Who would have ever thought that he—a thirty-seven-year-old man—would be slurping up sugared milk, but there it was!

While he crunched away, he pulled a news sheet over toward him. He still had trouble deciphering all the written words in this land, but one thing stood out: the date. June 30, 2003. A stark reminder of what he had been able to forget this past hour.

Magnus closed his eyes for a moment and raked his fingers through his hair, which had come loose during his bed romping. When he opened his eyes again, the date was still there, and he could not ignore the fact. He must have time traveled. What other explanation was there?

He flipped through the news sheets. Everywhere were glaring examples of what he should have seen before. Men had traveled to the moon on spaceships, for the love of Odin! People had heart transplants. Women bragged of breast augmentations. *Now, that is a type of surgery I would be interested in knowing more about.* Then there was computer sex. *That, too. Not that I know what a computer is.* Drug busts. Police brutality. Middle-East wars. Animal cloning. Comic strips. *Ah, who is this Hagar the Horrible? Methinks I would like to meet this dumb Norseman. He appears a fine, though misguided fellow.* And sports. Well-muscled men in this time were paid vast treasures to run about on a field kicking a leather ball or knocking their com-

213

rades to the ground. He liked that concept. Mayhap he would become a football player, if forced to stay here. Then again, he was probably too old. Nay, old or not, that occupation did not really appeal. He would much rather be a farmer.

Magnus shook his head from side to side in confusion.

Had he really time traveled?

Why?

Would he stay here or time travel off somewhere else? If so, would it be back to his own time, or forward? Was he doomed to be an eternal time traveler? *God's blood!* That would be a living hell.

What should he do now?

Well, one thing was certain: he would have to disclose all to Angela. That was a task he did not relish. He needed fortification for the disbelief he was sure to encounter. Since mead was not available, he would have to settle for pizza.

One question kept nagging at him, though: How would Angela react to having made love with a thousand-year-old man?

You're a what . . . ?

"Are you hungry, sweetling?"

Through a cloud of sleep, Angela heard Magnus's whispered question against her ear.

"Oh, no! Not again! I mean, really, Magnus, you are a magnificent lover, but let's not try to set an Olympic record here. Can't we save something for another day?"

A deep male voice chuckled as the mattress dipped

and he sat on the edge of the bed. "Not that kind of hunger, you suspicious wench, you!" He tweaked the side of her breast. "And do not try to paint me as the only insatiable one in this bed, oh you of the pop-sigh-call trick. You told me we could try it later. I can hardly wait."

Angela's eyes flew wide open at that reminder of the outrageous suggestion she had made mere hours ago, and Magnus's more than willing agreement to follow through. That was when she noticed the box of pizza sitting on the mattress between her and the insufferable, grinning rogue. *Oh,* that *kind of hunger.*

"You called Domino's?" She sat up in bed and pulled the sheet around herself. A bit of belated modesty on her part. Very belated, if Magnus's arched eyebrows were any indication.

"I did," he said, placing a paper napkin on her lap and handing her a glass of iced soft drink. "I already ate one."

She smiled at him. She *was* hungry, and she had soon devoured three slices and the entire glass of Pepsi.

"Now, about that pop-sigh-call trick?" Magnus asked silkily as he removed the box and glass from the bed and slid under the sheet with her.

Who knew Angela Abruzzi could set Olympic records?

Would wonders never cease?

Well, apparently not . . . because soon thereafter— with Magnus sitting up in bed propped against a pillow and the headboard, and she lying facedown on the bed, her face buried in her own pillow—Angela was hit smack-dab with the biggest wonder of them all.

"By the by, there is something important I must tell

215

you," Magnus said in a voice that was surprisingly serious . . . and oddly nervous.

"Oh?" Her response was muffled by her pillow.

"I am a thousand years old."

"Yeah? And I'm sweet sixteen and virgin to the . . . uh, bone." Her voice was still muffled by the pillow.

"I am serious, Angela. I was born in the year 963. I reached my thirty-seventh year two months ago, in the year one thousand."

"Puhleeze!" She raised her head to look at Magnus. Even though he was sitting, his height was still immense.

He stared back at her, looking concerned. He kept flexing his hands in an agitated manner.

She rolled over on her back so she could see him better. "You're mighty virile for such an old man."

"Do not make mock of me, Angela."

"How can I not make fun of you? You're trying to say I just made love with a man old enough to be my grandfather more than fifty times removed."

"Precisely."

"This is a joke, right? Next, you will be proposing another one of your sex games, though I can't for the life of me think what the appeal would be in senior-citizen sex games."

"Huh?" Magnus scratched his head and appeared to ponder her words. "Exactly what would senior-citizen sex entail?"

"I haven't a clue." She had to laugh at his interest in what would surely be a perversion. But then she sat up and wrapped the sheet around herself, sarong-style. It was obvious Magnus had something he wanted to discuss, and it wasn't sex, despite his momentary curiosity about yet another fantasy game.

"I do not know how to tell you this, Angela, except to blurt it out. Alas, I am a time traveler."

"Ha, ha, ha! You and Jules Verne. Quit joking."

"I wish I were joking."

"Okay, big boy, exactly how long have you known you were a time traveler?"

"Since yestermorn. I was in the winery cellar with Miguel and noticed the date on the bottles from your last year of producing wines. It said 1997. That gave me my first clue."

She rubbed her forehead with one hand to erase the headache that was beginning to throb behind her eyelids. "There is no such thing as time travel, Magnus."

"That is what I would have thought . . . till yesterday. Now it is beginning to make sense."

"How could it possibly make sense? By the way, Flash Gordon, did you come by spaceship? Ha, ha, ha."

"I came by longship, not a spaceship. And what I meant by 'making sense' is that all the wonders that have stunned me and my children since our arrival make sense when you consider that we are of another time."

"I do not believe in time travel. I'm sorry, Magnus, but it just doesn't pass the giggle test."

"I do not believe in time travel, either, but . . ."

"But what?"

"I do believe in miracles."

"You're crazy."

Still crazy . . . the next morning . . .

They were in a nearby Barnes & Noble before noon the next day with books on Viking history spread out

217

on the reading table before them. Angela was determined to prove to Magnus that he was not from the tenth century and therefore not a time traveler. In a way she felt foolish just making the effort.

"Before you start your proof-search, let me tell you some facts, and see if your books can back them up.

"I, Magnus Ericsson, am a Viking, born and bred. I lived in the Vestfold province of the Norselands . . . from 963 till the year 1000, when I started on my voyage. My father, Eric Tryggvasson, was a Norse jarl . . . comparable to a Saxon atheling, or high nobleman. My uncle, Olaf Tryggvason, was high king of Norway."

In addition, Magnus took a pen from Angela's hand and drew a quick sketch on her notepad. "That is our family crest. See, it is similar to that which is etched on my armrings, and those of Torolf, as well." Magnus's rough drawing showed writhing wolves intertwined with runic symbols, which meant "Honor before self," he explained. In addition, he gave her detailed information about his brother Geirolf, a famous shipbuilder, and the names of his ships, all of which began with the word *fierce,* as in *Fierce Wolf, Fierce Dragon,* and so on. He also told her of his other brother, Jorund, a warrior-for-hire who was known for his military prowess. His sister, Katla, was not famous, but she was married to a Viking of noble birth in Normandy. She had been married at the ungodly age of fourteen.

After an hour and a half of reading and note taking, Angela slammed the last book shut. Everything—*everything*—that Magnus had told her proved true, right down to the design of his family's crest, the wars in which his one brother had fought, and the ships his other brother had built. Had he somehow researched all this material ahead of time? If so, for what purpose? Just to get a part in a movie? To impress her?

None of it made sense, least of all Magnus's contention that he was a tenth-century Viking who had somehow shot through time to land in Hollywood.

She looked across the table at Magnus, who was leaning back in his chair, his ankles crossed and propped on another empty chair. He was flicking through the pages of two magazines—*Cosmopolitan* and *Playboy*—which he'd insisted she purchase for him after seeing the pictures and titles of articles on the front. There was a photograph of a nearly nude nubile young female on the one, which he'd proclaimed looked just like Girta the Great. She hadn't bothered to ask what Girta was so great at. The other magazine had articles such as, "The World's Greatest Sex Fantasy," "How to Get a Hard Butt in Half the Time," and "Best Methods of Oral Sex."

"Is oral sex like the pop-sigh-call game?" Magnus asked, putting his magazines aside.

"Shhh," she said, not wanting anyone to overhear. Her long, tall, way-too-handsome Viking was already garnering enough attention. Even in jeans and a plain black T-shirt, he was drop-dead gorgeous, with a butt that needed no hardening, thank you very much. Not that appearance mattered to her. Much.

He waggled his eyebrows at her. "Well?"

"Yes, it is." She felt her face heat up with embarrassment, though how she had a shred of modesty in her after the past twelve hours was beyond her.

"Tsk, tsk, tsk!" He flashed her a mischievous grin. "I

was wondering about the Norse history books you have been buried in."

"Oh." Her face heated up some more. "Yes, I have to admit that everything you say is true, but that doesn't mean you are a time traveler."

"What does it mean then?"

"I don't know, but I'll think of something." She bent over to pick up her purse from the floor and gather her papers. When she straightened, she caught him in the act of doing the one major thing women hated—ogling her behind.

"I am hungry," he said.

"You just ate four cheese danishes and two blueberry muffins with two lattes."

"I am hungry," he repeated.

She looked at him then, giving him her full attention.

He licked his lips slowly and sensuously, the whole time staring at her—and her behind—with unwavering . . . hunger. "I am hungry."

Angela thought of a dozen answers she could have given him, but the only one that seemed appropriate was, "Me, too."

Unfortunately—or fortunately—they made love on the front seat of her BMW, under a lap rug, in broad daylight, at the far end of the Barnes & Noble parking lot. It was by far the most scandalous thing Angela had ever done in all her life.

Who knew reading could whet such appetites?

A-viking he did go, via the TV. . . .

Angela had to go to her office to work that afternoon, but she had stopped on the way home to rent some videotapes for Magnus to watch while she was gone.

Magnus lay on the sofa for more than four hours watching one incredible tape after another on the tell-a-vision. First he viewed *The Vikings*, or started to. It was a very old move-he that starred Kirk Douglasson, and was silly beyond belief. If Dare-All No-Land thought Magnus was going to prance about a longship wearing a helmet with a giant eagle atop it, like this act-whore did, he had better think again. Magnus shut that video off after only a half hour.

Then he began another move-he called *The 13th Warrior*, which was bad . . . but not quite so bad as the Kirk one. In this story, the Vikings were portrayed as vicious and fanciful, believing in sea monsters and such, but the most unpalatable character was the Arab merchant as portrayed by Aunt-toe-knee-oh Band-arrows. Or was it Aunt-toe-knee-oh of the Band of Eros? Whatever. This fellow had a heavy accent more like an Italian than a Saracen. Plus, the move-he perpetuated the most outlandish theories about Vikings. First there was the claim that Norsemen were filthy in their daily habits; in truth, they were often fastidious to a fault. In addition, this Arab claimed that Vikings routinely had sex with their servants in front of everyone. Ironically, this move-he was based on a book that purportedly portrayed legendary events taking place in the tenth century . . . his very time period.

Finally Magnus began a series of five videos that were produced by Pea-Bee-Ess, entitled, *Vikings*, and narrated by a man with a fine Norse name, Magnus Magnusson. These were documentaries, according to Angela, and therefore more reliable historically. Some of the subtitles were, "Hammer of the North," "From the Fury of the Northmen," "Here King Harold Was

Killed," "Halfdan Was Here," and "England at Bay." He was riveted to the screen by these mostly accurate portrayals of the Vikings of his time, and he was still watching closely when Angela returned early that evening.

"So what do you think?" she asked as she sank down to the carpet next to the sofa and gave him a quick greeting kiss. He liked the way people in this country gave each other greeting kisses, farewell kisses, congratulatory kisses, sympathy kisses, kisses for each and every occasion. He could become accustomed to that.

"I think that there are many false rumors perpetuated about Vikings," he answered, "but these last videos are interesting. Even I am learning things about my own people."

She smiled gently at him.

His heart tightened with emotion, just looking at this woman. He had only told her one time, back at the Blue Dragon, that he loved her, but Magnus feared it was so. At this late date, in these unbelievable circumstances, he was falling in love. And it might very well be an impossible love . . . one with no future. That was why he had not repeated the words. Then, too, she had never said the words to him.

"Would you like to go out for dinner?" she asked.

If you only knew what I would really like! Hot, perverted, blister-my-bones sex, but I would settle for plain sex . . . for now. "Nay. Can we not eat here?"

"Sure, but no more pizza."

Just sex. He laughed and chucked her playfully under the chin.

"How about if I cook a steak and baked potato, with a salad?"

And sex. "Whatever you want . . . though I could do without the weeds."

It was her turn to laugh. "Okay, I'll put the potatoes in the oven, but I won't start the steaks for an hour. I think I'll take a shower first." She rose to her feet by bracing one hand on the low table.

This must mean sex. "All right," he agreed, and stood as well.

"All right?" She cocked her head to the side in question.

"What? That was not an invitation?"

At first she seemed not to understand. Then she smiled her understanding. "You are insatiable."

Sex, sex, sex! "Yea, 'tis one of the best things about us Vikings . . . but you won't find it on any of these documentaries."

"The best-kept secret?" She giggled.

He loved it when a grown woman like Angela giggled. It made her appear girlish and not so lofty. *Plus, it must mean sex.* "Only our special women know about it," he proclaimed.

"And I am special?"

"Oh, lady, you are more than special . . . to me." *And we are, for a certainty, going to have sex now.*

As it turned out, they never got a chance to take their combined shower, or to eat the steak dinner, or to engage in sex. The tell-a-phone rang just then, and it was bad news from Grandma Rose. There was a huge fire at the Blue Dragon in one of the grape fields, and it had been deliberately set.

223

Chapter Twelve

When life kicks you in the grape cluster . . .

It was the middle of the night by the time they got back
to the Blue Dragon, and Angela was frantic with worry.

The fire trucks were just leaving when they arrived,
and Grandma was waiting for them on the porch as
they drove up. All the lights were on in the house, and
spotlights illuminated the fields in the back.

"Is anyone hurt?" Magnus asked.

"No, thank God!" Grandma said. "Except for Jow.
The dirty rotten scoundrel kicked the dog in the ribs
pretty bad. Jow must have followed him into the field."

"Oooh! I could kill the guy, whoever he is, for that
alone. Anyone who hurts an animal is lower than low."
Angela grabbed her grandmother and hugged her
hard. She knew how much she and the whole household loved that damn dog.

"Where is Jow now?"

"Miguel tied his ribs up real tight with Ace bandages and took him home with him for the night."

"Boy, I am going to give Jow the biggest, juiciest marrow bone when I see him tomorrow."

"One tenth of the crop is lost," Grandma told her right off as soon as she finished hugging her. "Not as bad as it could have been, but devastating just the same." As an indication of her concern, Grandma was back to smoking furiously. But then, the children were probably off in bed by now.

"Don't you be worrying about how devastating anything is," Angela told her grandmother. "We'll survive this, just like we have everything else."

She noticed that Magnus was studying them both closely, his forehead furrowed with puzzlement. As the three of them began to walk toward the ravaged field, he asked, "Why is the loss so devastating to you? And what do you mean about 'everything else' you've had to survive?"

"Well, it's not the first time we've had suspicious arson or vandalism here at the Blue Dragon. We suspect it's either someone who wants to buy the place at a bargain price, or a competitor who wants to lower the price of our products." Angela shrugged. "We've never had any proof. And it hasn't happened for several years now."

"But each one of these events puts us further in the hole, financially, and we've never been able to crawl out," Grandma explained. "That's why Angela's job in the city is so important. Her pay helps to keep this place going."

"Now, Grandma. I only do a small part. You work

hard here, too, in your own way. Your contribution is immense."

Grandma blew out a huge cloud of smoke and nodded. No false modesty with her.

"I hope this won't interfere with Darrell and the film crew coming here," Angela mused aloud.

"It shouldn't matter. We can always let them use the south fields, far away from the devastation," Grandma said.

"Why . . . ?" Magnus started to say, then shifted gears. "It has always puzzled me why you would invite Dare-All and his crew to come here, when you so clearly are not fond of him."

"Money, honey." Grandma patted Magnus on the shoulder as if she spoke to a small child, which Magnus was not. She had to reach up to pat him. "It all boils down to money. Darrell is going to pay us up to seven hundred thousand dollars just to use the Blue Dragon vineyards as a backdrop for one of his movies."

"And if I decline to participate in one of his movehes?" he asked Angela. "Will that jeopardize his agreement to film here?"

"Probably," Angela said, unable to keep the desperation out of her voice. The fire and loss of Darrell's money would definitely bury them for good.

Magnus was silent the rest of the way.

They were all silent when they arrived at the field, where workers were still dampening the vines and making sure that the smoldering debris did not ignite a new fire.

"It is like the death of a child," Magnus murmured.

And that was the truth.

A Viking to the rescue . . .

Magnus spent the morning reassuring the children that everything was fine and would be back to normal soon.

More than one of them had confessed fears that they would be forced to leave the Blue Dragon soon, especially Kolbein, who was shivering just like he had in the old days. Did they not know that their visit here was only temporary? They were only guests, after all.

"I think we should get out our swords and go looking for these scoundrels who would do such a cowardly act," Torolf said. "Sword dew aplenty we could spill betwixt the two of us."

"Mayhap," Magnus agreed.

"Don't you dare," Angela said. "Violence begets violence, and then nothing is accomplished."

"Sometimes 'tis necessary to bring the guilty to justice," Magnus argued, "and if it takes a sharp blade or a battle-ax to do it, then so be it."

"If I had a sword, I would use it," Grandma Rose said, much to Angela's chagrin, and his and Torolf's delight. "I think I'll go buy myself a gun. An uzi, or something. Do they sell uzis in Wal-Mart?"

"I would stand guard all night long, if someone would just buy me a bow and arrow," Hamr said, walking into the kitchen where they were all sitting. The noon meal had ended some time ago. No one seemed motivated to go about everyday work.

"You will shoot your eye out," everyone said at once.

"Angela," Magnus said more seriously, taking one of her hands in his. Grandma Rose noticed immediately and her eyebrows rose with interest. She and Juanita, over by the stove, exchanged quick looks of approval. "I will investigate and find out who perpetrated this outrage against you. I will organize guards and enact safety measures to make sure it does not recur. Have you ever heard that famous Anglo-Saxon saying, 'God spare me from the fury of the Northman'? Well, this Northman is furious. But there is another problem that must be addressed first."

"And that would be?" Angela asked, and tried to pull her hand from his grasp. He could not understand why she would blush at mere hand-holding when they had done so much more.

"Money," he said. "And I have the solution."

"You do?" she said.

"I do." He rose from the table and went upstairs to his bedchamber. When he returned, he noticed that, though the baby still napped, all his other children had gathered in the kitchen to see what he was up to. He carried a small leather sack, which he proceeded to empty onto the table. "I will pay you *not* to have Dare-All and his crew come here . . . and to have him stop pestering me about becoming an act-whore. Is this enough?"

There were roughly two dozen coins on the table. "Since one of the previous ones brought me fifty thousand dollars, and I was probably cheated at that amount, I figure this should be more than enough . . . especially if you find me an honest coin tradesman."

Everyone's mouth was hanging open, except his children's. They were grinning at his cleverness.

"Magnus, you can't do this," Angela finally said.

"Try to stop me," he declared. "I am a Viking, and we are stubborn to the core."

"What you are," Grandma Rose said with tear-filled eyes, "is the answer to this old woman's prayers. Thank you."

Angela was too choked up to say anything. He took that for a good sign.

Mayhap she would agree to that totally outrageous *Cosmo* fantasy game to show her thanks. He had a few Viking twists he could add to it.

Then again, mayhap not.

He came to that conclusion when he looked at Angela and winked.

She did not wink back.

Company's comin' . . .

Angela had so many things she wanted to say to Magnus:

Like, "Thank you."

And, "No, thank you."

And, "Where did you get all these antique coins?"

And, "How many more are there?"

And, "Did you just offer me roughly one million dollars?"

And, "Is it possible you really are a time traveler?"

But she was unable to say any of that—for the time being—because company arrived.

"Hi, everyone. Angela. Aunt Rose. Juanita. And who are all of you?"

It was Carmen. Her cousin—five-foot-ten and model thin—was poured into black jeans and a tight white T-shirt that said, *Do It NOW!* over no bra if her prominent nipples were any indication. She wore no make-up and her black hair was straight as a poker. In essence, she was gorgeous.

Tagging along behind her was Carmen's fourteen-year-old daughter, Lily. Lily's short hair was bright red this week and curlier than a Chia Pet. She had on jogging shorts and a running bra over nubile young breasts, which immediately drew Torolf's attention, when he wasn't gaping at Carmen's nipples. The front of Lily's running bra had these words: *Guys have feelings too.*

And on the back, the message continued, *But, like . . . who cares?*

"I see your tits," Njal remarked to Carmen.

"Her den-ham *braies* are cutting her arse cheeks in half. Dost think she can bend over?" Hamr asked Njal.

"No duh!" Lily remarked rudely to their rude comments about her mother. "What cave did you crawl out of?"

"Your legs are free-can skinny," Njal countered to Lily.

"Chicken legs! Chicken legs!" Hamr chimed in.

Both of the little rascals thought they'd found easy prey in Lily, but Lily was a tough cookie who could give as well as she got . . . as she soon proved by ordering, "Chill out, birdbrains!"

"Bok, bok, bok!" Njal and Hamr clucked.

"Boys!" Magnus rebuked his two sons. "How would you like to eat some soap . . . or take on another scooping task?"

Njal and Hamr slunk away.

"Who . . . are . . . you?" Carmen asked, staring wide-eyed at Magnus. "Oh, don't tell me, Angela. You're into

muscle builders now. How could you? It is so . . .
so . . ."

". . . unfeminist?" Grandma finished sweetly.

"Yes. I expected more of you, Angela."

"Hey, I am not a muscle builder. I come by these
muscles naturally."

"Yeah, right. Steroid city would be my guess." Carmen continued to give him an impolite once-over,
which pretty much said that he was a man and
therefore his opinion did not matter. In fact, she tossed
out, "Do you know what God said after he created
man? He said, 'I can do better.' "

"Huh?"

"You prove my point, macho man."

Magnus appeared stunned by the vehemence of her
verbal attack. It was a common reaction from people
who didn't know Carmen and her politics.

"Any woman who thinks George Clooney is a dud
doesn't know anything," Grandma put in.

Yay, Grandma!

"Aunt Rose! Are you still fixated on that radio
broadcast? I told you, I have nothing against George
Clooney . . . just women who think looks are more important than brains."

"Who's George Clooney?" Torolf wanted to know.

"Some geezer that old ladies consider a hunk." Lily
was eying Torolf from head to toe, and her expression
said she would put him in the hunk category. Unlike
her mother, it seemed Lily had nothing against hunks.
"Awesome armrings, dude."

"Old ladies!" Grandma exclaimed indignantly.

"You consider George Clooney a geezer?" Angela
asked incredulously.

Carmen was beaming at her daughter, whom she'd apparently raised in her own feminist tradition.

"Aha! So, this is the man-hater kinfolk. I should have known." Magnus was speaking to Grandma.

Grandma nodded.

Exactly what had her grandmother been telling Magnus?

"Man-hater? Who's a man-hater? Just because a woman stands up for her rights, everyone thinks she has to be a man-hater." Carmen wagged a forefinger at Magnus's face . . . well, actually his chest, since he was so tall. "You know, some people think God is a woman. Personally, I do. How about you?"

Magnus just grinned, which probably infuriated Carmen.

"How about coffee and fresh-baked biscotti?" Grandma Rose offered, hoping to change the subject. "Lily, you can have milk, or fresh-squeezed juice."

"I totally prefer coffee . . . black," Lily said. "Mom lets me drink coffee. In fact, she said I can drink, like, anything I want . . . even wine. It's my decision."

Oh, boy! Angela could see where this conversation was headed.

Grandma's face turned bright red with outrage. "Feminist . . . scheminist, Carmen. You need to learn a few rules about being a good parent."

"Are you . . . are you . . . saying I'm a bad mother, Aunt Rose?"

"*Enough!*" Magnus roared.

Surprised, everyone turned to look at the big Viking, whose size overwhelmed the kitchen, despite its roominess.

"Have we not had enough disharmony here with the

fire? Let us start over on a peaceable note," he sug-
gested. Reaching out a hand to Carmen, he said,
"Greetings, m'lady. I am Magnus Ericsson, Angela's . . .
I mean, uh, a visitor here at the Blue Dragon."

Greetings? Carmen mouthed silently. But she shook
Magnus's hand and said, "I'm Carmen Abruzzo-Martin,
Angela's cousin."

"I thought as much."

"And what do you do for a living, Magnus?"

"I am a farmer . . . and a Viking, of course."

"Of course," Carmen said, but to Angela she silently
mouthed another question . . . actually, two. *A farmer?*
And, *A Viking?* It was clear what Carmen thought of
Angela's choice in men. "Let me guess, Magnus the
Magnificent—or is that Conan the Barbarian?—that
sword in Aunt Rose's umbrella stand belongs to you,
right? Just in case you need to fight a duel among the
chardonnays? Ha, ha, ha."

"And who is this?" Magnus asked pleasantly, ignoring the taunting words and looking at Lily, who hadn't
yet been introduced.

Sometimes you just had to admire his self-control . . .
in more ways than one. Angela would have to tell him
that later when he was using his self-control in other
ways.

"This is my daughter, Lily. She is a student at Sinclair
Academy for Girls."

"See, *Faðir,* girls go to school here, even when they
have seen fourteen winters, as I have," Kirsten said. "I
want to go to school."

"Me, too," Dagny said.

"Not me," Njal and Hamr said at the same time. She

thought they'd left, but they must have come back, not wanting to miss anything.

Just then Jogeir limped in, carrying Lida, who must have just awakened from her nap. Angela wished she'd known. It was hard on Jogeir's leg to go up and down the stairs. *Poor tyke!*

"Goo," Lida said in salutation to the visitors. If anything, the little one was consistent. As soon as Jogeir placed her on her bare feet, she proceeded to give Jow, who was still bandaged and not his usual energetic self, some slurpy kisses.

"Who . . . who are all these children?" Carmen asked.

"They are mine," Magnus said, raising his chin defensively. He probably knew what was coming next . . . from experience.

Carmen was doing a quick silent count. "All nine of them? You have nine children?"

Uh-oh, here comes the "male chauvinist pig" remark.

"Actually, I have eleven living children . . . and two dead. Do you have a problem with that?"

"Male chauvinist pig," Carmen muttered under her breath.

"Carmen . . ." Grandma cautioned.

Carmen literally bit her lip for a long moment to stem the flow of invectives she surely wanted to hurl at Magnus. Finally she inquired of Magnus in a supersweet voice, "Haven't you ever heard of birth control?"

"Not till lately. Believe you me, my life would have been different if I had." Then, realizing how that must sound, he added, "Not that I do not cherish every one of my precious children."

"Pfff!" Njal said behind him.

"Not precious enough to buy me a free-can bow and arrow," Hamr added.

Without even looking, Magnus reached behind him and took both boys by the scruff of the neck and proceeded to lead them toward the back door. "Boys," he said to Torolf, Storvald, Jogeir, and Kolbein, "we have work to do in the vineyards."

Jogeir reached down for Lida, who was playing with the tassels on a throw rug, and handed the baby to Grandma before following his brothers and father outdoors.

"Girls, why don't you show Lily the paintings you've been working on," Grandma suggested. "I bought them some paint sets at the mall several days ago, and they show remarkable talent," she told Carmen.

Gladly, the three girls went upstairs, chattering already like good friends. Lily could be heard saying something about a majorly cool guy who had just moved next door and already was playing tonsil hockey with her airhead girlfriend. Kirsten and Dagny looked duly impressed by this new language.

"I'll be right back," Angela said and went outside. "Magnus, wait a minute."

He turned and came back. With her standing at the top of the steps and he at the bottom, they were about the same height.

"Don't be offended by Carmen. She's like that with everyone."

"I was not offended, sweetling. I was more concerned about my bratlings offending her." He smiled softly at her and reached up a hand to caress her face. "Try to rest this afternoon. We were up all night driving.

235

Then you spent the morning with the fire inspectors. You must be exhausted."

"You were up all night, too," she pointed out.

"Are you inviting me to join you in a nap?" he asked, waggling his eyebrows at her. He was wearing dirty jeans and an equally dirty denim shirt, thanks to a morning spent clearing out the damaged vines in the burned field. His light brown hair, which appeared golden in the sunlight, was tied back into a ponytail, but it was more unkempt than usual. There was an ashy smudge mark on his neck.

Angela's heart turned over, just looking at this man who had become so important to her in such a short period of time. "Don't I wish," she said softly, and leaned forward to kiss him lightly on the lips. "Between Carmen and Lily, all your kids, my grandmother, and Juanita, I suspect it will be a long time before we can be alone again."

He nodded.

"Thank you, Magnus, for all your help. I'm not sure what I would have done without you."

" 'Twas nothing." He leaned up and kissed her then . . . not so lightly.

"And about the money . . . we need to talk about that."

"Nay, we do not. You may consider it a gift, or you may consider it a payment for my inevitable effect on your contract with Dare-All. Better yet, you may consider . . ." He chuckled as he let his words trail off.

"Yes?"

". . . me the answer to your prayers."

More trouble . . .

Magnus had been working all afternoon with the boys and Miguel and the Blue Dragon laborers, clearing out the dead vines. Miguel seemed to think the rootstock on most of the vines could be saved for another year, which was good news.

Fatigued and more than ready for that nap he'd mentioned to Angela, but knowing there was too much work to allow a rest, he leaned against his rake and stared down the hill.

Carmen's automobile was still there; she must have spent the day visiting. Poor Angela! Poor Grandma, as well! In his opinion, a person could take only so much of a person like Carmen. She reminded him of King Olaf's middle daughter, Ilse. Ilse swept into any great hall she was visiting like a big wind, carrying with her gossip, criticism, and general discord. What women like that needed were strong men to tire them out in the bed furs and strong hands to hold them in their places when not engaged in the primary activity for which females were born—sexplay. Mayhap he would share that thought with Angela later . . . if he could find a battle shield first, he thought, laughing aloud.

Just then Magnus noticed another automobile drive up. Even from this distance, he could tell it was a man who emerged and approached the front door of the house.

A premonition of danger swept over Magnus, and the fine hairs stood up all over his body. Jow's ears flared up with alertness, and he began to bark wildly even before he started galloping down the hill, despite his limp.

Magnus took off after the dog . . . not so much because he wanted to prevent the animal from doing harm, but because he feared this new visitor posed some threat to Angela.

When he got to the house, he found everyone gathered in the front hall. Juanita was trying to hold Jow back by his collar, but the dog was wild with excitement. The sharp words being exchanged could hardly be heard over his barking.

Magnus took the dog in hand and shoved him into the pantry, closing the door behind him. The barking could still be heard, but not so loudly.

He returned to the hall, where he found Grandma Rose, Angela, and Carmen speaking with a man dressed in an impeccably tailored gray garment known in this country as a suit. Not a strand of his whitish-blond hair or mustache was out of place. Even his fingernails were perfectly trimmed and dirt-free.

"What the hell's wrong with that damn dog? Someone ought to put the beast down, if it's that dangerous to people," the man complained.

"Anyone touches that dog, and he will find out what real danger is," Magnus said, stepping forward.

The man, who was of medium height, craned his neck to look up at Magnus. And gulped.

Magnus knew how he must look in his grimy work clothes to this well-groomed man, but he did not care.

"What business is it of yours?"

"What business is it of yours what business it is of mine?" Magnus countered.

"Huh?"

"You heard me. State your business and be gone. I will not abide anyone threatening those under the protection of my shield."

He heard Carmen murmur under her breath to Angela, "Maybe this brute isn't so bad, after all."

"Magnus, this is Gunther Morgan."

Instead of extending a hand, Gunther said in a snarl, "What shield?"

"The one that goes with this sword," Magnus said, drawing his weapon out of the pottery jar in the corner.

"I need a cigarette. Badly," Grandma Rose said, and scurried away to the kitchen.

"I need a cigarette, and I don't even smoke," Carmen said, and followed Grandma Rose.

That left just him and Angela and the stranger.

"I could have you arrested for assault," Gunther threatened, puffing his thick chest out in a bullish manner.

" 'Twould be hard to prove when you are trespassing, would it not?" Magnus said in an equally threatening manner, even as he fingered the sharp blade on his sword.

"Now stop it, both of you," Angela insisted, stepping between them. "Gunther is a neighbor. He heard about the fire, and . . . and . . ."

"And what?" Magnus addressed his question to Gunther.

"I made an offer to purchase Blue Dragon, if you must know. It's not the first time, but frankly it's foolish for these two women to hang on here. Everyone knows the place is in financial ruin, and that fire last night should be the last straw, I would think." His words dwindled off as he realized that Magnus and Angela were staring at him with hostility.

"How convenient—and offensive—that you would make another offer the day after our loss!" Angela said with a snarl.

"I was just trying to be helpful."

"If you want to be helpful, get your sorry arse out of here," Magnus said. "Angela doesn't need your money." If Magnus knew for sure that this man was responsible for the damage last night, he would attack him with his bare hands. But he needed proof . . . proof he would get eventually. For now he demanded, "Depart, or you will do so on the tip of my boot."

"Who the hell are you? A new foreman?"

"Nay, I am . . ."

He saw the fear in Angela's eyes that he would reveal they were lovers. That subtle insult he would have to ponder later.

". . . I am Angela's . . . new investor."

A woman's world . . .

That evening Angela found herself in a most uncomfortable position. She was teaching two young girls about sanitary protection.

Magnus was out in the vineyard with the boys and some hired security personnel, setting up twenty-four-hour patrols for the property. Grandma was rocking Lida to sleep in the adapted nursery . . . which was the former sewing room. And she was in her own bedroom instructing Dagny and Kirsten on the differences between tampons and sanitary napkins. They seemed awfully young, but even twelve-year-old Dagny had al-

240

ready had her first period. It must have been hard for both of them, not having a mother around at that important time.

"These are so easy to use," Dagny said, coming out of the adjoining bathroom. "And you say that we can just throw the soiled ones into the trash . . . wrapped in some toilet tissue?"

Angela nodded.

Kirsten was turning the tampon over and over in her hands, trying to figure out how it correlated with the instructions that came in the box.

"Maybe you should save those till you're a little older," Angela advised. "Just use the napkin."

Kirsten seemed relieved that she wouldn't have to use such an invasive product.

The girls, both of them, were adorable, really, with their blond braids and wide blue eyes. Even in jeans and T-shirts, they were Norse to the bone.

"What did you girls use before, if you didn't have sanitary napkins?"

"Rags . . . which have to be washed over and over. Or leaves, if there are no rags about. Sheep's fleece, too, but that is more rare, and a waste of good wool." Kirsten said this with a straight face, so Angela knew she spoke the truth.

The procedures were so primitive, they could only have been practiced by women in . . . *Oh, let's say the tenth century.*

With a thumping heart, she asked both girls, "Do you know what year you were born?"

"Nine eighty-six," Kirsten said.

"Nine eighty-eight," Dagny said.

Angela narrowed her eyes at a sudden thought . . .

241

an *incredulous* sudden thought. "What grade are you in school, Kirsten?"

"School? I have never attended school. The only ones who attend schools that I know of are monks and healers . . . and not all of them do."

"*What?* And, you, Dagny?"

She shook her head.

"But that's impossible."

" 'Tis the way of our land . . . naught unusual," Kirsten said. "Besides, Father Patrick—our grandmother's priest—taught us a little book learning and writing . . . on occasion. And we girls are instructed in all there is to know about running a household of three hundred. The boys master farming and fighting, or building ships, like Uncle Geirolf."

Angela shut her jaw.

"Our father told us not to discuss this with anyone," Kirsten was quick to add.

She gasped, not because Magnus had cautioned his children not to discuss their past, but because the dates and schooling information that Kirsten and Dagny had supplied reinforced their father's outrageous time-travel claim. The girls must have misinterpreted her gasp, because they rushed to their father's defense.

"Father meant no harm. He told us not to discuss those things to protect us." Dagny wiped a tear from her eyes as she spoke.

"Oh, honey, I didn't mean—"

"He is the best father in the world," Kirsten elaborated. "I know from watching the tell-a-vision and from talking to Lily that men like our father are looked down on here. They are considered crude and uneducated."

"Father grumbles mightily about the troubles we bring him, but he protects us always," Dagny added.

"You may not know this—and Father would not like my telling you—but half of us are probably not even his blood kin. People—especially women—take advantage of him by dumping babe after babe at his feet. He resists and complains loudly, but in the end he never turns any away. That is the way he is." Kirsten lifted her chin, as if defying Angela to disagree.

How could she?

Magnus was a grown man who might lie to her, but these girls were too young and innocent to have fabricated this tale. They were telling the truth.

"I won't say anything," Angela said as calmly as she could, so as not to alarm the girls, but her thumping heartbeat kicked up a pace.

Oh, God, oh, God, oh, God!

In a world that had become very uncertain to Angela, one thing became crystal-clear: She had some things that she needed to settle with Magnus. But first she needed to settle those things within her own mind . . . and heart.

A short time later, as the girls went off to the den to watch a movie and she was about to go downstairs, she passed the "nursery." It was not Grandma who was rocking Lida to sleep, but Magnus, who softly sang a song to her in a language she did not understand . . . probably Old Norse. As he crooned to her, Lida kept tugging at his war braids and saying, "Fa-Fa," baby talk for *father*. It was the newest addition to her vocabulary, next to "Goo." Even as he sang, Magnus would intermittently lean down and press a soft kiss to the baby's fine hair.

The sight of the big man and the tiny girl touched something deep within Angela's soul, and she accepted something then that she had known, deep down, for some time.

I love him.

Chapter Thirteen

Girls just wanna have fun. . . .

A week had gone by and there had been no more attacks at the Blue Dragon—thank the gods!

Despite the relative calm, everyone was restless and unhappy over what seemed like a forced confinement . . . though it was a wonder to Magnus how anyone could feel restricted on an estate this size. His children were getting spoiled, without a doubt, by all the niceties and conveniences of this land. They seemed to forget that just a short time ago they were content with privies and hearthfire cooking.

The girls especially seemed to want more and more, particularly after their visits with Lily, which had continued the past few days. If he heard "the mall" mentioned one more time, he just might scream. Or boys. Or makeup. Or shaving one's legs, which he had forbidden until Angela convinced him otherwise. Just so she didn't suggest that he shave *his* legs.

He, on the other hand, was restless and unhappy with good reason. Lovemaking with Angela had been off the menu since their return to the Blue Dragon, and he missed it mightily.

They had just finished eating a magnificent feast prepared by Grandma Rose and Juanita. He went out on the lawn with Lida to play a game of run-and-run—then run some more, if she had her way—in hopes of tiring her out before bedtime. Usually he was the one who got tired out first. His old knees were not accustomed to this type of activity.

In any case, it was no surprise that Kirsten and Dagny followed him outside to plead their latest causes.

"It is just not fair," Kirsten started out.

"When females say that thus and so is 'not fair,' a man does best to sit down, and preferably call for a horn of ale, because he is in for a long tongue-lashing." Magnus plopped down to the grass with great drama, lying flat out on his back with one forearm over his eyes.

"Faaaa-ther!" Dagny said in her newest long-suffering voice.

Lida giggled, thinking it was a game, and flung herself atop him. "Fa-Fa, Fa-Fa, Fa-Fa!" she kept squealing as she pounded on his chest.

Angela walked up to them then and said, "Here, Magnus. I bought you a present."

If you only knew what I am thinking, wench! His arm was still over his face. "I hope it is what I think it is," he said in *his* best long-suffering voice . . . an imitation of Dagny's.

"Not that, you fool," Angela retorted. "I bought this for you today when I was out shopping for groceries."

He removed his arm and looked up at her. She was handing him a frosty amber glass bottle. He lifted an eyebrow at her.

"It's beer."

I am thinking of her woman-honey, and she offers me honeyed mead. Ah, well! Magnus sat up and took the gift from her. "You bought me a horn of ale . . . well, a bottle of ale? What? Didst read my mind? Must be you are a Valkyrie. 'Tis the second-best thing you could have done for me."

He took the open bottle from her and immediately took a long swig of the cold brew. It was delicious. "Aaaah! Drink of the gods!"

"What is the first-best thing?" Dagny wanted to know.

How could I have forgotten that I have children about? Especially since I always have children about. "Never you mind, M'lady Curious." He chucked Dagny under the chin.

"I know what it is. 'Tis all boys ever think about." Kirsten wrinkled her nose with disgust.

He and Angela turned startled gazes to Kirsten.

"Kissing."

Whew! He and Angela smiled at each other.

That was Lida's cue to come up and give Kirsten myriad kisses.

"Yech! She tastes like grass. Have you been eating grass, Lida?"

Lida just grinned at her, revealing two tiny front teeth, and said, "Goo."

"Do you not even want to know what I consider unfair?" Kirsten asked.

Not especially. "Of course, sweetling."

She slanted him a scowl that pretty much said, *Do not patronize me, Father.* "Girls my age should go to school."

"I agree," Dagny said.

" 'Tis only fair that you hire a tutor for us *now,* then enroll us in school come fall," Kirsten went on. "And we need a proper wardrobe if we are to go to school every day."

"Every day! There is not enough to be learned to require daily schooling." *Besides, who knows where we will be come September? This is only July.*

"Also, I think my bedtime should be eleven o'clock, like Storvald's. 'Tis not fair that I should have to go to bed at ten, just because I am female."

"Well, I want a pair of jogging shoes. Njal says I am getting fat. I need to start jogging." Dagny blushed as she blurted out her needs.

"You are not fat, Dagny," Magnus told his daughter. "And since when do you listen to the opinions of a person who thinks it is attractive to let snot run down to his chin?"

"I will tell you what is really unfair," Kirsten continued.

Holy Thor! She is getting as bad as Madrene. Blather, blather, blather.

"Torolf gets to go to concerts . . . well, one concert, but I am sure there will be others. Lily is allowed to go to the mall whenever she wants, and she dyes her hair, and she has a boyfriend, and I want to go to her house for a sleepover, but you keep saying no, no, no. And

if I do not get a tiny little tattoo on my hip, I think I
might just die."

"Is that all?" Magnus asked as drolly as he could
manage.

Dagny and Kirsten actually had tears in their eyes.

"Dost anyone care to hear what I think is unfair?"
Magnus grumbled.

Everyone looked at him, and none of them asked
"What?"

"Well, I will tell you. There is something that I have
sorely missed since we left the Norselands, and does
anyone ever ask me what I want? Nay. It is, 'Give me
this. Give me that. This is not fair. That is not fair.' "

"What is it that you want, Magnus?" Angela asked,
putting her hand on his.

He took her hand in his, twining their fingers, stared
into her eyes steadily, and told her what his heart's
wish was.

"A cow."

The reason dumb-men jokes were created . . .

Magnus caught up with her just before she reached
the house.

"Angela, dearling, why did you storm off just now?"
I will ne'er understand women. Ne'er, ne'er, ne'er.

She stopped so quickly he almost ran into her.
"Don't you 'dearling' me, you dumb dolt."

I am a dumb dolt. But why now? "What? What did I
do?"

"A cow? Your dearest wish in all the world is to get
a cow? Puh-leeze."

249

That does sound a mite dumb. "You do not like cows?"

She told him something really foul that he could do with his cows. He guessed she must be angry about something . . . something beyond his comprehension. He was beginning to understand why women in this country told dumb-men jokes. Still, dumb man that he was, he decided to try to explain himself anyway. "I am a farmer, Angela. It is all well and good here at the Blue Dragon, but I miss the care of my milch cows, the satisfaction of seeing my gardens bear fruit, the regeneration of the earth year after year, springtime plowing, autumn harvests, the smell of fresh-mown hay—"

"Bullshit!" she said.

"That, too."

"You are impossible!" She threw out her hands in disgust, turned on her heel, and sprinted up the steps to the porch. He grabbed her by the upper arm and stopped her before she went inside.

"Explain yourself, woman."

"I was hoping you would say your dearest wish was to spend a lifetime with me, but I'm not entirely delusional. What I thought you *would* say was that your dearest wish is to spend the night with me."

Oh, now I am beginning to understand. But, bloody hell, where is all this hostility coming from? Must be that time of the month. But he was not dumb enough to express that thought. Instead, all he answered was, " 'Tis."

" 'Tis not," she replied, mimicking his form of speech . . . which was really unkind of her.

"Settle down, Angela," he started to say, and immediately realized his mistake. *Never, never, never tell a woman to settle down.* What was he thinking?

Her nostrils flared.

Time to cut my losses. There is only one way to stop a woman when she is on a rant. He picked Angela up off her feet by the waist, wrapped his arms around her tightly, and proceeded to kiss her thoroughly . . . so thoroughly that he hoped her bones were melting, because his certainly were. With his lips still firmly locked on hers and her feet still dangling off the porch floor, he turned and leaned his shoulders against the wall. His staff, which had been at half-mast for the past week, went full sail, pressing into her stomach.

How could Angela doubt how much he wanted her?

Certainly all his children, as well as Grandma Rose and Juanita, who were surely watching the spectacle he was creating, must realize how much he wanted her.

When he finally broke the kiss, he murmured, "How could you doubt my desire for you?" *Any more desire and I will burst into flames.*

"A hard-on does not equal true affection, and that is what I want."

A hard-on? A hard-on? That was certainly blunt enough. He did not need a translator to know what that crude term meant. Looking down at Angela's passion-dazed expression, he whispered, "It is my dearest wish to be with you . . . sex or no sex . . . for as long as I am able." Now, that was a stretch of the truth. "Do you believe me?"

She nodded.

He still wanted a cow.

But he was learning when to share his thoughts, and when to keep his big mouth shut.

We are family. . . .

Magnus and his children felt like family to Angela; so she decided to take them on a family outing the next day.

Oh, she was still annoyed with Magnus about his preferring a cow over her, but obviously not too annoyed, because her choice for their day away from the Blue Dragon was the regional Grange Fair and Craft Show, a preliminary to the state fair in the fall. The dolt would probably get to see a cow or two today.

Torolf's friend, Juan, was coming with them. He had borrowed a van for that purpose. The Universe Studios van had been returned days ago on the demand of a furious Darrell Nolan when he learned that his prize Viking was not going to be his prize Viking. He had threatened lawsuits and such for breach of promise, but Angela didn't think anything would come of that.

Also accompanying them was Lily, who had already proclaimed that she had a crush on Torolf. Kirsten was casting googly eyes toward Juan, who, at eighteen, was much too old for her.

Grandma said she'd rather stay home and relax . . . which meant that she was probably planning to chainsmoke the whole time they were gone. Magnus had organized hired security personnel and Blue Dragon workers to patrol the grounds while they were gone; he and his older boys would cover the night shift.

Fourteen of them piled out of two vehicles as they arrived at the fairgrounds.

After strapping an adorable Lida, with her Winnie the Pooh sun hat and matching jumper, into a fold-up stroller, and after Angela insisted that everyone slap on sunblock and wear baseball caps or sun visors, they made for the entrance.

"I have been riding a longship on the high seas and working my fields for thirty and more years without suffering a sunstroke or the skin sun-disease you speak of," Magnus grumbled as he began to push Lida's stroller. One of the things that amazed her about Magnus was how he took on certain caregiving tasks without ever questioning whether it was masculine or not. He was that secure in his own masculinity . . . as he had every right to be.

"Stop complaining. I could tell you enjoyed my slathering that cream on your face and arms."

"There was that," he conceded, flashing a wide grin her way, "though there are some other body parts of mine that could use equal . . . slathering."

Magnus looked just as adorable today as Lida, except he was wearing a soft plaid short-sleeved shirt, blue jeans with neat creases (God bless Juanita!), athletic shoes, and a Dodgers baseball cap over his tied-back hair. Surprisingly, his attire did not look out of place with the etched silver bracelets on his upper arms, which he never seemed to take off. Torolf never removed his either, and more than a few teenage girls were giving him and his armrings a second glance. It didn't hurt that he was wearing a black tank top and cutoffs, which showed off his muscles. He wasn't as tall or as muscular as his father, though. Not for the first time, Angela likened Magnus to a tree.

Just then Magnus caught her checking him out and

grinned. He gave her an equally thorough once-over, and his grin widened when he got to the spaghetti straps of her blue sundress, which left her shoulders and arms exposed. Like the other females, she wore a sun visor . . . in this case a clear blue plastic one, with her ponytail hanging out through the back. On her feet were sandals, which left visible her shocking pink enameled toes . . . something that seemed to particularly please Magnus.

In fact, he leaned close to her ear and whispered, "Methinks I have the perfect fantasy for later. Something involving toes and tongues."

"Oh, you!" she said, and slapped him playfully on the arm. But what she thought was, *Oh, boy!* It had been seven long days and nights since they'd last made love, and she missed him with a passion.

"Do you want me to take over with Lida?" Torolf asked. "The way you two are gazing at each other, I suspect you will be looking for the nearest hay byre."

"Torolf, you overstep yourself," Magnus cautioned. " 'Tis no way for a son to speak to his father. Mayhap you will learn some manners if I decide to send you to the same school Kirsten and Dagny want to attend so desperately."

"You would not!"

"Do not test me, son, or you may find out."

"All I did was ask if you wanted me to help with Lida."

"You asked more than that, and you well know it. You can help me, though." He handed Torolf several bills. "I put all the younger boys in your care, especially Njal and Hamr. Do not let them get in trouble."

"*Faðir!* You know bloody well that is impossible.

Njal and Hamr cannot breathe without getting in trouble. Oh, for the love of Frigg! Do you see that?" Torolf scurried off toward the gaming area, where Hamr and Njal were about to throw darts at balloons.

"What's so wrong with darts?" she asked.

"They will hit themselves with the darts, piercing an essential body part, or they will hit the man standing behind the plank under the tent, or they will hit some passerby. That, I guarantee."

"Maybe you are being overprotective."

"Would you like to make a wager?"

"A wager?"

"Yea. Something involving pink toes would suffice."

Where does he come up with this amazing stuff? Why do I find it so tantalizing? "And what do I get if I win? I'm not taking any more of your gold coins."

"Tongue."

Yep. Amazing and tantalizing.

Just then there was a shout of, "Hey!" The guy at the dart booth had fortunately ducked in time, but Njal had apparently almost hit him in the head with a dart. Torolf rushed up and grabbed both boys, apologizing profusely to the game-booth owner.

"I did not get my prize yet," Hamr was shrieking to Torolf, who had him and Njal by the upper arms, dragging them away.

"I will give you a prize . . . on your puny little arse," Torolf said.

Kirsten and Dagny were standing some distance away, red-faced and pretending not to know their brothers. The girls looked especially pretty today in matching, though different colored shorts and tank-top sets. Instead of their usual braids, their long blond hair hung loose down their backs almost to their waists. Lily had already commented on the pretty color of their hair, referring to them as Loxies . . . as in natural blondes in the vein of Goldilocks, as compared to Boxies, which were blondes born of boxed color.

Juan was staring at Kirsten with too much interest, but so were some younger boys who passed by. Angela wasn't worried about Juan. He was a good young man who would respect the invisible age taboo. Besides, he had a girlfriend. When Kirsten turned eighteen and Juan was twenty-two, that might be a different matter.

For the next few hours they walked around admiring the exhibits, everything from dried flower arrangements to fruit and vegetable preserves to fine needlework. Lida fell asleep in her stroller right away. When Angela fingered the finely crafted quilts, Magnus decided to buy her one in a star-and-heart pattern.

"This is much too expensive a gift," she said, even as he was paying for the item, and the woman was wrapping it in tissue.

"We Vikings love to give gifts more than anything else . . . well, almost anything else." He pinched her butt to show what he meant . . . as if she were clueless . . . as if any female over the age of twelve could misinterpret the hot look in his eyes. "Some say we are generous to a fault betimes, but methinks we get back what we give in life. And even if we do not, there is joy in the mere giving."

"So what you're saying is, 'Shut up and accept the gift.'"

"Something like that," he replied with a laugh. "Or, 'Shut your teeth and give me a gratitude kiss.'"

She did just that, gladly.

"You are so embarrassing, Father," Kirsten said in a mortified whisper. She had come up behind them with Dagny and Lily, who were hooting with laughter. "Men your age should not be interested in kissing . . . and, like, stuff."

"Men my age?"

"Old men," she said with disgust.

"Old? I am not old. Besides, men and women never get too old for kissing . . . and stuff." He lifted her by the waist then, twirled her around twice, then kissed her soundly and loudly on the mouth.

Kirsten just giggled, then hugged her father warmly.

"Can I get twirled, too?" Dagny asked.

"For a certainty," Magnus said, and gave the younger girl equal treatment.

What a father! Angela thought, and immediately added, *What a man!*

After that they ate and ate and ate. Hot sausage and meatball sandwiches. Corn dogs on sticks. French fries and onion rings. Fresh-squeezed lemonade. Funnel cakes. Popcorn. Lida, who was awake by now, favored cotton candy and cherry slushes, though she was given only a tiny taste of each.

Storvald found a woodworker who showed him how to use razor-sharp scalpels to create different effects on cherry-wood panels. His father promised to buy him a similar set.

Torolf kept winning at the anvil-and-bell game until he had six stuffed animals and a request from the operator to please move on.

Magnus almost had a heart attack when Hamr and Njal came over and discreetly dropped their shorts to show him the tattoos on their behinds. Fortunately they were removable ones. The boys danced away, laughing, when their father reached out to swat them. Those two really were little devils.

The others were off riding the amusement rides. A small Ferris wheel, which Magnus declared "for demented people only." A merry-go-round. A mixer. A loop-the-loop. And bumper cars.

She and Magnus moved on to the fresh produce displays. How a man could be so interested in turnips and carrots and string beans was beyond her, but Magnus surely was. Angela took a now-restless Lida out of her stroller, changed her damp diaper, then let her walk around as Magnus stopped at stand after stand to speak with the farmers displaying their wares.

"How do you get beans this size?

"Do you use fresh fertilizer? Do you prefer cow manure over horse or pig shit?

"Do you save your kitchen garbage for the pigs, or do you put it back into the soil? Compost? What is that?

"When is the best time to plant spring onions? How about winter wheat?

"What effect does the hot temperature here have on your produce? Is there enough rain?

"Can a man make a living as a farmer?

"Farm supports? What are they? . . . *What?* Your government pays you *not* to grow certain crops? That is insanity . . . surely, it is."

On and on Magnus went, asking question after question of the farmers, who loved talking about their work and their products. Angela could see that Magnus was in his element here. His questions were intelligent. His interest was genuine.

After that they entered the animal barns. And she might have thought Magnus had entered heaven . . . or his Viking Valhalla.

He touched each of the cows and examined them closely, calling them by name. Their names and those of their owners were on wooden plaques above the stalls. Messy Bessy. Madonna. Surfer Girl. Guernsey Girl. Holstein Hannah. Lucky Lady. Sylvia.

In one barn, modern-machine milking as well as old-fashioned hand milking was taking place. Magnus was incredulous over the milking machines and wanted to know all the details about the kinds and amounts of milk produced by the different breeds of cows.

Then there were the bulls . . . mean-looking dudes, these were. Brutus. Elmer III. Seventh Son. Brown Boy. Black Beauty. Cool Bull. Samson. Bull's-eye. Fred.

The animals had ribbons of various colors beside their stalls to denote how they had been judged in the various events at the fair. Many of them had been raised by youngsters as 4-H projects.

While Magnus mooned over the cows and discussed milk production, new breeds, and prices with the owners, Angela had a bigger job with Lida: keeping her from stepping in cow poop.

A little boy, about eight years old, was weeping over a calf at the end of one barn, where his father was trying to console him. Apparently the calf—which had been born at the fair—was ill and might have to be put down.

Magnus stepped forth and asked what was wrong.

The father looked at him askance, but answered nonetheless: "The calf is starving to death. Won't take milk from its mother. Won't eat any of the special feed

259

we mixed for her." He shrugged, and the message was clear: this calf was dying.

Magnus knelt down in the straw beside the reclining calf and said, "Let me take a look."

While he pushed the calf's eyelids back, opened its mouth and examined its tongue, even smelled its breath, the boy's father asked her, "Is he a veterinarian?"

She shook her head. "Nope. Just a farmer. A good farmer."

The man knelt down beside Magnus then and the two of them talked seriously while Magnus continued to examine every inch of the ailing animal. "The calf has mold disease in its stomach. 'Twas probably passed on by its mother. The disease has little effect on the adult cow, but is too much for the little one to fight," Magnus finally pronounced. "It must needs get a hot gruel mixture . . . a cupful at a time every hour till it will feed on its own. Force it down, if necessary." He then told the man exactly what ingredients should be in the gruel.

The man appeared skeptical.

"What have you got to lose?" Magnus said.

They both stood and shook hands. The young boy reached out his hand to Magnus, too, and whispered tearfully, "Thank you."

After that they moved on to pigs. Her favorite was a huge pig called Mud Stud. His "girlfriend," the sow in the next stall, was called Dirty Mary. According to Magnus, Vikings ate a lot of pork and used all parts of the animal, including the hide and bones—even the hooves and nostrils. That was true of the cows, too. *Yech!*

Next, they visited sheep, goats, chicken, and ducks.

At the "New Age" barn, they also saw ostriches, buffalo, trout, snakes, and alligators, which were also farm animals to some. Magnus couldn't believe his eyes. He laughed with delight. He talked excitedly. He shook hands and exchanged stories.

This was a new Magnus, one she had never seen before. Here he was in his element. Here he did not hesitate. Here he held himself with pride and authority. Here he acted as if farming was a noble profession . . . which, of course, it was.

If she hadn't known it before, she did now.

Magnus, the man she loved, was a farmer . . . plain and simple.

A man of many talents . . .

"Would you like to see me plow?"

Angela wiped the soapy foam from her eyes and stared at him through the frosty glass of her shower stall. "Magnus! It's midnight, for heaven's sake! What are you doing here?"

"All that exposure to farmers at the fair today reminded me where my true talents lie. I have come to show you my technique for . . . plowing."

"Naked?"

" 'Tis the best way," he said, stepping into the stall and closing the door after him.

She gave his form a long, slow survey, from his head down to his curling toes, then back up to his favorite part, which was behaving impressively, if he did say so himself.

"Great plow," she said, backing up slightly.

"Wait till you see the straight rows I harrow." Magnus stepped forward, crowding her against the tile wall.

"You'd better hope the ground is not too fertile." She combed the fingers of both hands through her wet hair to help remove the shampoo suds. Those motions caused her breasts to rise and fall in a very nice rhythm. In truth, there was a rhythm to her combing that set up a rhythm in his own body, down low.

But her words are like pouring cold water on a hot faggot. Be careful, my lady, or I may just fizzle. "You are right. What I don't need is more . . . uh, turnips."

"Turnips! Well, that's as good a word as any, I suppose. Where are the turnips, by the way?"

"Some of the turnips are asleep . . . I hope. The others are on guard duty in the vineyard."

"And how did you escape?"

"I told Torolf I had to visit the bathchamber."

"Oooookay."

"It was not really a mistruth." Actually, Torolf had wanted to know why he couldn't just piss against a nearby tree, and he'd told him he had "more serious business" to handle, which was not a lie either. Making love to a woman was serious business, indeed.

"You mentioned something about plowing, Farmer Brown."

Laughing, he lifted her into his arms, naked flesh pressed against naked flesh under the warm shower spray.

"Uh-oh!" Magnus said against her ear.

"What?"

"I sense some rough terrain. We must needs smooth it out afore doing any plowing. You would not want to break the tip, would you?"

"The tip?"

"The plow tip . . . you know, that iron-hard bit that is . . . well, you know what I mean."

"And how do you intend to do that smoothin' *thang*, plowboy?"

"Odd that you should ask. I just happen to have available two shovels," he said, holding out his big, splayed hands. Magnus took her wrists in his hands and arranged them high so that she gripped the shower head. Then he filled his hands with liquid soap and began to rub it into her "rough terrain." Hill and dale got equal attention. Rosy pebbles. Boulders. Limbs. Even "grassy" areas.

She was making that little mewling sound deep in her throat that he had come to love. The more he slathered, the more she mewled. And when he moved the slickness on his hands to the slickness between her legs, she almost shot off the floor with a jerk. Lowering her arms, she shoved his chest and said in a low growly voice that nigh melted his . . . plow, "My turn, sweetheart. The farmer's lady has got to work, too."

He couldn't argue with that.

So he was the one raising his arms to circle the showerhead, and it was Angela who was soaping him up and he was the one gasping his pleasure. With an expertise known to women throughout time, she rubbed his shoulders and neck, the muscled planes of his chest, the tendons in his arms and legs, the hard flatness of his belly, the hard curves of his buttocks and even the crease between them. She left the most important part for last. With slow deliberation, she poured more soap into her palms, encircled him, and began to milk him like a true farmer's wife. She must

263

have paid more attention today than he had thought.

But Magnus was a simple man, and he could only take so much. "Enough!" he roared, and backed Angela against the far wall of the stall, lifted her off the floor, arched her hips outward, and entered her. He felt as if every bone in his body were red-hot and rigid. He felt as if the blood in his body had turned molten. He felt as if every hair on his body were standing tall. All this because of the intensity of his arousal.

But then he looked at Angela, who was staring at him with wide eyes. And no wonder! Down below, her inner muscles were already contracting around him with the beginning of her "coming," as they referred to it in this land.

He could not wait then. He wanted to—desperately—but it had been too long—a sennight, by Thor!—and she had excited him too much with her farmer-wife play . . . and so he began the hard, hard, hard strokes that pressed her backside against the tiles with a delicious rhythm that was enticing in itself.

Angela's contractions were never-ending as he plunged in and out. Her fingernails dug into his shoulders. Her legs tightened around his hips. And still the ripples of pleasure in her inner walls tortured him with their clasping and unclasping till he thrust deep and hard and cried out his ecstasy.

For several long moments they both panted into each other's necks, neither noticing that water still sprayed over them, cold by now.

Finally, taking great joy in the passion daze that still covered her face, he leaned forward to give her a soft kiss of thanks. There was nothing he could say that would express how deeply she touched him with her response to his lovemaking. So he just kissed her softly once again.

"Have you naught to say, dearling?" he asked in the end, beginning to be alarmed by her silence. Mayhap he had misinterpreted her quiet. Mayhap she was offended by his hard and quick loveplay.

She studied him for a long moment and said, "You are some farmer, Magnus."

Relief thrummed through him at her playful retort, which was surely a sign that she had been pleased. Still, he had to ask, "I plowed straight and true, then?"

"And deep." She laughed.

But not for long.

Reaching behind him, he turned off the faucets, released Angela so that she sank weakly to the floor, then immediately picked her up in his arms.

"Now that you know about farmers, methinks you need a lesson in farm animals." He was carrying her into her bedchamber, which adjoined the bathing chamber. They were both very wet, especially their sopping hair, but neither noticed.

"Farm animals? That sounds kinky to me."

"Definitely kinky," he agreed unabashedly. *What is* kinky?

He dropped her to the bed and lay down on top of her. Angela would have some explaining to do to her grandmother the next day about the wetness of the coverlet, but he could not be concerned about that now. He was too aware of the wonderful naked woman beneath him.

"So what animals are we talking about here?" she inquired friskily, even as she combed his hair behind his big ears with the fingers of both hands. He did the same to hers.

"The stallion and the mare," he replied without hesitation.

Instead of shrinking back with revulsion, Angela surprised him once again with her laughing reply: "Yippee!"

Chapter Fourteen

A family Thing . . .

In the Viking culture, matters of great importance were settled at a meeting called a Thing, or an Althing. Everyone had a vote in these assemblies, though the chieftain's opinion usually carried extra weight.

Magnus decided the next day that it was past time to call a family Thing to discuss this time-travel dilemma in more detail with his children. He wanted Angela present, too.

So gathered that afternoon in the gazebo were Torolf, Kirsten, Dagny, Storvald, Njal, Jogeir, and Angela. He figured that the other children were too young to understand, or to keep a secret. In truth, Hamr would no doubt take great delight in announcing to the world that he was a "free-can time traveler" who had damn well better get a bow and arrow "free-can soon."

"Does everyone concur on this point at least . . . we

have time traveled to another country and a thousand years into the future?" Magnus asked.

No one immediately replied, which did not surprise him. It was hard to accept such a bizarre notion.

After a few minutes, though, each of them nodded reluctantly, except for Angela.

"What other explanation can there be?" he asked her.

"I don't know, but I live in a society that probes for scientific explanations for everything . . . and usually there is a sound, logical reason for even the most unusual events. But this . . ." She just shrugged.

"I think I know what happened." It was Kirsten speaking, and every one gaped at her with astonishment.

"My grandmother, Lady Asgar, was a Christian. She always said that she could not accept all the Norse legends and mystical ideas, like dragons and trolls and such, but she did believe in miracles. She said her One-God could do anything. That is what I think happened to us."

"A miracle?" Torolf scoffed. "For what reason?"

Kirsten shrugged. "That is not for me to answer."

"Why would the papist God care about us Vikings?" Njal wanted to know.

It was not such a ludicrous question.

"I suspect that God doesn't differentiate between cultures and peoples as much as we do," Angela said. "And I must tell you all, my grandmother has been praying a novena for a miracle for some time now . . . some knight in shining armor to come save the Blue Dragon."

"And she thinks I am that knight?" Magnus was horrified and pleased at the same time.

"Unfortunately, yes."

"Why unfortunately?" Magnus put his hands on his hips, a mite offended at her choice of words. It wasn't that he wanted to be a knight in shining armor, precisely, but he did not like someone—anyone—thinking he could not be one if he chose.

"Don't get your jockeys in a twist," she said with a laugh. "I just meant that if you were indeed the miracle she pleaded for, you were given no choice in the matter."

Mollified, he nodded his understanding. *I will show you a knight, m'lady skeptic. Just you wait and see. I can be knightly . . . especially at night. My brain is melting here.*

"Perchance you are correct, and the reason we time traveled is because Grandma Rose conjured us here with her papist beads, but methinks there may be another reason, as well." Torolf was rubbing his chin in a bemused fashion as he spoke. "I have been wondering if mayhap Uncle Rolf and Uncle Jorund time traveled, as well, and that for some reason we were meant to join them here."

A half dozen jaws dropped with amazement at this theory . . . a theory that was not entirely implausible. Actually, when he had first left the Norselands, Magnus had had a notion to search for his brothers, but somewhere along the way he'd forgotten, or been distracted by all the other things that had happened. Never had he considered, though, way back then, that his search might involve travel through time.

"And I have another idea," Jogeir spoke up, his chin

269

jutting out defiantly. It was so unlike the boyling to appear belligerent that they gave him their full attention. "Has anyone . . . just one person . . . considered that in this new land, with all its modern inventions . . . there might be a way to repair my clubfoot?"

It was such a simple question and so fervent that Magnus felt immediate guilt that he had not brought it up himself. He put a hand on Jogeir's shoulder. "You shame us, Jogeir . . . with good cause. We have all been so full of ourselves and our own complaints that we did not consider your greater need." Magnus looked toward Angela with an unspoken plea for help.

"I cannot promise anything, Jogeir, but as soon as I get back to the house, I will make an appointment with an orthopedic surgeon. We will find the best possible doctor. I should not say this without seeing a doctor first, but I cannot imagine that there isn't an operation to help you." She cocked her head in question then, staring at Magnus. "Didn't you ever consult a doctor about his . . . uh, handicap?"

"Of course. But those were tenth-century healers. I did my best, but that was then; this is now."

They were silent for a while, pondering everything that had been said and the implications.

"Okay, assuming I believe all this time-travel or miracle stuff, and I'm not sure I do, what next? Are you guys all going to bop off back to the past without warning one day? Are you deliberately going to try to go back? Or are you here to stay? Do you even have a choice?"

"That is *the* question," Magnus said, and he could tell by the somber expressions on all his children's faces that they agreed. Angela had good reason to ask the question, too, because she was involved in a relationship with a man who might disappear any moment.

"I do not want to go back," Kirsten said vehemently. "I like it here."

"It would be hard fitting in here . . . at first," Torolf said, "but I think I could adapt. Mayhap someday I would want to go back, but right now my vote is to stay . . . if our voting even matters."

"Me, too. Me, too. Me, too," the rest of the children said.

Magnus looked at Angela, held the eye contact, and said in as meaningful a way as he could, "Me, too."

"What would we do here, Father? What work would you do? Where would we live?" It was the ever-logical Storvald speaking.

"I can answer that," Angela said, much to his surprise. "Since your father invested almost a million dollars in gold coins into the Blue Dragon, you all are welcome to stay here indefinitely . . . at least till it's clearer what is happening and what you all want to do. There are some immediate things that can be done, like tutors for all the children, school enrollment in the fall, driver's training for you, Magnus, and for Torolf . . . and dozens of other things."

He cast Angela a thank-you smile. That was one worry off his mind—where they would stay and what he would do in the immediate future. The far-off future remained a mystery.

"But I would advise all of you to keep this time-travel theory to yourselves," Angela cautioned. "If the news got out, you would have every scientist and quack entrepreneur at your doorstep, dissecting you physically, emotionally, intellectually. You would never be allowed to live a normal life."

No one disagreed with that admonition as they sat contemplating how they would be regarded by this modern society. Not favorably, Magnus was sure. More like freaks.

"I have thought on everything we have discussed here today, and I have come to a conclusion," Magnus said. "My brothers are the key to our future."

"How so?" Angela asked.

"If I am able to locate my brothers in this new land, in this time, then my brothers would surely know, after all this time, whether 'twas possible to stay here or not. It would mean that time travelers can relocate and stay in the place where God, or the miracle, has sent them . . . if they so choose."

Angela focused on only one short phrase in all that he had said. "If they so choose?" she repeated.

He wanted to say that he did so choose, but he could not do that yet. Not till he had a surer idea of what the future held.

His silence must have been telling to Angela, though, because tears welled in her eyes before she turned, stricken, and left the gazebo.

If you don't succeed, try, try again. . . .

"Angela, Mrs. Abruzzi, be reasonable," Gunther Morgan pleaded.

He was sitting with her and Grandma in the front living room the next morning. After apologizing for his behavior the previous week, he began his usual campaign to buy the Blue Dragon. It was more than a coincidence that he chose to return at a time when Magnus and the boys were busy in one of the far vineyards with Miguel.

"Why is it so important to you?" Grandma wanted to know. "You have a bigger property than ours. Why can't you be satisfied with what you've got?" Since Lida was ensconced in a high chair in the kitchen with Juanita, and the girls were off at the mall with Lily, Grandma lit up a cigarette and took a deep, satisfying inhalation. The bliss on her face almost made Angela want to take up the filthy habit herself. Almost.

"I have four sons, Mrs. Abruzzi. Yes, I have a large property, but not big enough to satisfy all of them and their families. Plus, we are growing . . . the market is growing . . . but the amount of land remains the same."

"Look to the other sides of you, then," Angela advised.

"I have." Gunther sighed. "My neighbors are in the same situation as I am. They all have family dynasties they want to establish and only so much land."

"I won't be pressured to sell, Gunther. I won't," Grandma said fiercely. "As long as I am breathing, the Blue Dragon will stay in Abruzzi hands."

"But Angela isn't even married," he argued. "She may never have children to carry on your line here."

"Whether I marry or not . . . whether I have children or not . . . is none of your business." Angela wanted to slap the false pity off the man's face, but she fisted her hands instead. "Never lose your cool" had been her motto in business for years, and it had served her well thus far.

"You aren't even making wine here anymore, for chrissake!"

"We're planning on starting up again," Angela lied.

"You are?" Gunther asked, clearly shocked.

"We are?" Grandma asked, then quickly covered her tracks by saying, "I mean, we are . . . very soon now."

Gunther recovered his cool. "Be reasonable, ladies. You must have sustained severe damage from the recent fire. That, on top of your financial problems . . . well, it doesn't take a rocket scientist to see you're in trouble here."

"You know an awful lot about what's happening at the Blue Dragon, don't you, Gunther?" Angela inquired, her eyes narrowed.

"Only what everyone in the valley has heard." Gunther's beet-red face belied his words.

"The answer is no, Gunther," Grandma said, "and that is final."

Gunther stood and picked up his straw hat from the love seat where he had been sitting. "This is all because of that giant Viking, isn't it? He's convinced you to hold on here, hasn't he? Big, steroid-ridden ape! Doesn't know good wine from pig spit, would be my guess. Thinks he can run a vineyard with that old codger, Miguel. Hah! They will never make this place prosperous again. Never!"

Angela stood and advanced on Gunther. "Who are you to look down on Magnus? He's a better man than you are any day of the week. He's honest, hardworking, and a good father. Don't you dare disparage him. Don't you dare."

Grandma was staring at her strangely. "Way to go, granddaughter!"

"I'll tell you one thing," Gunther said, just before jamming his hat on his head and going outside. "Someone had better tell the Incredible Hulk to watch his step."

Never make a Norseman mad. . . .

"Magnus, why are you mad at me?"

Magnus was so blisteringly furious with Angela that his only response to her lack-wit question was to glare at her. She had dishonored him mightily by declining to call for his assistance and placing herself in danger's way.

For the past ten minutes, Angela had been sitting at the large kitchen table with Magnus and his family, and he had barely spoken to her. Everyone was uncomfortable with the silence that hung in the air between them. Grandma Rose and Juanita kept exchanging worried glances intermixed with the rolling of their eyes. The children sat with their eyes downcast, eating a tasty dish called shrimp paella over rice that Juanita had just served along with a long loaf of crusty bread and a zesty arugula, tomato, onion, and mozzarella salad. Rose kept refilling the frosty glasses of iced tea. Jow had his head between his two front paws under the table, where he awaited droppings from Lida. Even Lida was especially quiet as she dug into the rice with her own tiny toddler spoon and drank milk from her sippy cup.

"I will tell you why I am angry with you, Angela. You did not summon me when Gunther arrived, even though we have discussed in the past the threat he poses to the Blue Dragon and its people. Did I not order you to call me immediately if he came onto this property?"

He saw Angela bristle at the word *order*. He had noticed that women in this country—and time—misliked the idea of a man being in control. They associated too much with man-haters like Carmen. Could they not see that there were times when only a man's might and authority would suffice?

Lida must be turning into a modern female, because she made a little growly sound and flung a spoonful of rice onto his face with an almost gleeful-sounding, "Goo!"

"But I told you about Gunther's visit right afterward," Angela persisted.

He threw his hands in the air, after wiping the glob of rice off his face with a cloth. "What good did that do? He could have harmed you or Grandma Rose with no one nearby to defend you."

"He wouldn't have done that." Angela had the cheek to argue with him. "Gunther's methods are more devious than that."

"Are you never biddable?"

"Sometimes," she said, tossing her hair back off her shoulder in a challenging manner. The witch was reminding him of just which times she had been biddable with him. Like last night.

I can see you now, heartling, tossing your hair back in the same way while you practically neighed your pleasure. But I do not think I should remind you of that now. Mayhap later. He took a deep breath and said more patiently, "You did me grave insult by allowing Gunther to makes threats against me, then springing to my defense."

"What would you have had me do? Say nothing? Let him defame you?"

You are surely the most stubborn woman alive, Angela Abruzzi. Yield this once. Just free-can yield. "I do not need to hide behind a woman's robes."

"Oh, give me a break, Magnus. Maybe I should have called you back to the house when Gunther pulled up, but—"

Just then, the cell phone clipped to Magnus's belt began to beep. He could tell that Angela was surprised that he would carry such a modern device on his person. Hey, he might be over a thousand years old, but that did not mean he was unadaptable. He'd just purchased it that afternoon and was still getting accustomed to it. Gingerly he picked it up and spoke into the mouthpiece. "Greetings."

"Father, it is Torolf. We followed Gunther back to his house. Juan is hiding out front, and I am in the back. He is speaking to some rough-looking men just now. I do not think they are regular employees. They are carrying weapons, I believe."

"Keep a watch. The men we hired today should take over soon. I have arranged to meet with them in an hour."

"How will you get there?"

"Miguel will drive me."

"All right. Juan and I will stick on Gunther's tail till we hear from you."

"Do not let him out of your sight. And Torolf . . ."

"Yea?"

"Be careful, son."

Magnus clicked off and returned the device to his belt clip.

Everyone stared at him expectantly.

"Torolf? That was Torolf? Where is he?" Angela

asked in alarm. She stood abruptly and her napkin flew to the floor.

"He is busy on an errand I assigned him." He continued to eat, as if unconcerned. He was, in fact, very concerned . . . and excited. There was naught like a good battle to get a man's juices going. And he was bloody well sick of taking a defensive mode with the scoundrels who victimized the Blue Dragon. He hated just waiting for something to happen, like a milksop cowering in a corner. 'Twas past time to take the offensive.

"Does this involve Gunther?" Grandma Rose asked, just as disturbed as Angela. No doubt she would be sneaking off any moment now to smoke one of her toe-back-hoe sticks to calm her nerves. Juanita, standing behind her, was wringing her hands in her apron as she listened.

"You have no right . . . you should have consulted me . . . I mean . . ." Angela sputtered her outrage at him. "What have you done, Magnus?"

You do not want to know. Truly. "Nothing . . . yet." He continued to eat—even the dish of greens, which he was developing a taste for, especially when he put huge spoonfuls of creamy dressing on top to cover the bitterness of the weeds. His eating in the face of her fury made Angela even more furious. So he took another helping of everything. "Since you took action on your own, by excluding me from your meeting with Gunther, I have taken some actions on my own."

"I . . . Grandma and I . . . own the Blue Dragon."

"I have an interest in it."

"The money?"

"Nay, not the money." *You.*

278

Angela blushed. "Tell me what you are planning."

"Nay."

"Nay . . . uh, no?"

Women and their incessant questions! With all the inventions they have in this new land, you would think some man would have invented a zip-her for a talksome woman's mouth. "I cannot disclose our secret plan. What if Gunther returned and you decided to meet with him again, alone, and he tortured our plan from you?"

"Don't be ridiculous."

Ridiculous am I now? That mouth zipper is looking mighty good. "Well, I am done eating." He stood and motioned toward Miguel. "Are you ready to drive me into town, my good man?"

Miguel nodded and grabbed his hat, which was sitting on the counter. Juanita appeared as if she might have a worry fit.

"By the by, Angela, I have arranged to start taking driving lessons on Monday. Torolf is coming, too."

Her mouth dropped open.

Finally, a way to stop her blathering. Magnus walked over and gave Lida a kiss on the cheek, trying his best to avoid all the rice sauce.

"Goo," Lida said. Then, "Fa-Fa."

"That is what I like. A woman of few words."

He swore he could hear Angela gritting her teeth behind him.

Dirty Harry meets Mighty Magnus. . . .

Magnus had been working with a private detective agency and a team of security personnel for the past two weeks. The head of the troop, and owner of the agency, was Harry Win-slow, which Magnus thought was an odd name for an investigator to have, but then again, betimes winning slow was the best way.

Harry was a hard-as-nails former soldier with a haircut that was so short the scalp showed through. Magnus was thinking about getting a similar haircut, till he mentioned the idea to Angela. "Get a buzz cut, and you might as well buzz away, big boy!" she had exclaimed. Magnus was pretty sure that meant no. *Whatever.* He had other plans for her once this whole drama was over, and none of them depended on what was atop his head.

Her comment to him about the haircut was one of the few times she had spoken to him these past weeks. She was still fuming over his failure to share his plan for capturing "Big Bird." That was the code name Harry had given the culprit who was threatening the Blue Dragon. When he had asked Harry why they needed a code name, why they couldn't just refer to that *nithing* Gunther, he had said there was no firm evidence yet that Gunther was the one . . . or the only one.

Actually, there was another occasion when Angela had deigned to talk to him—when they took Jogeir to visit an orthopedic surgeon, who took pictures of the inside of the boy's foot and leg. An operation was scheduled for two weeks hence. He was nervous about putting his son under the knife, but Angela was optimistic about the operation's outcome, and Jogeir was wildly enthusiastic. In essence, he'd been outvoted from the start.

If Angela had been stingy in sharing her talk with him these past two weeks, she was even stingier with

her body. "No sex, no way, no how!" she had proclaimed when he had broached the subject.

When he'd grumbled, "There are some who say that
an organ in too much disuse could wither away," she
had rolled her eyes at him.

Wait till she hears what I have to say now.

Angela was in Grandma Rose's vegetable garden
when he walked up. Sitting down on a bench near the
bean trellises, he inhaled deeply, loving the smell of
moist earth, sun, and growing plants.

"Angela, come over here, please. I have something
to discuss with you."

She glanced up from the basket where she had just
placed several red toe-may-toe globes. "Go away."

Well, that was certainly short and sweet. "I need you
to do something for me."

"Dream on, buddy. You aren't coming near my bed
until I find out what you are up to. Even then, you
might not be welcome."

"Tsk, tsk," he chided. "I was not speaking of sex." *I
was thinking it, but I did not say it. Bloody hell, I am
always thinking it when around you, witch of my heart.*
"I need you to gather Grandma Rose and all the children, except Torolf, and go stay in your apartment in
the city for several days."

That got her attention.

She put the basket down on the ground, dusted off
her hands, placed them on her hips—*hips that look
very nice, by the by, in a pair of tight den-ham braies,
which mold her behind and slender legs and cup her
woman place . . . not that I consider any of that significant*—and said in a snarl, "Are you crazy?"

"Crazy for you." *Sometimes I astound myself. I can*

smooth-talk even in this modern language.

"Ha! Don't you dare try that smooth talk on me. I know what you are up to."

"You do?" *Caught in the act of being smooth. Ah, well!* He glanced down at his groin, where the only "up" thing on him was located.

"Not that, you dolt!"

"Oh." *She is losing her sense of humor . . . fast.*

"You think you can Softsoap me, and I'll agree to anything you want."

"Well, Softsoap did work in your shower when—"

"Oh! You are such a brute for bringing that up now."

A man will try anything. Trust me on this, sweetling. "Angela, can we start afresh? It is serious business I need to discuss with you. Events are building and I fear a climax here at the Blue Dragon sometime soon. I would not want you or your grandmother or my children to be at risk."

Angela walked up and plopped down beside him on the bench. "Why don't you start by telling me what's been going on?"

"We have been tracking Big Bird, and a trap has been set."

"Huh? Who has been tracking?"

"Dirty Harry and me."

Angela put a hand to her forehead and counted aloud. When she got to ten, she said, "Who is Dirty Harry? And please don't tell me it's Clint Eastwood."

"Flint who?

"Not Flint . . . Clint. Aaarrgh! Are you deliberately trying to confuse me?"

"Not deliberately." *Well, mayhap a little.*

She scowled at him fiercely, and when he tried to

put his arm around her shoulder, she slapped it away.

This appears not to be my day. Actually, there have been few of those lately. Mayhap I need to hone my skills better. "Dirty Harry is the code name for Harry Win-slow, the private detective I hired to help catch Big Bird, which is the code word for Gunther, or who-ever has been threatening the Blue Dragon."

"You hired a private detective? Without consulting me?"

"Yea, I did. And I got my driver's license today. Didst know that? Of course, I had to take the test twice. I almost hit a pole the first time. The policing man bit his tongue, drawing blood, and said a very coarse word. Mine is a license for foreigners living in this country, since I could not take the written test in your English—yet."

This woman needs to learn that men are men and women are women. I am the leader; she is the follower. That is the way of the world. Angela was staring at him as if he'd grown another nose . . . or bigger ears, which would be disastrous, of course. His were plenty big enough, thank you very much. Or mayhap she had read his mind and did not agree with his philosophy of life.

"Harry is a very nice fellow. In fact, when this whole investigation is over, he is going to take me out for a beer . . . to a local stripper bar. I did not want to ask him, but what is a stripper bar, Angela?"

Of course, he knew what it was, having asked Harry, but he was teasing Angela, or trying to. Unfortunately she just glared at him.

"Harry says the ladies there have tassels on their boobs. What are boobs?"

"You're a boob," she said angrily. Then she inhaled and exhaled deeply, as women were wont to do when exasperated with their men. "Magnus, how could you get a driver's license when you don't even have a birth certificate?"

"It helps when you know the right people. Least-ways, that is what Harry says. He got those parchments for me, and for all my children, too. And social security cards, whatever they are. Why do people need special licenses in this land to be secure in their social lives? Oh, and work records . . . Harry got those for me as well. The papers say I was a Green Beret. And I was in the Witness Protection Program." He beamed at her, sure she would be pleased at his enterprise.

She did not beam back. In fact, she murmured, "More like the Witless Protection Program." Mayhap she was not all that pleased.

"Let's start at the beginning. Just whom did you hire, and what has he discovered?" she demanded to know.

She is a demanding wench betimes. "I hired a private detective, and he in turn hired some professional hit men—"

"Hit men?" Angela screamed in his ear.

He rapped the side of his head with the heel of his hand as if to clear his ears. "I was just teasing, Angela."

"This is no teasing matter."

Yea, she is definitely losing her sense of humor, and the best place to restore it is in the bed furs. Unfortunately I couldn't lure her to my bed furs at this moment even if I had the smoothest tongue in the world. "Harry hired some professional security and detecting men. I realized the day Gunther came to visit that I needed help . . . that *you* needed help. I have often been a soldier for my king in the Norselands, but fighting is direct there. You lop off a head or pierce a man's gullet with a sword. Or he does the same to you. We use none of these devious attack-and-hide tactics. Well, actually, we Vikings employ a bit of that when out a-viking, but that is neither here nor there." *I have got to stop rambling. I am beginning to bore myself.*

"How much is this going to cost?"

Money, money, money! I am sick of talking about money. "You are not to worry about that, sweetling."

"Don't call me sweetling. At this moment I feel anything but sweet toward you. And you can't keep shoveling out money on my behalf."

Oh, really? Try to stop me. "We can discuss that some other time. What Harry and his troop have discovered thus far is very alarming. Not only did Gunther probably set fire to your vineyard, but he has sabotaged your good standing with bankers in the area. If you had gone to them for a loan to recover your losses, you would have been denied."

"Oh, no!"

"He is the one who lured your winemaker away, as well. He found him employment in the Franklands. 'Twas he who conspired to raise the price of the glass bottles you use for your wines. 'Twas he who was responsible for the bad brakes on that load of grapes that was lost last year when the truck careened off the road."

"Is Gunther really that evil?"

"I think so," Magnus said, taking her hand in his. "Harry's men are experienced in gathering evidence . . . everything from fingerprints to car tracks to a paper trail, whatever that is. But Harry warns me that Gunther is getting desperate. He was moderate in his methods in the past because he thought he could afford to wait you out . . . that eventually you would surrender, being helpless women. But now . . ."

"Now?" she prodded.

"Now he perceives that my presence may change things. He is not sure who I am and what our relationship is, but to his mind I am here to save the Blue Dragon, and that he cannot allow."

Angela quietly pondered all he had told her. He saw the moment understanding dawned. "Gunther is going to try to kill you. That's why you want us all back in Los Angeles. That slimeball plans to kill you. Ha! Over my dead body!"

Methinks I am making progress now. Leastways, she cares if I live or die now. He smiled grimly at her vehemence.

"Nay, not over your dead body . . . because your sweet body is going to be far from the Blue Dragon."

It's not over till it's over. . . .

For two days Angela walked around like an automaton in her L.A. apartment.

She went into her office both mornings, managed to show a half dozen homes, and even sold one, pulling in a hefty commission. But the rest of the daytime hours she spent with Grandma and the kids, all of whom fought the strictures of confined living. None of them wanted to go out, though, in case Magnus called, which he did once a day.

When she asked how the "plan" was going, Magnus was always infuriatingly elusive in his answers. "On target." "Biding our time." "Do not worry." She felt like screaming into the phone at him, and she would have . . . if she weren't so very worried about him.

To make matters worse, Darrell Nolan was being a real pain, now that he knew she was back in town. The man just wouldn't give up on signing Magnus to be the next big star in his stable. Apparently Magnus had taken to hanging up on Darrell on those occasions when Darrell managed to connect with him by phone. Even that rudeness didn't daunt the persistent producer.

"Why don't we go to the mall?" Angela suggested in the late afternoon of the second day. If she had to put up with much more MTV, video games, the quack-quack of Lida's pull-along duck toy, makeup makeovers of Dagny and Kirsten in her bathroom, and general overall shrieking, Angela was going to pull her hair out. She loved Magnus's kids—each and every one of them, even the rascally Njal and Hamr—but all of them all at once in such a small space . . . well, even a saint's patience would be taxed. "We can have dinner at Chi-Chi's or Red Lobster. Even McDonald's . . . God forbid! Then spend an hour or so walking around the mall."

"Quack, quack, quack . . ." It was Lida coming through on her established route, living room to bathroom.

"How about if I stay here and take a nap while the rest of you go to the mall?" Grandma suggested. She was probably dying for a cigarette. But more than anything Angela was afraid Grandma would scoot back to the Blue Dragon, which she hadn't left for this long in more than five years.

"Quack, quack, quack . . ." Lida was on her return trip.

"If I go to the mall, Grandma, you go to the mall," Angela insisted. "Unless I can leave Lida and the duck here."

"Quack, quack, quack . . ." Lida was passing through again.

"I'll go to the mall," Grandma said.

"Can I have my ears pierced?" Dagny wanted to know.

"Well, I don't see any problem with that . . . as long as it's only one hole per ear." Lots of girls her age had their ears pierced, so Magnus probably wouldn't object. Heck, some people even had infants' ears pierced.

Kirsten sat up straighter, suddenly taking her eyes off the Britney Spears video playing on TV. "I would rather get a piercing in—"

"No!"

"You did not even let me finish," Kirsten complained.

"It doesn't matter. No piercings anywhere except the ears without your father's written permission."

"*Faðir* said I could buy a bow and arrow," the sly little Hamr said. It was such a bold lie that Angela had to laugh.

"Good. Show me his written permission."

"He does not write so well. 'Twas a message he gave me in person."

"Any witnesses to that exchange?"

"Nay, just the two of us." The little snot was beaming. He actually thought she was buying his story.

"Good try, Hamr, but the answer is no."

"I'm thinking that we should get Rollerblades for everyone," Njal suggested. "I saw them on some young people when we were driving into town. They look like great fun."

Rollerblading sounded harmless enough, but then Angela got a clear picture in her mind of all these kids Rollerblading around her apartment, or down the condo halls. "Maybe sometime later . . . when we're back at the Blue Dragon."

"You are no fun," the usually quiet Kolbein commented.

Luckily she was spared any more requests by the ringing of the phone. She was laughing when she picked it up. "Magnus?"

"No, Miss Angela, it is me, Miguel."

The fine hairs stood up on the back of her neck. "Miguel? What's wrong? Oh, God! Are those sirens I hear in the background?"

"*Sí*, but you are not to worry. Mr. Magnus told me to call and tell you it is all over. Gunther has been arrested, and the police have taken him to jail."

She exhaled loudly, not even realizing that she had been holding her breath.

"There are six police cars here. My Juanita is making coffee for the men now . . . and sweet buns. Ay-yi-yi! What a scene it was here tonight, but it is all over now. Will you be coming back tonight or tomorrow? Juanita wants to know."

"Tonight," she replied without hesitation. "Where is Magnus? Can I speak with him?"

"That is the thiiiiiiing," Miguel drawled out ominously. "He cannot come to the phone."

"Why?"

"Because they have taken him to the hospital."

Chapter Fifteen

Falling for a fallen hero . . .

By one A.M. Angela had dropped Grandma and the
children off at the house and was on her way to the
hospital.

She knew from frequent cell-phone calls she had
made to Miguel and Torolf during her return trip that
Magnus had sustained a gunshot wound to the shoulder. Although not a deadly wound, it could have been
if the bullet had entered only a few inches lower.

She also knew from her phone conversations that
doctors were still holding Magnus in the hospital emergency room, where he was resisting being admitted . . .
even for overnight observation. Torolf said they finally
had to knock him out with a tranquilizer just to settle
him down for the examination.

When she walked through the hydraulic doors leading into the emergency room, Torolf was waiting near

the entrance for her. Standing next to him was a physically fit older man with a GI haircut, whom she assumed was Harry Winslow.

"May Odin be praised, you have arrived," Torolf said, after giving her a quick hug. "Father is acting like a bear in a hunter's trap."

"Ms. Abruzzi, so glad to meet you. I'm Harry Winslow," the other man said, extending his hand.

She wanted to ask for the details of what had happened, but she needed to see Magnus first.

"You are not sticking another needle in me," she heard a male voice roar out suddenly.

Magnus. Following the voice, she found him in a curtained area arguing with a hefty nurse who appeared well able to handle herself with the difficult Viking.

"Look," Magnus was saying. "I pissed in a cup for you. I let you take large amounts of my blood to be tested. I let you sew up my wound, even though 'twas a mere scratch. No more bloodletting, I tell you."

"Buddy, one more shot. That's all. You either roll over and show me your pretty butt, or I'll strap you down."

"Angela!" Magnus had just looked up and noticed her standing there. He opened his arms wide for her to come to him. "Best you beware, healing maid, my lady is here now, and she will protect me from the likes of you."

Thank God, he's all right. He couldn't be hurt too badly if he's roaring like this. Angela sat on the edge of the mattress, on his good side, and hugged him gently. She didn't realize how pent-up her emotions had been till the tears began to spill out with her loud sobs.

"Angela! What is wrong? Has someone been hurt?"

Is he for real? "*You're* hurt, you thickheaded fool," she wailed. "That's why I am crying."

"Oh," he said, immediately followed by, "Get me out of here, Angela."

Angela glanced over at the nurse, who stared pointedly at the needle in her hand.

"One more shot," Angela told Magnus. "Then I'll go see about getting you released."

"All right," he said, rolling over onto his stomach. "But then I am walking out of here, even if I have to wear this arse-baring garment."

His behind was in fact bared by the hospital gown. And a fine-looking behind it was, too. Even the brusque nurse thought so. Angela could tell because the woman winked saucily at her after giving his butt a good once-over, then jamming the needle into the firm flesh.

While he was dressing with Angela's help, Magnus spoke with Harry and Torolf. "You did a fine job, Harry. We ne'er would have been able to catch Gunther without your help."

"Thank you. It's what I do. But you are the one who made yourself a target. Can't tell you how much I admire your courage, man."

"Target?" Angela repeated.

"Yep, we set Gunther up. Magnus made himself very visible the last few days . . . at the Blue Dragon, around town. Had him boasting in bars and local stores about how things were going to improve at the Blue Dragon now that he was here. Despite all the evidence we had gathered, we needed to catch the perp in the act . . . which we did."

Angela glared at Magnus, who gazed back at her with utter innocence.

Calm down, Angela. You can't smack a wounded man. Inhaling deeply for inner strength, she said, "I love the Blue Dragon, but I never wanted you to put your own life on the line."

"Sometimes a man must be a man."

She rolled her eyes. *Is there such a thing as an adorable male chauvinist?*

"We will discuss this later . . . that I promise you," she said, now that he was dressed and frankly looked a bit white-faced and weak, despite his macho bravado, "but for now, let's go home, honey, and put you to bed."

"Will you come to bed with me?" he cajoled in an exaggerated little-boy voice.

"No." She laughed. "You never give up, do you?"

"Never." He laughed, too, then winced when that slight movement pained his shoulder. " 'Tis the third-best thing about a Viking."

She wasn't about to ask him what one and two were. She was pretty sure she already knew.

Sleepless in Sonoma . . . not . . . !

The trouble at the Blue Dragon was over. All that was left was the cleaning up . . . both physically and legally.

But first Angela slept till noon the next day, so exhausted was she by the night's events. Magnus was even worse . . . or better. He slept off and on for a full twenty-four hours. Every time she heard him up and about, whether just visiting the bathroom or brushing his teeth or taking a quick shower, she was waiting for him in his bedroom with a glass of juice and more pills. Sleep was the best aid to healing at this point, the doctor had said.

It was one A.M. of the second night, and Angela was sitting at the kitchen table with a glass of wine, working on the Blue Dragon account books. She heard a loud noise, as if someone had tripped over something, followed by what was probably a swear word in Old Norse. It must be Magnus.

She put together a tray of chicken-salad sandwiches with dill pickles, Juanita's famous potato salad, and a pitcher of lemonade. Magnus would be starving once he finally awakened for good.

When she got there, though, he was sleeping again. The sheet covered him only to the waist, making visible in the moonlight the white bandage wrapped around his shoulder and under his armpit. Her heart dropped every time she saw that evidence of his wound . . . a wound that could very well have been fatal to him.

The sheer curtains were billowing inward with a building breeze that portended rain. In fact, heat lightning was already flashing across the sky, filling the room with short-lived brilliance.

Because there was a chill in the air, she attempted to raise the bed linen up over Magnus's bare skin. She wouldn't want him to catch a cold on top of everything else. Bending over the bed, she had managed to draw the sheet upward without awakening Magnus . . . or so she thought.

A hand snaked out, grabbed her by the waist, and pulled her down onto the bed beside the prone figure.

Luckily it was Magnus's good side where she hit.

He lifted the sheet high, tucked her up under his arm, with her face resting on his chest, then covered them both. She was wearing a thigh-length nightshirt and nothing else. He was wearing a shoulder bandage and nothing else. All that cool bare skin touching cool bare skin was giving her warm ideas . . . ideas that were out of the question considering Magnus's condition.

"I thought you were still asleep," she said, snuggling closer. "I brought you some food."

"Later." He kissed the top of her head.

"You could have died, Magnus."

"Yea, I could have. But then, I could have tripped over a rake, hit myself in the head, and died on the spot, too . . . just like Hord the Hairy did. Do not make too much of this incident. Death is a part of life."

"Even so, when you are feeling better there are some things I need to tell you . . . things I would have been devastated to have never told you if you had . . . well, died."

"Secrets, eh?" He laughed softly, then winced when that movement apparently caused him some pain. "Actually, there are some things that I have neglected to say, too."

Her heart soared suddenly.

"It is about my children."

Her heart deflated just as suddenly.

"It occurred to me afterward, in the hospital, whilst the healer-witch was jabbing needles into me, that I had been negligent in regard to my children. I made no plans for their future, if something happened to me. Would you have taken on that responsibility?"

295

"Of course." That she responded in that way, without hesitation, was a marvel to her. Magnus wasn't her husband; they were not her children. But then the answer came to her. "They feel like family to me."

He nodded. "I thought as much, but it might be best if we call on a lawmaker one day to make legal provisions for such."

"Are you planning on dying soon? Is there something you're not telling me?" She was only half kidding.

"Nay! I am much better, except for this dull ache in my shoulder, but 'tis best to be prepared."

"You know, Magnus, this might not be the right time to mention this, but since you mentioned lawyers . . . well . . . I'm not sure how to say this. . . ."

"Just spit it out, sweetling."

"I've been led to believe that not all of your children are your blood children. Did you know that you can have DNA tests done that would prove beyond a doubt whether they are truly yours or not? And all it takes is a simple swab of saliva."

"Really? That is amazing. But what purpose would it serve me? They are my children, regardless of what any tests show."

"That makes sense. It's not like you're back in the tenth century and could return them to their mothers or other relatives."

He shook his head. "I would feel the same even then. Once I took those children under my shield, they became mine. No turning back. Ever."

Her heart swelled with pride that he felt that way. In an age when absentee fathers were often the norm, this man knew the meaning of fatherhood.

"Now, what did you want to tell me?"

She raised her head so that she could look at him. It took all the nerve she had, but the words had to be said. "I love you, Magnus."

He leaned up and kissed her lightly on the lips. "I know that, heartling."

"You know that?" she asked, softly at first, then added more shrilly, "You know that? And that is all you have to say?" Tears filled her eyes and she started to roll out of bed.

He tightened his arm around her shoulder and would not let her move.

"What? What is wrong now?"

"Surely you aren't so thickheaded that you don't understand what is expected of you when a woman says she loves you."

He thought a moment. "But I already told you that afore."

"*Once!* Once, you told me, and then it was in the middle of sex . . . or almost-sex . . . and that doesn't count."

"It does not?"

"Not by a long shot."

"Aaah, Angela, do you really need the words? I thought it was apparent in everything I do how much I love you."

She wanted to be angry with him, but she couldn't be, not with her pleasure at his heartfelt words.

"I think of you every moment of every day . . . when I am hoeing Grandma Rose's vegetable garden . . . when I am spraying the grapevines . . . when I am playing with my children . . . when I watch you eat, or drink, or walk, or sleep. You have become the most important person in the world to me."

"A woman needs the words, Magnus."

"I love you, Angela."

She put the back of her hand against her mouth to stifle a sob.

"Why are you crying? I hand you my heart and you cry. Truly, I will ne'er understand women."

"I'm crying because I'm happy. These are good tears."

"Uh-huh," he said dubiously. "If women need the words, then men need action. We want to be *shown* affection."

It took her several seconds to understand. "You can't make love. You're hurt."

"*That* part of me is not hurt. It is hurting, but only for want of you."

"Magnus, you are in no condition to make love to me."

"True. But I am in perfect condition to have love made to me . . . by a woman who purports to love me. Of course, she would have to be very gentle. Hmmm. Gentle love. I like the sound of that. You and I have engaged in almost-sex, bed games, hard loving, and everything in between. 'Tis time for some gentle love, do you not think?"

"Magnus, no."

The hand that was wrapped around her shoulder dropped lower, under her back, and the fingertips caressed the side of her breast. Even with the nightshirt, she felt his touch, and it was tempting.

"Magnus, no."

The hand slipped lower and began to bunch up more and more of her nightshirt, thus raising the hem inch by inch till not just her legs were exposed, but some other places besides.

Oh, Magnus. "No, Magnus."

"Come on, Angela," he coaxed. With his mouth he nudged her face up so that he could kiss her. Between his kisses he kept murmuring, "Please . . . please . . . please . . ."

Don't tempt me like this. I shouldn't. I really shouldn't. "I'm afraid I'll hurt you," she groaned out. He was nibbling at her ear now, when he wasn't inserting his tongue in it, then blowing softly.

"I'm afraid you'll hurt me if you don't. Take off that *shert* now, sweetling. You are making me hot."

"That's not why you're hot," she said with a laugh as she looked down between his legs. Still, she sat up and pulled the shirt over her head.

"I know." He put his hand on her nape and pulled her down so that he could kiss her in earnest now. She lay on her left side with her right hand cupping one side of his face. Her breasts rested against his chest, and his hand continued to press against the back of her neck, but that was the only way in which they touched. His other arm lay useless on the mattress . . . useless as far as their lovemaking, that is. When he moved that arm, his shoulder would hurt.

"I love you . . . I love you . . . I love you," he said against her mouth, in between kisses.

And she responded with, "I love you . . . I love you . . . I love you," as well before taking the aggressive role he seemed to want. Opening her mouth over his, she licked his lips and moved from side to side till he allowed her entrance. Then she used her tongue to taste and plunge, over and over, in the movements he usually employed to simulate the sex act.

He must have liked what she was doing because he groaned . . . then groaned again.

"On top," he grunted out. "Lie on top of me, Angela."

Oh, boy! It's a lot harder playing the lead than I thought it would be. She followed his directive and arranged herself carefully over him. She couldn't resist then. She moved her breasts from side to side over his chest hairs, thus proving that "playing the lead" had some advantages. That sensuous abrasion was enough to send ripples of pleasures coursing across her skin in wave after wave. *Yep, definite advantages.* She closed her eyes briefly, wanting to savor all the delicious sensations.

"More . . . do it more," he urged hoarsely.

"Whatever you want, sweetie. Whatever you want."

A laugh escaped through his gritted teeth. "Never say that to a man. You ne'er know what he might ask of you."

Well, she didn't know about that, but she was more than willing to comply with his simple request for more. She undulated against him so that now her breasts and her pubic area brushed his chest and stomach in rhythmic fashion. Between her thighs, behind her buttocks, she could feel his hardened penis . . . which seemed harder and longer now. A hot wetness pooled in her most secret places.

"Sit up," he urged now. When she did, he added, "Higher," and motioned her to shimmy her body farther so that her bottom rested on his belly. Then he told her exactly what he wanted. "Give me your breast,

Angela. You take it in your hand and put it in my mouth."

She hesitated. It was such an intimate thing to do.

"Do it, dearling."

She put an elbow on the pillow beside his head. Then she placed her other hand under her breast, lifting it high so that the nipple stood out turgid and proud. Lowering herself, she gave him her breast, which he immediately began suckling.

She whimpered at the intensity of excitement he generated there with his lips and tongue and teeth. His other hand played with her other breast, pinching it slightly into prominent pleasure-pain. She couldn't hold her body still, so aroused was she. Because she straddled his wide body, her legs were spread to their limits. Thus, rotating her hips in a circle, she managed to rub the slickness of her engorged folds and the protruding bud. *Is this masturbation or lovemaking?* She decided that it didn't matter if it pleased the man she loved, and there was no doubt in her mind that Magnus was pleased.

"Come closer," he choked out.

At first she thought she hadn't heard right. She glanced up and saw that his lips were slack with arousal and his eyes were glazed with passion. He waggled his fingers at her, indicating he wanted her up higher on his body.

She knew instinctively what he wanted, and, as much as she loved him, she was not sure she could do *that.* But then some inner voice nagged at her. *What greater love is there for a woman to give a man than her total trust . . . her total surrender?*

With a heated face, Angela placed herself so that

Magnus could pleasure her with the fingertips of one hand . . . and with his mouth . . . without even raising his shoulder. It was the most embarrassing . . . exhilarating thing she had ever done. And when she came in this way, she felt as if she'd given him a great gift . . . and herself, as well.

"You are so beautiful," he said, watching her face closely while she came to orgasm.

Angela felt beautiful. Tomorrow she would probably be mortified. Today she felt beautiful.

"Ride me now, sweetling," he said in a voice that was husky with emotion.

"Don't you want me to . . . uh, reciprocate?" she asked as she moved her hips lower again.

"Not now. Mayhap later. For now what I want is to be inside you."

Magnus was a big man, and he was big *there*, so it took a little doing to lower herself down over him. She need not have worried about how she looked, though, because Magnus had his eyes scrunched tight and he was panting heavily. She was pretty sure she had excited him to the point of mindlessness. She was pretty mindless herself.

"A little help here, Magnus," she said with a laugh.

Opening his eyes, he laughed, too, especially when he arched his hips up off the mattress, and her eyes almost bugged out. Then, with his one good hand and his other weakened arm, he showed her the way he wanted her to move.

Just before they exploded with mutual bliss, he whispered against her ear, "I love you, Angela, more than life itself. I do not know what tomorrow will bring, but for today, just know this. I love you."

Angela thought that was more than any woman could want.

Then Angela was unable to think at all.

Summertime, and the livin' is . . .

August in wine country was a little bit of heaven.

There was a lush greenness everywhere the eye could see. The air smelled of growing things . . . vegetables, flowers, grass—and, yes, grapes, most of all. The cycle of life so apparent in the land always drew strong emotions to the surface of even a big man like Magnus.

Grandma Rose reveled in this time of year, too, especially since dozens and dozens of her prized rosebushes were in bloom. She grew almost one hundred varieties, of all sizes and colors, which was amazing to Magnus . . . first, that anyone would spend so much time and money to cultivate a flower, which yielded only beauty; and second, that so many varieties existed. There were not enough cows in all of the Norselands to produce the amount of fertilizer that Grandma Rose used.

Now that Magnus's shoulder was almost healed, he worked daily in the vineyards, and it was a labor of love. The people in this new land—California—took for granted the good weather, which would have been considered a gift of the gods back in the cold Norselands. Good weather was critical to all growing, and thus far the grapes at the Blue Dragon were flourishing. If there was frost in the spring, the grapes would never reach maturity. If the sun got too hot, the vines would just shut down in self-preservation. Too much rain and the flavor of the grapes was diluted.

There was an element of gambling to a farmer's life, whether the product be wheat or grape. But now Magnus was nervous. Only a few short weeks till harvest, and anything could go wrong.

The vintners who would be buying the Blue Dragon's grapes this year stopped by almost on a daily basis, wanting to make sure the fruit was just right. The man who had come this morning had walked all the aisles with Magnus and Miguel, randomly checking for phylloxera, which had apparently hit a vineyard north of them. Phylloxera was a licelike parasite that killed the vines with its saliva while eating away at the roots. There was no cure, except for digging up all the stock. Luckily the Blue Dragon was safe . . . thus far.

Traveling workers, known as migrants, would be arriving in early September to help with the harvest. Angela had told him that they would hire at least a dozen for a three-week period to supplement the regular workforce.

Speaking of Angela . . . well, thinking of Angela . . . there she was now. He put down the clippers he had been using to thin the clusters of grapes and walked down the aisle toward her. She was looking especially lovely today in silky white *braies*, leather sandals, and a black tanking-top. But mayhap she was looking so good to him because he had not seen her for the past five days while she worked in the city.

She walked into his arms, gave him a long greeting kiss, then walked back toward the house with him, their arms linked. Dinner would be served in an hour or so.

"Did you stop to see Jogeir?" he asked.

"Yes, and he has improved so much, Magnus. It's hard to believe that the operation was done only a week ago. He'll need lots of physical therapy, and of course we won't know for sure how successful the operation was till the cast comes off . . . still, the doctors are amazed at his improvement so far."

" 'Tis a miracle," he concluded.

She laughed and laid her head against his shoulder. "Well, a miracle of medicine," she conceded.

"I visited him last night, and will go in again this evening. The healer told me that he might be able to come home tomorrow."

"I know, and he's so excited. Grandma fixed up a bed for him in the den so he won't have to go up and down the stairs with his crutches. He's already planning on lording it over his brothers that he will be having a TV in his bedroom."

As they approached the house, they saw Matt Delaney, the young man from You-See-Ell-Aye who had been tutoring Magnus's children these past two sennights. Right now he had Kolbein, Hamr, Njal, and Storvald, even Torolf, sitting at long tables, writing on parchment. Hamr and Njal looked up at him with pleading eyes and Hamr mouthed silently, *Torture!* while Njal mouthed, *Help!* Dagny and Kirsten had no doubt already finished their lessons for the day, being the more willing students.

"Hello, Mr. Ericsson," Matt said, standing to shake his hand.

"Greetings, Matt. How are they doing?"

Matt rolled his eyes. "Actually, they're doing very well, considering."

"Considering?"

"Kolbein would rather be watching *Sesame Street.*"

Kolbein glanced up at his father, but he did not appear too unhappy, in Magnus's opinion.

"Torolf would rather be working in the vineyard with you, but he has the motivation of knowing that if he enters high school in the fall, there will be dozens of pretty young girls to meet."

Torolf glowered at Matt, but it was probably the truth.

"Storvald is a pretty good student now that he understands how important measurements are to his woodworking skills."

Storvald did not even look up from the parchment, where he was drawing lines with a pencil and ruler.

"Now, Hamr and Njal, they are a different story," Matt said, and sighed deeply.

Magnus understood that sigh completely. Matt need not say any more.

"These two would rather be doing anything—I mean anything—rather than read or write."

"Or do numbers." Njal groaned.

"Methinks the worst thing is reading," Hamr said, "though I would like to learn what happens next to that Harry Potter fellow."

"I have an extra hour each day, Mr. Ericsson. You said you wouldn't mind some tutoring yourself," Matt pointed out.

Magnus's face grew warm and he shifted from foot to foot, even as his sons clapped and hooted with laughter. "A man is never too old to learn, but I must wait till after harvest. That is when I will commence."

"I'll be back in grad school then, but my girlfriend,

Marcy, is student-teaching nearby. Maybe she would be interested in tutoring you."

Magnus said, "That sounds fine."

Angela said, "I don't know about that."

Torolf said, "Hey! How come Father gets a female tutor? No offense, Matt, but you are not pretty at all."

Kolbein said, "I need a nap."

Hamr said, "If I get all the answers right on my numbers tomorrow, can I get a bow and arrow?"

Storvald said, "I am thinking of building a longship."

And Magnus escaped into the kitchen with Angela. The smells emanating from the stove and table were marvelous. Grandma Rose was making peach and strawberry preserves.

Angela went up and gave her grandmother a greeting kiss on the cheek. Apparently Angela had come to see him first on her arrival home after being away five days.

"Sweetie, I didn't know you were back. I'll be done here soon. Juanita is out in the garden picking some eggplant for dinner." Grandma Rose glanced at him then, making a quick *tsk*ing noise when she noticed him taking some cookies from the cookie jar. "You'll spoil your dinner."

"Never!" he replied with a laugh.

Grandma Rose laughed, too. "By the way, a Dr. Neville called you today. Said he'd see you at the hospital."

He nodded and started toward the stairs. "Do I have time to shower before dinner?"

"Plenty of time," Grandma Rose said.

Angela caught up with him in the hall. "Who's Dr.

Neville? I don't recall that name among Jogeir's physicians."

"He is a physician I met one day whilst you were gone. I am thinking about having a little snipping done myself. Would you like to take a shower with me, sweetling? I have missed you sorely . . . and I do mean sorely."

"No, I am not taking a shower with you in broad daylight with Grandma and all the kids about. What kind of snipping?" She had picked up a small piece of leather luggage at the bottom of the stairs and was carrying it up to her bedchamber, he presumed.

"A vasectomy."

Angela stopped dead in her tracks, dropped the luggage, and didn't even look backward as it toppled down the steps. "You? *You* are having a vasectomy?"

"I agree it is hard to fathom how a man like me would consider being cut *there*, but Harry assures me that it is painless and very effective. I have not made a final decision yet, though. What . . . what troubles you, Angela?"

She was staring at him as if he had stabbed her. "You were going to make such a monumental decision without consulting me."

He was about to advise her that she was not his mother or his wife . . . but luckily he curbed his tongue. She did have some rights. After all, she shared her body and her home with him. She was the woman he loved, who loved him in return. "Angela," he began more patiently, "I have bred eleven living children. 'Tis more than enough for any man. Truly, I cherish each of my children, but I would not want another."

"Not even one of mine?" Her voice broke on a sob.

"Oh, God! You are with child," he concluded, putting a hand out to clasp her on the shoulder. "I thought you said that you were taking birthing-control pills, but then, they do not work perfectly; that is what Juan told Torolf. Oh, God!"

She slapped his hand away and charged ahead of him the rest of the way up the stairway. When he followed her into her bedchamber, she informed him icily, "No, I am not pregnant. Lucky you!"

Whew! "Angela, what is this about?"

"I'll tell you what this is about," she said, but then she seemed unable to speak. When he started to approach her, she put up a halting hand. Finally she calmed herself and asked, "Having no father here, let me be the one to ask. What are your intentions toward me?"

"Huh?" *Uh-oh, I know where this conversation is headed.*

"Are you even remotely considering marriage?"

Remotely. "Of course, but there are many other things to be settled first."

"Like vasectomies?"

"Why do you keep harping on that operation? I will not have it done if you do not want me to. Really, 'tis not important."

Carmen was right. You are a dumb man. "Yes, it is important, Magnus."

A prickling of suspicion rippled through his thick brain, but he waited for Angela to say it herself.

"I want to have a baby myself. Just one. I want to experience childbirth. To breast-feed my own child. To have a child *with you.*"

Oh, nay! Nay, nay, nay, nay, nay! Ask me for gold.

Ask me for jewels. Ask me to swive you silly. Ask me to lay down my life for you. But do not ask me to have another child. He knew his inner thoughts would be hurtful to her, so he kept them to himself. But he could not think of any words that would soothe her spirits.

Apparently his silence was telling to her. Her shoulders slumped and tears misted her eyes.

"I would not mind marrying you, but no more children," he said as gently as he could.

"You would not mind . . ." she sputtered, then spun on her heel and rushed into her bathing chamber, where she locked the door after herself, but not before telling him to do something to himself that he was fairly certain was anatomically impossible . . . although Balki the Braggart had once claimed to do such. But then, Balki was the same person who claimed he could tie his man part in a knot and still engage in sexplay.

In any case, it was not the homecoming celebration he had envisioned.

Chapter Sixteen

Gimme a good dumb-man joke . . .

Angela couldn't sleep much that night, so she went down to the kitchen at five A.M. and plugged the coffeepot in. She had decided to return to the city for a few more days, to give Magnus breathing room and herself a chance to figure out where she wanted to go with this relationship. Besides, she had more than enough work piled up at the office, and her boss was beginning to gripe about her erratic hours.

Magnus had hurt her deeply with his comments last night. He was clueless in his dumb-man finesse—or lack of it—but if nothing else, he was honest to the bone. And what he had said to her was his heartfelt sentiment. He loved her, but he did not want any more children. Furthermore, he probably preferred not to marry again, after all his past bad experiences.

"Angela!" Magnus exclaimed, coming into the

311

kitchen in his work clothes—faded jeans and a T-shirt. She should not have been surprised to see him downstairs so early. He liked to start his day at sunrise. "What are you doing up?" Just then he noticed her luggage sitting near the door. "Oh, nay! You are not leaving again? Please let us talk about this."

She shook her head. "Not now. Give me a couple of days to get my emotions under control. When I'm able to think more clearly, we can talk."

"Do you want me to leave the Blue Dragon?"

"No!" she practically screamed. More softly she said, "No, I don't want you to leave here. Please stay. I'll be back."

He sat down dejectedly on the bench across from her. "I do not want to lose you."

"I'm only going to L.A. I'll be back by Saturday. Carmen invited all of us to the Cultural Awareness Festival at her college. It's a two-day event featuring all different cultures, their history, their arts and crafts, their foods, their music."

"In other words, boring. If Carmen is involved, it will be 'politically correct,' as well. That is the right term, is it not? Holy Thor, I can just see it. Vikings who use their swords to chop wood. Indians who eat no red meat. Saracen soldiers who recite poetry. Saxons who abhor fighting. Byzantine warriors who discover their feminine sides."

"I promised Carmen that we would come . . . or, at least, that I would, with some of the kids." She raised an eyebrow at him, clearly inquiring whether he would join them.

He groaned. "Carmen hates me."

"She does not hate you."

"Then why is she always telling those dumb-man jokes in front of me? 'Why is a man's sperm white and his piss yellow? So he can tell whether he's coming or going.' " He told the joke in a perfect imitation of Carmen's condescending voice.

Angela had to smile, despite the grimness of her mood. Carmen did like to jab at Magnus a bit, and he always rose to her bait ... which was her point, of course.

"Do not go, Angela," Magnus pleaded, reaching across the table to take her hand in his.

"To the cultural festival?"

He shook his head. "Do not go back to the city today. I am a lack-wit betimes. I say lack-wit things. Give me a chance to make it up to you."

"Magnus, you didn't say anything that you didn't mean. You might find a way to sugarcoat your words, but the facts remain the same. You want different things from life than I do."

"I want you."

"I know that." Angela rose from the table and walked toward the door. She had intended to wait till Grandma awakened before leaving, but her nerves were strained to the point of breaking. Much longer in Magnus's presence and she was going to commence bawling. That was something she didn't want her grandmother or Magnus to witness.

She was picking up her bag and opening the door when Magnus said, "But I love you."

Before she left, she turned slightly and told him, "There are a lot of things I'm unsure of right now, but there's one I'm certain about. Love is not enough."

Sandra Hill

Getting back in m'lady's good graces . . .

One week later, Magnus had grudgingly agreed to attend the half-brained culture festival at Carmen's college, but he was not happy about it. In the end, he'd had no choice. It was either tag along with Angela and the children, or stay home brooding.

He'd decided to tag along *and* brood.

Carmen started in on him right off. No sooner had they exited their cars and begun walking up the steps to the big brick building than she gave him an insulting once-over examination. Then she asked, "Do you know why dumb men get married?"

Stricken, he looked quickly at Angela. Had she been discussing their personal problems with her cousin? She shrugged her ignorance of what Carmen was talking about.

"Someone ought to tell Carmen that the smirk on her face is highly unattractive. I am thinking about introducing her to Harry, who would be just the man to put her in her proper place," Magnus told Angela in an undertone.

"Don't . . . you . . . dare," she replied.

"So they don't have to hold their stomachs in anymore," Carmen said, answering her own question.

Magnus exhaled with relief that Angela had not betrayed him by discussing their intimate lives. But then he immediately glanced down at his flat stomach. Was Carmen intimating that he was getting fat?

Carmen let loose a hoot of laughter that she had caught him once again.

He shook his head from side to side. "Carmen, you are a comely woman, though far too skinny, with way too many brains. 'Twould do you a world of good if you would dumb down—'tis an expression I heard on the tell-a-vision—which you are already doing, of course, by displaying those nipples of yours like arrowheads about to spear your next target." Well, that should shut the bothersome wench up for now.

Dagny, Kirsten, and Lily put hands over their mouths, trying to suppress their giggles. Torolf was laughing outright. The other boys were waiting with great delight for what would come next . . . no doubt hoping that Carmen would whomp him over the head with that arse-pack she wore around her waist.

Carmen was, indeed, speechless for a moment. She glanced down at her white tee-*shert,* which displayed the message, *I am woman. I am invincible. I am tired.* It should have had one more line: *And I have big nipples.* In truth, her nipples, without any undergarment, did stick out prominently. When she regained the power of speech, she said with great vehemence, "You are so crude. Why do you . . . why do men . . . keep fixating on physical appearance?"

"You started it. You are the one who mentioned my stomach."

She ignored his words and continued: "Women will never be equal to men till they can walk down the street with a bald head and a beer gut and still think they are hot stuff."

"There you go again, implying I have a big belly."

"Every conversation in the world is not about you . . . you farmer. Did you hear why the dumb farmer watered his garden with whiskey? So he could grow stewed tomatoes."

"Are you maligning farmers now?"

315

"No, honey, just dumb ones."

He said the only thing he could think of to say, and it was really dumb: "Nipples."

But apparently it was the right retort if he wanted to further anger the woman. Her face turned red as a . . . well, stewed tomato . . . and her painted fingernails were curving into claws.

He stepped away slightly, not taking any chances with those lethal weapons.

"Carmen . . . Magnus . . . let's call a truce here. It's going to be a long day if you two are scrapping from the get-go." It was Angela who was trying to be the peacemaker.

Magnus noticed then that all his children were watching the exchange between him and Carmen with great interest, except for Lida, who kept reciting her newest word over and over, "La-La, La-La, La-La . . ." It was short for Angela. He could tell that Angela was immensely pleased by Lida's affectionate chanting of her name, especially when she interspersed her babbling with wet kisses to her cheek. What was it about women throughout the ages that they went all soft and melty over kisses? He would like to plant a few on Angela and see if she went all soft and melty for him.

"I agree," Carmen conceded, "but I'll tell you one last thing, Angela. You are a wine maker, so you should recognize that men are like fine wines. They start out like grapes, but it takes a good woman to stomp them till they mature into something even remotely above the level of a slug."

"So you recommend a lot of stomping, eh?" Angela asked.

"You can stomp on me anytime you want, sweetling," Magnus told Angela. See, he could be peaceable, too.

"Oh, good Lord! You look at Angela as if she's a piece of candy. It must be true what they say. Some men drink from the fountain of knowledge, but most of them just gargle."

"Nipples, nipples, nipples," he said.

"Dumb, dumb, dumb," Carmen said.

Magnus made a low growling sound in his throat and had to tighten his hands into fists to keep from strangling the witch. Seeing how upset he was getting, Angela handed Lida over to him, probably figuring that with a baby in his arms, he wouldn't commit any violence.

"Dost think you have gotten the last word, Carmen? Well, mayhap so, but just let me end our discussion with this thought: If women knew what men were really thinking, they would ne'er stop slapping us. And my thoughts right now are extremely slappable with regard to you . . . and not in a lustsome way, either, even with your wanton display of nipples."

Carmen bared her teeth at him and no doubt would have indeed slapped him if Angela hadn't taken him by the upper arm and led him into the building.

"You have to learn to ignore Carmen," Angela told him.

"She does not bother me overmuch," he boasted, now that he had put his back to the irksome gnat.

He should have known that Carmen wouldn't let him go so easily.

"Hey, Magnus," Carmen called to his back. "Do you know why doctors slap babies' butts right after they're born?"

He faltered, but continued to walk.

"Don't turn around. Just keep walking," Angela told him. To Carmen, she merely said, "Tsk, tsk, tsk."

"To knock the penises off the smart ones."

"Can I please lop off her head?" he asked Angela. "Or leastways her tongue?"

"No!" Angela shook her head, laughing. He was not certain if she was laughing at Carmen's jest or at him. It mattered not. She was laughing. He would take her good moods any way they were handed to him these days.

So to Angela he said, "Whate'er you say, dearling."

And to Carmen, he said, "Whatever!"

The shock of a lifetime . . .

They were having a good time this afternoon—a *really* good time—and that surprised Angela. For some reason all her bitterness and anger toward Magnus had melted away—probably because she had missed him so much this past week—and replacing it was a real joy in just being in his company and that of his children.

This was no group of rank amateurs who had gathered here at the cultural fair. Oh, there were the usual Society of Creative Anachronism types, but even these knew their subjects well. Many of the exhibits were commercially sponsored by jewelers, soap makers, painters, and wood sculptors, but that in no way diminished the quality of the lore and exhibits.

Magnus purchased a beautiful Mexican turquoise pendant for Angela and turquoise beaded necklaces for Dagny, Kirsten, and Lily, and even a turquoise brooch in a sterling silver setting for Carmen, who accepted it grudgingly, not really wanting to be beholden to Magnus.

Hamr and Njal got Native American feathered headdresses, but were not entirely happy because their father refused to add hatchets to the ensembles. Lida was already wearing the soft leather moccasins Magnus had acquired from the same Indian tribe. He bought Torolf a handworked leather vest made by Eskimos. Storvald was practically ecstatic over the carved and painted Mallard duck created by some group purporting to represent American frontiersmen. Kolbein kept rubbing a softly woven Scottish plaid throw blanket against his face. Jogeir, who had stayed behind at Blue Dragon, still recuperating from his operation, would be delighted with the Chinese gazing ball that would be his gift.

Angela had made some purchases, too, including a Scottish plaid kilt for Magnus. When he'd asked her if that meant she would be letting him model it for her, she answered honestly, "I don't know."

Carmen came up to them just as they were about to go out the back door. She told them that there were dozens of exhibitors outdoors, especially those with large products, or those who had working craftsmen at their booths. Plus, the SCA was staging a number of events there, including a Highlander log-throw contest, a performance by Lippizaner stallions, kung fu demonstrations, and even a mock battle between the Saxons and the Vikings. Angela was excited to see how Magnus and his kids would react to these modern re-enactments of his people. The children ran off ahead of them, but she and Magnus were slowed down by

Lida, who was balking at the stroller and wanted to walk herself.

Just then Torolf came back and stammered out, "*Faðir.*" His face was white and his hands were shaking. "*Faðir,*" he repeated.

"What is it? What happened?"

Torolf, who appeared to be speechless, waved a hand in the air to indicate everyone was okay. "You will not believe this. I have found a most unusual display . . . shipbuilding . . . longship building."

Magnus shoved his son aside and looked ahead of him to where a very tall man wearing Viking attire stood staring at him, mouth agape with shock. He had an adze in one hand and a chisel in the other, which he proceeded to drop, just before shouting, "Magnus!"

And Magnus, in turn, shouted, "Rolf!" Then the two Viking men rushed toward each other and embraced warmly.

They both had long, blondish-brown hair and whiskey-colored eyes. The similarities were uncanny. It must be Magnus's long-lost brother, Geirolf.

It was the shock of a lifetime for all of them, but especially for Angela, who was already having trouble accepting the reality of time travel. Now she was faced with two time travelers meeting in the far distant future, by chance.

Or was it chance?

Lotsa catching up with two thousand-year-old men . . .

When they'd had time to recover from the initial shock, introductions were made all around. Magnus had his arm looped over his brother's shoulder, not about to let him get away again.

"You know all my children, Rolf. Torolf, Kirsten, Storvald, Dagny, Njal, Jogeir, Hamr, Kolbein." As each of them stepped up, Rolf shook their hands in the modern tradition, or hugged them warmly.

"And the little one?"

"Ah, that is Lida. She came to us after you left."

Rolf raised an eyebrow at that news, but luckily he did not make jest of his brother, as was his usual wont.

"Angela, come here, dearling; I would have you meet my little brother, Rolf, whom I have told you so much about."

"Li-little?" Rolf sputtered. Magnus was just slightly taller than Rolf, and a little bulkier, but Rolf was the youngest brother, so Magnus always delighted in giving him that appellation.

Rolf turned his attention to Angela then, and his eyes widened with appreciation.

"This is Angela Abruzzi. My . . . uh, friend."

He saw Angela flinch at his naming her his friend. What did she want him to say? Lover? He thought not.

"Angela and her grandmother have offered me and my family great hospitality these many weeks at the Blue Dragon, her family vineyard."

"You are living at a vineyard . . . here in California? But . . . but how did you get here? I mean, did you come from the Norselands direct to California?"

"Ha! I wish that were so. Nay, we came by way of Vinland and Hollywood."

"You have been in Hollywood? *You?* I cannot credit such a thing."

"Why? Think you that just because you are prettier

321

than me I would not be material for Hollywood? On the contrary. I have been invited to be an act-whore in a move-he, but I declined."

Rolf's mouth was slack-jawed with disbelief.

"But that is a story for another day. You will notice that Madrene and Ragnor are not with us. They stayed behind in Vestfold. Madrene wed recently. She and her husband run my farmstead. Ragnor is taking my place at Father's court."

Rolf nodded, but he was clearly confused.

"You know our parents died last year?"

Rolf nodded again, solemnly.

"Who are all these smiling people behind you?" Magnus asked.

"Bloody hell! How could I have forgotten?" He extended an arm, and a tall woman with auburn hair and beautiful green eyes stepped forward into his embrace. Both Rolf and this woman, along with the workers in his large tent, were wearing Viking attire. "This is my wife, Profess-whore Merry-Death Ericsson. She teaches at a college."

"A wife? You finally wed, eh? Didst have to travel across time to find a female who had not heard of your reputation?" he teased, and reached out to give Merry-Death a big hug.

"It is so good to meet you, Magnus. Rolf talks about you all the time. Is it true that you have . . . Well, we can save that for another time." She hugged him back in genuine welcome.

"And this boyling is my son, Foster," Rolf said with much pride, lifting high in the air a little boy of about five years. "And that little mite chasing after your Lida is our Rose. She is almost three years old."

Rose and Lida were indeed having a grand time running around in circles. Personally he thought his Lida, though younger, was the faster, but then she had her new, light moccasins on, which probably gave her an advantage, and Rose was wearing a long gown with an open-sided apron in the Norse style.

People were gathering about, watching with interest the reunion of the two brothers. Mayhap it was not such a good idea to garner that kind of attention. So he and Rolf walked to the back of his exhibit, where the rudimentary frame of a longship had been erected. Angela and Merry-Death followed them with Lida and Rose in hand. They were chatting softly.

"What are you doing here? Do you live in California?"

Rolf shook his head. "Nay, I live on the other side of the country . . . in Maine. I operate a Viking village called Rosestead, where the people do everything we did back in Vestfold . . . and in the old ways, too, which is ridiculous, really. I would much rather use a drill and electric sander, but people like to see me expend all that energy doing everything by hand." Rolf rolled his eyes at Magnus, a silent message that the old ways were not really so old to them. "We raise our own animals, weave our own cloth, make soap, design jewelry, even build longboats. Rosestead is open to tourists six months of the year. That is why I am here at this culture festival. Our appearance here brings us publicity, and therefore we attract more tourists."

"And you make money doing this?"

"Yea, we do. Mostly the village was financed in the beginning by my selling my armrings." He looked pointedly at Magnus's armrings and those on Torolf.

"Do you have any idea how much those things are worth here? More than seventy-five thousand dollars."

"Really?" Magnus said without much interest. "Dost know how much just one gold coin from our time is worth? Close to the same amount. These people are barmy here, if you ask me. They call my coins antiques."

Rolf narrowed his eyes at him. "Just how many of those gold coins do you have with you?"

Magnus just grinned.

His brother laughed. "You ever were the thrifty one, Magnus . . . always saving for bad weather."

"Whatever," Magnus replied, not about to rise to his brother's jibes.

Rolf laughed even more at his use of that modern word.

"We are quite a pair, are we not?" Magnus said, hugging his brother once again. "Two thousand-year-old men meeting by happenstance in a field a world away from home." But then he thought of something and pulled away in alarm. "Rolf, I cannot believe that I did not ask earlier, but what of Jorund? You know, he left after you and never returned."

"I know."

"You know?"

"Yea, Jorund is living in Texas with his wife, Maggie, his two adopted daughters, and his son, Eric. In fact, he would have been here this weekend, except that Maggie is big with child. I mean, really big. They expect twins."

Magnus knew how devastated Jorund had been when he'd lost his own twin daughters to famine several years back. It was good to know that he had gone on with life.

"Does Jorund run a Viking village in Tax-us, as you do in Maine?"

Rolf shook his head, and his eyes twinkled merrily. "Nay, he teaches demented people how to lose fat and gain muscle."

That was the most incredulous thing Magnus had heard all day. Jorund was—or had been—a warrior of great word-fame. And now he worked with demented people?

He and Rolf glanced at each other and shared a smile.

"You and I and our families will go to Texas and surprise Jorund with your presence here in this land," Rolf suggested. "He will be so pleased."

"Magnus," Angela said, coming up to his side. "Would you like to invite your brother and his family to stay with us at the Blue Dragon tonight? They plan to exhibit here again tomorrow. It would give you a chance to catch up some more. I can call ahead to Grandma. You know she would love the company."

"Yea, that is a good idea, sweetling." He looked toward Rolf, who nodded his agreement. Then he kissed Angela on the top of the head and said, "Thank you," before she walked off to make her call.

When he turned back, Rolf was watching him with clear amusement. "And who exactly is Angela?"

"The reason for my being here," he answered truthfully. And that was all he could say for now.

Leaving on a jet plane . . .

Angela was at the airport, seeing Magnus and his family off with Rolf and his family. They were all going to

San Antonio, where they planned to surprise the third brother, Jorund, and his wife, who was about to give birth to twins.

"I still don't see why you won't come with us," Magnus said to her.

"This is your family," she told him for about the twentieth time since yesterday, when he'd been reunited with Rolf.

"You are my family, too," he insisted.

She shook her head. "No, I'm not, but please let's not rehash that conversation now, Magnus. I want you to go and have a good time." She couldn't explain to Magnus how hard it would be for her to be there with his family and not be able to explain how she fit in . . . or didn't fit in. She was too old-fashioned to settle for "lover." Furthermore, with her yearnings for her own child and Magnus's firm refusal to have another, Angela was afraid she would burst out weeping if Jorund's wife Maggie gave birth while they were there. She had so many emotions she was holding inside.

"You will be here when I come back?" Magnus asked.

"Of course." *Maybe.*

"I will return in one week . . . plenty of time before harvest," he assured her, but she wondered if he wasn't trying to reassure himself, as well.

"Don't worry about the vineyards, or the harvest. Everything is under control, now that Gunther is behind bars." Besides, they had gotten along without him before. They would do so again. It would be a lot harder, of course, but they would survive. They would have to, because they could no longer depend on Magnus now that he had other alternatives provided by his family. Would he move to Maine—or Texas—or would he choose to stay here in California? Angela honestly did not know, and that was scary in itself.

"I feel this big empty space growing betwixt us. I do not want to leave if things will be different when I come back."

"Things will be the same." *Things will never be the same. Never.* She shoved him forward to the boarding line. She'd already said her good-byes to everyone else, including a tearful hug from Lida, who kept saying, "Bye-bye La-La, bye-bye La-La."

Magnus gave her a final kiss, and she hugged him hard . . . harder than she probably should have. But this might be the last time. No, she couldn't think like that. She had to hold herself together till Magnus was on the plane. Just a little bit longer.

"I love you, Angela."

"I love you, too, Magnus. Always."

She could see that Magnus was torn. Excitement over his first plane ride and seeing his other brother conflicted with his unease over leaving her. The least she could do for him was to pretend she was happy he was going. She waved her hand gaily and threw him a kiss just before he went into the corridor leading to the aircraft. A short time later, she watched as his plane took off.

Like a zombie Angela walked through the airport, willing herself to be brave. It was only when she was in her car in the parking lot that she broke down. Loud sobs and huge tears. She cried for the wonderful weeks she had shared with Magnus, and she cried for the future she could no longer conceive of having with him.

He didn't know it yet, but things had changed. She had not lied to him the previous week, but now she knew better.

She was pregnant.

Chapter Seventeen

Loneliest guy in the crowd . . .

It was utter chaos at Jorund's home in San Antonio, Tax-us, with six adults, one semiadult—that being Torolf—and thirteen children, all under one roof.

There were people everywhere . . . not just his huge family, but Rolf's and Jorund's, as well. Plus, demented people that Jorund taught at his exercising business showed up at the oddest times, including a woman who thought she was a chicken—not just any chicken, but a Kentucky Fried chicken—and a three-hundred-pound fellow with glittering garb who claimed to be a long-dead singer named Elvis. Since Elvis was a Norse name, meaning *sage,* he tried not to be too harsh with him, but try getting back to sleep in the middle of the night on the living room sofa after hearing someone screech in your ear, "You Ain't Nothin' But a Hound Dog."

Then there was the fact that Jorund's wife, Maggie, had gone into labor the night they arrived . . . probably from the shock of their unexpected appearance. She'd given birth ten hours later to twin boys, Magnus and Mikkel, whom they'd given the nicking names of Mack and Mike, which was utterly ridiculous, though he was honored, of course.

It had been great fun to surprise the spit out of Jorund, and it was even more fun reminiscing with his brothers all this week, but in the midst of it all Magnus was miserable. He missed Angela desperately, and he missed the vineyard, and he missed the hard work it entailed. It might not be farming, but he had come to enjoy toiling in the vineyards. He even missed the grapes. Mostly he missed Angela. But every time he called, he felt Angela slipping farther and farther away. Even worse, she hadn't come to the phone at all yesterday or today. Grandma Rose had not answered directly when he asked where she was.

He suspected that Angela was avoiding him, and he did not know why. Well, that wasn't entirely true. He knew why. They hadn't really resolved their problems since the night he'd told her that he did not want to have any more children, even with her. That had been two long weeks ago. An aeon.

It was past midnight, and all the children were abed, including the new babes. He was sitting on a lounging chair near the pool in Jorund's backyard, knowing he would be unable to sleep once again, especially if Elvis showed up. If he did, mayhap he would have the odd fellow teach him how to play his guitar. Besides that, Elvis had taken to making them fried peanut-butter-and-banana sandwiches, which he was developing a taste for.

Just then his two brothers walked up and sat down in the chairs next to him. They both had bottles of beer in their hands and they handed a spare one to him. *Uh-oh. I sense a gang-up here.*

"What is the problem, Magnus?" Rolf asked.

"Everyone can see how unhappy you are," Jorund added.

"Of course I am unhappy. I have the world's worst headache from being confined indoors during the past two days of rain with my nine children—not to mention your children—and crying newborn babes."

"You adore those children of yours," Rolf charged.

"*Adore* is too strong a word. Did you hear that Lida said a whole string of words today? She said, 'I lub you, Fa-Fa.' And she was talking to me."

"We heard, we heard," Jorund said with a smile. "About a hundred times now you have told us."

"What are you two doing here at this time of night, bedeviling me? You should be in your beds a-slumber, or keeping your wives happy. Need you some advice on how to do that? The latter, I mean."

His brothers just grinned at him.

"Methinks I should go home on the morrow," he said of a sudden. And for some reason, having said it, he felt a world of heaviness lift from his shoulders.

"And where is home, Magnus?" asked Jorund, who always was the more serious one. "Back to Vestfold?"

"Nay, back to California, and the Blue Dragon."

"And Angela?" Rolf offered.

That was the crux of the matter. Wherever Angela was would be home to him, he realized in an instant.

He was a thickheaded lack-wit not to have realized that before. Nodding slowly in response to Rolf's question, he asked, "Dost really think we have a choice . . . to stay or go back?" He and his brothers had discussed this issue over and over the past few days. They were convinced that there was a choice, and once they had made theirs, there was no going back.

"I repeat my first question: What is the problem, Magnus?" Rolf persisted.

"I do not know if I can have a future here."

"Why the bloody hell not? Do you love her?" Jorund was ever the one to get at the heart of a matter.

"Yes," he said without hesitation.

"Do you want to stay here in the future?" Rolf was crossing his eyes at him as if he were being deliberately stubborn in not seeing the answer.

"I think so. Yes. Yes, I do. I worry betimes about Ragnor and Madrene, and I would miss them sorely, even that shrewish Madrene, but they are well able to take care of themselves."

"Then what is the freakin' problem?" Rolf pretended to tear at his own hair.

"The free-can problem, my brother, is that I have nine children here in Ah-mare-ee-ca . . . tagging along behind me, attached to my sides like burrs, hanging around my neck. Then two more back in the Norselands. I do not want any more children."

"Aaah," said Jorund. "And Angela does."

He nodded. "Yea, she does. Leastways, one. But knowing her, it would not stop there. My seed is virile, and she is voracious. I told her I would be willing to wed with her, but no more children. She told me to do something obscene to myself." He threw his hands in the air in a hopeless gesture. "That is the problem."

Jorund looked at Rolf, and Rolf looked at Jorund, and they both burst out laughing.

"Vor . . . voracious . . . the man has a voracious female, and he is complaining. Oh, holy Thor, that is the most mirthful thing I have heard in ages." 'Twas Jorund speaking. The half-brain!

"Willing . . . you told her you were *willing* . . . oh, I wish I had been there. Merry-Death would have slapped me witless for such a remark." Rolf was still laughing. "And exactly what obscene thing did she tell you to do?" Rolf was even more of a half-brain.

When Jorund had stopped laughing and wiped tears of humor from his eyes, he turned more serious. "Magnus, you always were one to make a mountain out of a molehill. Is Angela willing to act the mother to your existing children?"

He shrugged. "She already does."

"Then is one more child really such a big favor for you to give her?" Jorund's voice was gentle with compassion.

"People will make jest of me . . . even more than they do now. Her cousin Carmen—you met her, Rolf . . . the profess-whore—already makes dumb-man jokes about me."

"Since when does laughter hurt a big man like you?" Rolf scoffed.

"Well, the dumb-man jokes do not bother me as much as I pretend. In fact, I get great satisfaction in throwing back nipple jests at Carmen, so we are even . . . usually."

Jorund and Rolf stared at him, openmouthed. No

doubt they were impressed with his great finesse in handling bothersome females.

"Actually, I have been thinking about this baby problem, and the more I think on it . . ."

"Yea?" his two brothers prodded.

"I really want to have a baby with Angela."

His brothers let out a whoosh of relief, as if they'd already known he would come to that conclusion.

"But just one," he quickly added.

"It is a gladsome thing that the three of us have been rejoined in this new land," Jorund said then.

"Yea, 'tis." Rolf nodded, deep in thought. "At one time, after deciding to stay here in the new world, I was convinced that I would be the last Viking in history, but now it appears there will be three last Vikings."

"And many more to come," Jorund added with a twinkle in his eyes. Jorund never used to twinkle. Must be Maggie who'd taught him to do that.

Magnus cared not about any of that other business, though, whether he was first or last Viking . . . or whether there were others to come. All he knew was, *I am going home.*

Home is where the heart is . . . he hoped. . . .

Angela was in the vineyard with Miguel, checking the various varieties of grapes for ripeness. A wonderfully satisfying experience it was, too, knowing that all the hard work of many months was about to bear fruit. And soon it would all be over, and the cycle would start again.

She knew from years of doing the same task with

her grandfather how to tell from touch, taste, smell, and texture how many more weeks it would be till harvest. It was her and Miguel's opinion that it would be another week at least. He would begin hiring migrant workers this afternoon.

Angela needed something to do with her hands and body to dispel her out-of-control nervousness. Magnus and the children were coming back today. He had left a message on the answering machine, telling her when their flight would arrive and asking that she pick them up. Angela had sent Juan and Grandma in her place with two vehicles, unable to bear the thought of being reunited with Magnus in a public place.

"Look! They're back," Miguel said with excitement, pointing down the hill to the house and driveway, where the cars were just pulling up.

Her heart began racing wildly. Stuffing her hands into the pockets of her denim coveralls, she began to walk slowly down the vineyard aisle.

"I must go tell Juanita," Miguel said, rushing ahead of her toward the back door leading to the kitchen. "She will want to have food and drinks ready."

Angela smiled, despite her somber mood. She understood Miguel's enthusiasm. Everyone had missed Magnus and all the children. The Blue Dragon had seemed quiet without them.

But it was a quiet they might have to become accustomed to if things went as Angela expected they would.

She saw Magnus hand Lida over to Juanita, who was already out in front of the house, welcoming everyone. She also saw him hold out his arms, halting his other children and pointing toward the house, as if ordering them inside. *Uh-oh.* She knew what this was about. He wanted to talk to her alone first.

That suspicion proved correct when Magnus began to stomp angrily around the side of the house and up toward the vineyards. She met him halfway.

Magnus was so angry at Angela he could scarcely breathe, and he was so happy to see her he could scarcely breathe.

She looked beautiful to him today, with her black hair drawn high on the back of her head in what modern people referred to as a ponytail. Her sun-bronzed face was clear of its usual paint and rouge. The mole he adored above her mouth stood out.

Is she happy to see me? Why does she look so serious? "Well, wench, you did not come to greet me at the airport," he accused right off. *That was certainly a smart greeting to make. Why not alienate her from the beginning?* The whole time his eyes were practically devouring her. She seemed to be doing the same, or mayhap she was examining him with disdain. He was so blind with worry he probably could not tell the difference between lust and loathing.

"I couldn't."

"Why not?" *Oh, please, just talk to me, Angela. I am dying inside.*

"I'm too emotional right now. I was afraid of how I might react."

Too emotional? That sounds good. Does it not? "I was very angry. It seemed an insult to me."

"Are you still angry?"

"Yea . . . and nay."

She raised her eyebrows in question. "Yea, I am angry, but it matters not because I am so very happy to see you again. I have missed you sorely."

Her eyes misted over and she blinked to hold back the tears.

"Do not dare cry afore I have done and said everything I have come to say. 'Tis hard enough for me to bare my soul without your heartrending tears."

She blinked some more.

"Angela, take your hands out of your pockets," he ordered with a loud sigh.

"Why?"

"Because I intend to kiss you mindless, and you will need something to hold on to. Hopefully, me."

Before she could blink again, or say him nay, he lifted her high in his arms and kissed her hard, then softly, then hungrily, then softly persuading, then hungrily again. She moaned under his lips, but he would not end the kiss for fear she would say something to break off their relationship. His hands roamed her buttocks and back and shoulders; he wanted to touch every inch of her, to make her his by physical force if necessary.

Through the haze of his emotion, he finally realized that Angela was indeed holding on to him, one arm wrapped around his shoulders, the other hand caressing his face.

When she pulled away, ending the kiss, she stared back at him in wonder. "You have tears in your eyes. Oh, my God! You have tears in your eyes. Why?"

"Because I am afraid of losing you."

A soft sob escaped her lips.

He acted quickly, before she could say anything more, and carried her down the rest of the aisle, then set her on a bench. Going down on one knee, he took both her hands in his, as he had been told by both Rolf and Jorund was the tradition in this land. "Angela Abruzzi, will you consent to be my wife?"

"You said . . . you said you wouldn't mind getting married, Magnus. I don't want a husband under those conditions."

"I am a half-brain. What can I say? Words do not flow from my lips with the smoothness of a polished swain."

She smiled slightly, which he took for a good sign. "I never wanted a polished swain."

Yea, a good sign. "All I know is that I want to spend the rest of my life with you by my side. I love you, Angela. You already know that, and if marriage is what will keep you with me, then that is what I want . . . with all my heart."

She squeezed his hands, which still held hers. "But that's not all."

Here it comes. The crux of their problem. Please, God . . . or gods . . . let me say this right. "Angela, 'tis true I have far too many children. You have to admit that. But whilst I have been away, I realized something important. There is naught in this world that would give me more pleasure than to have a child with you. I would cherish it, and you. I would even put up with Carmen's dumb-man jokes, which would surely increase on that blessed event. If you would be mother to my children, then surely the least I can do is be father to your—*our*—child."

"Yes." Tears were streaming down her face now.

"Yes what?" *Oh, God, if you are going to be on my side, now would be a good time.*

"Yes, I will marry you. Yes, I love you. Yes to everything."

"Thanks be! Can I get up now? My aging knee is about to crack." *I knew I could count on You. Thank You, nonetheless.*

She laughed gaily through her tears as he picked her up once again and twirled her around in his arms. As he hugged and kissed her, it was unclear whether the wetness on their faces was her tears, or his.

"Did she say yes?" Torolf wanted to know. He was rushing up from the house with the whole troop following behind, including Grandma Rose, who had her rosary beads in hand, Juanita, who was drying her eyes on her apron, Miguel, who was drying his eyes on a linen pocket cloth, and Lida, who was waddling up at a fast pace, arms outstretched, saying, "La-La, La-La!" As Angela picked up his little girl, Hamr said, "I know just what to get you for a bride gift."

Everyone answered for him: "A bow and arrow."

Kirsten asked, "Can we have a big wedding feast? Please, please?"

"I want to wear flowers in my hair," Dagny said.

"Well, I am not wearing a suit, and that is that," Njal declared.

"Perchance I could carve a statue of the bride and groom for the nuptial cake," Storvald offered.

"Well, you had all best wait a few weeks for this event so that I can dance at the wedding," said Jogeir, who was still on crutches.

Kolbein, ever the soft-spoken one, piped in finally, "I could be the ring bearer."

"Wouldst you have me for your best man, Father?"

Torolf inquired hopefully. "That is what they call the main witness in this new world."

"Please, sweetie, tell me that you will have the wedding soon after harvest . . . while my roses are still in bloom," Grandma Rose said.

"Ay-yi-yi! The preparations we will have to make. The priest, the food, the wines, the music." Juanita was speaking to Grandma Rose, and they were both smiling at each other, clearly jubilant at all the work facing them.

As everyone gathered around to congratulate them then, all of them speaking at once, Magnus put his arm around Angela's shoulder and hugged her closer to him. An immense warmth came over him then, a feeling of rightness that he had found his place in the new world.

"You know, heartling, Rolf told me that he once considered himself the last Viking, and he took much pleasure and pain in that prospect. But I find there is only one thing I want to be."

"And that is?" she asked, reaching up to kiss him lightly on the lips.

"I only want to be your Viking . . . Angela's Viking."

Epilogue

Vikings sure know how to party. . . .

Magnus Ericsson and Angela Abruzzi were married on the lawn of the Blue Dragon on September 27, 2003. Father Sylvester officiated at the Christian rituals, but it is said that the Norse gods smiled down on them that day, too.

She wore her grandmother's Italian lace wedding gown, and white roses in her hair. Magnus wore a black tux with a snow-white shirt. All of Magnus's sons wore tuxes, too, and, boy, were they fuming! Kirsten, Dagny, and Lida were pretty in pink—organza gowns, with matching pink baby roses in their hair, just like Angela's.

Rolf and Jorund had tried to convince Magnus to have a traditional Viking wedding, complete with Norse attire and foods and rituals, but Magnus had balked at that. He said he was a modern Viking, and he was putting aside the old ways. Rolf had tried to tempt him by offering to bring several well-fattened acorn hogs from Rosestead for the feast, but Magnus had declined the offer. Thus it was that Magnus allowed his children to select the menu; to no one's surprise, they settled on dome-nose pizzas and chocolate layer cake. Scattered about the heavy boards were tubfuls of feast ale and Kool-Aid, not to mention the Blue Dragon's own fine wines.

The band played Britain Spear and Arrow-smith music, among other tunes. Everyone danced, even Magnus, who claimed to be too big and clumsy, but turned out to be smooth and sexy in his moves. His children were, of course, mortified.

Lida and Kolbein were the flower girl and boy, respectively. Torolf, Rolf, and Jorund stood up for Magnus . . . though they professed to be standing him up, so shaky were his knees. All three argued over who was to be the "best man," and finally settled on the three being the "best men."

Carmen made only one dumb-man joke: "Why do only ten percent of men make it to heaven?"

Magnus had declined to be baited this day, and prided himself on his silence.

So, when she answered her own jest by saying, "If they all went to heaven, it would be hell. Ha, ha, ha," Magnus just smiled at her and mouthed the word, *Nipples.*

Carmen gave them a huge box of condoms for a wedding gift.

Magnus repaid the favor by introducing Carmen to Harry Winslow, who took one gander at her big nipples and professed to be in love. Carmen, who'd recently separated from her husband, surprised everyone by blushing.

When the wedding feast was well under way, Angela took Magnus by the hand, leading him toward the old wine-making shed. "I have a groom gift for you," she said with a decided gleam in her eyes.

To Magnus's immense surprise, what he heard when he opened the door was this greeting: "Moo!"

He peeked inside, then peeked again. "You bought me a cow for a wedding gift?"

"Yes, yes, yes!" she said, practically jumping up and down with excitement. "Do you like it?"

"I love it," he said, hugging her warmly. " 'Tis the best wedding gift I have ever received."

"Well, I have another one," she said nervously.

He cocked his head in question.

She put his hand over her stomach. "I'm . . . I'm going to have a baby."

"But the birthing pills?"

"They don't always work, Magnus. Please don't think that I lied to you about being pregnant when you asked that one time. I was wrong."

"Well, I was wrong about the cow."

"Huh?"

"This baby is the best wedding gift I have ever received. Oh, sweetling, do not look at me like that. Didst doubt I would be anything but happy about a child of your womb . . . even when I was being blind and bullheaded?"

They hugged some more; then Magnus announced, "I forgot. I have a wedding gift for you, too." Taking her hand, he ran toward the house with her, forcing her to lift the hem of her gown high off the ground to

343

keep up with him. When they got inside the house, he started to lead her up the stairs.

"Not *that* surprise," she said. "Not with all these people here."

He laughed and chucked her under the chin. "Even I would not be so crude." Lifting her in his arms, he carried her all the way to the third floor, where his bedchamber was located. On a low table sat a sloppily wrapped package in floral paper.

Tentatively she opened the package. Inside were six empty bottles of wine, each with the Blue Dragon label. Pinot noir. Chardonnay. Cabernet sauvignon. Sauvignon blanc. Zinfandel. Sangiovese. But the most amazing thing to Angela was the date on each of the labels: 2004. That was next year.

"Magnus?"

"My gift to you is that we will be resuming wine making at Blue Dragon."

"But that's impossible. Oh, I thank you for the kindness of your gesture, but it would take a monumental amount of money to start up again."

"Well, that is my second surprise, sweetling." He opened the door to the closet, where there were four antique chests stacked one atop the other. He opened one and out spilled dozens and dozens of old gold coins. Likewise the second chest. And the third. The fourth one was different. It had precious gold and silver jewelry . . . chains, armrings, necklets, brooches . . . many set with amber, amethyst, or chrysalite stones, and a few with rubies and emeralds.

"You've had all of this and kept it a secret from me?"

"Well, not precisely a secret."

She put her hands on her hips and tapped her foot.

"Not a secret. A surprise."

"This is worth a fortune!"

"Yea, 'tis. More than enough to open the winery again, I figure."

"Oh, Magnus. Thank you so much."

"Save your thanks, wench, for I have a third surprise for you."

"You are full of surprises, aren't you?"

He nodded. "I lied on the stairway when I said I was not so crude a man." He made this confession with total lack of contrition. "In truth, I am very crude. 'Tis one of my better traits. In fact," he said, and picked her up, tossed her on the bed, flipped her gown up to her waist, and crawled up over her, "I have saved the best gift for last. 'Tis something I want to show you."

"And that would be?" Luckily, she was laughing.

"The famous Viking S-spot."

Author's Note

Dear Reader:

I never intended to write a story for Magnus Ericsson, the third brother from *The Last Viking* and *Truly,
Madly Viking*. Why else would I have created a man
who was crude, a farmer, and the father of thirteen
children? Definitely not hero material! More like a humorous secondary character destined to stay just that.

But then one day, the title *The Very Virile Viking*,
came to me, and I realized that there was only one
man who deserved such a description. Virile, indeed!
But how to redeem a man who had had all those
wives, mistresses, and "passing fancies"—that was the
question.

It is my intention that this will be the last book in
this particular series. However, you must note that I
left Magnus's son, Ragnor, behind in the Norselands,
and I have portrayed him as quite a roguish fellow,

even at sixteen. Do you think that was my subsconscious's way of leaving a door open?

I hope you will let me know what you think of Magnus. I personally think he developed into quite a guy.

Your thoughts on my books, your support, and your loyalty are always appreciated. And I'm always willing to listen to what you would like to see next on my creative palette. Another Viking? If so, should it be the twins, Toste and Vagn? Or young Jamie, the Highland Viking? Or one of Tyra's many sisters? Or Alrek, the clumsy boy from *My Fair Viking*?

But perhaps it shouldn't be a Viking at all. Instead, maybe another contemporary Cajun story, in the vein of *The Love Potion*? Better yet, another Baptiste from the historical Louisiana bayous might not be a bad idea (think *Frankly, My Dear* and *Sweeter Savage Love*). Isn't it wonderful that there are so many choices?

I love to hear from you readers—that your husband or significant other now calls you *heartling* or *sweetling*, that you stayed up all night reading one of my books, that you laughed out loud at times and shed a tear at others. This is why I write.

Sandra Hill
P.O. Box 604
State College, PA 16804
e-mail: shill733@aol.com
Web site: www.sandrahill.net

Turn the page to read an excerpt from
KATIE MACALISTER'S newest historical romance:

Noble
Destiny

We join Lady Charlotte Collins in the midst of her
exciting adventure. A poor widow, she has returned
to London eager to take her place in the *ton*, only
to find herself shunned by all. The answer to her
problems clearly lies in marriage, and she knows
the perfect man to be her husband. Now, she just
has to convince the gorgeous Scotsman
to be her groom. . . .

AVAILABLE MAY 2003!

Four nights later the moon was rising full, shedding its cold, mercurial light down upon the city of London, setting a ghostly glow upon the lamplighters who clambered up and down their short ladders as they lit the new gas lamps along the Pall Mall, casting the paving stones into variegated pools of black and silver through which carriages and horses plodded heedlessly as they went about their way, washing pale the portly figure of a man dressed in early Elizabethan garb as he climbed over the solid stone-and-wrought-iron fence surrounding the garden belonging to Lady Jersey. The moon, had she been able to express an opinion about what she saw from on high, would have no doubt commented that the portly man in costume was by his very actions suspicious. Rather than entering the garden through the gate, as most people chose, the gentleman straddled the fence, vaulting down to the soft flower beds below with a distinctly heard, "Damnation! I'll get Caro for this!"

When, rather than strolling the graveled pathways as was the normal means of locomotion in a garden, the gentleman skulked about the shrubberies, racing from one clump to another, dodging behind topiaries shaped as fantastic beasts, finally emerging close to the stone steps leading up to the veranda at the rear of the house, surely any watcher would be well within his right to express surprise.

Truly, the gentleman was acting in a peculiar manner. From where he crouched next to the steps, he suddenly stood, fluffed up his ruff, tugged his doublet down over a pronounced belly, pulled a handkerchief out of his codpiece, and brushed the dirt from his dainty white hands, and finally, after a quick look around to make sure no one was looking, hiked up his Persian silk stockings. What anyone would have been driven to say when this same portly man was arrested in midstep by the sight of a dark-haired young woman bursting from the house and hurtling down the stairs was lost, but certainly the conversation that followed, hushed and whispered though it was, in all likelihood was not what would have been expected.

"Caro," the gentleman whispered urgently as the young woman dashed by him. Lady Caroline stiffened at the repeated hiss of her name, turning slowly to give the beruffed figure a cold and cutting glare.

"Sir, I do not have the honor of your acquaintance."

"You most certainly do. You piddled in my sand pit when you were only three. I remember quite distinctly how Matthew laughed when Nurse blamed me for the implement."

The silent, still figure of Lady Caroline, dressed charmingly in the wide panniers, rose silk, and silvered lace of her mother's era, came to life again under the influence of that familiar, if annoyed, voice. "Incident not *implement*. Char? Is that you?"

The portly man moved from the shadow of the balustrade onto the middle of the steps. "Yes, it's me; just where the devil have you been? I waited at that gate for an eternity! You were supposed to unlock it at half of midnight, Caro! It's well after midnight now!"

"I'm terribly sorry, but dearest Algernon insisted on having a waltz with me. Charlotte"—Caroline squinted to make out her friend's face in the shadow—"I thought your costume was to be of good Queen Bess? You appear to be dressed as a man."

"Yes, yes, I changed my mind. I thought I would be less conspicuous if I were dressed as Henry the Eighth." She twanged the leather protrusion curving gracefully from her groin. "No one who knows me would ever expect to see me in a codpiece."

"No, indeed," agreed Caroline with alacrity. "Say what you will about your propensity for shocking the *ton*, codpieces are simply not part of your everyday apparel."

"And yet, in fairness," Charlotte admitted, "I must say it's very handy. Because I was so late waiting for Mme Beauloir to deliver my costume, I did not have time to dine at home. Tremayne Three was kind enough to give me one of the horses' apples, which fit quite snugly in the codpiece. It's of no wonder to me that men wore them for so many years—they're much handier than a reticule!"

The two women considered that piece of male apparel in silence for a moment.

"Why do you suppose they call it a codpiece?" Caroline asked. "It doesn't look anything like a fish. Yours looks like . . . well, rather like an overly ambitious squash."

"It was the finest codpiece Mme Beauloir had," Charlotte answered with dignity, stroking the smooth leather-and-brass object that, she had to admit, did somewhat resemble a squash. She was about to defend her codpiece's honor further, but the noise and light spilling out as a veranda door was opened returned their attention to the circumstance at hand.

"Take my arm," Charlotte demanded, "and pretend I'm a gentleman."

"You don't walk like a gentleman," Caroline objected.

Charlotte stopped at the top of the steps and pulled Caroline to the side, where an urn erupted in a screen of greenery, providing a modicum of privacy. "What are you talking about?"

"No one will believe you're a man if you walk like a woman. Surely you must realize that. It's just common sense. Men don't sway their hips when they walk."

"Some do," Charlotte pointed out, squirming slightly as she adjusted her codpiece. "Drat the thing; it's tickling."

"True, but those aren't gentlemen we are supposed to know. What are you doing now? Char, you can't do that in public; someone will see you!" Scandalized, Caroline hurried to stand between her friend and the nearest group of people enjoying the cool night air.

"I can't help it," Charlotte muttered, her chin

jammed against the starched linen of the ruff. "This codpiece is most uncomfortable. It's . . . moving."

"*WHAT?*"

"Shhh," Charlotte hissed, glancing around quickly before returning her attention to her nether regions. "It's as if there were something in there. Something other than my handkerchief, that is."

"Moving?" Caroline asked through her teeth, smiling a bit wildly at a couple dressed in red dominoes as they strolled past. "What do you mean, moving? What could be in there that could move?"

"I don't know." Charlotte grunted, trying without success to unattach the buckles holding the polished leather piece onto her costume. "But I suspect something claimed occupancy while I was hiding in the bushes outside the gate waiting for you to let me in. Thus, it's quite clearly all your fault that my codpiece is now rife with wildlife."

"Don't be ridiculous; what could climb into a codpiece? There's no room in there for anything but an apple!"

"Caroline," Charlotte snapped, turning abruptly so the codpiece whapped her friend smartly on the hip. "A family of dormice could have set up shop in this dratted thing and I'd be none the wiser, so if you don't mind, I'd appreciate a little help evicting them from the premises so I can fulfill my destiny and become Lady Carlisle, something I simply cannot do if I have rodents inhabiting my groin!"

"Oh, good heavens." Caroline moaned softly. "We're doomed!"

"It's not that bad," Charlotte answered, placing both hands on the protuberance of the codpiece and tugging. "I just need help getting it off. The buckles seem to be frozen or caught on something."

Caroline, her back to Charlotte as she attempted to block the sight of her friend's codpiece-related actions, reached behind to tug at Charlotte's arm. "Char, stop," she whispered in an anguished, choked voice, trying as she did to summon up a smile. She raised her voice in a clear, "Good evening, Lord Carlisle."

Charlotte, for once alert to the nuances around her, froze and peered over Caroline's shoulder as she bobbed the earl a curtsy. "Damnation."

Dark, midnight-blue eyes met hers.

"Quite," Dare replied.

"I . . . er . . . if you'll excuse . . . my husband is waiting for me," Caroline murmured apologetically and, with a worried glance at her friend, hurried off to rejoin the ball.

One of Dare's eyebrows rose as he studied Charlotte's costume. "Henry the Eighth?"

"Yes, how very clever of you." She turned as if to gaze out in contemplation at the darkened garden, rubbing the codpiece on the railing in an attempt to force it loose. It didn't help. With a quick sidelong glance at the handsome man staring out into the garden next to her, she tugged at the obstinate bit of leather with what she hoped was unobtrusiveness.

Dare's second eyebrow rose as she realized she would need to practice her unobtrusive-codpiece-tugging skills in the future. Clearly this was one of those times when it was more prudent to admit her folly than to encourage the man whose children she would someday bear into thinking her the type of woman who would stand on a balcony during a very fancy costume party and grope at her codpiece. "There's . . . I think there's something in there," she whispered, nodding toward the leather protrusion.

Dare pursed his lips.

"Something alive," she added, trying not to squirm under both his look of disbelief and the surety that it was hundreds of tiny little feet that were brushing against her sensitive flesh. Overwhelmed by the need to explain further, lest the earl think she was ten cards shy of a deck, she added, "I think something crawled in while I was hiding in the shrubs."

He blinked.

"Perhaps you would be kind enough to extract it for me? Lady Beverly assures me there is a private room at the end of the hall we could use briefly."

"Madam." Dare finally spoke, but in tones so frigid Charlotte expected ice to form upon his manly lips. "The contents of your codpiece do not interest me in the least."

"I understand," Charlotte answered somewhat ruefully. "I'm out of apples. I'm afraid I had room for only the one, you see. I didn't know you'd want one, too, and a two-apple codpiece just seemed a bit too extravagant."

She smiled, wondering briefly about the wild, dazed look in his eyes, finally putting it down to too much champagne. Gentlemen always had too much champagne at masquerade balls. In fact, she had counted on that very fact to aid her in drawing him into her net. Her smile brightened as his look of confusion increased. He was no doubt so well oiled by now, she'd have no difficulty in proceeding as planned.

* * *

As Dare reentered the ballroom in search of his sister he shook his head in disbelief. He knew he was in trouble. Charlotte had cozened him into meeting her a few minutes from now to help her remove her codpiece. He had tried to heed the warnings of the sane voice in his head, but he had been unable to resist the lure of spending a few moments in private with her. The situation was so ludicrous, so utterly Charlotte, that despite the harsh words he had spoken to her, it would have taken a group of strong men and quite probably several draft horses to keep him from the explanation of what she was doing dressed as Henry VIII with an animal stuffed down her codpiece. He couldn't begin to imagine what her explanation was, but he was certain it would be the most entertaining thing he had heard in a long time.

As for the sane voice warning that he was courting trouble by assisting her . . . well, she was a widow, after all. Rendezvous with men at balls were no doubt requisite in her set. A few moments spent alone with her would do her reputation no harm at all. There was, however, the matter of *his* reputation, and it was with an eye to that grisly relic that he took the precaution of murmuring a few words into his sister's ear.

"Where's Mrs. Whitney?"

The small, dark-haired woman dressed as the infamous pirate Anne Bonney turned and smiled at her brother, her dark eyes sparkling with happiness. "She's dancing with David. Isn't this a lovely party? I'm so pleased you agreed to let us attend, although it wouldn't have hurt you in the least to wear a costume. What are you looking so worried about? It's not me, is it? Dare, I'm perfectly capable of standing here by myself while David dances with his aunt. Unless, that is, you wished for me to join the set with you?"

Dare tweaked a dusky curl nestled next to Patricia's ear and ignored the teasing glint in her dark brown eyes. "Minx. I detest *ton* parties, as you well know. The only reason you're here is because I couldn't stand the incessant grizzling about not having anyone attend your wedding if you weren't present tonight, not that I see the connection between the two events. However, even if I wished to dance with you, I am not free; I have an appointment I must keep. I want your promise you'll stay here and await Mrs. Whitney's return."

"Oh?" With one eyebrow cocked in the manner of her brother at his most quizzical, she looked him up and down. He was an impressively austere man in his dress blacks—there was no disputing that—but he had about him an unexpected air of suppressed excitement that intrigued her. Dare was so seldom excited about anything other than his steam engine, surely if something—or *someone*—had caught his attention, it behooved her to learn more. "What, pray tell, do you have an appointment to do? You're not gaming, are you? No," she answered her own question before he had a chance to protest her accusation. "No, you wouldn't do that; you're much too careful with your money to be throwing it away on nothing. Hmmm. Perhaps you are meeting with a gentleman who wishes to invest in your steam engine?"

Dare glanced nervously toward the door. He hated leaving his sister alone, especially since his entire future hung upon the goodwill of the woman acting as her chaperon, but he had promised Charlotte he would be with her momentarily. The thought of what might happen should she stroll into the crowded ballroom and announce that she was awaiting his help with her codpiece made his flesh crawl. "I must leave. Give me your word you'll stay here and wait for Mrs. Whitney until I return."

"Not a gentleman investor, I think." Patricia ignored his request, her eyes laughing as she tipped her head to better consider him. "For if you had an investor, it would not matter to you in the least whether or not Mrs. Whitney recommends you to her husband, and thus you wouldn't be so worried about placating her. Not to mention keeping your scandalous past from her ears." She tapped a finger to her lips, her eyes growing bright with interest. "If it's not gaming and it's not an investor, then it must be . . . good Lord, Dare, you're not intending to have an assignation with a woman, are you?"

"Well, I'm not likely to have one with a *man*," he snapped. "Now, will you—"

"It *is* a woman!" Patricia crowed.

Dare scowled as he abruptly shushed her. "If you can't behave any better than this in public, I'll think twice about giving my permission for you to attend any other such festivities."

"After next week, you won't have any say about where I go, but that's neither here nor there." She waved away her brother's objections. "Tell me about this woman you're meeting! Who is she? Do I know her? Are you courting her? Oh, Dare, I do so worry about who will take care of you after I'm married— please tell me you've fallen in love and are about to offer for a woman who will love you in return."

"Love." Dare snorted, momentarily distracted by that unwholesome thought. "That sort of foolishness is what comes from reading those novels you devour weekly."

Patricia watched her brother steadily for a moment, the light of laughter dying in her eyes. "No, I can see you're not in love with anyone, but I haven't given up hope that you will someday find the woman meant for you. I know you believe yourself too scarred by the events in the past to ever give your heart again, but truly, brother, not all women are like the one who hurt you. You must have hope. You must leave yourself open to loving again."

The blank, shuttered look that accompanied any reference made to the events of ten years past left Dare's face a cold, unyielding mask. "Yes or no—will you stay here and behave until Mrs. Whitney is free?"

There was no hope for it; he would not discuss the past. Patricia allowed herself an inner sigh of concern for him, but found a cheerful smile as she saluted smartly. "Aye, aye, *mon capitaine*. Hoist your mainsail and belay those worries, brother mine. I shall stay here becalmed until my own darling captain comes to hoist my anchor."

Dare paused as he turned to leave. "Patricia, just because you're marrying a sailor—"

"Captain, if you please, of the finest Whitney ship ever to sail the seas!"

"—captain, does not mean you must talk like Halibut Harry, the fishmonger's delight. And there had best be no anchor hoisting before the wedding," he warned, his eyes dark with meaning.

Patricia grinned and shooed her brother off. With a

361

shake of his head at the folly awaiting him, he started for the small room off the darkened end of the hall that Charlotte had indicated. Surely it would be a simple matter to help her, one quickly attended to. He would assist evicting whatever it was that had taken up residence in her codpiece—women were so often squeamish about such things—then perhaps engage in a few moments of the particularly delightful form of word games that passed for conversation with Charlotte, after which, with a polite but firm excuse, he would take his leave. The nagging desire he felt to be near her would be assuaged, she would receive discreet assistance with regards to her codpiece problem, and none would be the wiser.

He was mentally forming the excuse he would use to make his escape when he entered the room. "My apologies for being delayed, Lady— Mmrph!"

Dare didn't have time to do more than catch a glimpse of heated blue eyes before he was pulled into an intimate embrace.

With Henry VIII. A very well padded, bearded, codpieced Henry VIII.

He unwound the arms clasped behind his neck in order to detach his lips from the mouthful of scratchy red-orange wool that covered Charlotte's lower face. "I never thought the opportunity to voice this opinion would arise, but there is much to be said for women who shave."

Charlotte, dismay filling her eyes for a moment at his rejection of her advances, smiled instead. "I beg your pardon; I forgot about the beard. One moment— I'll remove it; then we may continue with the ravishing."

Dare shook his head in hopes of clearing away whatever it was that was keeping him from hearing her correctly. He knew Charlotte's verbal acrobatics were sometimes filled with leaps in logic that even a learned man would be hard-put to follow, but the one she had just made was surely beyond even her fertile mind.

"About the problem with your costume—"

"That's been remedied," she replied, frowning as she tugged on the side of the woolly beard. " 'Twas just a leaf, not a family of dormice, as I had suspected. Drat this thing—Crouch must have used extra glue on it. I can't seem to peel it off, and I ask you, how on earth am I ever going to attend to the ravishing in time if I'm wearing a beard?"

An ugly suspicion flared to life in Dare's mind. "Exactly who do you expect will be ravishing you?" a morbid sense of curiosity forced him to ask.

Charlotte frowned as she muttered something about needing glue remover. "Pheasant feathers! You'll just have to keep your lips clear, is all. As for your question, no one will be ravishing *me,* Lord Carlisle. I shall ravish *you.*"

"You *what?*" Dare couldn't believe that even Charlotte, outspoken and uninhibited as she was, would suggest such a thing. A moment of honesty had him amending the thought to a disbelief that she would plan his ravishment in someone else's home, certainly not anywhere they could be easily . . . He sucked in his breath at the horrible realization that she had set a very clever snare for him, and he, a man who had prided himself daily on avoiding just such entrapment, had blindly walked right into her clutches.

"You needn't worry; I shall take care of everything.

363

You won't have to lift a finger," Charlotte promised.

He stared at her, dumbfounded. Having removed the black-and-gold velvet doublet, she was spinning in a frustrated circle as she attempted to reach behind herself to untie the tapes holding a large pillow bound over a linen shirt. "Foo! I can't reach the dratted thing. If you could just unbind me, my lord, I will be happy to begin the proceedings. I don't imagine we have much time, and although my experience with ravishing gentlemen is limited, I assume it will take more than a minute or two."

Dare stared in continued disbelief, his emotions tangled and confused as anger and outrage battled with a very unwelcome desire to laugh. He should leave that exact moment. He should walk out of the room and leave Charlotte to whatever horribly convoluted plan she had hatched in that Gordian knot of a mind. He should turn his back on her and never see her again, never again feel the velvet brush of her voice, never experience the brilliant, brief surge of joy that swelled within him when he caught sight of her, and certainly he should never, ever hold her in his arms again.

It just was not sane.

So be it. I'm mad. Dare told himself as he leaned against the door and crossed his arms over his chest, watching as Charlotte muttered and swore as she attempted to wriggle out of the pillow. He clamped down firmly on the wave of desire that swept through him at the sight of such unintentionally seductive movements, damning his eyes and his lust equally. No one would ever believe he could be aroused by a large, hairy, long-dead king, but with each wiggle of her rounded hips his desire, amongst other things, swelled. "This ravishment you're planning . . . do I assume it has something to do with your proposal of marriage a few days ago?"

Charlotte triumphantly kicked herself free of the pillow, turning upon him a look of innocence so profound it would make an angel feel impure. Dare wasn't fooled for a moment.

"Marriage? Proposal? Oh, that silliness! Good heavens, my lord, I'd forgotten all about *that*," she replied with what he knew were dimples beneath the beard. "No, this is totally unrelated."

"Ah. Would you mind, purely to satisfy my curiosity, informing me exactly what the goal *is* of your intended ravishment of my person?"

She paused for a moment in the act of unbuttoning her breeches. "You want to know why I wish to ravish you?"

Dare nodded. Yes, he did. He wanted her to admit that she was no better than the rest of the women in society. He wanted his disillusionment to be complete and inexorably final. He wanted to kill the hunger for her that grew stronger within him each time he saw her. By God, he needed to exorcise himself of her!

"Oh. Well. That. Er . . . it's quite simple, actually. You look exceptionally well against me."

A bubble of laughter threatened his iron control. "I do?"

"Yes." Charlotte gave him another bearded smile, and continued to work nimble fingers down the line of mother-of-pearl buttons on her purple-and-black breeches.

He resisted the almost overwhelming and completely irrational urge to take her in his arms and kiss away what infinitesimal bit of wits remained within her. "I see. I apologize for my incorrect deduction. I had imagined that your ravishment of me was part of a plan to trap me into marriage."

Charlotte paused. "Oh?"

"Yes. It had occurred to me—luckily you have shown me the error in my thinking—that you might have arranged to be discovered with me here."

Her hand stilled upon the buttons. "Ah."

"In this room."

She blinked.

"In a state of extreme undress."

She licked her strawberry-sweet lips.

"That isn't the case?"

She raised an outraged chin and shot him a steely look. "I am sorely offended that you could think me capable of such a heinous and unworthy act, Lord Carlisle. You would think a gentleman would be pleased with an offer of ravishment, but no, you have to be obstinate and suspicious and ruin the whole experience! I'm of half a mind to not ravish you at all!"

One heavy gold eyebrow cocked in question.

"But I shall," she continued, nodding righteously as she resumed work on the buttons. "I shall overlook your petty thoughts this once, but don't be expecting me to be so generous the next time."

"So your intention in removing all of your clothing and making love to me is not to be discovered, compromised to the point that I will be forced by honor into wedding you?"

"I just said that!"

"Then you don't mind if I lock this door?" Dare

turned the small brass key in the lock and pocketed it.

"Er . . ." Charlotte watched him warily.

"I thought you wouldn't. Where would you care for the lovemaking to take place?"

Her lovely blue eyes didn't even blink. "Er . . ."

"That couch looks comfortable. Or perhaps you would like to have your wicked way with me on the rug before the fire?"

She glanced at the fire. "Er . . ."

Dare gave her a scandalized wiggle of his brows as he strolled over to stand next to a large leather armchair. "Don't tell me you prefer more *inventive* positions? The armchair, perhaps?"

Charlotte looked with blossoming interest at the armchair. "How could that be possible?"

Dare couldn't help but laugh. She really was the most refreshing woman he'd ever met, uninhibited, direct, every word and deed unexpected, but he had had enough of playing her game. He had spent well over the few minutes he had allotted to attending her codpiece needs, and his future relied upon his keeping his sister's soon-to-be aunt satisfied of his character and morality. "Lady Charlotte, I'm afraid I must turn down yet another of your charming but irregular offers. I have left my sister alone too long. If you will forgive me . . ."

Charlotte approached the leather chair, prodding gently at it as if she expected it to explode before her eyes. "How exactly does one conduct a ravishment in a chair?"

Both of Dare's eyebrows rose.

"Where, for instance, do the legs go?"

His eyebrows rose even higher.

"And what about the . . . instrument? How exactly is it wielded in such a situation?"

Dare mused upon his luck in having thick hair, for if he had not, his eyebrows would have found themselves at the back of his head. "Lady Charlotte—"

She stared at the chair with a puzzled frown, one hand holding her unbuttoned breeches together. "I simply cannot picture it. Not even in Vyvyan La Blue's famed *Book of Connubial Calisthenics* is an armchair mentioned."

Dare opened his mouth to take his leave once and for all.

"I would have remembered such a thing if it were!"

He shook his head. He had to gather his wits—and do it now—else he'd be lost in the mad twirl of her thoughts.

"It wouldn't be an easy thing to overlook, and I paid diligent attention to the chapters on creative use of furnishings as Antonio, my late husband, was so very fond of brocade."

"Regardless—" *Brocade?* Surely he was not hearing her correctly.

"You wouldn't think a man would find brocade a thing of enjoyment, but Antonio loved to have me wrap him in long lengths of it, then use a carpet beater on him."

"I must be . . . Did you say carpet beater?"

She nodded, tracing a finger down the curved back of the chair. "Yes, he said it made the brocade soft and pliable and soothing to the skin, although how he could appreciate that with all the twitching and spasming and moaning he did as a result of the application of the carpet beater is beyond my understanding."

He thought that was the least of what was beyond her understanding.

"Still, he looked forward to the brocade-beating sessions, so I guess there must be some merit in what he said."

Dare took a good, firm grip on his wits, and made one last effort to save his sanity. "Lady Charlotte?"

Charlotte turned to him with a sweet, completely misleading expression on her bearded face. "Yes, my lord?"

He looked deep into her lovely eyes, fathomless and clear, and he knew a yearning he had not felt since he was young and foolish and in love for the first time. But he was no longer young, and foolish though he might be, he had no place for love in his life. "Good evening."

"But, my lord . . ."

He walked to the door and unlocked it, glancing back over his shoulder to forever burn the image in his mind of the woman who had somehow, against his will, stayed in his heart after five lonely years. She was beautiful. Ethereal. A goddess, still as marble, clad in rumpled silk stockings, her ruff skewed slightly to one side with her exertions, the long lace fall of her linen shirt tangling with the hand that clutched her breeches together, the codpiece dangling in disarray. Her face was pale against the burning red of her beard, making her eyes glitter bright and clear as the bluest of summer skies.

He would leave town after Patricia's wedding. He would never see her again. "Good-bye, Charlotte."

The latched turned under his hand, forcing him to step back quickly lest he be struck by the opening door.

"Ah, Lord Carlisle, there you are. A little bird told me I could find you here."

Dare looked with growing horror at the smiling, suspicious face of his hostess.

"Lady Jersey. I . . . er—"

"Your sister was worried about you, weren't you, Miss McGregor?"

Dare took another step back as Patricia slipped in next to Lady Jersey. Both women looked beyond him to where Charlotte had scurried behind the chair. "I was. It's not like my brother to disappear when he promised me a waltz, although if you have some business with that gentleman, Dare, I am willing to forgive you the oversight."

Lady Jersey stepped farther into the room, inclining her head toward Charlotte as she held out her hand. "Sir, I do not believe I've had the pleasure?"

Charlotte, with a strangled sound and a quick, indecipherable glance at Dare, reached out to take the proffered hand, but snatched it back quickly when her breeches started to slide down her hips.

"Good God in heaven!" Lady Jersey exclaimed, her sharp eyes missing nothing of Charlotte's rumpled appearance. "Lord Carlisle, I had no idea you are a . . . that you preferred . . . "

Luckily the presence of Patricia put a halt to any further utterances. Dare opened his mouth to explain, but he couldn't. If he mentioned who Charlotte was, the parson's noose would be around his neck before he knew it. Yet if he didn't, Lady Jersey would be sure to spread word of his alleged sexual preference, which, given his luck of late, would find its way unerringly to the ears of the very straitlaced Mrs. Whitney, and that would spell a disaster from which he could not recover. He tried to rally his wits, but the full horror of the situation had struck him, leaving him with a sick, clammy feeling in the region of his stomach, hands that were suddenly damp, and the knowledge that if his goose was not yet actually cooked, it was next in line. Before he could do more than sputter an objection, however, the matter was taken from him.

"Lord Carlisle was merely helping me with my codpiece," Charlotte said in a deep, obviously false approximation of a male voice. Two more people crowed into the doorway as she cleared her throat and added, "That is, he was assisting in removing an object from it."

Dare's mind went numb around the edges. He hadn't thought matters could be made worse, but when Mrs. Whitney leaned toward him and in a scandalized whisper asked why a half-clad man was standing before Lady Jersey, he felt the leaden weight of despair clamp itself around his heart. Dare glanced at her, over to the sympathetic eyes of Patricia's betrothed standing beside his aunt, and felt the cold hands of the feather plucker approaching. He was caught. Ensnared. Trapped. It had come to this, to a choice. If he wanted any hope of selling his engine design to the Whitney shipyards, he would have to salvage the situation, and assuming his prayer for the earth to open up and swallow him whole was not going to be answered, salvage meant sacrifice. *His* sacrifice.

He took one last breath as a free man.

"When I say he was assisting me, I mean that he offered to look inside and determine what exactly was in—"

371

"What Lady Charlotte is trying to say is that she has done me the honor of bestowing upon me her hand."

Five pairs of eyes stared in surprise at his pronouncement. Dare looked calmly back at all of them, beyond feeling anything but stupefied.

"She? That person is a woman?" asked Mrs. Whitney.

"I knew it!" Patricia exclaimed, saluting her brother with her wooden saber before kissing him on his cheek. "I'm so pleased!"

"Best of luck to you, old man," said David, the sea captain, as he clapped Dare on the back.

"*Lady Charlotte?*" Lady Jersey said in annoyance as she turned to face the person in question. "Lady Charlotte Collins? The Lady Charlotte who ran off with an Italian nobody despite my warning her it would all end in despair? The Lady Charlotte whom I specifically forbade to attend my ball? The Lady Charlotte who, upon hearing my refusal, referred to me as 'that jealous old she-cat who wouldn't recognize a good opportunity if it bit her on the bottom'? *That* Lady Charlotte?"

Dare looked at Charlotte. She looked back at him, her eyes round with surprise; then suddenly she whooped with delight and threw herself across the room and into his arms, murmuring into his ear, "I knew this would turn out well! I knew you wouldn't fail me! Now we will be wed and you shan't be hunted any longer, and Lady Jersey will have to receive me, and I shall have gowns and go to balls and dance, and best of all, your instrument will be happy to apply itself while you delegate the armchair's usage to me."

"*Demonstrate,*" Dare corrected softly, flinching slightly as the hunter's arrow pierced him with a mortal blow. The question was, had he been saved or damned?

Improper English

WIN A TRIP TO LONDON!

KATIE MACALISTER

Sassy American Alexandra Freemar isn't about to put up with any flak from the uptight—albeit gorgeous—Scotland Yard inspector who accuses her of breaking and entering. She doesn't have time. She has two months in London to write the perfect romance novel—two months to prove that she can succeed as an author.

Luckily, reserved Englishmen are not her cup of tea. Yet one kiss tells her Alexander Block might not be quite as proper as she thought. Unfortunately, the gentleman isn't interested in a summer fling. And while Alix knows every imaginable euphemism for the male member, she soon realizes she has a lot to learn about love.

Dorchester Publishing Co., Inc.
P.O. Box 6640 ___52517-8
Wayne, PA 19087-8640 **$6.99 US/$8.99 CAN**
Please add $2.50 for shipping and handling for the first book and $.75 for each book thereafter. NY and PA residents, please add appropriate sales tax. No cash, stamps, or C.O.D.s. Prices and availability subject to change.
Canadian orders require $2.00 extra postage and must be paid in U.S. dollars through a U.S. banking facility.

Name _____
Address_____
City_____ State_____ Zip_____
E-mail _____
I have enclosed $_____ in payment for the checked book(s).
Payment <u>must</u> accompany all orders. ❑ Please send a free catalog.

CHECK OUT OUR WEBSITE! www.dorchesterpub.com

ATTENTION
BOOK LOVERS!

Can't get enough of your favorite **ROMANCE**?

Call **1-800-481-9191** to:

✳ order books,

✳ receive a **FREE** catalog,

✳ join our book clubs to **SAVE 20%**!

Open Mon.-Fri. 10 AM-9 PM EST

Visit **www.dorchesterpub.com**
for special offers and inside
information on the authors you love.

We accept Visa, MasterCard or Discover®.
LEISURE BOOKS ♥ LOVE SPELL